RIVERS OF THE SKY

An Epic Fantasy Misadventure

M.A. LIGUORI

Hydra
Publications

ISBN: 978-1-937979-30-0

Hydra Publications
Goshen, Kentucky
www.hydrapublications.com

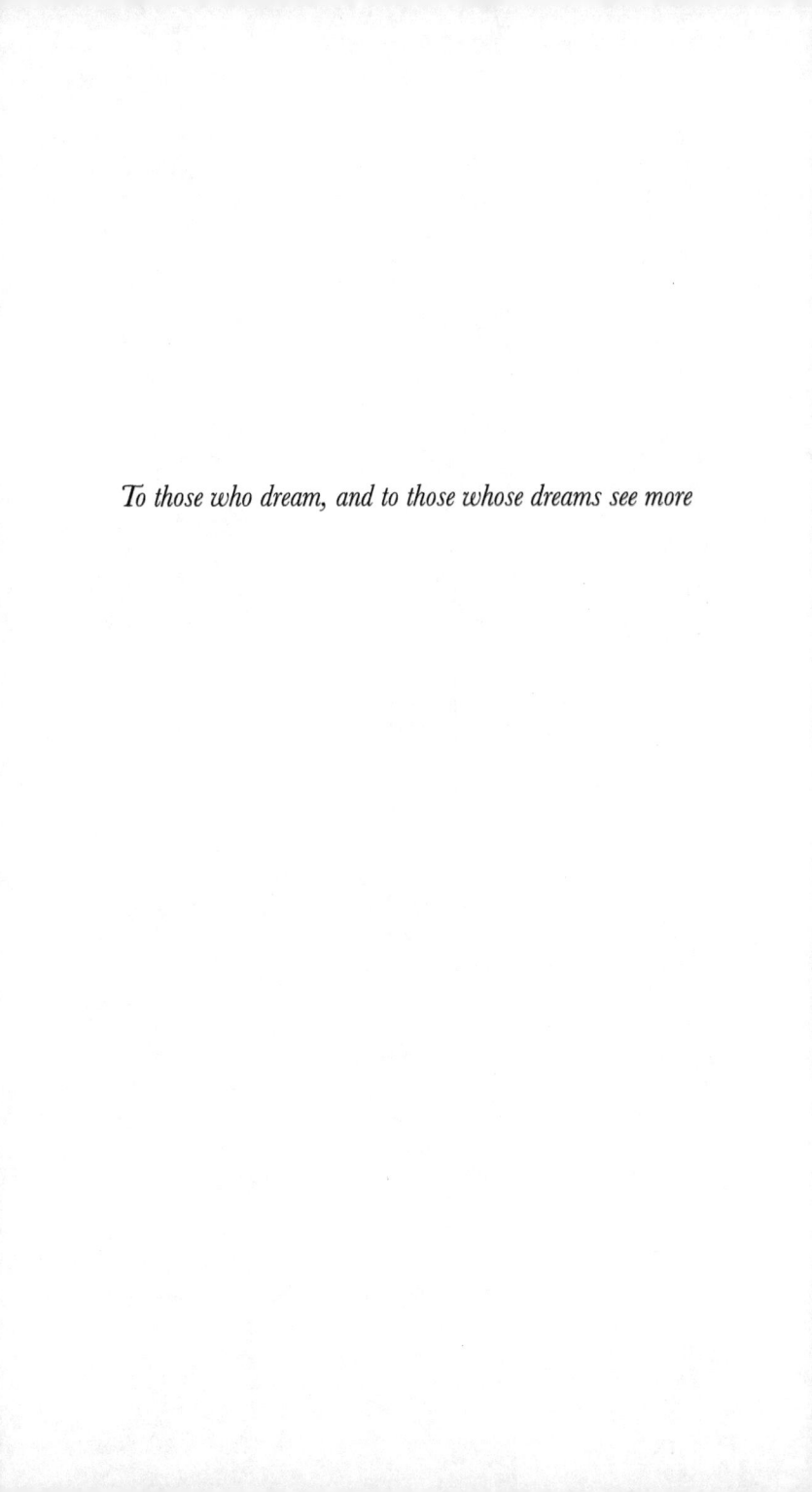

To those who dream, and to those whose dreams see more

a river to carry, cleanse, create
a mushroom, like a shield against the slash,
maybe some mush
a dog, three-legged, clairvoyant to the receiver
so claims the boy with the aged face

Chapter One

*a*drian Renn stared down at his gloved hand. Beneath the worn doeskin lay a charred, crippling, and career-ending wound. He tried not to focus on it. Not now, at least.

It was another balmy day after the spring thaw, just before noontide and while the third-quarter moon still lingered in the soft blue sky. A field of low grasses fluttered lazily in the breeze, empty save the row of archery butts positioned at the northernmost end. Spectators lined the outskirts of the field, courtiers and ministers and noblemen all chattering and gossiping as they awaited the capital city's annual contest of marksmanship.

Well, all except Adrian.

His eyes rose to the high marble terrace of the imperial tower, where the overweight prime minister and his slew of imperial toadies sat. Yes, there it was —the luxurious robe of rare firemouth silk hanging cheerfully from a gilded display stand, its fancy filigree lining and sleeves of studded garnets glittering under the blaze of the rising sun. It was a magnificent prize, a lord's guerdon, but one that was meant solely for the victor of the contest. Adrian, however, intended to have it in his grasp long before that.

His gaze shifted from the robe to the prime minister, Lord Talrin Haroden, who sat on a wide throne-like chair and sipped overpriced wine from an overpriced goblet. He was draped in his usual formal attire: a horned ceremonial headdress, pearl-studded sash and shoes, and a heavy fall of gray robes that resembled a pachyderm's hide. The people called him the Rhinoceros Lord because they loved him, and they loved him because he had protected and guided the people since the emperor's untimely death left a successor too young to rule. Lord Haroden was, in truth, a benevolent and evenhanded leader, and that meant Adrian didn't like having to steal from him. But the decision had already been made, and Adrian couldn't back out now. Niall would never forgive him.

Where the hell is that little steward anyway?

Adrian studied the host of hangers-on that surrounded the prime minister. Now Niall was a difficult man to keep sight of—since he stood no taller than a woman and no wider than a boy—but Adrian's eyes were still keen in his thirty-four years, and soon he spotted the little steward mingling with the other courtiers nearby. So affable and trustworthy the man appeared, and yet Niall, like most men of ambition, was nothing more than a weasel with an insatiable appetite for personal gain.

Now why would Adrian think that? Well, for one, the steward wanted more than half of the profit from the robe. That was simply outrageous. Sure, Niall may have secured their southern buyer and organized all the details of this little ploy, but it was Adrian who had to smuggle the garment out of the city and travel hundreds of miles to the south to sell the damn thing. *It's my neck on the block here,* Adrian thought, *and for that I deserve more.*

He lowered his eyes from the tower and placed them back on the field. A company of mounted military officers cantered in from the south, hardened men strapped in thick plates of dark steel armor that protected every point and crevice from shin to hip to shoulder. They bowed their helmeted heads and waved to the crowd while perched in the saddles of their caparisoned chargers, powerful beasts arrayed in hues of warm chestnut to deep roan.

High Commander Krall Vyren was the last officer to appear. Even from a distance you could tell he was a massive man, a mountain of old muscle and grizzled hair, with bone-hard eyes and a crooked nose that had been broken more times than a lesser soldier might ever see battle. He sat astride a coal-black charger whose spiked barding matched the spikes of his own armor. Krall the Conqueror he was styled, but many called him Krall the Ashen or Cinereous Krall, or a handful of other names he'd acquired during his many years of military service. Point was, no other man inspired such reverence from the crowd —although in Adrian, he only inspired consternation.

A pair of robed courtiers bickered as they strolled in front of Adrian. "You can't compete with these men, you clod," the shorter one said. "Do you know how difficult it is to fire an arrow while moving at a full gallop? It's not about sight or timing, no, a master marksman simply *feels* the precise moment to loose. It may look easy, but such skill requires a lifetime of—"

The men were gone then, and Adrian's attention returned to the terrace. His head was beginning to throb. Maybe it was the heat, maybe it was the nerves, or maybe it was the odor of unwashed bodies mixed with all these cloying perfumes. He took a deep breath, thumbed the sweat from his brow, and adjusted the fit of his fancy satin outer jacket. Niall had given it to him so he could blend in with the other courtiers, but in truth, Adrian hated the garment. He hated it because it was an ugly and uncomfortable thing with oversized sleeves and garishly embroidered roundels, but more than that, he hated it because he could never afford it himself. No, these days he was nothing more than a penniless wretch who had to scrape miserably by.

But not for long.

Chargers galloped down the line, arrows twanged and thudded, tallymen made announcements, and the crowd erupted in cheers. This happened again and again until the afternoon sun finally began its descent over the western mountain line. It was then Adrian spotted a tendril of smoke drifting skyward near the base of the tower. It was a dark smoke, the kind produced by the dung of the whitest wolves of the farthest north, and yet, none of the spectators seemed to notice, not at first, not until the smoke thickened and thickened and nearly wafted into their faces. Even then, most onlookers simply nudged each other and murmured at what they saw. A few even cheered, thinking it was part of the event. But then more smoke appeared in different locations, more and more until the spectators were nearly surrounded by it. A woman screamed, and next Adrian knew panic had exploded through the crowd.

Frightened courtiers fled in all directions, shouting and shrieking and shoving their way forward. The guardsmen didn't even try to restore order. No, they focused only on clearing a path for the water carriers, but the two-man teams who carried the massive wooden containers never stood a chance against the crowd. Bodies collided and wood splintered and water drenched the earth, and passing courtiers in sandals slipped and fell into the mud and called out for aid. It was a terrible commotion but also a rather exceptional ruse—and that was exactly what Adrian and Niall had intended. No fire, no harm, just smoke.

Adrian stepped back and stared up at the terrace. Lord Haroden made his escape through a raised door curtain. His councilmen and ministers all followed without any notion of etiquette. *Hurry, Niall,* Adrian thought. *Hurry, goddamn it.* At last the little steward appeared. He snatched the robe from the display stand, crept to the far side of the terrace, extended his arms over the marble balustrade, paused, and then opened his hands.

Adrian was running now, running toward the luxurious firemouth silk robe that was drifting down the western face of the tower. He did his best to keep an eye on it, but the mob of sweaty men and shrieking women did better to distract him. *Move, move, get out of the way, goddamn it.* A sudden gust carried the robe behind the walls of the imperial orchard. Adrian broke from the crowd and dashed along the tower. Faster and faster he went, faster and faster as he stormed inside the unguarded entranceway . . . and came to a sudden halt before a sea of blazing red blossoms.

No, no—what the hell is this? Apricot trees, rows of them, each pruned and trimmed and brushed with painstaking precision. The robe was lost among them. *Damn it, I don't have time to search every goddamn tree.* But that was exactly what Adrian began to do. He went from one to the next, searching the base and boughs and blossoms, until he'd been through a dozen, then a score, then so many that he lost count. *Where are you, where are you.* Only after backtracking down several hedgerows and circling the same square three times did he finally spot the damn thing.

There it was, dangling from the canopy of a twenty-footer whose branches were gnarled and twisted and covered in toothy, ovate leaves. Easy climbing for a child, sure, but what about a man with only one usable hand? Adrian frowned. *Is this some god's cruel jest? Making a disabled man climb a goddamn tree.*

No time for self-pity. The robe was nearly his.

Adrian grasped a bough with his good hand and planted his feet on any knot and latent bud he could find. Up and up and up he went, a slow and difficult ascent, which only grew worse when a honey bee began buzzing in his ear. Like a fool Adrian swatted at it, and like a fool his balance faltered and he slid down a painful four or five feet. *Idiot, what is wrong with you?* He remained there for a moment, catching his breath and taking in the sweet-smelling blossoms that flourished all around him.

He cursed the apricots for being early bloomers, then up and up and up he went. It was another slow and difficult ascent, but with care and patience he reached the upper limbs, seized the robe by its trimming, and gave a gentle pull. The damn thing wouldn't budge. He tried again, harder. No use. He found another foothold and climbed a bit higher. Another bee zipped past him, or maybe it was the same one, who the hell knew, but Adrian ignored it this time. He leaned onto a branch that groaned under his weight, and with gentle fingers he unhooked the robe and brought it down to his chest.

Got you.

It was just as beautiful up close, but it was also divinely soft and flawlessly stitched. Any sericulturist worth his salt would tell you just how extraordinarily rare a single firemouth silkworm was, never mind how many were needed to create a garment of this size. That thought alone made Adrian smile as he unslung the haversack from his shoulder, stuffed the robe inside, and slid down the tree until the ground rose up with a *thud*. He made his way out of the orchard and back into the crowd. The exit from the palace district lay ahead. *Don't stop*, Adrian told himself. *Beyond the gates is the city itself, and after that is—*

"Where are you going with that?"

The voice was cold and deep and dangerously calm. Adrian's heart shot up his throat. He refused to turn; he simply ignored what he heard and kept moving, doing his best to blend in with the other stragglers from the mob. The question came again. Louder this time, more forceful. Adrian ignored it a second time. *Don't stop, Adrian, don't stop.*

An arrow screamed past his ear, striking a wooden arbor no more than an arm's length away.

Adrian froze. For a long moment he simply stared at the arrow. This wasn't a poorly crafted thing; no, it was an expert's missile, as evidenced by the sleek birch shaft and decorative motifs and expensive eagle-feather fletching. Never had Adrian come so close to being struck, not once in his three years of military conscription. And yet, he knew the arrow was intended only as a warning. He also knew that if he took another step, the next one would not be.

Slowly, ever so slowly, Adrian turned.

High Commander Krall Vyren rose from the saddle of his charger, arms outstretched, crimson horn bow drawn, black-tipped arrow nocked and pointed.

Adrian lowered his eyes. His life was over. Done. The end. Lord Haroden may have been an even-handed ruler, but such blatant theft would undoubtedly come at a hefty cost . . . and that cost would be a swift sentence followed by an even swifter punishment.

But no, a careless runner in oversized gray robes slammed into the crupper of Krall's charger. The horse bucked and whinnied, the high commander lurched forward, and the arrow snapped beneath the weight of his armor. Krall fought to regain control of the beast, and while doing that he growled, "Don't you dare move, thief."

"I won't," Adrian said, then turned and bolted.

He ran and ran and didn't stop running, and every passing moment he feared an arrow would pierce him in the back. But it never did, and somehow, by some ridiculous measure of good fortune, the next avenue he turned down brought him directly before the gatehouse of the palace district. The exit was so close—but the giant double-leafed doors were already groaning to a close. Adrian's legs pumped harder. *No, no, no, no, no.* The groaning deepened as the gap between the doors narrowed. *I'm not going to make it, I'm not going to make it.*

BOOM. The doors slammed shut—not a moment after Adrian had flung himself through. *By the gods that was close. Too damn close.*

Adrian's doeskin boots pounded down the main

avenue's uneven cobblestones. He glanced back and saw sentries on the parapet shouting at him to halt. Moments later a sally port opened and a company of mounted soldiers came roaring out. High Commander Krall Vyren was in the vanguard, shouting orders and waving a quirt and looking rather furious.

Goddamn it, the bastard's not giving up.

Adrian cut through an alleyway and burst into the busy market district, and suddenly he was dodging hawkers and rug peddlers and acrobats and entertainers of all kind. Men gasped and grunted at his rudeness, while women started in surprise. Dogs loped and barked all around him, which caused pigeons to squawk and take to feather. From inside butcher stalls, burly men grunted and mallets pounded. Street urchins dashed this way and that. Adrian dodged a handful of them and also a barefoot pregnant woman, but the portly fellow with the shoulder pole he never saw coming. He slammed into the man with a heavy thud, then stumbled headlong into a stallholder. Wood cracked and rattan snapped and figs and fruits of all sizes and smells and textures flew into the air. Adrian sprang back to his feet and continued running, ignoring the curses from the angry merchants behind him.

The crowds eventually thinned as Adrian exited the market district. He continued to run even though his calves burned with cramp and his lungs begged for relief. *Don't stop, you're almost out.* The North Gate rose above him, the city's central exit, its massive jutting towers clad in stone and perched on a solid foundation of loess and tamped earth. The gates were still open. Listless sentries barely spared a glance as Adrian dashed under an enormous archway. Darkness gobbled him up only to spit him back into the light, and suddenly the grand city of Scarlet Sun was behind him.

I did it. I'm out of the city. By the gods, I'm out.

Without stopping Adrian stripped off his fancy outer jacket in favor of his homespun and inconspicuous tunic and trousers. Around him the urban sprawl soon faded into a more idyllic view of suburban developments—taverns and hostelries and outbuildings and workshops that clung to the city's massive outer wall. Porters and draymen clogged the main roadway, the axles of their carts groaning under the weight of their loads. Adrian maneuvered around the yokes of oxen and teams of draft horses and fled through an open stand of gray pines. Behind him, high above in the city's watchtowers, clappers clacked and conch horns wailed as sentries raised the hue and cry.

The robe was his, but Adrian was now a wanted man.

Chapter Two

*T*he Dusty Daisy was a tired old brothel that stood on a tired old hill two miles from Scarlet Sun's outer wall. It certainly wasn't the most inviting of places—not with its broken roof tiles and weathered façade and partly rotted mortise and tenon joints—but to Adrian it had served as a welcome respite after his wife's death some years ago.

He lowered his head and sneaked past the tired old gatekeeper, careful to avoid familiar eyes. Inside, the common room was crowded with patrons who were laughing and shouting and downing huge gulps of flavorful wine from earthenware cups. Adrian hopped over a sozzled fool who lay curled up on the floor, then weaved around a serving girl who nearly spilled a tray of jellied meats on him. He paused to ogle a half-dressed bawd emerging from the private screens beyond the common area, only to be distracted by the cheers of the rowdy gamblers in the rear dens.

The proprietor was a short fellow with a short temper, and right now he was shouting at his bruisers and his servers and whoever else set him off. Adrian usually found the man terribly obnoxious, but today he was glad for the distraction. It allowed him to reach the stairs unnoticed, though his ascent was a bit clumsy since his legs still ached from his frantic escape from the city. Sure, Adrian was exhausted, but he couldn't stop to rest. Not yet. Bands of mercenaries and companies of soldiers were surely being organized to hunt down the fugitive. The very thought unnerved him. He wasn't supposed to be seen—he'd assured Niall that he wouldn't be seen—but he was seen, so now Adrian was alone and without supplies and standing at the doorstep of a four-month journey. He needed help, and he could think of only one person who could help. Jessamine.

He rounded the corridor and approached the first private chamber on the left. Vacant. Maybe she was still downstairs? Adrian moved to the balustrade to overlook the rowdy common room below, his eyes focusing on the bawds. Some were comely, others were curvy, and a few were both, but not one was Jessamine. *Where are you, goddamn it.*

"You look in need of company."

15

Adrian turned. A woman approached, dark of hair and clad in little more than a red chemise. When she joined him near the balustrade, he couldn't help but notice how tall she was—even barefoot she still managed to stand eye to eye with Adrian. Not that Adrian was ever the tallest man in a room, but he usually stood above most women.

"Is Jessamine here?" Adrian asked. "She's not in her room."

She frowned playfully at that, pretending to be insulted. Her face wasn't unattractive by any means, though she would've been prettier with a smaller nose and without those dark circles around her eyes. "She's with a client. Some wealthy robe from the imperial palace, a secretary to a high minister or some other." Her bangles clinked as she motioned to a private room on her right.

Adrian bowed his head and headed for the room. The bawd called after him. "I said she's *with* someone."

Adrian ignored that. He raised the door curtain and went inside.

Jessamine stood in the center of the room before a large wood-framed featherbed. At the sound of his footfalls she turned. Tresses of brown hair flowed past her shoulders like a shimmering cascade, framing a narrow face and eyes as warm as autumn leaf litter. Though she was a pleasing enough sight from the neck up, Adrian couldn't help but stare lower, at the lovely curves accentuated by the tight floral slip she wore.

A man sat up from the featherbed, bare-chested and potbellied but still wearing his trousers, thank the gods. He frowned at the visitor, but made no move other than to scratch his hairy chest with a pair of hairy fingers. His rheumy, drunken eyes followed Jessamine as she stepped away to cover herself with a silk robe. He seemed disappointed to see her fully clothed again, but Adrian couldn't fault him for that.

Jessamine turned to Adrian and puckered her lips. "You'll have to come back, handsome."

Adrian motioned her closer. His voice was low and grave. "I need to talk to you now. I'm leaving the city, I'm leaving the north."

She stared at him for a long moment, so long he wondered if she was just going to outright deny his request. But then she turned and padded back to her client. She placed his silk outer robe and scarf and pearl-studded shoes by the bedrail and bent down to pick up his sash and tunic. "Dress yourself. We're done."

Adrian had seen pomegranates that were less red than this man's face. "We're done? No, no, no, you don't tell me when we're done, I tell you when we're done. Do I need to remind you of just who I am? I'm the assistant secretary to the Minister of—"

The tunic landed on his face, silencing him. "I know who you are," Jessamine said. "You still have to leave."

Adrian couldn't help but smile at her. Such a spirited little lady.

The man huffed and puffed for a while, but in the

end he pulled on his robe and shoes and fastened his scarf. He looked a bit more distinguished in his attire, certainly an improvement over the paunchy old frog he was without. He stomped to the door like a spoiled child, glaring at Adrian the whole way. Adrian replied with a smirk that surely did nothing but infuriate him more. Wasn't the shrewdest move but Adrian wasn't about to let some imperial lickspittle throw his weight around.

The nobleman gone, Jessamine was left shaking her head. "I shouldn't have done that. That wasn't some no-name fool, Adrian, that was—"

He cut her off. "I need coin, and I need a horse— and not some sorry nag, I need a courser capable of riding all the way to the southern coast. Please, Jessa, I need your help."

Jessamine threw her arms around Adrian and kissed him. Her lips tasted of citrus and cinnamon, and so comforting was her embrace that he couldn't find the strength to pull away. Adrian could feel his baser urges overbearing the practicality of reason. Jessamine was well trained in the art of lovemaking, which meant she knew just how to touch him, just how to move her body against his. When their lips parted she purred in his ear, her hands moving from his shoulders to his chest and stomach, then lower to his—

Adrian pushed her away.

Her face sank into a childlike pout, but at last she seemed to grasp the urgency of the situation. "You really are leaving."

"I have to. I'm sorry."

She stared at him for a long moment, then without a word she went over to open a trunk beside her bed, pulling out a leather purse and tossing it to him. Adrian untied the thongs and looked inside. Strings of coin, two hundred shimmering ounces at least. She also fastened him in a lightweight traveling cloak, and handed him a sheathed knife. By the gods she was good to him, and he told her that.

"You've always been my favorite," she replied.

Adrian believed her. Why shouldn't he? He wasn't considered an uncomely man; no, he had a look that was both rugged and playful, along with a head of thick russet hair that complemented perfectly the richness of his eyes. And though he could stand to be a little taller and perhaps hold a little more muscle, he generally had little to dislike about himself—well, except for his burned hand of course.

"The stable master recently took in a charger," she told him. "Needs to be groomed and re-shod, but it was once a soldier's horse, well trained in single-handed commands and subtle aids."

"What about the stable master? He won't be happy."

"Don't fret over that oaf, I'll handle him." Her dark eyes blinked, and a frown slowly found her face. "Adrian, what's happened to you, what's wrong?"

He sighed. "Listen to me, Jessa, tell no one I was here. Do you understand?"

"Were you not seen coming in?"

"Just that client of yours and some bawd, but neither knows who I am."

Jessamine nodded. Her fingers moved down to raise the sleeve of his tunic and touch his single gloved hand. She never teased him about it, nor did she ever ask him to remove it, not even during the warmest summer nights. Few had ever shown him such consideration. That must've been why he favored her. He favored her and now he wished he didn't have to leave, but soon enough imperial guards would be crawling all over this brothel, questioning the patrons and panders and of course the proprietor. Adrian had to get out of here, and he had to do it quickly. "The horse," he said. "Please, Jessa."

Without a word she led him down the stairs and into the stable yard. A young groom worked quickly to have the horse curried and saddled and ready to ride. It was a long-bodied beast with a slight sway-back, dun in color save the black of its fetlocks and dorsal stripe. The grooms helped Adrian into the saddle since he was tired and weak and long out of practice. The horse adjusted immediately to his weight, as if Adrian had been its master for years. "I think I'm meant for this horse," Adrian said. He patted the beast's flank with his good hand, then reached up to take the reins. "Yes, I can feel it. We're going to be together for a long time."

Chapter Three

*I*n a week the horse was dead.

It was so sudden, the way those nasty boils broke out all over its body. The worst was that Adrian knew how to treat the poor thing, but being a fugitive and all, he couldn't just head into town and visit the local druggist's shop. What then could he do? Nothing. And as he did nothing, the boils continued to spread and the horse grew weaker and weaker until one afternoon it simply collapsed. Adrian ended the beast's suffering by opening its throat with the knife Jessamine had given him. Well, he *meant* to end its suffering, but sadly, it took a long goddamn time for the beast to die, and all Adrian could do was sit there and listen to the poor thing wheeze and wheeze before death finally decided to take it away.

The next morning Adrian did his best to skin the carcass. It was large and heavy and unwieldy, and when he began his cuts, blood and gore spilled all over the place, and when cutting out the liver, he accidentally cut into the bile duct which further made a mess of things. Still, he managed to salvage a few good portions, and using a bit of tinder fungus he prepared a fire and cooked the meat, then ate a hearty meal and smoked the rest for later. And although the following days of travel left him tired and footsore, he never once went hungry. Still, it was difficult to ignore the lure of a roadside inn, difficult even though good sense told him that imperial riders and mercenaries and informants were surely swarming these places. Lord Haroden must've promised quite a sum for the foolish thief who stole the imperial robe.

And so Adrian had no choice but to sleep in the wild, under the protection of the pines and broadleaves and surrounding foothills. His days were filled with sunshine and birdsong, his nights alive with wolf howls and katydid calls and the occasional high-pitched wail of a puma. Three years of military service had taught him how to survive well enough, but the weight of solitude was difficult to bear, and even the lush springtime landscape wasn't enough to lift that weight. Still, there was one small bit of solace to hold onto. Out here, Adrian was neither an impoverished wretch nor a wanted criminal. Out here, he was just a man. Well, a man with a burned and deformed hand. But a man nonetheless.

He traveled along the outskirts of the main road, avoiding imperial checkpoints and post stations and all the settlements that appeared every dozen or so miles. Sometimes this required him to traverse difficult terrain: dark forests filled with tortuous paths, upland slopes fraught with poisonous flora, and stony ledges with steep drop-offs. He mildly sprained an ankle after slipping on a patch of uneven gravel, and he was nearly bitten by an adder whose nest was unintentionally disturbed. Once he awoke with strange rash marks on his chest, so he slept off the ground on a suspended bed constructed out of branches and grasses that were tied together using the gut salvaged from that poor dead horse.

His thoughts often drifted to the stolen imperial robe in his haversack. Funny how all that fine silk and fancy filigree and rows of studded garnets meant nothing out here. The natural world cared not for material possessions. Sadly, Adrian once had all the coin and property and purpose a man could ever want in life, but that was before the accident with his hand. Something good taken away was much worse than never having it at all.

Supplies dwindled as the days passed, and hunger soon took precedence over other concerns. He paused from his travels to forage for grasses and greens to supplement what little horsemeat he had left. He dug for dandelion roots, plucked blades of goosegrass, picked fresh knotweed by the riverside, netted small red crabs that scuttled along the banks, and collected limpets that clung to the underside of rocks. It was the very bloom of spring, and Adrian was thankful for that.

The waterway inevitably led him to a quaint lake-side village. Steeply pitched thatch-roofed houses rose out of the surface of the water, their back ends supported by hardwood stilts. Nearby, flat-bottomed boats drifted lazily across shallow waters, manned by sun-beaten fishermen equipped with fish gaffs and barbed hooks and sinkers and nets. From the sides of their boats dark-feathered cormorants plunged into the water to snap up fish, although their necks were tied with a cord to prevent the seabirds from swallowing their catch.

The simplicity of a fisherman's life warmed Adrian's heart. Sure, they were poor and overworked and overtaxed and occasionally they went hungry, but they were generally unfettered by the daily pressures of urban life. It certainly seemed a respectable way to spend one's days, and certainly one in which most men found comfort. But Adrian wasn't like these common folk. He couldn't bear the thought of never returning to his former life of prosperity and privilege. He wanted more for himself. He deserved more. And this robe was the key to obtaining it all.

Farther along was a private property of ramshackle longhouses rising over rows and rows of rectangular garden plots. Vegetables. So many vegetables. Adrian's eyes widened at all the colors and textures. *Don't be a fool,* he told himself. *You've already stolen enough, haven't you?*

But Adrian couldn't help himself; his horsemeat had run out, and he was tired of eating grass and tiny crabs. He moved a little closer. So many delicious choices. Spinach, beetroot, coriander, sweet potatoes, cabbages, artemesia, broad beans, and more. He just wanted a little taste. Why not? Dawn had not yet broken, and no one was around. Besides, it wasn't like stealing a goddamn lamb. He just needed a few hand-fuls—enough to keep himself nourished for a day or two. He saw purple-tinged rutabagas and colorful aubergines and tender sorrel. Red amaranth and purple mustard plant and tomatoes so ripe their glossy flesh looked about to burst. He saw gourds, sugar cane, taro corms, barberry, onions and garlic and sword beans and—

The ground vanished. Adrian pitched forward, and darkness rose to swallow him whole.

Thud. He landed on his hands and knees, hard, so hard he was sure he'd twisted or fractured something. But no, as the pain began to ebb, he realized the dirt wasn't as solid as he thought. It wasn't packed earth— it was mud, thick and wet and . . . no, wait a moment. Adrian cringed from the stench. It wasn't mud at all. *What the hell is this?*

An ordure pit, he realized, then bent over and vomited.

Chapter Four

*H*e was covered in it. Excrement. On his hands, his face, his clothes—even in his mouth. Maggots clung to his hair. Flies buzzed all around him. The smell was like a hot acrid gas burning his nostrils. *I have to get out of here. Now.* Adrian staggered to his feet. Earthen walls rose above his head, jutting and uneven but just low enough for the average man to climb out of. But Adrian was not your average man. No, his burned and blackened hand was too crippled by pain and weakness to use, and his good hand wasn't strong enough to pull himself out alone. Desperation seized his heart. *Oh no, oh no, oh no. I have to get out of here.* He wanted to shout for help but he was a felon and a fugitive—what if the wrong ears heard him?

He tried again and again to climb out, but the more he tried the more difficult it became. Self-control swiftly vanished. He called for help. No one came. Adrian began to shout, louder and louder until his voice became a painful rasp, and when that happened he kicked the wall so hard the pain made him wince, and then he punched and clawed at it until every ounce of strength oozed from his body. Then he fell back on his rump, splashing onto the floor of excrement.

The haversack slipped from his shoulder and landed beside him. The leather thong loosened; the studded sleeves of the firemouth silk robe spilled out. Adrian didn't care. He despised the stupid thing right now. *Here I am . . . the most wanted criminal in the north, trapped like an animal in a pit of waste.*

He raised his head to gaze at the sky. Clouds, fat and white and billowy, drifted lazily overhead, as if to remind him just how carefree and joyful the world was. This was a cruelty of divine proportions. Yes, only the heavenly deities could've arranged something so heinous. Surely they were *laughing* at him, laughing and laughing and laughing, and so Adrian cursed at them, cursed all the goddamn deities he could think to name—but they didn't stop laughing. "I hear you, goddamn it. I hear you laughing at me. DAMN YOU ALL, STOP—"

"No one's laughing."

Adrian froze. He didn't see until now—a man

standing above, peering over the edge of the pit. No wait, two men. The first was enormously tall and enormously thick, a bearded beast of a man who looked like he could strangle a hound with a single hand. Brown locks of shaggy hair poured messily down his head, partially concealing a pair of cheekbones that were rigid as fists. The second man was beardless and more compact, with a half-lidded, expressionless face and only a few wisps of dark hair clinging to his head. When Adrian spoke he directed himself to that one. "I'm trapped," he said. "Can you help a good fellow out of a scrape?"

Neither man responded.

Looking closer now, Adrian saw the resemblance in the faces of these two. Both shared the same deep-set and downturned eyes, the same frowning mouths, and the same wide and bulbous noses. Obviously they were brothers. "Please help me."

Again, no response. *What is wrong with these two?* Adrian contemplated a more diplomatic approach. He offered up a fake name, introducing himself as a minor emissary on an imperial mission for an administrator of Scarlet Sun. "I left my entourage to enjoy a jaunt through these lovely gardens when I stumbled into this pit," he explained. "A careless move, I know, but I injured my wrist in the fall, and I can't seem to climb out. Would you be kind enough to help? Your assistance will not go unrewarded, I promise you that."

The larger of the two gave a low growl. He lifted an arm to rest something against his shoulder. At first

Adrian thought it was a crude farmer's tool, like a handheld hoe or harrow, but no, it wasn't any of those at all . . . it was a cleaver.

The hackles rose on the back of Adrian's neck. He was neither a coward nor untrained with a weapon, but something about the shaggy-haired man unnerved him. The bastard was huge for one, his bare chest and shoulders corded with muscle and covered in hair, like a bear standing on two legs. Also, his weapon wasn't just some dull and dinted thing. It was a massive two-handed cleaver, likely used on the largest of animals, and probably so heavy that Adrian couldn't wield it properly with just his one good hand.

"Your boots, your belt, and your traveling cloak," the shaggy-haired man demanded.

Adrian swallowed a throat lump. "You're robbing me?" Still, as awful as that sounded, it also came as a bit of relief. Common brigands—yes, that was all these men were. *They don't know who I am.* That meant the robe was safe, so long as he kept it hidden—wait, where was the robe? *Oh, there, half buried in excrement. Can they see it? No, it's too dark down—*

"Your bag there, too," the other brigand said. Unlike the sonorous growl of the shaggy one, the second man's voice was softer and calmer, but by no means was it any less threatening.

Adrian didn't move. "Not this. There's nothing of value inside it."

"Open it."

Adrian bent down and untied the already loosened thong. He paused. "It's just a robe, an old and tattered robe. Please, it has no value beyond my own sentiment."

"Show me."

Adrian pulled the robe from the sack. He held it up. By some stroke of luck, the deep reddish light of dusk managed to mask the color of the garment. Even Adrian had a hard time seeing its true magnificence, and he was holding the damn thing.

The shaggy-haired man dismissed it with a wave. The other brigand wasn't so quick. He stared at the robe quietly for a time, then the faintest hint of a smile touched his otherwise emotionless face. "This is no emissary. I believe we're looking at a wanted man."

The shaggy one turned. "Who is he?"

"The imperial notice I read to you, do you not remember?" He spoke to the shaggy-haired man in a voice that seemed tired of explaining things. "They're hung at every city gate and every roadside inn from here to the southern border. The roads are swarming with soldiers, and travelers are being checked at every city gate." His dark eyes refocused on Adrian. "There's quite a reward for your capture."

"Oh, how much?" Adrian was genuinely curious.

"Three thousand strings of coin and two bolts of silk from the prime minister's own private wardrobe. The whole northern realm is looking for the thief who ran off with the imperial robe."

Adrian nodded. "Well, too bad a meager pair of brigands won't be able to claim such a reward."

The two men didn't respond to that; they simply

glared at him. Adrian wasn't sure who unnerved him more. The shaggy-haired one certainly had a look of danger about him, especially with that giant frame. But the other one—while more husky than tall—seemed to carry an air of authority about him, as though he was the one who made the decisions here. Clearly he was a man of intellect, clever and patient and difficult to read.

"We'll take the robe and sell it elsewhere then," the shaggy-haired one said.

"You'll get nothing if you do that," Adrian countered. "Do you think you can just stroll into any city and sell Lord Haroden's most luxurious treasure? No, you'd be arrested for collusion. Only I know where to sell it, and only I know whom to sell it to. The robe is worthless without me."

The husky brigand's face darkened at that. It was so subtle that even Adrian, who considered himself quite adept at reading others, barely saw it. "Allow me to offer another way," Adrian said. "A better way. Serve as my escort to the south and I'll reward you with a share of the profit. What do you have to lose? You're both outlaws, am I right? Both forced to live the life of hardship because of some unjust regulation. If we work together, only the imperial government stands to lose."

The husky one didn't speak for quite some time. At last he said, "You have a buyer waiting?"

Adrian hesitated.

"Tell me or you stay in this wretched hole."

"In Swallowtail, yes. A privateer with a crooked

eye and horseshoe mustache who answers to the name of Broden."

"How much is promised from this buyer of yours?"

"Five thousand ounces of gold. Enough to buy fifty households, one hundred plots of land, two hundred servants, and the best guard dogs around."

"We want half, or we kill you and take our chances with the robe."

A terrible deal, but Adrian was in no position to bargain. "Fine. Agreed."

The husky man nodded curtly. "My surname is Zerei, my given name is Eldred. My brother here is Olan. Olan's going to help you out of there. Go on, you heard me."

The shaggy-haired Olan gave a snort of disgust. "He's covered in dung." Nevertheless, he came over and knelt at the edge of the pit, then lowered a hand that was as large as a vinegar keg. Adrian grabbed it and was hauled onto solid ground. He spent a few moments uselessly wiping the filth from his clothes. "I'm going to the river, I need to wash up."

Neither man let him pass. Both simply stared down at him as if planning to bash his head in. Adrian froze. *Stupid, stupid, stupid! What kind of an idiot trusts a pair of outlaws?*

"First you must come with us," Eldred said.

The two men led Adrian into a woodland copse that was thick with broadleaves and yellow poplars and bristly bushes. A group of white-necked jackdaws cawed from the limbs of a gnarled deadwood, but at the approach of the three men they spread their glossy black wings and took flight. Nightfall was quickly descending, and the faces of the outlaws had all but vanished in the darkness. Fear twisted Adrian's gut and stole the moisture in his mouth. He tried to hide it, but it must've been so plainly written on his face.

They set him down on a flat bank of earth surrounded by a wall of thicket as twisted as a serpent's body. The shaggy man began rustling through small pouches and packs, likely his little cache of stolen items. Adrian turned his head and looked up. Stars shimmered softly overhead, framing the waxing crescent moon and a thin veil of wispy clouds. A breeze careened through the nearby trees, while a loon's distant call complemented the soft tranquility of cricket song. It was a beautiful night that could only have followed a beautiful day, and certainly it didn't seem like a day in which Adrian might die. He wished he knew what these two were planning, but Eldred had gone off somewhere, and Olan was gathering stones and digging a shallow pit. Before long a small cook fire flashed to life.

No one spoke. Olan brought out a haunch of salted mutton and placed it over the flames. The smell was heavenly, but the twisting ache in Adrian's stomach was hell. When had he last eaten? He'd lick the excrement from his hair just for one bite of that mutton.

"Are you going to kill me?"

Olan downed a huge swig from his gourd-bottle,

then corked the top and belched. He had the soaked stare of a man who enjoyed his wine, and something told him that Olan could outdrink a thirsty bear. "No."

"Then what is your brother doing?"

Olan took a bite of the meat. Grease dripped into the dark curls of his beard. "Preparing the serum."

"What sort of serum?"

"To see if you're telling the truth."

Adrian frowned. The last thing he wanted to do was be the subject of some strange man's concoction. It sounded like a heap of rubbish, yet Adrian wasn't foolish enough to admit that aloud, so instead he asked, "Are you two some sort of occultists?"

"Not me."

"Then what is it you do?"

His mouth was full. "Rob people."

"Well, no, I mean what *did* you do before . . .?"

"Ox butcher."

"That explains the cleaver," Adrian said. "Can I have a taste of that meat?"

Turning, the shaggy man glared with red-rimmed eyes. "You talk too much." The eyes moved up and down, examining Adrian slowly and pointedly. "Where's your other glove?"

"I only have one."

Eldred returned and crouched beside Adrian. In his hand was an old mortar and pestle, which he used to crush and mix several different herbs and reagents together. Then he dumped the trituration into an earthenware bowl that was filled with a strangely glutinous liquid.

"What is that—blood?" Adrian asked.

"Snakelion blood. Do you know what a Snakelion is?"

"Do you need to ask? Snakelion. A lion's body with a snake's head, am I correct?"

"Sarcasm is the sanctuary of the weak," Eldred replied. "A Snakelion has many forms and many features, but always it possesses a leonine body covered in imbricated scales. They're found only in the far southern wastelands, where they sift through the black dunes and strike unwary travelers. Not uncommon to find men propped in the sand with their limbs torn from their sockets."

"How gruesome," Adrian said dryly. "What are you doing with its blood? Are you an herbalist?"

Eldred paused from his work to gaze flatly at him, as if offended by the amateur remark. "I'm a pyromantic examiner who specializes in the arcane principles of mendacity. You see, a Snakelion's blood is the very crux of my procedures. To yield this powerful concoction it must be mixed with the ancillary herbs of star anise and milfoil and wormwood, along with the hind legs of nineteen male grasshoppers."

"Nineteen male grasshoppers? Must be a pain to scrounge the woods searching for those things. How do you even know which are males?"

"Males lack the rod that the females use to deposit eggs into the soil. It's called an ovipositor. Also, only the males make that distinctive chirrup sound—they do so by rubbing their hind legs against their wings. Fascinating, I know. Any other senseless questions or observations before we begin?"

"Nineteen's a strange number. Why not make it twenty? Seems a much more fitting figure. Have you ever found a male grasshopper with only one hind leg? I can imagine how difficult it must be to make that chirrup sound, don't you think?"

"Are you finished?"

"Yes. No, wait. What exactly are you doing?"

"The veracity of every man's intentions is revealed by the Celestial Deity of Skyfire. If you are telling the truth, the ingestion of this concoction will reveal warmth and tranquility to the eye. Do you understand?"

"Yeah, you want me to consume a bunch of bloody grasshopper legs."

Eldred's face softened just a touch. "Look, it's plain that you are a skeptical man. Most intelligent minds are. But the revelation of truth is achieved regardless of the recipient's beliefs. Now take off that glove and put your hands together."

When Adrian didn't obey, Eldred motioned once again. "The glove, I said take it off."

"No."

Olan leaned close and pressed something sharp under Adrian's chin. The ox cleaver. "I would love to hear you say 'no' again." His deep-set eyes were colder than murder.

"Better remove it," Eldred insisted.

"You don't understand. It's not—"

Eldred grabbed Adrian's wrist, hiked up the sleeve of his tunic, and yanked off the glove. His eyes widened. "What in the . . .?"

It was a charred hunk of necrotic flesh, black and withered and sloughing eschar from the tips of the fingers to the middle of the forearm. The old and torn bandages wrapped around it offered little in the way of concealment. Adrian withdrew his hand at once, hiding the disfigurement beneath the folds of his traveling cloak.

"Did you see that," Olan blurted. "It's blacker than the devil's bunghole."

"What the hell happened to you?" Eldred asked.

Adrian clenched his jaw. "What difference does it make? You wanted to see my hand, and now you have. Don't touch it. I'm warning you, you will not like what happens if you do."

"It's diseased," Olan said. "Tell him to put the goddamn glove back on."

Eldred handed the glove back to Adrian. "Fine, no matter, we'll continue with you wearing it. Here, sit up. Straighter. Now bring your hands together. Like this, yes, that's it." He poured the foul liquid into Adrian's cupped palms, made him repeat a string of mumbo jumbo, and told him to drink but not to swallow.

Adrian grimaced at the vile taste. He wanted to spit it out, but he knew Eldred would just make him drink it again, so he kept his mouth shut and breathed through his nose and tried not to taste anything. A foulness rose in his stomach, one that didn't hesitate to inch up his throat. *How disgusting. How absolutely disgusting.* He pushed down the urge to vomit, and waited and waited and waited . . . and just when he couldn't wait any longer, Eldred told him to spit it into the fire. "Do it quickly."

The liquid sizzled when it touched the flames, producing a blast of heat that punched Adrian's face like an open furnace. He shut his eyes and leaned over, retching and spitting and spitting and retching, yet he couldn't get rid of the taste. Nothing satisfying about blood and dirt and grasshopper legs, no matter how hungry you were.

When his eyes reopened, Adrian saw the flames licking and lapping the air. It was hard to discern at first, but beneath the flickering oranges and reds and yellows . . . he glimpsed another color, an undertone of blue—not bright and soft like the sky, but a deep blue—like the waters of a midsummer lagoon. Adrian couldn't believe it. Blue flames! In moments, the warm and tranquil tones faded back to the radiant oranges and reds, and the fire returned to its former self.

"I saw it," Adrian blurted. "I saw blue flames— that means I'm telling the truth, yes?"

Eldred nodded. "The celestial deity has revealed the truth behind your words."

"Thank the gods," Adrian said. He hawked and spat a few more times to rid himself of the foul taste. "Anything else you need me to do? Perhaps lick a poisonous toad or shove a spider up my nose?"

Eldred shook his head. "There's that sarcasm

again." He turned to regard Olan. "The truth has been revealed, Brother. We will escort this man to the southern lands."

Olan nodded but the cleaver remained clenched in his oversized fist. "Fine, but he'd better keep that dead hand away from me . . . or by the gods I will cut it off."

Chapter Five

The three men journeyed without incident for the next fortnight.

Adrian's new companions proved to be quite the adept travelers, Eldred especially. The man seemed to recognize every rustle and peep from every creature, and could identify the inherent properties of every tree and shrub and creeper they came across. But he moved swiftly and spoke only when speaking was necessary, so that meant silence ruled for most of the day. Adrian tried to engage the brothers in conversation, but his efforts were squashed like a beetle under a boot. The outlaws were entirely devoid of cordiality.

Adrian wasn't like them. He would never be like them.

The roads they traveled were narrow and difficult. Most twisted and snaked along the outskirts of the various mountain hamlets. Foot travelers were rare, and the lack of wagon ruts in the road meant porters were even rarer. They did spot the occasional grog shop or roadside inn, but these places were wisely avoided. Olan huffed and grumbled when his gourd-bottle ran empty of wine, but Eldred ignored the complaints.

The brothers seemed to examine every passerby they saw. Adrian knew what they were thinking—he was no fool. For the life of an outlaw, survival meant always looking for the next victim, always looking at the next possible advantage. Robbing travelers and ransacking merchant wagons was a basic necessity, so naturally the brothers spent time gauging and analyzing their possible targets. They did this with a frightening degree of profes-sionalism, one that was surely honed by years of experi-ence. Adrian sorely lacked such experience. He felt like a child tagging along with a pair of elder siblings, and the more the two brothers began to murmur and whisper secretly to each other, the more Adrian grew irritated and resentful. He couldn't let this happen. He wouldn't.

The next morning, just after they broke their fast and prepared to set out, Adrian squared his shoulders and stood his tallest before the brothers. "Before we go any farther, I have something to say."

Both men frowned.

"If you two are to accompany me all the way to the southern city of Swallowtail, then I must make something clear. There will be no robbing, no looting, and no murdering. None. That is all I ask."

Olan's bulbous nose twitched. "Do you want to make it to your destination or not? We've got little food and even less coin."

"I know," Adrian said. "But you both know how to survive in the wilds. I'm certain we can get by without causing any grief."

Olan let out a throaty laugh. "Do you think your hands are not as soiled as ours? Err, hand."

"I know I've committed a capital offense, but I didn't cause any pain or suffering. The only wound was to the pride and dignity of a powerful and beloved ruler. Now, I want to be clear. No robbing, no looting, and no murdering. That is my rule, and it must be obeyed, or our little partnership disbands right here."

Adrian was sure they'd see through his bold words and laugh at the scared man beneath. Worse, he feared Olan might cut him down with that giant cleaver of his. Thankfully, Eldred replied before any of that could happen. "Fine. We agree to your terms."

Olan spun on his brother, nostrils flaring.

"Relax, Brother." He looked back at Adrian. "You have my word. Though it may not seem as much, I assure you that your precepts will be honored."

Adrian nodded, but by no means did he trust him. How sincere was an outlaw's word, after all?

They traveled in silence for a while. Just before

high sun the company wended their way around a branching gorge and found themselves surrounded by tall beetling crags, mountain brooks bristling with wisteria, and stands of black pine and cypress. Such a beautiful panorama—even disgruntled Olan seemed alleviated by the sight.

Eldred pointed at something in the distant ranges. A secluded cluster of outbuildings and temples and cottages, enwreathed with clouds and neatly tucked neatly away from the hooks of civilization. "A monastery," he said. "We'll find sanctuary there. Simple fare, heated water to wash ourselves, a few nights' rest on cushions of chaff."

"Is it safe?" Adrian asked.

"All monks have forsaken concerns of the material world. They'll not ask questions."

"Any chance they'll have wine?" Olan chimed in.

"No," Eldred said.

Adrian gave a nod. "Fine, but we must remember what I said earlier. No robbing, no looting, and no—"

Olan grunted. "It's hallowed grounds. What sort of man do you take me for?"

A cruel and violent one, Adrian thought.

The path narrowed as it climbed a bare and winding ascension, then narrowed even more before halting at a steep drop-off. A rickety wooden bridge built against the mountainside was their only crossing —it was not so much a bridge as a frail ledge of uneven planks that were held in place by hempen rope and rusty nails and jutting lower support beams.

Adrian went to the edge and foolishly looked

down. The black maw of a rocky ravine gazed up at him, a long and ceaseless gaze that buckled his knees and dizzied his thoughts. *Don't be a coward,* he told himself. He watched as the brothers moved across, their heavy tread causing the thin horizontal planks to wobble and groan. They made it look so easy, but then again, they made everything look easy.

Adrian used his good hand to grip the mountain-side since there were no railings. He took a single step forward, then another, and another. The brothers were growing impatient, but Adrian didn't care. The bridge wasn't solid in the least, the wood old and dilapidated and the ropes frayed and gray. *Don't think about them, don't think about falling, just think about taking one step at a time . . . one small, simple step.* Adrian exhaled and took another step. One more and then another. He was doing fine. He was going to make it. Already halfway across and he was doing fine.

The sun decided that now was the best time to appear between the jagged mountain crags. Blinding light spread in all directions. Adrian had to let go of the mountainside in order to shade his eyes. He squinted and lowered his gaze and did his best to keep moving. Another step. Another and another. *You're doing fine. You're going to make it. You're definitely going to—*

Wood cracked and the bridge moaned, ready to give way. Adrian's legs burst into motion. Planks rattled underfoot, each one louder than the last. His heart pushed up his throat. *I'm going to make it, I'm going to make it.* Solid ground was just ahead. He used his good hand to push off the jagged rock wall. Pieces of stone broke free, plummeting silently into that terrifying maw of darkness. *Almost there . . . almost there . . .*

Adrian flung himself onto solid ground—but he overcommitted to the jump, careened out of control, and crashed into Olan. It might as well have been a wall of mortared granite, because the big man didn't budge. Adrian stumbled back a few steps before landing on his rump with a pronounced *thud*.

The two brothers looked at him, blinked, and broke out in uproarious laughter. It was the first time Adrian heard such sounds from either of them. Eldred's was a raspy, subdued laugh, while Olan had more of a hearty, thunderous guffaw. Adrian didn't care that the laughter was at his expense. He was just happy to see them laughing, and he was even happier to be alive. Yes, that was all that mattered.

Eldred helped him up. Adrian turned to face the monastery. The tall wooden gates stood open, and a footpath of white stone led to the cloisters. Patches of passionflowers and trellises overgrown with clematis vines surrounded the company. A rocky overhang to the east served as a waterfall spout, as the gentle cascade poured down into the lower tarns. Men in sackcloth habits sat in meditative mudras. All were thin and ragged and leathery of flesh, and their heads were shaved to the skull. Most were silent and motionless, save one or two who spared a quick glance at the unannounced visitors.

Eldred led the way into the inner compound. Up an old and twisted stairway and across the forecourt, they saw a pair of goat-headed statues guarding the arched entranceway of the monastery's main hall. Somewhere inside, a man was shouting.

"YOU HAVE SHAMELESSLY BROKEN TWO OF THE FIVE PRINCIPLES THAT BIND EACH MONK TO THIS VERY MOUNTAIN."

Adrian halted. "Maybe we should go back."

Olan gave a derisive snort. "Is your mettle so easily dulled?" He walked through the archway and disappeared inside the hall. Eldred followed. Adrian turned and gave one last look at the monastery grounds. Nothing seemed amiss, so he turned back and went inside.

Huge wooden rafters ran across the ceiling, supported by tall pillars that were bent and cracked and stained with bird droppings. Crude sculptures of goatmen in meditative mudras were positioned in various places, their horns spiraling decoratively around the nearest pillars. An altar stood on an uneven dais at the far end of the hall, its surface covered in incense holders and censers and caprine idols. Two monks stood at a small table beside the altar, one meek and silent, the other livid and shouting.

"HOW COULD YOU COMPORT YOURSELF WITH SUCH DISGRACE?!"

The scolder was obviously a man of high importance—the abbot, most likely—as he wasn't dressed in regular rags, but in a rich raven-black cassock. The sleeves of his garment were drawn to his elbows, exposing a pair of skinny arms. His face was skinny as well, his features delicate and hawk-like—neither old nor unpleasant.

Olan stopped in the middle of the hall. He brushed away the shaggy brown hair from his eyes and gave a pronounced cough.

The two monks turned.

"Forgive our intrusion," Eldred said. "We are but simple travelers, we mean no harm or disrespect."

The abbot regarded the uninvited guests with a detached gaze, but after a moment he bowed his head, though it seemed more out of duty than warmth. "No words are needed, as no judgment is passed." He took a few steps forward and opened slightly his arms. "Silver Wind Monastery is a welcome refuge to all. Take comfort in the monastic order of the Sacred Argali." He sounded pleasant enough, yet there was something about his eyes—something about the way the man was looking at Adrian . . . a curious look, one that Adrian didn't like it at all.

"We seek a place of rest, a bit of honest fare, nothing more," Eldred told him. "We'll pay what is customary for lodgings."

The abbot was quick to shake his head. "You know I cannot accept your coin. Our fare is crude, but what we have is yours to enjoy." He sent away the scolded monk and offered the three visitors to join him at the kneeling cushions. A moment later two attendant monks approached with bowls of pears and sliced quinces and loquats. Adrian chose a quince and swallowed a fresh cut of the tart yellow fruit.

The abbot said, "My Argalist name is Sincere Sunlight, my given name Yared. You must forgive my earlier outburst—such anger is never acceptable in a holy place. But I believe your sudden intrusion may have been a blessing. You see, there are no accidents or errors in the Great Path of the Sacred Argali. What I mean to say is perhaps I've been a little harsh with my prior. I will reconsider his punishment."

Eldred asked, "What offense has he committed?"

"In my absence, he has shamed the monastery by drinking wine and spending coin on women. Standard punishment is forty lashes of the switch and expulsion, but this was his second offense. He was condemned to a slow death by starvation."

"A bit excessive," Adrian said.

"Wait a moment," Olan blurted, wiping the fruit juice from his lips. "You have wine and women here?"

"Wine shops are found in the lower hamlets," the abbot replied, though his tone was rather listless. "It seems the temptations of the outside world are proving too great for some of us." He seemed lost in his thoughts for a moment, as if he'd forgotten that he was sitting among strangers.

Olan swallowed a halved loquat and said, "Wouldn't mind a young bawd to keep me warm tonight. You could use one, too, you know. A little flower on your pillow and maybe you won't be so goddamn cranky."

The abbot smiled at that, though it was without mirth. "Our monastery has seen enough broken principles as of late."

Eldred said, "Shopkeepers in your jurisdiction shouldn't be authorized to sell wine to a monk."

"And they're not, but you know that a well-greased palm overrides any regulation."

Olan growled. "Well, I don't see the problem. A man has needs."

Abbot Yared shook his head at that. "The monks of Silver Wind are beyond such primitive desires." He rose to place a pinch of incense in a censer, then performed a handful of simple reverences to the idol. He turned back to the guests and said, "You three have a haggard look about you, as though you've been running from someone. Now I don't know who that someone is, but as I said earlier, no words are needed, as no judgment is passed." He seemed to take a long moment to himself. "But I do wish to say one thing. The day will eventually come in which you separate from your mortal coil. When that happens, you will ascend to the Great Rivers of Transmigration and stand before the Five Deathkings of All That Becomes. Now my question is this: how do you think you will be judged? Will you return to the world of the living in a new body, or will you be sent to the underworld to face an eternity of suffering. Only your heart knows the truth."

No one answered that, and after a long and silent moment the abbot said, "I must retire for the evening. I've been suffering from an acute liver imbalance since returning from my recent pilgrimage. Difficult is the life of an itinerant monk. To inform others of the Argalist Path in a non-dogmatic and non-authoritarian manner, without inquisition or coercion . . . well, sadly, many are no longer convinced this way, nor are they touched by prayer or parable." He gave a heavy sigh.

"We thank you for your time and hospitality," Eldred said, bowing his head. "The moon is waxing; we will be gone before it turns."

"No, please, stay as long as you wish. After your meal my attendants will escort you to your private room. We'll talk again soon."

The guestroom was lightly furnished with wooden couches and two small altars that were sprinkled with incense and bowls and paper crafts. Novice monks brought in buckets of heated water so the travelers could wash their hands and feet. Scrubbing the filth and dirt encrusted on his skin was among the greatest sensations Adrian had felt in a long time. Olan seemed to share his mirth—the big man only complained once about the lack of wine. Afterward, they lay down on cushions of chaff, and next Adrian knew it was morning. He urged the brothers to wake up. "We need to leave."

Olan rubbed the sleep from his eyes and snorted. "The hell are you afraid of?"

"I don't trust him, the abbot," Adrian said.

"Never seen a holy man with a bellyful of wrath?" Olan remarked.

"I don't know . . . the way he was looking at me. He knows something."

"He's a monk," Eldred reminded him. "Monks live unfettered by the concerns of the outside world. Besides, leaving now would be seen as an affront—it would disfavor us with the Sacred Argali."

"I don't care about some bull-spit deity," Adrian said. "It's not safe here."

Olan went to reply but it was Eldred who spoke first. "Only fools leave such decisions to their meager selves. I will call upon the Celestial Deity of Skyfire to reveal the truth of the matter." He began gathering his materials.

Adrian shot him a dubious frown. He didn't even mean to do it.

Eldred raised a single bushy eyebrow. "Still doubting the principles of pyromantic examination?"

Adrian looked down at his gloved hand. "Hard to believe a little blood and a few grasshopper legs can predict the truth of a man."

"Small-minded men fear what they don't understand."

"And fools believe in something just because they are told to."

That made Eldred sigh. "Since the earliest records of the imperial annals, emperors have employed men of otherworldly abilities to decipher auguries and discern truths and chart the course of imperial rule. Do you think of these men as fools? There are many methods of divination, do you think them all fraudulent as well? Extispicy, haruspicy, water scrying, cloud gazing, divinations that require complex components. Each subset requires years of study, decades even.

Some say it takes a lifetime to fully understand the smallest and subtlest intricacies of such arcane and powerful—"

"Have they ever been wrong?"

"What?"

"Your examinations, have they ever been wrong?"

Eldred gave him the look of an adult amused by a child. "There is no 'wrong' in my examinations. What is revealed to be truth . . . is truth."

"Fine," Adrian told him. "Call upon this deity. Do you have enough grasshopper legs or should we start scrounging around the cloisters?"

Eldred shot him a frown, then gathered his materials and left the room. He was back in a few minutes. He walked to the low table and set down his mortar and pouches. A faint cough escaped his lips.

Adrian was staring at him. "Well?"

Eldred didn't look up. "The abbot's gone."

"Gone?"

"He was called away from the monastery, some kind of urgent matter. Should return tomorrow after dawn."

Adrian's heart began to pound in his chest. "Pack your gear. We're leaving. *Now.*"

Chapter Six

"We're not going anywhere," Olan growled, and it was obvious that his word would brook no further debate. "You know I never cared for you to begin with, Deadhand. But now . . . your cowardice makes me think even less of you."

"Quiet," Eldred said. He was staring out of the unlatched window. "We're too late. Soldiers."

Adrian moved to look outside. Serried ranks of heavily armed men appeared on the forecourt, the dark steel of their armor shimmering in the moonlight. Adrian cursed. *I knew it, I goddamn knew it.* He turned and grabbed Eldred's shoulder. "The bastard abbot betrayed us."

"How many?" Olan asked.

"Thirty at least, all footmen," Eldred answered. "They must've dismounted at the bridge. No one's crossing that on a barded charger."

"Mounted or not, it makes no difference. We've nowhere to run." Adrian didn't mean to sound so desperate, but he couldn't help himself. He turned and gathered his belongings, adjusted his traveling cloak, and slung the haversack with the imperial robe across his chest.

Olan was twitching and flexing, as if preparing to take on all the soldiers himself. Adrian said, "You must have some bugs in the brain. There's no way we can fight our way out of this. Hey, are you listening to me?"

"Adrian's right," Eldred said. "Only way out is across that bridge."

Fear crept up Adrian's throat and froze his words on his tongue. *We're trapped. It's over. Just as my journey begins, it so quickly ends.* His mouth opened, but all he managed to utter was, "We'll never make it."

"Probably not," Eldred replied, and the three men started across the room. Just as they reached the door, it swung open and the scolded prior appeared. He didn't spare a moment. "A hidden recess, there, behind the wall curtain. Go quickly."

The space was small and untidy and reeked of stale grain. Olan shifted uncomfortably in the dark, while Eldred moved only to unhook the cudgel at his

54

hip. Adrian could hear the sound of voices growing louder and closer and closer and louder. He peered out from behind the folds of the handwoven fabric. A company of northern soldiers burst into the room, boots stomping and armor clanging. Leading them was a huge grizzled man in a spiked helm and polished steel breastplate. "Who's that?" Olan whispered, his head so close Adrian could feel the bristles of his beard.

"That would be the high commander of the northern army, Krall Vyren," Adrian replied softly.

Krall's head turned as if listening. Adrian released the fabric and slid away from the recess. *Did he hear me?* Adrian thought. *How the hell did he hear me?* His good hand gripped the hilt of his knife . . . but the moment passed and Krall turned away. The soldiers began ransacking the room, overturning the wooden couches and trashing the altars in search of the fugitive. Adrian waited for an armored hand to pull aside the wall curtain but it never did, and before long the same boots rumbled and the same armor clanged as the soldiers exited. Adrian emerged from the hidden recess and crept to the window. The soldiers had returned to the outer forecourt, and now High Commander Krall Vyren was ordering the abbot to stand before him. Yared looked so small and frail before the ranks of these heavily armored men.

"Don't play me false, monk," Krall growled. "Is this some sort of diversionary tactic? Complicity is to be harshly punished."

"No, my lord, I had my prior personally prepare

the guestroom for our visitors," the abbot pleaded. "He can attest to my innocence."

All eyes turned to the prior.

The meek man looked squarely at the abbot. "Forgive me, master, but you didn't order any such preparations. We've no guests."

Krall ordered the guards to seize the abbot.

"Liar," the abbot shouted at the prior. "You don't deserve the cloth."

A mailed fist struck the abbot in the gut, dropping him to his knees and shutting his mouth. The soldiers then hauled the poor man off, while Krall Vyren turned to face the remaining monks. "Any man who harbors and feeds a known fugitive will suffer as his accomplice. Don't think you are the exception, monks. Lord Haroden is not above the punishment of holy men." With that, Krall turned and left, his company of soldiers trailing behind him.

Adrian moved away from the window and released a deep breath. The relief was like a huge wet comber washing over him. He would live this night. By the gods he would live.

When the prior returned to the hall, Adrian greeted him with a deep bow of his head. "You risked your neck to spare the meager lives of strangers. Why?"

"I would've suffered a slow and painful death if not for your arrival. How could I not offer my aid? Besides, that virtueless scoundrel of an abbot needed to be relieved of his title, and judging by the lack of monks that came to his aid earlier, I'm assuming I wasn't alone in that notion."

Adrian bowed his head once more. He wasn't sure what to think about all this deception, but the prior did save him from certain capture, and for that he was grateful.

"I overheard the officers before," the prior went on. "Pickets have been posted along every road from here to Beetleburr. The mountain paths are no longer safe. The Rhinoceros Lord is spending a small ransom to find you. They say his financial officers are working tirelessly through the evenings, allocating funds to military officers and districts for the capture of the infamous thief."

For some reason Adrian smirked at that, even though it meant his journey would become that much more treacherous.

The prior was staring at him. "Does that please you? You are a curious man. Best to move south by southwest."

Eldred frowned. "That'll lead us to the Darkwing Gap."

The prior nodded. "It's the only place even High Commander Krall Vyren won't pass through."

"What? Why not?" Adrian asked.

Eldred looked askance at Adrian, as if he were dealing with a child. "The people of the northern villages have a little saying: 'When you hear birds and squirrels but see not a thing, beware, beware, the Chitterers of Darkwing.'"

Adrian said, "Chitterers. What the hell is a Chitterer?"

The silence that followed was strangely unsettling. Olan broke it at last when he broke wind. The four men shared a brief laugh, but it wasn't enough to lift the mood.

"Diabolical creatures," the prior said. "Ambushers and slaughterers of unwary travelers."

"Sounds exciting," Adrian said. "I'm all atwitter with anticipation."

Eldred sighed. "That sarcasm again. You know it's quite unbecoming."

Adrian responded to that with a dramatic nod, but when he looked up he realized the other men were staring at him as though he were either a halfwit or a madman. Maybe he was a bit of both.

Chapter Seven

$\mathcal{D}$ays drifted into weeks as the company moved farther and farther from civilization. Adrian had never been so deep into the wilds with so little concern. Eldred knew how to make the most efficient snares, knew where to find the best waterholes, and knew what herbs and vegetation were safest to consume. Wax currants and chokecherries were among their daily nutriment, while occasionally they foraged for gooseberries and edible mushrooms that looked no different from their poisonous kin. On less fortunate nights they prepared soups with pinecones and nettles, but those nights were rare, as the land had much to provide during these spirited spring months.

They reached the Darkwing Gap a week later. It was a wondrous sight . . . an enormous rift in the mountains carved by a river that twisted like a serpent in tall grass. Red pines dominated the lower slopes and plateaus, while the higher rises were draped in robust firs and spruces. The long sweep of conifers was occasionally broken by stands of hickories and aspens whose yellow-gold leaves streaked across the land like trails of corncob.

They traveled mostly through an undergrowth of bushes and bracken and bramble. In the nearby brooks water chestnuts and other sedges flourished, while lethal black henbane gathered in malodorous clumps along the hillsides. They used makeshift nets to catch the shad migrating upriver, while taking precautions to avoid the black bears that wandered along the lower streambeds. But the deeper into the gap they traveled, the sparser the surrounding wildlife became. Gone were the titmice and chickadees caroling from outstretched boughs, the same of the gray squirrels that tittered from higher tree limbs. There was nothing in sight—and yet they began to hear a quiet chittering . . . a dulcet, indistinct sound that was lost among the trees. A knife of dread twisted in Adrian's gut. *When you hear birds and squirrels but see not a thing, beware, beware, the Chitterers of Darkwing.* Every step he took, every twig that crunched underfoot . . . it was as if someone were watching them, stalking them like a silent predator. But nothing ever appeared, and as the day wended its way into night, no one spoke about it. The brothers didn't seem rattled in the slightest, so Adrian convinced himself he wasn't rattled either. But that wasn't entirely true.

Sleep didn't come. Maniacal faces filled Adrian's mind whenever he closed his eyes. He didn't even know what a Chitterer looked like, but his mind had no trouble conjuring up some ghastly images. Worse, the darkness brought a menagerie of sounds that was like crossing over the threshold of some nightmarish plane. Harrowing croaks and hair-lifting grunts and ghostly drawn-out moans all filled the midnight sky. Even the cricket song was more ominous in tone, sounding less like the chirps of tiny insects and more like the snarls of palm-sized bruins. And once, when it was deep in the night, Adrian heard an absolutely awful howl that was so loud it woke both brothers. *Beware the Chitterers of Darkwing. Beware the Chitterers of Darkwing.* Adrian sat clutching his knife until at last dawn's golden light decided to reappear.

Later that morning, Eldred spotted a corpse.

It lay at the bottom of a rocky pit, silent and motionless and stretched out in a tangle of thorns and shrubbery. The three men peered over the steep precipice for a better look. Despite the distance and the fact that the body was lying in an awkward sprawl, Adrian could see that the face was of a man . . . a man who died with a terrible fright in his heart. This must've happened recently, because the scavengers had not yet gotten to him.

"Looks like the poor bastard fell," Eldred said. He scanned the area, searching for a way down.

"What are you doing?" Adrian protested.

"He might have something useful on him."

"Eldred, remember my rules. They apply to the dead as well. Besides, it's too treacherous a descent. Best to just move on."

"Foolish to pass up something of value. A weapon, some food, or perhaps a new pair of boots large enough for my brother, so he can finally stop whining about his blisters."

Olan grunted. "Big feet have big blisters, goddamn it."

Adrian shook his head and reiterated that they must move on. Surprisingly, Eldred respected his wishes, and a few days later they exited the Darkwing Gap. Adrian was terribly exhausted and terribly unfocused and even a bit unhinged, but that night, for the first time in a while, he slept. He slept and he didn't even dream, which was a rarity for him these days.

When he awoke he shielded his eyes from the flicker of warm light. A cook fire crackled nearby, the smoke vanishing into the hazy sky. Was it dawn? No, twilight. The brothers were feasting on a pair of plucked grouse and apparently sharing a bowl of wine from a bucket.

Olan's eyes drifted to Adrian. "Back from the dead." He ladled out wine into a bowl, then offered a cut of roasted meat. "Eat. Drink. You slept through the entire day."

Adrian looked suspiciously at the offering. "Where did you get this wine?"

The firelight danced on Olan's face, casting shadows and highlighting the skin around his deep-set eyes. "We met a traveling wine seller just after high sun. Good tidings, Deadhand, the Centipede Road is no more than a few miles away. That'll take us straight to Swallowtail. What? Don't look at me like that, we didn't break any of your precepts. We used the coin in your purse."

Adrian pushed the bowl away. "Are you mad? Lord Haroden is expending every last resource to hunt me down. You can't just purchase wine from some wandering merchant. How do you know it's not drugged?"

Olan shifted a leg and broke wind. "It's not."

"Adrian's right," Eldred said. "You need to be more prudent, Brother." He looked at Adrian. "And you need to eat. You're starting to look a bit scrawny."

Adrian wasn't sure how he looked, but by the gods he was hungry, and even though the meat was over-cooked and the wild rice and hazel nuts were all clumped together like duff on the forest floor, Adrian savored it all. He had a lot to be thankful for. The Darkwing Gap was behind them, the Centipede Road just ahead, and goddamn it the food tasted like something from the main course of an emperor's banquet.

"We should've listened to you earlier, Adrian," Eldred admitted. "Back at the monastery. You were right about the abbot—we should've left right away."

You could tell Eldred was not a man used to displaying such humility, so Adrian took it as an enormous compliment. Before he could reply, however, Olan belched so loud the surrounding woods echoed, and Eldred gave him a good upbraiding.

"What?" the shaggy man questioned. "We're out of the gap. Safe from the Chitterers, are we not?"

"That doesn't mean we're safe from fox fiends and ogres and whatever else might lurk in this goddamn forest. You know, Brother, sometimes I don't know if you're a toper or just a fool."

Olan's bearded face twisted in confusion. "I don't know what a toper is. And I'm not a fool."

Eldred clarified by calling him a drunkard, and the two brothers began to quarrel, in the way that only brothers did. Adrian leaned back and licked the grease from his lips. It pleased him to see the more human side of these two outlaws. The coldness of their exteriors seemed to be slowly melting away, revealing the emotions of two somewhat ordinary men beneath. It was as if Adrian was finally being allowed inside their world, and he was thankful for that.

"You used to drink so much you beat your apprentice bloody," Eldred snapped at his brother. "Do you not remember?"

"The bastard was stealing from me."

Eldred scowled. "He began stealing *after* you battered him in one of your many drunken rampages."

Olan shook his shaggy head, growled something unintelligible, and turned to Adrian. "My elder brother sometimes thinks he's better off without me."

Eldred scoffed. "I'm a goddamn outlaw because of you."

Olan looked grimly at him. "I didn't mean to kill the prick. You know that."

"I don't understand," Adrian said.

"Well, you see, my brother here"—his eyes flicked to Eldred—"you want to tell him? No? Fine. I'll do it." He turned back to Adrian. "My elder brother was once a rather respectable man . . . a man whose truth-telling readings granted him a rather comfortable life-style. But all that changed when a comely woman came to him for an examination. You should've seen my brother around this broad, what a bumbling goddamn fool. Anyway, the woman was suspicious of her husband's activities, both in his personal and business affairs. Turns out, she had a right to be. The Celestial Deity of Skyfire decreed the husband not only an adulterous cad, but a real crooked mother-screwer who made his fortune through exploitation and a heap of other crimes. Well, needless to say, the husband wasn't happy about losing his wife's faith."

"He was a prick," Eldred said flatly, his arms crossed.

"Yes, but he was a well-to-do prick, and so he used his coin and his muscle to defame my good brother's name. Within a moon's turn poor Eldred had lost all his customers, and worse, the bastard husband hired a pair of thugs to knock him around. That of course didn't sit well with me."

"What did you do?" Adrian asked.

"What any loyal brother would do. I grabbed a jointed bludgeon and smashed the two wretches and then went after the husband. I meant to give the prick a light drubbing, but I guess I took it a little too far. I don't care, the damned fool deserved to die. A real worm of a man, that one. Why are you looking at me like that, Deadhand?"

Adrian swallowed a charred piece of meat. "I expected an offense that was . . . less honorable, you could say."

Olan's cavernous eyes twinkled in the firelight. "Does it shock you to know that I am not a vile man?"

It did. After all, Olan's crime wasn't some base act targeted at an innocent victim. No, he had simply doled out a punishment that was duly deserved.

"Obviously all men are not what they seem, Deadhand. Like yourself. You stole the prized garment of a powerful ruler, and yet, something tells me you're not just some dishonest little thief."

Adrian took a moment to find the right reply. When he spoke his voice was distant and small. "I was an artisan once. A stone carver."

Olan snorted at that. "Oh, an artsy fellow. That explains a lot."

"A rather successful artisan, I might add. I was a young man when I mastered the finest techniques of the north, techniques well beyond their time, and my carvings were sold to some of the wealthiest men in the city. I had access to the highest quality carborundum sanders and the finest minerals, everything from nephrite to jadeite to malachite and serpentine and skystone. By the gods those were the brightest of times . . . twenty-two years and already I had my own guild and my own apprentices and servants. My days were spent in creative work, while my evenings were spent hobnobbing with powerful aristocrats. I even married the daughter of one, a master ironsmith with so much gold it was said to leak from his pores. You should've seen the dowry . . . brocade sacks filled with strings of silver and gold, gilded candles and vermeil vases and mosaics of glazed tesserae, bolts of silk and satin and—" He stopped suddenly and looked down, not speaking again for a long moment. "My wife died two years later, in childbirth."

Olan didn't reply to that, and silence passed for a time. Crickets and katydids chirped in the distant bushes. The shaggy man's eyes eventually moved down to Adrian's gloved hand. "So is it burned? Diseased?"

Adrian looked down. Something persuaded him to pull off the doeskin glove, and when he did he raised the black and blistered hand eye level, turning his wrist as if to display the horrible disfigurement. "Burned. I didn't even realize what happened until after. It didn't hurt, but the eschar . . . it spread up to my fingers and down my forearm, through the skin and into the underlying muscle and bone. But the strange thing is that it still hurts, even though the nerves were destroyed. And more than that—and you may not believe this, but every living thing I touch with this hand begins to burn. I don't know why. A curse, maybe."

Eldred was looking at him with incredulous eyes.

"A curse? Didn't expect a skeptic to utter such a word."

"Yes, well, I don't know what else to call it. I sought every physician I could find, and spent most of my coin on surgical incisions and medical debridement, but nothing could heal the necrotic tissue or improve the blood and lymphatic circulation. I squandered the rest of my coin on alchemists and herbalists who offered fancy decoctions and elixirs and medicaments." He gritted his teeth. "They were all frauds. Every last one of them. But it was too late. I was out of coin, and I couldn't even work to make more. My apprentices and servants all left me, my households were repossessed or foreclosed. In a year's time I went from being a prominent artist to an impoverished wretch living in a tiny shack like some goddamn base-born drudge."

The brothers were silent for a time. At length Olan said, "At least you survived."

"What?"

"Fires are deadly. Smoke inhalation will poison your lungs. You're fortunate it didn't take your life." Olan ladled out another bowl of wine but didn't drink it.

Adrian's nod was slow and hesitant. "Part of me wishes it had taken my life. I would've journeyed through the Great Rivers of Transmigration, faced my judgment, and returned to the earth as a whole being once again. You know, Abbot Yared asked us how we would be judged by the Five Deathkings of All That Becomes. He thought me a corrupt man, a thief and a scoundrel, but in my heart I believe I've led a virtuous life. I don't deserve——"

"*Quiet,*" Eldred hissed. His eyes were cast on the surrounding forest, his expression sober and alert.

Adrian looked around. Nothing in sight. No, wait, that wasn't true. There were shadows flitting here and there, faintly in the dull moonlight. For a moment he thought High Commander Krall Vyren had somehow found him, but then he heard the sounds . . . the soft and eerily dulcet sounds, and his heart froze in his chest. These were not the sounds of gentle birds or squirrels. No, these were something far more sinister.

Chitterers.

Chapter Eight

Chitter Chitter Chit . . . Chitter Chitter Chit.

Adrian's knife was in his hand but he didn't remember unsheathing it. He was on his feet now, though his calves quivered like jelly. Panic fought like two unseen hands to constrict his throat. He might have loosened his bladder, but he didn't bother to check.

Chitter Chitter Chit . . . Chitter Chitter Chit.

"The hell is that?" Olan growled to his brother. "You better not say Chitterers, because you told me we were well beyond their territory. We lit the damn cook fires because you were so sure, remember?"

A shadow removed itself from the bole of a tree

and became a tall humanlike figure in the moonlight. It was wrapped in a tattered cloak that looked to be stitched from a hundred different tree rodent pelts. Shards of bone hung from the belt at its hip, small bones, animal skulls and whatnot, with more fastened to cords that dangled from its neck. Despite these rather macabre accouterments, it was the Chitterer's face that frightened Adrian most. Like an artist's portrait gone awry, the face was a twisted mash of grisly features: bulging jaw, hollow cheeks, eyes like two spheres of soulless light. Instead of a mouth there was only a gaping hole, and like a shark this hole overflowed with jagged triangular teeth, with many chipped and broken.

Eldred gave the slightest shrug. "Perhaps I was wrong."

A swath of cold fear cut through Adrian's heart. *Oh no, oh no, oh no . . . do something, damn it. Anything.* All men could be reasoned with, or bribed, or at worst, you handed over all your belongings and your life was spared. But this Chitterer didn't look like any man to be reasoned with—or any man at all for that matter. No wait, that wasn't true. Despite that wickedly hideous face, something about this creature's disposition seemed . . . oddly human.

The Chitterer spoke in a voice that was raspy but articulate. "Everybody runs. Why didn't you run?"

"Because you're ugly," Olan muttered, clutching the haft of his ox cleaver. "Look at you. Your ugly, stupid face."

"Wait, Olan," Adrian said. "Wait a moment." He

raised his voice to address the Chitterer. "Forgive us for trespassing in your lands. We didn't intend to offend you. Please, accept our meager offering of wine as payment for safe passage."

Olan scowled. "Are you mad? That's the last of the wine, goddamn it."

"Just give it," Adrian said.

Olan hesitated. He looked at the bucket, then at his brother. The two outlaws began bickering, just as they did the other night. It went on for so long that even the Chitterer looked bored. Finally, Olan relented, and the big man went forward and placed the bucket before the creature.

The Chitterer snarled. "Don't want your flavored piss." It raised a booted foot and knocked the bucket over. The lid popped off, and the earth eagerly drank the dark liquid.

Olan gnashed his teeth. "Why'd you do that? Now I'll have to cut you down."

"Stop it, Olan," Adrian said. He turned to acknowledge the creature. "What do you want from us?"

"The weapon in your hands. Your traveling gear. What else . . . oh yes, your *skins.*"

The way the creature had spoken that last word chilled Adrian to the marrow of his bones. He swallowed a lump of cold dread, and did his best not to sound like a frightened child. "But we need those. We're journeying to the south. A long journey."

The creature shook its head, an all-too human gesture. "You can forget about that journey now. You see, there's a whole host of us, and only three of you. Now cast your weapons to the dirt. Make it easy for yourselves."

Adrian wasn't ready to give in to the demands of this creature, even if it meant a quick end. The brothers hadn't moved either, nor did they seem to show any desire to do so. When the Chitterer seemed to realize this, its head turned and a low growl poured from its gaping hole of a mouth. An obvious command of some sort, as more Chitterers emerged from the shadows of the underbrush. A dozen, fifteen —no, at least a score or more. Adrian and his companions were surrounded.

"Stay behind me," Eldred urged. "Don't give them your back."

Adrian tried to obey, but a thousand thoughts were racing through his head, and not one was useful. *Oh no, oh no, we're trapped. We're all trapped.* Dull yellow eyes were everywhere—observing from the shadows, peering through the thicket, staring down from the boughs of trees. Adrian spotted an open pocket of low shrubbery where no eyes glowed. "Through there. We can make it. If we run we can make it."

"It's what they want," Eldred said. "Not about to make it easier for them."

"No, we can make it," Adrian said. "I'm going. I'm going. Follow me."

"No, you stupid—"

Too late. Adrian bolted, his legs pumping and pumping as he raced for the gap. Branches slashed at his arms and leaves rattled in his face and vines reached out to tangle his legs, but no Chitterers swarmed him. He could hear Eldred calling after him, but Adrian didn't stop. *I'm going to make it. I'm going to—*

Something slammed into him. The world spun and the earth rose to smash him like a stone. Dazed, Adrian staggered to his feet, only to find that his knife was no longer in his hand, and a particularly large and nasty Chitterer stood snarling over him. *This isn't good.* The creature lunged at him, but Eldred appeared and shouldered the gangly thing to the ground. A second Chitterer leaped from the shadows, but Olan seized the beast and drove it headfirst into the trunk of a crooked pine. There was a sickening *crack*, and the creature hit the ground with a flop.

A bold display, but it wasn't enough to deter the other Chitterers. Four or five now advanced upon the brothers. Adrian had to do something. This was his fault, goddamn it. He dashed forward but a pair of yellow-eyed shadows rose like sentinels in his path. He turned but another Chitterer appeared, this one so large it caused Adrian to stumble back, trip on a jutting root, and fall hard on his knees.

All Adrian saw was the club in the Chitterer's hand, a large and misshapen thing with a head covered in bony spikes and bits of old gore. The creature grunted as it raised the weapon. *Get up, get up, get up,* Adrian told himself, but his legs wouldn't obey, so he did the only thing he could do: he ripped off his glove, threw out his blackened hand, and seized the Chitterer's exposed shin. Fingertips seared soft white flesh, which caused the creature to shriek and curse and yank its leg back to examine the wound. For a moment nothing happened . . . and then, something happened.

Specks of black appeared on the leg, a few at first, then more and more, until it looked like blotches from a spilled inkstone. They raced up and down the creature's body, blackening and blistering and stretching apart the skin like old fabric in the midsummer heat. The stench of charred flesh punctured the air, a fetid smell, like someone squashing a black puffball and blowing the spores in your face. The Chitterer began to shudder, then convulse . . . but despite the flailing limbs and the obvious agony wracking its body, the expression on its face didn't change. How was that possible? That was when Adrian realized the truth.

The Chitterer screamed a terrible scream, but the sound died midway as the flesh of its neck dissolved into a soft pink windpipe, which then melted away to reveal upper vertebrae. Hands clawed at the sky like a drowning man fighting to surface, but those hands also melted into bone, and then the entire skeleton crumbled into a fine powder. A soft breeze scattered the powder like ashes, leaving nothing more than a heap of mismatched leather armor, a half-scorched cloak of tree rodent pelts, a giant spiked club, and of course . . . one terribly hideous mask.

With the Chitterer's death there was a great pause, a sudden and enveloping stillness that surged through the land and reached toward the firmament. It was the stillness that one feels in the dead of winter, when the weather is so cold you could see wisps of frost-smoke twirling in the air. And then, just like that, the earth began to tremble. The Chitterers were fleeing for their lives. Adrian watched them. He watched them all run away like the frightened rodents they were, and when the earth was silent and still once more, he shook his head, wiped the moisture from his eyes, grabbed the Chitterer's mask, and rose, examining it.

The hard outer shell was decorated in strips and patches of what appeared to be dried skin. The dull yellow of the eyes seemed to be achieved by a glossy dye, perhaps one of saffron or calendula. The mouth that was crammed with teeth looked frightening from afar, but up close he could see how shoddy the work was, as if done by a neophyte or child. For some reason, Adrian smelled the mask, and of course it smelled awful. He saw something protruding from the underside. A hollow little object, the perfect size for a man to blow into. Adrian put his lips around it and did just that. The sound that came out startled him. It was, of course, the dreaded Chitterer call.

Adrian marveled at the ingenuity while laughing at his own foolishness. Eldred was standing a few feet away, observing with widened eyes. Adrian handed him the mask. The husky man held it gingerly, as if it were about to come alive. A long moment passed before he finally spoke, and all he said was, "Son of a mother-raping clod . . ."

Adrian showed him the small pipe-like instrument on the underside of the mask. "And this is what makes the Chitterers chitter."

Olan came racing through the brush. The shaggy man was breathing hard and nursing a bruised shoulder, but goddamn it if he wasn't jubilant. "Did you see those bastards break? Like swine running from the chopping block. Glorious, I tell you. Absolutely glorious. What is that, a mask?"

"That it is," Adrian said.

Olan looked confused. "What kind of creature wears a mask?"

Eldred sighed at his brother. "No kind."

Chapter Nine

"Y̲ou know, Deadhand, I tend to despise men of your stamp."

"My stamp?"

"Yes, skeptics. Non-believers. You're bad for business. You ruin the mysteries of the mystic, rain on the visions of the oracle." Eldred's boots stomped across the hard-packed earth. He came to a halt before the rocky precipice of a wide overlook. "Last night, I learned something about you. You're not like other skeptics."

Adrian smiled at the compliment. "You don't think so?"

"No, you're *worse*. You're a goddamn hypocrite wrapped in a skeptic's rotten shell."

The smile twisted into a frown. "What the hell are you talking about?"

Eldred didn't answer. His eyes closed and he took a moment to inhale the crisp alpine air. The late afternoon sun was sinking below the mountain ranges, and the sky was overrun by a host of crimson clouds: fat puffs in the foreground, wispy striations in the rear. Below, the undulating hills teemed with mountain heather and fiery red wildflowers. Crepuscular birds shrieked from the boughs of towering broadleaves, while a lone and persistent goshawk circled the meadows from above.

The skirmish with the Chitterers had ended only yesterday, but in the face of such a beautiful and tranquil landscape it seemed a month or more had passed. "Eldred, you said you wanted to speak in private," Adrian said. "Well, here we are . . . so speak."

Eldred placed a hand on Adrian's shoulder; his grip was so strong that for a moment Adrian questioned his safety. "In matters of conflict you would do well to listen to me. Do you understand? Look at me. Never go against my word in the heat of battle."

Adrian started to reply, but Eldred wouldn't hear it. "You may have completed your three years of military conscription, but you seem to have forgotten two of the most basic yet unforgivable offenses: disobeying orders and abandoning your fellow rankmates. I don't mean to sound harsh, Adrian, but I've followed you this far, respecting your rules and your wishes . . . and

I must say: if you go against my word again our little partnership is through. Do you understand?"

Adrian wisely refrained from a retort. "I understand."

"Good. Now that we've settled that . . ." The husky man released his grip and folded his powerful arms across his chest. "What manner of sorcerer are you?"

Adrian stammered. "W-what?"

Eldred's eyes narrowed in a way that made Adrian fidget. "You touched a man and he *died*, Adrian. I saw his skin melt away like pork fat, saw his bones crumble into dust. Now I ask you again, what manner of sorcerer are you?"

"I told you, it's a curse. I can't explain it. I . . ."

"It's happened before, yes? Tell me."

Adrian nodded. "An old physician, the first to offer treatment for my hand. I didn't know at the time . . . I didn't know *that* would happen. Why? Do you know something about my condition?"

"No. Never in my years have I seen a clearer display of the supernatural arts."

"How could you say that? You're a pyromantic examiner or whatever."

Eldred lowered his gaze. "Yes, well . . ." His sigh was like a soft whisper against the trees. "You know, Adrian . . . you and I are not so different."

"Oh, no, please don't do that. Please don't gurgle up such a sad, tired cliché. We are different, trust me, we are *very* different."

"Maybe, but not in our affinity for skepticism. You

see, the examinations, the herbs and reagents, the ritual words . . . it's a racket. All of it. But you already knew that, didn't you? Just as you knew the Chitterers were nothing more than men in masks."

"I suspected."

Eldred turned to survey the landscape. The last remnants of daylight highlighted the coarse stubble growing on his cheeks, and the crisp breeze mussed what little hair he had left on his head. The shadow of that overhead goshawk finally departed, and the echoing birdcalls had also faded away. "From the days as far back as our founding rulers, there have always been men gifted in the supernatural arts. These men were said to be more than flesh and blood; they were heavenly figures so in harmony with the universe they could travel through the nebulae and touch the light of distant stars. Astronomers have written of such accounts after observing the constellations through the use of armillary spheres. What a godly sort of people they must've been, don't you think?"

Adrian opened his mouth but couldn't find a suitable reply, so he said nothing.

"But the truth is . . . it's all a bunch of rot. In my recent years I've realized there was never a single man of any supernatural talent. They are all just shrewd deviants and eccentric wretches whose sole purpose is to sway public opinion and staunch groundswells of dissent." He sounded disenchanted, like a child losing a beloved pet. "I'm nothing but a fraud . . . a charlatan. Please don't tell my brother. He's a simple fellow, two-fisted and hardheaded as an ox. The truth will weaken our fraternal bonds."

Adrian promised he wouldn't, and the two men stood silently at the overlook for a while longer. At length Adrian said, "So the reagents . . . the milfoil and wormwood, they're all without purpose?"

Eldred nodded.

"The nineteen grasshoppers?"

"I just like the number. Sounds mystical."

"What about the Snakelion blood—does such a thing as a Snakelion even exist?"

"Only in myths and fireside tales . . . although they were briefly mentioned in the annals of the second era of rule, not in name but it does mention a giant snake fiend that guards the eastern edge of the realm. Obviously, the source material is questionable at best. What I use is pig's blood mixed with a precise extraction of woad to give it that bluish tint. To make the flames blue, specks of copper or arsenic work very well."

"So, ultimately you decide whether or not the person is lying."

He nodded. "An examiner's greatest skill is self-possession. He must have the confidence and conviction to back up his truth-revealing statements, no matter how absurd or implausible they may seem. The declaration of the Celestial Deity of Skyfire must be revealed so firmly that the client would be ashamed to dispute the point. It requires practice, you know, the same as painting or poetry or disbudding a calf." His lips grew wider, as if he found something amusing. "In my younger years I became so overblown with confidence that I foolishly believed I had some sort of gift. Those days I fattened my money belt by hoodwinking a lot of poor souls. You know, there's something intriguing about that. If a man didn't believe my examinations outright—and sometimes he didn't—the truth of my words often became so ingrained in his heart that it eventually became the man's reality. It is a showing of how pliable we truly are, how weak the waking mind is in contrast to the subconscious."

"The woman," Adrian said. "You lied about her husband—he wasn't a cheating, swindling bastard after all, was he?"

Eldred shook his head. "That was the only time I ever mixed personal interest with professional judgment, and clearly it backfired. The poor bastard was killed, my brother and I became outlaws, and I've only myself to blame. The desire to win the woman's affections clouded my judgment. By the gods she was a heavenly creature. I wasn't always so bald and rough around the edges myself, you know." He paused. "I expect you will think less of me."

Adrian told him no, and it was the truth. "The day we met, after Olan pulled me out of the ordure pit . . . I'm glad you chose to make the flames blue. I wouldn't have made it this far without you or your brother, even though I've yet to gain Olan's respect."

"Give it time. Olan's rather soft beneath all that hair and muscle." Neither man spoke for a while. At last Eldred said, "We should head back before my brother wanders off."

*O*ver the next few days the three men moved along the thick woods that skirted the Centipede Road. All was quiet. Checkpoints were rare and riders were rarer, and only the occasional porter or carter or pilgrim passed them by. Once, they spotted a horse-drawn carriage that was bedecked with luxurious silk curtains and driven on gilded axles. Immediately, you could see the cogs turning in Olan's head. Eldred too. Hell, even Adrian was tempted. What sort of riches lay inside such an opulent conveyance?

But Adrian reiterated the precepts to Olan, and the big man's shoulders slumped and he went off grumbling to himself. The entire next day, as if to punish Adrian, Olan did nothing but complain about his sore feet and sore back and sore whatever. Adrian barely listened to any of it. Truth was, he hadn't been feeling well himself. For one he was tired . . . not sleep-tired but deeply fatigued in both heart and spirit. His balance was off, his mind clouded as though every thought had to be squeezed through a fog. But he couldn't disappoint the brothers, so instead of slowing their travel, he fought against all pains and discomforts and simply pushed on.

But after another three or four days, Adrian couldn't push any longer. His legs decided to quit and he collapsed on a sun-dried patch of grass, dizzy and sweating and sapped of strength. A fit of coughing turned into a bout of retching. Pain churned in his gut. He tasted blood in his mouth.

Olan seemed unconcerned. The big man said, "He's fine. He's fine." But when Eldred came over and studied Adrian, he shook his head and said, "Face is wan, pupils are dilated. Look at his mouth, it's covered in some kind of rash." He lowered his head to stare into Adrian's eyes. "Did you ingest something you shouldn't have, my friend?"

Adrian thought about it, then said no.

Olan didn't believe him. "You sure, Deadhand? Just because a stream runs clear doesn't mean it's safe to drink, you do know that, right?"

"Of course," Adrian said. "It wasn't that." He tried to think about it once more, but he couldn't focus on any particular thought. "I don't know what's wrong with me. Perhaps I'm not made for an outlaw's life."

"This isn't an outlaw's life," Olan argued. "Not with your goddamn rules. What sort of outlaw refuses to rob and loot and waylay? You've turned us into skulking, gutless vagabonds."

"Nothing gutless about abstaining from wrongful acts," Adrian countered.

Olan spat. "That's funny, coming from a thief."

Eldred sent his brother off to fetch some herbs, but Adrian figured it was just to let Olan cool off. When the big man was gone, Adrian said, "I'll be fine tomorrow. I just need to rest for a little while. Please make sure your brother doesn't ignore my precepts."

Eldred nodded. "I will. Now shut up and rest."

Sleep came and went. Adrian awoke for a few minutes here and there, only to be pulled back into that ever-draining darkness. One moment the sun was shining like a white pearl, the next it was absent and dark. One moment birdsong filled the surrounding forest, the next it was crickets and katydids. The world came and went, and time was relinquished to an unstoppable juggernaut that dragged Adrian along as it willed.

When next his eyes opened, he saw Eldred sitting on a hollow log of deadwood, cleaning his teeth with some kind of root. Olan was standing nearby, bare-chested and scratching his hairy belly. "What else can we do," the big man grumbled. "Let's just take the robe and leave."

Eldred pulled the root out of his mouth and examined it. "I told you, we can't do that."

"Why the hell not? He might be lying, you know."

Eldred shook his head. "The flames turned blue. The Celestial Deity of Skyfire deemed his heart truthful." He flicked the root into a patch of undergrowth. "There's a hostelry no more than half a day away. We'll take him there as soon as . . ."

The darkness returned, and Adrian succumbed to its embrace. Dreams came to him, along with the same recurring night terror he'd had since the day he burned his hand. There was fire and smoke and screaming and a strange three-legged dog, and when next Adrian awoke, the bright rays of sunlight blinded his eyes. He was in movement; he could feel

Olan's massive arms carrying him, could hear the big man panting with exertion. Adrian tried to twist himself free but it was no use. He was just too weak. Birds chirped from the nearby trees. Mountain argali clashed from somewhere far. It was a bright spring day, so full of life, and yet all Adrian could feel was the coldness of death. *Put me down . . . please, put me . . .*

Once again the darkness came and went, and suddenly Adrian was no longer in the wilds, no longer surrounded by the bright and beautiful landscape. He was lying on the dusty wooden floor of a dark and dusty room, and judging by all the muddy remnants of foot traffic, it was the anteroom of a hostelry or tavern. Olan was crouching to his left, breathing loudly through his mouth as he always did. Eldred was standing on the other side the room, arguing with a man who sounded like the proprietor of the establishment.

"I'm sorry but I must have your names," the tortoise-faced man explained. "The law requires me to maintain a register with all the proper seals, and to make sure every guest's name is entered along with his place of origin and destination. If an officer discovers any missed or incorrect entries, I will lose my license —or worse, my freedom. So please, tell me your . . ."

Darkness. Adrian's eyes closed and opened once more. He was lying on an old featherbed, beneath coverlets of musty wool. Soft candlelight flickered from somewhere nearby, highlighting the cracks in the wood-paneled walls. He could hear the muffled yet unmistakable clamor of drunk and rowdy inn patrons from a nearby area.

A shadow crossed the room—it was Eldred, holding an earthenware bowl of something that smelled extraordinarily foul. "Drink it," he said.

Adrian did. It tasted awful, like old tree fungus mixed with mud taken from a sty—not that Adrian had ever tasted such a combination. Still, it was awful enough that he had to resist the urge to spit it out. "Where are we?" His voice sounded as though he'd swallowed a pound of sand.

"A hostelry."

"I know that . . . *where* are we."

"Province of Acanthus, fifth prefecture of the Autumnal district. About twenty miles north of Beetleburr."

Adrian placed the bowl on the nearby stand. "We shouldn't be here. You know it's not safe." He pulled the coverlet off and went to rise.

Eldred placed a hand on Adrian's chest. "Don't."

Adrian intended to push the hand off him, but then his eyes caught a look at his own body. The grime and muck embedded in his clothes was gone, and his chest and arms were scrubbed clean. The only untended part of him was his single gloved hand, as evidenced by the ring of encrusted dirt that ran along his skin beneath the material's edge.

Eldred handed the bowl back to him. "Drink, damn it. The concoction wasn't cheap, and neither was this room."

"What's in it?"

"A tisane of peppermint and rosehips and a mix of other demulcents. An effective blend to purge the toxins you ingested." He leaned in. "You need to be more careful, Adrian. I thought you knew coralberries were poisonous."

"Poisonous berries? No, that couldn't have been the cause." He thought for a long moment. "The berries I ate weren't white or yellow or anything like that—I'm not a goddamn clod. They were a pale red. Now I know reds aren't always safe but they weren't growing in little clusters, they were growing alone. And oh, I saw birds eating them, so I'm sure they were safe."

Eldred sighed and shook his head and muttered Adrian's name a few times in disappointment. "Birds can digest toxins and poisons that can kill a man within hours. I thought you were sharper than this. Why didn't you just ask?"

Adrian stammered. "It was early . . . you were off taking a piss. I don't know, our loop snares were empty and our box traps were untouched. I was hungry. I guess I *am* a clod." Adrian swallowed another sip, his face scrunching from the taste. "I don't think we should linger here any longer."

"You need to rest, my friend. We didn't make it halfway to Swallowtail to lose our guide now. Besides, we're safe here—for the moment at least."

Adrian didn't like the way that last part sounded. "What does that mean?"

"My brother . . . he spent all last night in the common area, deep in his cups. I overheard him carrying on about our encounter with the Chitterers, bragging about how they broke and fled. Damn drunken fool talks too much."

"We should leave," Adrian said. "Remember the monastery, it will happen again."

"Two days, Adrian. We leave in two days. You'll be ready then."

*T*he tisane gave Adrian the most vivid dreams, but these eventually twisted into that same recurring night terror. Flames flailed all around him like giant red tendrils, causing waves of heat to blast and blister his face. Adrian searched and searched but couldn't escape the blaze and the smoke and the awful sounds of men and women and children burning and dying. It was then the three-legged dog appeared. The black-furred beast stared at Adrian with a pair of black-pooled eyes, then it turned and hobbled off through a passage of smoke.

Adrian followed the dog around every curve and through every twist and turn, until at last the smoke dissipated and he found himself standing before a single tree in an otherwise desolate strip of gray land. The animal was sitting on a single haunch and staring up at him. Its mouth opened. A ghostly, disembodied voice escaped its maw. *Save us, save us, save us the innocent from agony. The gods know we've suffered enough. Only the rivers can carry us home.* It was an old man's voice, though sometimes it was a younger man's voice, or a woman's voice, or a child's. When it was done the dog turned and limped off, and suddenly Adrian was falling . . . falling and falling down a bottomless chasm, falling and falling and—

SMASH.

The wooden door burst open. Armed men marched inside in a deafening clangor of steel and mail. Adrian tried to scramble out of bed but he slipped and fell hard onto the floor. When he looked up, a row of spear tips was thrust in his face.

"Hello, thief."

Adrian was expecting to see the face of High Commander Krall Vyren, but no, it wasn't him and these weren't his soldiers. These men wore thick coats of imbricated lamellar plates over long capes that were streaked in pink and ruffled along the edges. Wait, pink? Adrian was about to make a snarky comment about that, but then he saw Olan and Eldred kneeling in the center of the room, ankles and wrists bound. "Sorry, Deadhand," was all Olan said. Eldred didn't even look up.

Adrian gave a resigned sigh. *Damn you, Olan, damn you and your big drunken mouth.*

The commander of these pink-caped fools entered last. He was a lissome man, his face smooth and comely but in a way that a woman's face was comely. The scales of his polished armor glistened like serpent skin, while a fancy floral belt secured the fancy floral sash at his waist. Like the soldiers he also wore pink, only a bit more of it. By the gods he looked like a walking tulip.

"Seems your big friend here has a big mouth," the

commander said. He had a mellifluous voice, but his smarmy expression dearly deserved a smack. One of his soldiers brought him the haversack that was hanging from a peg on the wall. Looking inside, the commander nodded and turned to acknowledge his men. "I want them all chained and racked, with extra iron on the giant fellow. We're marching double-time back to the fortress garrison. Don't like it? Don't care. I'm tired and I want to go home." He turned back and winked at Adrian. "My partner and I just adopted a young orphan boy, and I'd like to be with them."

"Congratulations," Adrian said.

Chapter Ten

*A*drian raised his good hand to adjust the hinged wooden rack locked around his neck. It was an awkward and heavy thing that both hindered his movement and stole his strength. Eldred and Olan were racked in the same fashion, but neither seemed to struggle as much as Adrian did. Both were much stronger men, he supposed.

The commander's name was Layne Rey. He was a distinguished military general styled as the Pink Pangolin, though he also had a slew of other titles that were outshined only by his ego. The strict and prissy man carried a look mirror and shouted at his attendants whenever his wavy hair wasn't exactly how he liked it, and yet his soldiers showed him a great deal of respect and admiration—which Adrian didn't fully understand.

They rose in the predawn darkness, traveled until the sky turned ruddy, and sometimes continued marching into the night. The soldiers ate little and infrequently: usually cuts of smoked beef or handfuls of dates or figs or some other dried fruit. A complaint occasionally arose but General Layne was always quick to quash it. "Never mind your tired bones, never mind your sore and blistered feet, never mind the rumble in your belly and the dryness in your throat. March, march, *MARCH.*"

Adrian struggled to keep up. For one, he had a goddamn prisoner's rack locked around his neck, and secondly, he hadn't fully recovered from his earlier bout of food poisoning. But the more he lagged behind, the more the soldiers mistreated and berated him. Today they were in especially foul moods, which must've meant their commanding officers were in foul moods, which must've meant the general himself was in a foul mood. Such was the way of military order.

As if things weren't awful enough, the surrounding countryside was downright miserable. The sky looked like someone flung a tarp of undyed linen across it, and the trees appeared frail and wilted against the deep-reaching fog. The heavy rainfall of last night left the company battling through mud and muck today. Fortunately, after a few more days the sunshine returned and the earth grew firm and dry. With the mood lightened, the soldiers began trolling a tune from a bygone era. Something about a man and a fly and an unclothed woman . . . Adrian couldn't really tell what it was about—there was a lot of whooping and collective shouting going on—but he didn't care so long as the attention was off him.

Sometime later the fog broke apart and a pair of watchtowers rose in the distance. These were intimidating structures, immensely tall and sturdily built with corner piers, latticework screens, and thick cantilevered brackets to support the overhanging tile roofs. Farther along, Adrian could see the outer walls of the fortress, serpentine in shape and constructed with a base of tamped earth and thick blocks of stone. Missile holes and drainage spouts gaped at various intervals, while armored sentries eyed the prisoners from their positions along the battlements, crossbows in hand.

The portcullis rose with a cringe-inducing screech. Adrian was led up an exterior stairway, past a turret, and back down another stairway before entering a small room that smelled of sweat and old fabric.

A turnkey greeted them with a toothy smile. "Don't get comfortable. The head keeper is coming to take you to the warden's quarters for registration."

"How long will that take?"

The turnkey's lip curled up. "You have somewhere else to be?" He left.

Olan immediately began fussing with the rack

about his neck, but after banging the thing against the wall, he accomplished little except giving himself a headache. Adrian had a headache, too, and it only grew worse when the two brothers began quarreling.

The head keeper never showed up. Strangely enough, it was General Layne Rey himself who came for them, though it must've been a good two hours later. "Our esteemed provincial viceroy requests an immediate audience with the thief," he announced. "Stand up, One-glove, that means you."

When the door creaked open, Olan made a foolish attempt to rush forward, but the rack around his neck obstructed his movements, not to mention the handful of soldiers who waved their spear-points in the shaggy man's face.

General Layne seemed amused. "Stand down, big fellow, don't get yourself in a tizzy now. It's you who caused this mess, is it not?"

"And it's me who will rip out your heart and liver," Olan growled.

General Layne ignored the remark, though his handsome face turned grave. "Come now, thief, best not to keep our illustrious viceroy waiting."

Adrian was taken inside a large room furnished with cressets and stools and tables that were covered in parchment maps and military charts. It was every-thing you'd expect to see in a commander's quarters —except for that sculpture of a pink-plated pangolin perched on the officer's desk. The quality was rather exceptional, and Adrian didn't hesitate to admit that to the general. "Though I've never seen a pangolin that color before," he went on. "A female, perhaps. Tell me, do they stay in the burrows and knit while the males go out and forage?"

General Layne chuckled at that. "You've got cheek, One-glove. In ancient days the pangolin was known as the Mountain-Borer, the giant scaly digger who could smash rocks into powder and carve gracefully through crags. It is the only mammal in the realm covered entirely in scales yet gifted with a mouth sharper than an auger. It is considered the very essence of protection, like an impregnable fortress that brings great comfort to both lord and land."

"I see. And the pink?"

"Pink is the heavenly combination of a man's mind and body. The red of his blood and the white of his brains as one. You see, pink has the uncanny ability to neutralize disorder and calm hostility, in any situation, in any heart."

"Well, if you say so. You are the Pink Pangolin."

"That I am. Now, have a seat. Lord Marius Murden will see you now."

The provincial viceroy entered in a fit of coughing. He was a shriveled graybeard of a man whose body moved like a sloth that hadn't slept in a year. His eyes were small and scrunched beneath the folds of his many wrinkles, but his nose was wide and fleshy and cinnabar red. An oversized silk outer robe trailed so far behind him that his little steward had trouble keeping in step.

Adrian didn't like the old viceroy. Not because of his shrew-like features or his oversized robe or his constant coughing, but simply because he reeked of cruelty. He was also rather volatile. When he'd lifted a silver-enchased goblet to his lips, he took one sip and slammed it back down on the officer's table. "What is this? I said *fresh* hawthorn berry, not this flat and astringent piss." The little steward apologized a dozen times before scurrying off.

When Lord Murden finally received the wine he wanted, he drank deeply and gave a contented belch. As soon as the goblet touched the table his steward was there to refill it. Only after a few more measures did the provincial viceroy acknowledge his guest. "Scarlet Sun, the annual marksmanship contest. You committed a capital offense that day. My fastest rider stands by to send word of your capture to Lord Haroden. A single command from me and your little journey is over."

"Well then, let's cut the cackle," Adrian countered. "Your rider hasn't gone yet, and I'm here talking to you instead of being whipped raw in the warden's quarters, so you obviously want something from me."

He paused before answering. "General Layne told me you're a man of quick wit, Adrian One-glove. Silver-tongued and plainspoken." He drained his goblet. *Bang.* The steward scurried to refill. "I've also been told that you are the hero who routed an ambushing party of Darkwing barbarians, otherwise known as Chitterers. Is that true?"

Adrian gave a nod—well, the best he could with this rack around his neck.

Lord Murden coughed about a hundred times. "What was I saying? Oh, yes. It just so happens that we've had some longstanding trouble with these barbarians. Goddamn bastards hiding behind masks . . . they are wreaking havoc on our northern supply lines and trade routes."

"You are a provincial viceroy, a man of exceptional imperial power. Surely you can petition the capital for help. Lord Haroden will acknowledge your request, he is an honorable and evenhanded ruler, after all."

Lord Murden laughed so fiercely that he had to spend the next few minutes regaining his breath. "Poor fool. You truly are from Scarlet Sun."

"What does that mean?"

"Lord Haroden may be loved within his own walls, but discerning fellows like myself know him for what he truly is: the savage who seized the throne and split the empire in two." Another fit of coughing. "Truth is, I have petitioned the capital for aid, many times, but what does that bastard always say? He doesn't have the resources for such an undertaking." Lord Murden's wrinkled face looked livid. "Not enough resources? And yet, here he is, spending half his treasury tracking down a snot-nosed little thief who made off with his precious little robe."

Adrian didn't reply to that, and Lord Murden coughed some more before continuing. "I am tired of being overlooked and underappreciated. Tired, tired,

tired. Honorable men can only be denied so many times. Hell, if I wasn't such an old fool I would've pledged my faith to the south long ago. Don't look so surprised, thief, I can't afford this conflict with the Chitterers any longer. My depots and granaries are running empty, my roadways are under constant harassment. The people are growing desperate, some are ready to rebel. You know how much an ounce of salt costs these days? How about a bushel of rape-seed? No, I won't even bother with the details. Anyway, these masked cowards are holed up in a pass of the Darkwing Mountains, east of the gap. They've overtaken a major military checkpoint called the Sala-mander Gateway, and goddamn it they are ruining every bit of trade and traffic." He gave a sigh that turned into a cough. "I don't know what to do. I begged and begged the heavens for an answer—and then you show up. Auspicious, my advisors tell me."

"I didn't show up. You captured me, brought me here."

"Nevertheless." He gave a brief pause. "I've read your military records. You served three years in the Wolftail Regiment, where you trained the sixteen blades and nine defenses under the most prominent arms instructors in Scarlet Sun."

"Yes, but that was a long time ago. My regiment saw conflict only once. I haven't wielded anything heavier than a knife in over a decade."

"Yet you managed to put the masked barbarians to flight, so what does that tell me? Not only can you hold your own in conflict, you must also possess some degree of shrewdness in you. Now I'm sending a regiment of pangolin soldiers in a full offensive campaign. General Layne Rey will lead them. Don't fret, you won't be directly involved in the battle. But you will serve as the general's chief advisor."

Adrian blinked. "You don't understand. What I did back there was not strategy . . . you want me to drive off an *army* of those things? Forgive my insolence but is there henbane in your wine? Because you are talking rot."

General Layne Rey went to reprimand Adrian, but Lord Murden raised a hand to stop him. "Listen closely, you little churl, if you drive the Chitterers off a second time, I'll pardon you and your outlaw friends and personally hand the imperial robe back to you. How does that sound?"

Adrian looked down at his gloved hand. "You'll break faith."

Lord Murden looked wounded. "Why would you doubt my honor?"

"Judging by the way your steward trembles before you, I'd say you have as much honor as a tapeworm in a man's belly."

"I won't deny that I am cruel, my one-gloved friend. But just because I am cruel doesn't mean I lack honor. You'll have the robe back, along with your freedom. Now those are my terms, and I expect that you will agree to them. If not, you'll be sent back to Lord Haroden with that fancy robe stitched to your rump."

Adrian took a moment to consider the viceroy's

words. Could he be trusted? Of course not, but what other choice did he have? Either aid this old bastard for a chance to get the robe back, or be sent back to Scarlet Sun to face his punishment.

"Fine," Adrian said. "Now get this goddamn rack off me."

Chapter Eleven

*T*he battle hadn't even begun and already Adrian was exhausted.

He was crammed foot to crown in overlapping plates of scale mail, an enormously heavy suit of armor that left him sore and sweating beneath the layers of thick underpadding. His spaulders and cuisses were cumbersome and uncomfortable, his pink-streaked cape smelled old and rank, his greaves and vambraces were far too tight, and his halfhelm was a tad oversized so the upper rim kept slipping forward to obstruct his vision.

Was all of this protection necessary? Probably not, but Adrian was a pangolin soldier now, and only a fool would complain when surrounded by such a grim host of other pangolin soldiers. About two thousand pink capes in all, not to mention the auxiliary troops and the extra bodies to guard the supply wagons in the rear. The army had been marching for nearly a week now, and already they had to overcome a host of obstacles that would send lesser men into retirement. Slippery slopes, tortuous paths, steep drop-offs, and mudslides. Yes, mudslides. While climbing a narrow foothill a sudden shift of land caused the earth to come roaring down upon the vanguard. A handful of veterans were swept away like lambs in white water, while another ten or so were left with fractured bones and sprained ligaments. Adrian had never seen anything like it.

Of course some of the softer soldiers saw the disaster as an inauspicious sign, but General Layne Rey quashed such concerns at once. "All men fear the shadows of the unknown. The only difference is the man who runs from them is a coward, while the man who continues the march is brave. Which man will you be? Don't choose the first one. I don't want to march alone."

Adrian was beginning to see why the soldiers were so fond of the general. The Pink Pangolin had a confidence about him that was rather infectious. Also, the man never wilted under pressure; he was a rock, a great big pink rock. And sure, he may have been annoyingly handsome and a bit prissy and rather strict in his ways—but he wasn't cruel like Viceroy Murden. No, General Layne Rey knew just how to command his men, and he did it with such skill and tact that Adrian no longer found it strange to see a full regiment of hardened veterans all marching in capes that were streaked in the softest hue of pink.

But for all the general's strengths, there was also a cockiness about him that Adrian disliked. At thirty-one the general had never lost a skirmish or battle, so of course he thought himself unconquerable. And the Chitterers he perceived as nothing more than a ragtag group of undisciplined barbarians. Adrian tried to tell him differently; he even tried to present a stratagem that would outsmart the deceptive barbarians, but the general didn't want to hear it. A shame, since Adrian had been devising this maneuver since the day that damn prisoner's rack was removed.

A week later they reached the Salamander Gateway. The checkpoint was strategically located along the narrow defile of a pass, and this pass was surrounded by jagged mountain ranges that assaulted the sky like sharpened talons. The main gate of the palisade was weatherworn and weak and uneven, and for that a simple ram would suffice. But once inside, an overhanging ridge to the east could serve the enemy as a defilade for a ranged assault, yet General Layne wasn't concerned about that. "Only a skilled battalion of bowmen could threaten us from that position," he said. "Chitterers don't have bowmen, and they are anything but skilled."

The afternoon had just passed the zenith when a crack team of siege rammers went to work on the tall wooden gates. After ten blows it buckled, after twenty it broke, after thirty it burst. War drums roared to life in thunderous cadence, while a host of bearers raised their pangolin standards and pennants. This was the signal for the full regiment of pink-caped soldiers to storm inside the Salamander Gateway, and storm inside they did.

Adrian wasn't among them. No, his place was with the rear guard, and from a keen vantage point he watched the advancing ranks of pangolin soldiers smash into the defensive host of Chitterers. Things quickly turned bloody, but the pink capes had superior weapons and superior armor and superior numbers and superior training and superior discipline, and the impetus of their force was so powerful that the Chitterers immediately buckled and looked ready to break. Then they *did* break. They turned and fled from the front lines, a clear rout. It was so swift, and yet victory seemed all but certain—until Adrian began to see the shapes and shadows forming high on the eastern ridge.

Boom. Massive boulders and jagged chunks of rock came caroming down the ridge. *Boom.* Over and over and over, each sound shaking the earth like thunder at your feet. The pangolin center was caught in the firing line; they could do nothing but brace for impact. *Boom.* Scores of men, entire squadrons, were smashed and crushed and knocked off the edge of the defile. The pangolin army was thrown into confusion, and it was then the routed Chitterers turned about, rallied, and charged.

They tricked us, Adrian thought. *The bastards tricked us.*

Adrian could hear General Layne's voice rising above the clamor, shouting for his men to reform and fight, fight, *FIGHT*. But it must've been hard to fight when you couldn't see, and it must've been hard to see when giant rocks were crashing down all around you. *Boom.* More men were smashed and more were scattered and more were cut down by the advancing Chitterer host. Some of the pangolin soldiers began to flee. Others followed, then more and more and more, and suddenly there was a horde of bodies rushing Adrian's way. He scrambled for cover, but someone must've slammed into him because next Adrian knew he was lying face down in the dirt while heavy boots stomped all around him. *Get up, goddamn it, get up before you're trampled to death.* Adrian crawled and crawled until he was out of the darkness and back on his feet, but before he could reorient himself, a Chitterer rose over him, steel in hand and masked face twisted in a perpetual snarl. *I'm dead, I'm dead.* But no, a rankmate appeared and smashed the Chitterer's throat with the haft of his curved sword. But another Chitterer appeared, then another and another, and suddenly Adrian was swept away by the undertow of battle.

Time moved so slowly. It was a strange, almost woozy contrast of rapid thought and sluggish motion that every soldier referred to as the drunken spirit of war. For every second that trickled by, a thousand thoughts flitted through Adrian's mind. Unfortunately, not a single one was helpful. But as the hideous faces of the Chitterers came and went, Adrian tried to stab and slash and hurt them, but there was barely enough damn room to wield his knife, so his whole body became a weapon, every armored piece of him. Still, for all his efforts, his time was mostly spent bouncing between his rankmates like a lobster in an eddy. Blood spilled like burst bladders all around him, and the metallic smell of struck steel was like an acid in the air. The heat of conflict was so intense and disorienting that Adrian couldn't focus on anyone or anything.

So he stopped trying to focus, and instead he bullied his way through the dense throng of battle, and once he found an exit he ran as fast as his heavy armor allowed of him. Other pangolin soldiers were running with him, but the Chitterers didn't pursue. Why the hell not? Adrian realized they didn't want to give up their advantageous position. He realized that and still he ran and ran and ran, and soon the battle became a distant dust cloud, so he walked for a while longer before rejoining the defeated ranks of General Layne's army on a northeastern plateau, where gulches and chasms dipped and dropped and fortified their position. At last safety and clarity was found, but morale was crushed and the soldiers were left humiliated and in despair.

The next few hours were eerily quiet. Adrian spent them observing the physicians and bone setters at work. Now these were experienced men, many former soldiers themselves, so their eyes were unsympathetic and their hearts unaffected. Adrian was the opposite. His heart ached to see his fellow pangolin soldiers in such pain and distress, but it was the ones who went from motion to motionless that troubled Adrian the most. Especially when their eyes remained open.

Obviously sleep didn't come that night. When his eyes closed all he could see was huge rocks tumbling down the ridge and smashing into the hapless pangolin soldiers. The sound of bones breaking was nauseating. Adrian wasn't a coward but he wasn't a hardened soldier either, and he certainly didn't belong here. Hell, he almost *died* today—and this was after Viceroy Murden had assured him that he wouldn't even see battle. But he did see battle, and now he wanted to escape this hellish nightmare. But there were scouts posted all over the area, and these scouts would find him and haul him back like a shameful dog. Not only that, but his defection would place Eldred's and Olan's lives at risk. It was all too much to bear. *How the hell did I get myself into this mess?* Adrian had no choice but to stay and fulfill his oath, even if that meant getting himself killed. But a soldier's death was considered a brave death, and that wasn't so terrible, was it? Maybe not, but he'd still rather pass from this world as an old man in his warm featherbed; too bad that wasn't an option right now.

When dawn broke Adrian headed straight for the general's tent. Inside, a slew of military officers and advisers were all in a frenzy of strategizing and debating while pointing at parchment maps and paper markers. Adrian crossed the room toward

General Layne Rey, who sat alone on an uneven stool with his eyes closed. Adrian wanted to yell at the effeminate fool, to rail at him and call him a prissy little prick whose arrogance outweighed his abilities. But he couldn't gather the courage to do any of that, so instead he muttered, "So much for pink's uncanny ability to neutralize disorder and calm hostility, in any situation, in any heart."

General Layne didn't respond to that. But he did open his eyes. He opened his eyes and stood up and demanded silence. Silence was immediately his.

The Pink Pangolin spent the next few moments studying his officers and advisors. At last he gave a disappointed shake of his head, then his slender body turned and a hand gestured to Adrian. "My chief advisor just spoke to me. Do you want to know what he said? He said, 'So much for pink's uncanny ability to neutralize disorder and calm hostility, in any situation, in any heart.' "

The advisors and officers shook their heads and mumbled and frowned at what they heard, but General Layne silenced them at once. "Does that displease you? It shouldn't. It shouldn't because it was the truth, and the truth is something I haven't heard in quite some time. You see, I was warned not to underestimate our enemy, but I didn't listen. Instead I flung my soldiers headlong into the behemoth's jaws, and as a result we were crushed under the boot-heel of deception. I was cocksure when I should've been cautious. Brazen when I should've been prudent. Victory can only be guaranteed when a general knows his enemy as well as himself." He looked down.

His advisors immediately offered soothing and sympathetic words, but the general silenced those as well. "Did you not hear me? Over a hundred men died yesterday because of my negligence. Twice that number are lying in the physician's quarters, broken in body and in spirit. Make no mistake, this is my loss to bear. And it is a terrible loss—but that doesn't mean I intend to limp back to Viceroy Murden with my tail tucked between my legs. What about you?"

When the advisors offered a collective no, General Layne nodded and said, "Good, but victory cannot be achieved with all of this petty quarrelling. I need us to be as one, to exist as one heart and one mind. Can we do that?"

When the officers agreed, General Layne Rey turned back to Adrian. "You have our attention now, One-glove. Please, we're ready for your counsel."

All eyes were on him. It was such a sudden and surprising shift that Adrian didn't know what to say. When he finally did speak his voice sounded so small and foolish. "I know my appointment as a chief advisor doesn't mean much to any of you. Why should it? My three years of military conscription are nothing more than a distant memory, and sadly I've forgotten so much that I might as well be a fresh-faced greenhorn again. Hell, I barely understand all the technical jargon required of a military strategist, words like fusillade and defilade and enfilade and such. So for me to step inside this tight military hierarchy and even think of advising such an upstanding lot of veteran officers . . . well, I certainly understand all the hard stares and cold shoulders being tossed my way.

"That said, I do know one thing that many of you may not. I know that the Chitterers are masters of deception. It is their greatest strength . . . but it can also be their greatest weakness." He produced his Chitterer mask and made sure they all saw it. "Listen to what I have to say, that's all I ask." He took a deep breath, cleared his throat, and spent the next half hour or so detailing his stratagem against the Chitterers. It seemed flawless in his head but when it came out of his mouth it sounded rather trite and amateurish, and he certainly didn't expect General Layne to consider any of it, but the very next morning his officers were busy reconfiguring their maps and diagrams, while his soldiers were out hunting and crafting and gathering supplies. Adrian couldn't believe it.

Three days later, a picked detachment of one hundred soldiers tightened the straps of their makeshift Chitterer masks and fastened the cloaks that were stitched from the pelts of squirrels and chipmunks and other rodents. With the aid of hempen rope and under the cover of darkness, the men began the treacherous climb up the southeastern cliffs. Three hours later, at dawn, as the main battle reignited inside the checkpoint, the detachment of disguised pangolin soldiers swarmed the unsuspecting Chitterers on the eastern ridge. Suddenly instead of falling rocks there were falling barbarians, one after another, some shrieking in terror as they tumbled and rolled and landed in a twisted heap of broken bones. It was hard to watch and even harder to stomach, yet never before had something so brutal filled Adrian's heart with such relief.

The main host of Chitterers split in an attempt to bolster their allies on the ridge. This maneuver was expected, and a flanking host of pangolins appeared to push the enemy into a pincer, where they were mowed down like grain before the sickle. Even the barbarian overlord, an enormous fellow with an enormous club, couldn't repel the onslaught. He did manage to dash the brains of two, three, even four pangolins, but by then the entire vanguard was on him, stabbing, stabbing, stabbing until the enormous man was nothing more than an enormous lump of red meat.

It was then the Chitterers folded.

The ones who tried to flee were swiftly cut down from behind. The rest discarded their weapons and knelt in surrender. For a while pangolin soldiers kept killing them anyway, until at last General Layne regained control and ordered a full cease. The drudgery didn't stop then. The surrendered were rounded up and organized into rows for branding or beheading, while parties were sent to scour the base of the mountain for dumped gear and fallen soldiers. Scouts were sent for reporting, contingents were sent to the commissariat, and squadrons were arranged for a handful of other duties. Everyone had a job to do, and it was all very sobering work, very quiet . . . but all that changed the moment Adrian entered the Salamander Gateway.

He was so cautious of the carnage that he didn't notice the oncoming swarm of pangolin soldiers. They surrounded him and called out his name and cheered for him, and soon those cheers escalated into a song, and this song was one of joy and victory and thanksgiving to the gods. At first Adrian tried to sneak away, but when he saw the calm approbation in General Layne Rey's eyes, he removed his helmet and wiped the sweat from his brow and did his best to sing along.

Chapter Twelve

For the weary and the wounded, the march back to the fortress garrison proved as arduous as the battle itself.

Adrian had sustained only minor injuries, but after days of marching he added stiff legs and a sore lower back to his list of cuts and bruises. Forget about freedom and forget about the robe, all he wanted was a soft featherbed, a warm meal, and a washbasin of hot water. The simplest of amenities, really.

As the northern infantrymen footslogged through the surrounding villages, farmhands and husbandmen dropped their hoes and mattocks and rushed over to cheer and kowtow before their saviors. The attention renewed the spirits of the weary soldiers—Adrian included—and morale only grew stronger as the watchtowers of the fortress finally came into sight. At last, they had returned.

Adrian was escorted into a private room where an eager young squire helped remove his armor. By the gods it felt like slabs of solid stone were chiseled off his body. He was given a fresh tunic and trousers, but before he had a moment to rest, the viceroy's steward came and led him into a crowded dining hall where Lord Marius Murden was waiting. Eldred and Olan were there, too, free of their prisoner racks and looking rather contented. Olan the big bastard had a cup of wine in his hands.

To Adrian's surprise, Lord Murden didn't break faith. He personally handed Adrian the haversack with the imperial robe inside, along with a purse that jangled with coin. "What do you think of my honor now," he said.

Adrian bowed his head deeply, then turned and beckoned to the brothers. It was time to leave.

"Don't be in such a hurry," Lord Murden said, coughing. "My talented staff has prepared an exquisite banquet in your honor. Please, sit and enjoy."

"I thank you for your overwhelming generosity, but we'd like to leave as soon as possible, with your consent of course."

The old viceroy's wrinkled eyes shrank in disappointment. "If I can't make you stay then at least allow yourself to be feted one last time. My daughter has just arrived from Beetleburr to honor the heroes who subjugated the Darkwing barbarians. Amelia's a rather delicate flower, you see, and to deny her request would be considered the gravest of insults."

The viceroy gestured to his left, where a young woman in a sleeveless gown of embroidered gray silk sat. Adrian swallowed. How had he not noticed her before? She was a beautiful thing with porcelain-smooth skin and eyes that were both cheerful and alluring. Her dark locks of curly hair were pinned up in a cloud coiffure, which was accented by a single pink pomegranate flower. "An honor, truly," she said with a bow of her head.

Adrian bowed in return before turning back to the viceroy. "Of course we'll stay for the evening."

"Of course," Lord Murden said, then coughed.

There was music, there was dancing, and there was a lot of drunken revelry. Servers appeared bearing trays of delectable courses, and each was accompanied by wine, wine, and more wine. Adrian chose the steamed muttonchops and mallow fruits, while Eldred and Olan gobbled down the devilled whitebait and braised pork patties with sides of bean sprouts and salted squash. Speeches were given and poetry was recited, and before Adrian knew it the banquet was over and he was stumbling back to his private quarters, his head clouded from the excess of wine.

He lay down on the featherbed and closed his eyes. It didn't take long for his inebriated mind to wind down into a state of quiet peace, but just as the darkness of sleep began to overtake him, he was pulled back out by a firm knock on the door.

Adrian opened his eyes. "I said no visitors. Please."

Silence for a few moments, then a soft, feminine voice called out. "Forgive me. Another time then."

Adrian sat up. *Lady Amelia?* He scrambled to dress himself. "Please come in, my lady."

The door opened and the viceroy's daughter entered. She wasn't wearing that same elegant gown from the earlier banquet, but a simple evening robe over a patterned chemise that looked no less stunning. "I wanted to personally thank you for all you've done. With the barbarians subjugated the populace will be at ease, which means my father will be at ease, too."

"It was General Layne Rey and his soldiers, not me."

"Please, don't insult me. I am the daughter of a provincial viceroy."

Adrian looked down. "It was luck, nothing more."

She smiled. "Modesty is a quality found in great men. May I?" She gestured to the nearby wooden couch.

Adrian obliged her request. Perhaps it was the wine, but he couldn't help but stare at her. Such a gentle smile and such cheerful green eyes . . . how could any man not desire her? Her perfume was a sweet scent of jasmine, strong but not overwhelming. Again, it was probably the wine, but right now, he found this highborn young woman more beautiful than any other woman he'd lain with since his wife died. *But what do you want from me, beautiful woman?*

A pair of attendants bustled about the room, one hanging locust twigs on the walls for freshness, the other filling two goblets of wine. As if Adrian hadn't drunk enough already.

"You've done well for my father," Lady Amelia said. "Now I've come to see if you would lend your counsel to me."

Adrian accepted the wine from the attendant but didn't drink. "I am honored, my lady. Truly, I am. But I am not a man of any experience or merit."

"Let me decide that."

"Well then, how can I be of service?"

"My father has arranged for me to marry a man I do not wish to marry."

"And who is this suitor?"

"Lord Haroden."

Adrian laughed. He didn't mean to, but the image of this beautiful young waif standing beside the obese prime minister was too comical to ignore. "Forgive me."

"No, go on, laugh. Trust me, I don't desire such a union."

"Well, perhaps you should. He is a powerful man."

She frowned at the remark. "Yes, but he's not so benevolent and honorable as the people may believe. My father says he is a choleric sort behind closed doors."

Adrian scoffed at that. "Lord Haroden is the

noblest ruler our realm has seen since the second era. Your father's talking rot because he feels slighted."

"Yes, well, that said, a man such as that could never please me as a husband."

"Are you telling me that you prefer a simple rustic with a kind heart over an enormously wealthy aristocrat? If so, you are the vision of every lowborn man's dream."

That made her smile. "Well, I'm not reckless enough to marry solely for love, but let's just say I prefer the selfless heroic types who may or may not wear a single glove."

Adrian felt himself blush. "You're too kind, my lady. I'm not worthy of even talking to someone of your status. You are the daughter of a provincial viceroy."

"Stop it, I have enough toadies to flatter me. You haven't touched your wine. You don't like? A little thick on the hawthorn, but the tannins give a unique complexity to the mouthfeel. Please, drink with me."

Adrian didn't want to insult her, so he obliged her request. The wine flowed and flowed and kept flowing, and before long they were chatting freely like two lovebirds on a moonlight tryst. Finally, after a lull in the conversation, she asked, "What would you do in my stead?"

"About what?"

"My father's demands. Should I agree to extend my hand to Lord Haroden?"

Adrian thought about it for a long moment. With a playful grin he said, "I would defy my father's wishes and bed the lowborn hero who wears a single glove."

She smiled at the jest, but later that night, she did just that.

*T*hey spent the next evening together, and the next after that, and soon the days of idle dalliance drifted into weeks. The fortress garrison had become a comfortable place. Adrian and Lady Amelia enjoyed nightly strolls along the wall walks of the double parapet, and often they'd spend hours talking and laughing and sharing secrets beneath the beauty of the night sky.

She seemed genuinely interested in Adrian's former life as an artisan, and so he went on and on about the history of hardstone carving, from when the first of men mined the precious skystones and created zoomorphic motifs using iron tools and abrasives. He spoke of later times in which craftsmen honed their skills in relief work to create a vast range of decorative objects such as personal jewelry and ceremonial batons and ritualistic scepters and even full-sized body suits. Some artisans even carved small figures that were placed in the tombs of the wealthy to serve them in their journey to the next life. There was so much knowledge to impart, but Adrian didn't want to pontificate or bore her. "Of course, this is all in the past for me," he said at last. "When I burned my hand I lost everything. My clients, my guild, and all my coin. Such hardships must be difficult for a woman like you to understand."

He didn't mean to insult her, but her sudden frown made him immediately regret his choice of words. "I've known hardships," she said sharply. "Just because I live a life of wealth and privilege doesn't make me any less susceptible to adversity. Truth is, I'd gladly give up this life. It is a rather empty one."

Adrian nodded, but inside he didn't agree. These past few weeks had been among the greatest that he could remember. He had a full belly, clean attire, a beautiful woman in his bed, and courteous attendants who catered to his needs at all hours of the day. What more could a man ask for? This was the life Adrian hoped to attain once he sold the imperial robe. It was the life he always wanted. The life he deserved.

And yet, he knew it was all a ruse.

The hour was late when Adrian rose from the featherbed. He put on his tunic and trousers and traveling cloak, then slung the strap of the haversack over his shoulder. Lady Amelia remained asleep on the bed, her chest rising and falling like a gentle tide. Before heading to the door, Adrian kissed her gently on the forehead. "Thank you, my lady."

She smiled, but her eyes remained closed and her voice was distant with sleep. "For what?"

"I may be a fool to your beauty, but that doesn't

mean I'm a fool to your father's scheming." He kissed her a second time. "Goodbye," he said, and left.

Eldred was waiting in the corridor. Olan wasn't with him. Adrian cursed under his breath. "Where is he? I told him to meet us here, right before third watch."

The husky man shrugged. "Nothing ever goes as planned with that oaf. Come on."

They had to double back to Olan's quarters and yank the drunken giant from his drunken stupor. The courtesan sharing his bed gasped and snatched the coverlets to cover her nakedness. A rather pretty little thing, Adrian admitted, even though he had no time for such thoughts. Olan was trying to dress himself, but the big fool kept stumbling around the room. *Hurry, hurry, hurry.* The sentries changed shifts every night at third watch, or about an hour before midnight. Time was running out.

When the three men finally exited, they noticed the arched doorway at the end of the corridor remained unguarded. Adrian urged Olan to move quickly and quietly, but the big man was as coopera-tive as an untrained ox. *Hurry, hurry, hurry.* The exit was close now, but Adrian could hear the heavy tread of the next shift of sentries approaching from the east wing. He hastened his pace. *It's fine. Don't worry yourself. We're going to make it out, we're going to make it out . . .*

They nearly *did* make it out, except Olan the drunken fool managed to stumble into a silvered cresset in the wall niche, which resulted in a great echoing *clang*. Adrian and Eldred rushed to help the giant man to his feet, but it was too late. A pair of armored sentries turned the corner and blocked the way. The taller of the two wore a captain's badge. He had an ugly wen on his chin, and an even uglier scowl. "A bit late for an evening stroll, yes? You three haven't been given authorization to leave."

"Well, we're leaving anyway," Adrian replied.

The night captain's face twitched with irritation. "Gates are closed. The hour is late."

Adrian stared at his nasty wen. "Am I a prisoner here?"

"No."

"But I can't leave?"

"Yes."

"So, I'm not a prisoner but I can't leave."

He thought for a moment. "Yes."

Olan stepped forward and placed himself between the two. The sentry wasn't short by any means, but the giant man had a way of dwarfing most men.

"Don't, Olan," Adrian warned.

The shaggy-haired man ignored that. He was sloshed to the gills and raring for a fight. Oddly enough, the smaller captain seemed ready to give him one. "The hell do you want? You're too damn drunk to stand, you big wretch."

Olan smiled, clenched a fist, and slugged him.

Everything happened so fast. The man fell back, Olan fell on top of him, and now the two were rolling around on the floor, grunting and growling and pounding each other with powerful fists. Eldred tried to pull his much larger brother off, but Olan must've thought he was another sentry, because he threw an elbow that clocked his brother in the face. Eldred fell back, and the giant man returned to pummeling the captain. One, two, three more blows, and now Olan's giant hands were wrapped around the captain's neck. He squeezed and grunted and squeezed some more, and the poor captain's face began to turn a shade of purple, while his wen was turning white.

More sentries came pounding down the corridors. It took about six or seven of them to subdue the drunken bear of a man. The rescued night captain fought to regain his breath. "I think the bastard broke my jaw. Goddamn it, it hurts." A bludgeon appeared in his hand. "Hold him."

They restrained Olan like a wild horse while the captain wailed on him. Adrian tried to pull the sentries off but he had only one working hand, and that hand wasn't strong enough to do much. Nevertheless, his efforts were cut short when a mailed fist slammed into his stomach, stealing his breath and dropping him to his knees. The same hand yanked his head back by the hair, and a knobbed bludgeon rose over him . . .

"STOP IT. ALL OF YOU."

Hands froze. Heads turned. Lady Amelia was standing at the end of the corridor, her hair tousled from sleep, her unfastened robe offering a revealing glimpse of the chemise she wore beneath. Not that she was in a revealing mood. No, the woman looked downright furious. "Let them go."

"My lady . . ." the night captain said. "Your father issued an edict, I—"

"I am his *daughter*. Do you think he will be pleased when he hears of your defiance? I said let them go."

The night captain spat a wad of bloody phlegm. "Can't do that, my lady."

"You will or you'll never wear that badge again. In fact, I'll make sure you spend the rest of your miserable life working the cesspits and privies with the rest of the soil workers. Does that sound just to you?"

It was enough to turn the captain into a meek little hound. He gave an order and the captives were unhanded. Eldred helped his brother up, and together they staggered toward the exit of the barracks. Adrian followed—but not before taking one last look at Amelia. Maybe it was the poor lighting or maybe he was just a spoony halfwit, but he swore he saw a touch of longing in her eyes.

No matter. Back on the road again.

Chapter Thirteen

The midsummer heat was unforgiving. The three companions gave in to frequent stops simply to find relief from the sun. Adrian knew it was bad when Olan filled his empty gourd-bottle from a running stream. The big man *never* drank water. Still, it was nice to see him sober for a change, even if that meant he was a bit of a sourpuss.

Three weeks had passed since they'd left the fortress garrison, and the aches and bruises endured by all three companions had long healed. The area they traveled through now was a dense floodplain supplied by the many tributaries of the Caterpillar River, a grand waterway whose strength was drawn from the glacial meltwater of the eastern mountain ranges. Fortunately for them food was aplenty here— but there were also some rather nasty creatures as well.

Huge muskrats. Water spiders with legs as thick as a man's finger. Skimmers and dragonflies the size of pinecones, midges with fangs, and leeches that drained enough blood to make you woozy. Snakes slithered through the reeds or across the water's surface, cottonmouths and smooth-liners and the three-banded poisonous ones that could kill you with a single bite. The flora was no better. On more than one occasion, Adrian brushed against a plant or nettle only to later develop a skin rash. Thankfully, Eldred always had an assortment of counterirritants on hand, from jewelweed salves to poultices of chickweed and comfrey. The man may not have been a true pyromantic examiner, but by the gods he was resourceful.

Evenings in the wild were long and lonesome. Adrian's thoughts naturally drifted to Lady Amelia. The time spent with her was like a half-forgotten glimpse of a reality that would never be realized. Was he wrong to mistrust her? No, Adrian couldn't deny his suspicions. The lady's affections, whether sincere or not, were surely meant to stall him. Such a clever ploy could've only been orchestrated by Marius Murden. The viceroy had gotten what he wanted from Adrian, and so he intended to hand him over to Lord Haroden. So much for honor.

After a few more days of travel the river stopped them in their tracks. Their only crossing was a two-span arched bridge that ran along a southern fork of the Centipede Road. The good news was that the bridge was arrayed with olive green banners, which meant it was manned by southern soldiers. The bad news was that Adrian still didn't trust what he saw. "It's too convenient," he said.

"No other crossing," Olan muttered.

"We can hire a boatman," Eldred said. "Shouldn't be difficult to find among the fisherfolk villages."

It was a sensible idea. The three companions traveled along the banks and entered the nearest hostelry they saw. It was an old weatherworn structure with an open common area that provided a lovely view of the river. The proprietor was a stout gentleman who looked friendly but wasn't friendly at all. When Adrian greeted him, the man scowled and said, "I'm not your goddamn servant. Sit down, someone will find you."

"I need to cross the river," Adrian said.

The proprietor didn't even spare the decency to look up. "Bear Belly Bridge, less than a quarter mile to the south. Toll is minimal. Thank me later."

Adrian leaned forward, placing his gloved hand firmly on the counter. "We know where the bridge is. We can't take the bridge. Do you know someone who can ferry us across or not?"

The stout man stared at the hand. "Will cost you."

"I have coin."

"How much coin?"

"Enough."

Only then did the proprietor lift his eyes to meet

Adrian's gaze. But after a long, scrutinizing moment, the eyes went back down to steal a look at Adrian's single glove. "I knew a master fisherman once. A good man, loyal, hardworking, whatever. He always wore this ugly hat of black straw, but I never thought anything of it. Then one day the breeze stole it from his head, and wouldn't you know the bastard had the mark of a criminal carved into his forehead, right here, just below the hairline."

"I'm not a criminal," Adrian said.

"Well, that glove says you're hiding something. Lucky for you I don't give a kid's rump. And by kid I mean a baby goat. Or an actual kid, whatever." He paused. "The old sculler moored out back is mine. My boatman will come by later to take you. Fifty ounces, silver."

The amount was so absurd Adrian almost spat in his face. "Ten ounces, and I won't tell my big shaggy friend just how much of a gouger you are."

His eyes narrowed but he didn't miss a beat. "I have big friends, too. Twenty ounces."

"Fifteen, and not an ounce more."

The proprietor nodded at that. "Half up front. If you're not here an hour before dusk you're out of luck."

Adrian handed him the coin. By the time he was finished, Olan was already seated at a table and calling for a server. Damn him and his wine.

The three companions spent the day enjoying the riverside view from the waterfront common room. Wild geese and mottled mallards patrolled the reedy banks, pecking at water chestnuts and feeding on duckweed. Farther out, merchant boats and barges came and went, with salesmen and tradesmen conducting all manner of business as usual. There was a lot of talking, a lot of dickering, a couple of altercations, and one terrible miscommunication that led to a fistfight. Adrian was surprised to see such an influx of waterborne traffic, but this village turned out to be one of the few hubs of clandestine trade between the north and south.

The bustle of the day eventually faded as the red light of dusk bled the sky. The boatman still hadn't arrived. The proprietor said to be patient, but Adrian's patience had already grown thin. Worse, Olan was becoming more and more obnoxious as he consumed more and more wine, and now looks were being cast their way. When the giant man belched like an overfed bear, Adrian could hold his tongue no longer. "Do you always drink yourself dumb wherever you go?"

Olan took no offense to the remark. In fact, he threw an arm around Adrian's shoulders and gave a fairly gentle squeeze. "You know, Deadhand, I've grown to like you. I have. But for a guy who can incinerate a man with a single touch, you sure fret a lot." His fingers curled to form a twisted sort of claw, and then the big man let out a bellow of a laugh. "That's some goddamn mother-raping sorcery you have there."

Adrian lifted the shaggy man's arm off him and sighed. No use arguing with him now. He glanced outside. Twilight was threading into night. Still no boatman. "Maybe we should find another way across."

"A bit late for that," Eldred said.

Adrian drummed his fingers on the misshapen table. "I don't know if we should trust this proprietor or his boatman."

"Let's give it more time."

Olan gave Adrian a nudge. "Like I said, Dead-hand, you fret too much. My brother's a gifted pyro-mantic examiner, have you forgotten? The truth can be revealed through the Celestial Deity of Skyfire."

Eldred lowered his eyes. Before he could reply, however, Olan blurted, "That our guy?"

Adrian turned to see a lean and leathery-skinned man exchanging words with the proprietor. When the proprietor pointed to Adrian the man came walking over. Without stopping he rapped a single knuckle on the tabletop and headed to the outer docks. Adrian and his two companions followed. They found the boatman standing on the pier and working the hawsers that attached the sculler to a dockside bollard. It was a flat-bottom boat, propelled by a single stern-mounted oar. Simple but effective.

"Don't stand there," the boatman muttered in a voice that sounded raspy from disuse. "Help me unmoor it so we can set off."

Traffic on the river was sparse at this hour. The gibbous moon bathed the water's surface in a coat of ivory, and the surrounding reeds gleamed like sword tips in a forge. The old man wasn't much of a talker, but he was an expert at angling the oar blade and directing the craft. His thin yet muscled arms worked with the tireless repetition of a farmhand after years of wielding a sickle.

Out of the dark and distant fog rose the city of Beetleburr. It sat perched on a wide promontory, its looming, stone-faced towers protected by thick outer walls and massive gates. Adrian glanced at his companions and saw the exultation in their eyes. They did it. They crossed the river. Soon they would be free of the north, which meant they would finally be free of Lord Haroden's grasp.

Or so Adrian thought.

"Who's that behind us?" Olan asked.

Adrian turned. Silhouettes of mounted figures appeared on the riverbanks, like ghosts materializing out of thin air. Adrian couldn't see their faces, but he saw the outline of the spiked helmet worn by the center rider. "Krall Vyren. Goddamn it, the bastard followed us. I knew it. I knew Lord Murden was stalling me."

"They're on horseback and strapped in heavy armor," Eldred said. "They won't be crossing the river like that."

The horsemen turned and rode south, cutting swiftly through the reeds.

"Now where are you headed?" Olan wondered.

It was hard to tell in the growing darkness, but it looked as though they were heading straight for—

"The bridge," Eldred said.

Adrian spoke quickly. "They won't be able to cross, will they?"

Eldred shook his head. "Bear Belly Bridge is southern occupied and heavily garrisoned. Northern soldiers wouldn't be foolish enough to try. They'll be detained at once."

But they weren't detained. No, somehow, the horsemen were *advancing*. Adrian could see them now: a host of black figures galloping across the bridge, completely unhindered. "They're crossing," Adrian said. "They're crossing the bridge."

"Stay calm," Eldred advised.

"I am calm. They're *crossing* the bridge." He turned to the boatman. "You need to go faster."

The man must've seen the fear in Adrian's eyes, because his arms began working the oar like a well-rested strongman. Still, it wasn't enough. Hell, even if he had eight arms and four oars it wouldn't have been enough.

"They'll be waiting for us at the shore," Adrian said. "They're going to run us down like frightened hares."

"Listen, both of you," Eldred said. "If we get separated—"

"We won't get separated," Adrian told him.

"If we do . . . the Stone Laurel is one of Beetle-burr's most prominent inns. We meet there, got it?"

Olan gave a low grunt.

"Adrian?"

"Fine." He couldn't tear his eyes away from the riders. "But we won't get separated."

No one spoke after that, and it seemed an eternity before the shoreline was in sight, and another before the sculler finally waded into the shallows of the inlet. It slowed as it hit a patch of silt; the boatman jabbed his finger and said that he could go no farther. Eldred and Olan dove overboard. Adrian hesitated. "You *have* to get closer. My arm . . . it's difficult to swim with—"

The boatman gave Adrian a shove. The world spun, and the river smacked him like the crash of a cymbal. When at last he righted himself and surfaced, the boatman had already turned his vessel around. Ahead, Eldred and Olan were swimming in overarm strokes. Adrian tried to follow, but with one working arm he could barely manage to stay afloat, let alone muster any measure of speed. Something beneath the surface snared his foot and yanked him to a sudden halt. He tried to pull it free. Not happening. He tugged and turned and twisted but for all his efforts, he managed only to get himself more stuck. And now the river threatened to swallow him whole. Panic set in; he tried to shout but fistfuls of dark water poured into his mouth. *Idiot! Do something before you drown.*

He unsheathed his knife, held his breath, and dove below the surface, groping around in the darkness. He imagined his foot was trapped in the jaws of some powerful creature, but it turned out to be a clump of weeds wrapped around an underwater snag. Adrian slashed and slashed until he came free. Then he resurfaced, took in a huge gulp of air, and swam on and on until his feet sank into mud. He crawled clumsily onto the shore, coughing up river water like a broken fountain.

The brothers were gone.

Adrian darted through the sedges and cattails to find cover in the surrounding woods. He was soaked to the bone and his stomach ached from gulping down all that foul river water—but at least he was safe.

Wrong. He wasn't safe at all.

A horse snorted from somewhere nearby. Adrian didn't even look. He just bolted. Hooves pounded after him. *Clop, clop-clop, clop-clop.* No matter how fast he went, his mounted pursuer seemed to be gaining on him. *Clop, clop-clop, clop-clop.* About twenty yards away now. Ten yards. *CLOP, CLOP-CLOP, CLOP-CLOP.* Five. Four.

Adrian leaped aside as the charger came barreling past, hooves kicking up clumps of earth as it skidded to a halt. The beast turned. High Commander Krall Vyren, mounted in the saddle, drew his crimson horn bow and aimed a black-tipped arrow at Adrian's heart. "There you are," he said.

Adrian's hands rose in surrender.

"You impressed me, thief. I never thought you'd make it across the Caterpillar. In fact, I lost fifty ounces of coin wagering against it."

"A shame," Adrian said, panting from exertion. "I hope you don't want me to reimburse you."

The high commander snorted at that. "No, what I want is for you to remove that haversack from your shoulder. Slowly, very slowly, or I will put this arrow between your ribs."

Adrian did as he was told.

"Good. Now kneel. Now untie the thong and remove the garment. Place it on the ground."

The firemouth silk robe glimmered softly in the moonlight. Krall dismounted from his charger for a closer look. Adrian placed his hands behind his back and quietly removed his glove. "You impressed me, too," he said. "You must tell me how your company was able to freely pass the southern soldiers at the bridge."

The high commander gave another snort. "Northern soldiers disguised as southern soldiers waving southern banners." He advanced another step. "A simple deception, but not enough to fool a clever thief like you." He took one more step and reached down for the robe . . . a slight extension . . . but just enough for Adrian to lunge forward and seize the man's fingers with his blackened hand.

Krall Vyren didn't react at first. No, his dark and brooding eyes simply stared at Adrian like two obsidian stones. A long moment passed—a moment that seemed an eternity—and then the man recoiled as though singed by a hot poker. The crimson bow fell from his grip. His hand began to blister and blacken and crack. The high commander could only watch in horror as flames swarmed up his arm and across his chest and up his neck, scorching everything in its path. It happened so fast that all he managed was a single shrill cry before the flesh of his entire body burned away, and his bones disintegrated into ash.

Silence then. A long and terrible silence that was shattered by the gallop of barded chargers and the shouts of mounted soldiers.

Adrian ran.

He ran deeper and deeper into the woods, higher and higher uphill. The moonlight turned the blue-black junipers into gnarled and shadowy things that looked ready to come alive. Then something *did* come alive. Up ahead—it wasn't a horse but a much smaller animal. A wolf? No, a dog. It was a three-legged dog. *No, I don't believe it.* The beast was scurrying uphill so quickly that Adrian could barely keep it in sight. For some reason he followed it. He didn't know why, but he kept following it even when the shouts of the soldiers had long faded and Adrian's legs began to stiffen with fatigue. He kept running and running and eventually the aches vanished. For a moment he thought he was flying—and after tripping on something he really *was* flying—but then he smashed into the ground and tumbled through a patch of wild-flowers before finally rolling to a stop.

He lay there, grimacing away the pain. His lungs began to calm. There was only silence now. No galloping, no shouting, nothing except the faint evening breeze and the dulcet symphonies of the nocturnal denizens. Adrian listened to it all, too afraid to move.

Chapter Fourteen

"*L*ook at you," a voice said. "All footsore and frightened. What are you running from?"

Adrian tried to rise, but exhaustion and vertigo smacked him in the face and sent him back down. He blinked and blinked and rubbed his eyes until the blurriness began to fade, and then he looked up.

A figure stood over him—a young boy. The darkness made it hard to see clearly his face, though from his size he looked no older than nine or ten. The little fellow was studying Adrian curiously. "What are you running from?"

When Adrian didn't reply the boy must've gone

away, because the world became quiet again, so quiet that Adrian decided to remain where he was. The night sky stretched out overhead, dark and blue and full of wispy silver clouds. Adrian watched it until his eyelids grew so heavy they were like two slabs of iron. It was a battle he couldn't win, a battle that he didn't want to win, and as his eyes closed the world began to fade into that familiar darkness . . .

Chitter Chitter Chit . . . Chitter Chitter Chit.

Adrian's eyes shot open. *What the hell?* That was a Chitterer's call. But no, it couldn't have been—the Chitterers were broken and subjugated. Adrian reached for the mask he kept tied at his hip. Gone, the damn thing was gone. He sprang to his feet. It was the boy—that little thief! Adrian chased the runt down and ripped the mask from his tiny hands. He almost backhanded the brat—by the gods he probably would've had the boy not run off once more, this time skipping and capering near the crest of the hill.

"You little rogue," Adrian shouted. "What is wrong with you?"

"I just wanted to try it," the boy replied. He cocked his head like a confused hound. "What are you so afraid of?"

Adrian grunted and looked around, fearing at any moment High Commander Krall Vyren's riders would burst out of the surrounding thicket. But they never did. Adrian took a moment to collect his thoughts and brush the dirt off his trousers. The boy remained nearby, skipping and capering and singing a stupid song. Adrian was in no mood for childish games. "Can you be quiet," he said. "You're too damn loud."

"Loud? That wasn't loud. *This* is loud. *THE MAIDEN GIGGLED AS THE BRUIN DANCED AND THE FIVE-TAILED DOE PRANCED AND PRANCED—*"

"BE QUIET," Adrian hissed. His hand went to his knife, but thankfully he had enough sense not to unsheathe it. "Just go away. Go home. You shouldn't even be here. I'm a dangerous man."

The boy cocked his head but made no other move. "You don't look dangerous."

"Well, I am. Now leave me the hell alone." Adrian turned to the east and started off. He passed a small cottage of knotted gray wood, then pushed through thick stands of wild plum thicket until he found himself at the edge of an overlook. Below, the grand city of Beetleburr hummed on the promontory like an old waterwheel. It was an immense city, among the largest Adrian had ever seen, but even from his distance he could see how incongruous it was. There were no straight avenues like in Scarlet Sun, but hundreds of winding ones that overlapped one another and left the buildings haphazardly crammed together like mackerel in a cask. The hour was late so the main entrance gate was closed and the streets were vacant, although he did spot an occasional light from a night worker's lantern.

"What are you running from?" The boy was standing behind him.

Adrian turned. "I thought I told you to go away."

The boy tilted his head down, his face hidden in shadow. "Are you going to Beetleburr?"

"It's not your concern," he said, but after a moment of thought he muttered a curse to himself. He'd already forgotten the name of the inn, the one Eldred had designated as their meeting place.

"You must be looking for the Sapphire Moon," the boy piped up.

"No."

"Are you sure?"

Adrian ignored the brat. *What was the name of that goddamn inn again?*

"You would be wise to avoid a man named Dravid. An ill-bred little trickster, that one."

Stone . . . yes, it was stone something—was it a fruit? No, a flower. Adrian couldn't focus on his thoughts, not with that little imp talking so much. *Something with the letter L. Stone Lilac, no, Stone . . . "*

"Dravid once threw a man down a well over an ounce of unpaid interest. Do you believe that? An ounce! What a horrible thing to do."

Stone Lily . . . no, Stone . . . Larkspur?

"He steals too, and robs, and does all the things a crooked man—"

"Would you *be QUIET*, you little *BRAT.*"

The boy flinched. "I am merely trying to help."

"I don't need your help, you little monkey. Now if you don't get the hell awa—" The words died on his tongue as the boy stepped into the moonlight. The face was not a child's face but an old and wrinkled one, with heavy eyes that seemed wise beyond the years of any boy. Adrian stammered. "W-who the hell are you?"

The little fellow stared at him with those old, old eyes. "I'm the one whose cottage you came stumbling to."

Adrian couldn't help but stare at this strange individual. He was so small, yet he wasn't like the stumpy and disproportionate half-men Adrian had seen in Scarlet Sun. No, this fellow's body was underdeveloped but in good balance, like that of a typical boy. He had a preadolescent's unblemished skin, a preadolescent's strong hairline, and a shock of messy brown hair that came complete with a preadolescent's cowlick. *So strange.* He'd never seen anyone with the face of an old man but the body of a small child. "How many summers have you seen?"

The way Adrian said that made the old child frown. "I don't know. Is that strange? I feel like I've seen so many . . . yet I remember so few. I can tell you more about it, if you'd care to listen."

"Sorry, I need to keep moving."

"It's past the curfew hour. The city gates are closed. Besides, you're wheezing. You may be suffering from what islanders call secondary drowning. You need to rest, perhaps I can offer you an herbal antihistamine to reinvigorate your lungs."

"I'm fine. Just go. Please."

The old child turned away hastily, so hastily that Adrian suddenly regretted his decision. But the little fellow soon vanished among the trees, and Adrian had no choice but to turn and head down the hill toward the city of Beetleburr. He didn't get far before his breathing became shorter and more ragged. Was the old child speaking the truth? No, Adrian was just tired. He decided he could go no farther. He wrapped his traveling cloak around him and curled up beneath the trunk of a massive oak. Sleep didn't come at first, but then his eyes closed, and soon the world drifted into darkness, a long and peaceful darkness that was broken only by the light of dawn.

Birds chirped and chipmunks chittered and sunlight poured into the crevices of the distant mountains like molten gold. A beautiful morning, in truth, but Adrian had no time for beauty. He gathered his belongings and fastened his cloak and ensured the imperial robe was safe in his haversack. The air was crisp today; the canopies of ash and toothed aspen were swaying as though gentled by an autumn breeze. Adrian's wheezing had stopped. He couldn't quite explain it, but he felt renewed—invigorated even. Now, if only he could remember the name of that goddamn inn . . .

The Stone Laurel, he thought triumphantly, and with that, he headed down the hill toward the bustling city of Beetleburr.

Chapter Fifteen

*H*e searched the city for days, but the Stone Laurel Inn was no more real than a castle in the clouds.

It didn't help that Beetleburr was the most neglected, most miserable city he'd ever had the misfortune of visiting. The arbitrarily designed avenues were teeming with all manner of foul-smelling, foul-tempered, and foul-mouthed city folk. Adrian spent most of the time combing the lower districts, dodging oxcarts and draymen and crossing gray and rickety bridges over gray and turbid waterways.

He visited the local wine shops and brothels and

inquired with the patrons and proprietors and panders. They all looked at Adrian as if he had just confessed to murdering a child. Were they hateful, reticent, or simply untrusting? Adrian couldn't tell, so he decided to grease some palms to get an answer.

The first man he'd given coin to turned and bolted, disappearing into the crowded avenues like a twig among brushwood. Adrian decided to approach a woman next. She took his coin and slapped him and shouted that she was not some whore to be solicited. The outburst caught the attention of a few local bruisers, so Adrian had to flee the area at once.

This isn't working. At all.

As daylight began to diminish Adrian entered the nearest inn and rented a room. Yes, the place was filthy and yes the featherbed was infested with bed lice, but he didn't care. Anything was more comfortable than sleeping in the hot summer wilderness. Still, he longed for the companionship of the two outlaw brothers. Even Olan, that big drunken bastard. But more than that, he longed for Lady Amelia. Her eyes were so cheerful, her touch so gentle. He couldn't help but regret leaving her that night. Even though she had been a pawn used by the provincial viceroy to stall Adrian, he *still* regretted leaving her. *What a fool I am.*

Someone must've been tipped off about how much coin Adrian had in his purse, because the next day Adrian received several visits from some needy and greedy folk. They tried everything from subtle manipulation to shameless begging in order to get a share of his coin, but Adrian refused them all. Bawds also came to importune him, but Adrian wasn't in the mood to pillow a whore. Well, maybe just one. A tall ashen-haired beauty with legs like poplars and a pair of breasts to make even the most faithful husband blush. She talked a bit much and smelled of too many oils and perfumes, but by the gods did she ever please him that night.

At cockcrow Adrian awoke alone. He went downstairs to the common area and broke his fast on a bowl of rice congee. A man was stealing looks at him from behind a wooden pillar. Middle aged, above average height, thin build. Adrian did his best to ignore him, but eventually the man crossed the room and bowed his head in greeting. "I'm told you are looking for the Stone Laurel."

Something about him made Adrian uneasy. Maybe it was his eyes; they were small and squinty, as if he were constantly staring at the sun. Or maybe it was his posh accent, which was odd because he was dressed in homespun and had a frame no thicker than a rib of celery. A scar at the top of his balding pate ran down to his left brow, but that wasn't nearly as noticeable as his ears. By the gods they were huge and lumpy and red, as if someone had smashed them with a club.

"Let me guess," Adrian replied. "You just happen to be the man to disclose such information."

He nodded. "Well, my information comes at a price, of course."

"Of course," Adrian said, a little more abrasive than he intended. Still, he had a right to be standoffish. No one else in this awful city had offered him any information about the Stone Laurel. *Now this big-eared wretch shows up and wants to graciously tell me where it is?* Adrian didn't trust him—and yet, he had nothing else to go on, so in the end, he decided to at least hear him out.

"You'll find the Stone Laurel in the western district, in a ward overrun by thieves and gangs," the man explained. "You should stay away. A fresh-faced outsider like you, you'll be robbed to the bone."

"Thanks for the warning. I'll manage."

"I have a few contacts there, I could escort you myself."

"And you are?"

"Most call me Kit, like the fox, and yes, it's because of these." He touched his giant ears and smiled. "They do have certain advantages. Being a keen listener and all, I tend to know how to get people things—and quickly."

The self-deprecating remark made Adrian lower his guard just a touch. *At least the man has a sense of humor.*

Kit sat down and called for a server. Then to Adrian he said, "Share a measure with me?"

Adrian politely declined. The wine was cloudy yet pricey, and Kit only took a single drink. Afterward he said, "The way you talk, you're not from the borderlands area. You sound like a northerner, you from Scarlet Sun? Moonflower?"

Adrian didn't answer.

"Forgive the intrusive question. Clearly you're a

long way from home, and clearly you must be seeking the inn for good reason."

Adrian gave him only the slightest of nods. "Clearly. So how much does an escort cost these days?"

"Thirty ounces, silver preferred."

Adrian sighed. Why was every man so greedy? "I could hire three men for that amount."

"Three regular men would be useless compared to someone who knows what I know."

"I'll give you ten."

"Twenty."

"Ten."

"Fine. Half up front."

"Done." He reached into his pouch, weighed the coins, and paid the man.

The man's eyes caught a glimpse of Adrian's glove. "A bit warm for that, my friend."

His hand went under the table, a subconscious action.

"You shouldn't hide it. To do so only strengthens the very thing you wish to forget."

Adrian couldn't help but agree. His eyes drifted to the scar on Kit's head. "What are *you* trying to forget?"

"Well, it's a bit of a long story . . ."

"Make it a short one."

"Very well. My family owned a hillside terrace in the far south. This was years ago, before I was a man grown. You know, I loved the south. I spent my springtide years with my trousers rolled up to my knees and my hands buried in the paddies. Some say it's a life of drudgery, others say it's a life that enriches the soul."

"Which is it?"

"A little of both, I guess. But it didn't last. Civil outbreak caused a sudden tax hike that jeopardized ownership of our land. My father went to the county magistrate to plead with the district tax collector. The bastard was all nods and smiles, granting us all sorts of pardons and reliefs. But the very next day, the tax collector and his soldiers rode up and doused the paddies with buckets of toxic oil. But that wasn't the worst of it. Bastard ordered my father's throat slit right in front of me." He sighed and pointed to his scar. "That was when I got this. The tax collector said it was to make sure he knew who I was in case I was foolish enough to seek revenge." He decided to take another drink. "A real sob story, eh?"

"A tearjerker for sure. Did you ever seek revenge?"

He shook his head. "The tax collector moved to another district, I moved north, and life moved on. Funny thing about getting older . . . you just stop caring about things. My father was a bit of a prick anyhow. So, what about your hand, can I see it?"

"No."

"Don't be sore. At least tell me what happened."

"It's a bit of a long story."

"Well, make it a short one."

"Funny thing about that," Adrian said, "I don't want to."

"A real witty fellow, aren't you?"

*T*hey set off at noon. The sky was cloudless and crystal and cheerful, but the midsummer heat was stifling. Crowds of impatient people moved like riffles in a river, each one sweatier and smellier than the last. Kit seemed to have an easier time sifting through the bodies, probably because he was no wider than a poppy stem and tall enough to have a good view of oncoming traffic. Lucky bastard. Well—except for those ears.

At the market square, Kit purchased a plump greengage from a plump grocer. He ate it beneath the awning of a low-rise hockshop. Adrian joined him there, a bit surprised by the number of old stores and merchant stalls still in business. Apothecaries, clothing boutiques, teashops, calligraphy stands, fortune-telling booths—and quite a few were fairly busy at this midday hour. In the streets Adrian saw foot masseurs, storytellers, hair cutters, candymakers, and a never-ending flow of hawkers and peddlers who sold everything from reed baskets to stuffed sea urchins on a stick. At the farthermost corner of the square, entertainment was offered in the form of acrobats and jugglers and singsong girls who performed in open-air theaters.

Adrian asked, "When did it happen? The gangs, the corruption at the Stone Laurel."

Kit chewed a while before answering. "Last year. Not long before the spring thaw. Some purse-proud bastard hired a group of ruffians to terrorize the local establishments, forcing the proprietors to pay outrageous fees under the guise of 'protection'. The Snakeheads, they're called. Fitting name, don't you think?"

"Where was the local magistrate in all this?"

"Paid to look the other way. Corrupt bastards, every one of them. The city council included. This shouldn't be much of a surprise to a worldly fellow like yourself."

"I know nothing of politics."

"But you do know of greed."

Adrian nodded. Just as he went to reply a man emerged from the crowd, knocking shoppers to the ground as he bullied his way past. Behind him, an irate hawker raised the hue and cry. The sentries, however, were either too hot or too lazy to spring into action, and by the time they arrived the thief was long gone. Kit just snorted, as if such criminal activity was commonplace here—which it probably was.

"I've seen a lot of cities," Adrian said at last, "but never one so run-down, and with so many . . ." He paused.

"Bottom feeders?"

"I was going to say unsavory figures, but bottom feeders works."

Kit threw away the half-eaten fruit. "Wasn't always this way. Constant sieges and skirmishes between the north and south decimated the city and razed the surrounding farmsteads. I kid you not, one day the banners atop these walls changed from north to south and back no less than six times." He turned his head and spat over a stand of rusty animal cages.

"Now that there's nothing left, no one cares enough to reclaim this city."

"Sounds like the people here have truly suffered."

"Not all. Hard times for honest folk means good business for scoundrels. The second ward of the western district is proof of that. Just one of the many byproducts of a divided realm." He started walking. "Not much farther now. Come on."

The crowds thinned as the streets narrowed, and soon they were crossing unpaved alleyways that were just wide enough for the two men to walk abreast. Around them rose tall and uneven buildings whose upper stories leaned forward like the branches of old willows. Aged wooden beams occasionally groaned under the unforgiving sun.

Adrian didn't like this area. He wanted to turn back, but Kit urged him on. "It's just around this bend. See the fountain clock over there? The inn's behind it. Come on."

They rounded the corner and approached a circular fountain whose three-tiered centerpiece was actually a clepsydra. Around it were twelve bronze-cast sculptures depicting horse and ox and goat-headed figures sitting in cross-legged positions. Kit explained how water once spouted from each of the fountainhead's mouths at every hour, and at noon all twelve would fire in unison. It must've looked magnificent in its day, but now it was cracked and discolored and the stagnant water was thick with black sludge. The old inn behind the fountain looked no better. Its pillars were worn, its insides were gutted, and its roof was marred by broken and missing tiles. It was a sad sight, yet one that was all too common in this wretched urban blight.

Two rough-looking men stepped out of the doorway.

Adrian's heart began to pound. He'd made a mistake. By the gods what was he thinking? *I have to get out of here. Now.* He turned. Three more figures appeared behind him, blocking the alleyway.

"What's going on here?" Adrian demanded. A stupid question, since he already knew the answer.

The ruffians advanced in a nonchalant manner, as if they were enjoying a stroll along a quaint promenade. Closer, Adrian saw hard and grizzled men, their features dented and misshapen and indicative of a life of physical combat. Blood-red kerchiefs were tied around their muscled necks, while cudgels and daggers and hatchets were clasped in their scarred hands. They stopped behind Kit, who scratched a large ear and tossed Adrian a noncommittal shrug. "I told you, hard times for honest folk—"

"Means good business for scoundrels," Adrian finished. He let out a defeated sigh. *How could I be such a goddamn fool?*

They took everything but his life.

Chapter Sixteen

*A*drian spent the following days wandering the streets, homeless and penniless and weak with hunger. His robe and belt and haversack and boots and coin pouch and knife and mask had all been taken, but what truly stung was the loss of the imperial robe. A part of him had died at that moment. Everything he'd worked for over the last few months was gone . . . snatched away like a rag doll from a child's hands.

They hadn't actually taken everything. Kit had let him keep his trousers and tunic and underclothes and —surprisingly enough—his glove. A shame, since Adrian would've loved to grab that bastard's neck with his blackened hand. Yes, he would've happily drained the life out of that big-eared robber and every one of his thugs. *My precepts don't apply to law-breaking scoundrels. And those bastards need to be punished.*

But he had other problems now. Three days passed and Adrian had barely eaten. He was light-headed and worn out and the pain in his stomach burned unlike anything he'd experienced before. He'd been reduced to a scavenger and a scrounger and a street beggar, who spent most of his time hanging around the market square like a pesky mosquito. Passing citizens ignored him, ridiculed him, scowled at him, spit on him. One burly fellow even slapped Adrian across the jaw when asked for an ounce of coin. Damn these people were cruel. Adrian was less than a man in their eyes—no, he was less than the vermin in the streets or the excrement on the outsoles of their shoes.

By the fourth day he was too sun-drained and weak to panhandle. He stood in the shade beneath the eaves of an abandoned shop, watching an extraordi-narily old street merchant hawk dried dates. He was a small man with a small presence, but his dates drew a formidable crowd of eager customers. Adrian asked for one but the old bastard ignored him. He just wanted *one*. One measly little date, goddamn it.

At dusk, the drum tower sounded the closing of the market. Foot traffic began to disperse. The date seller was among the last to depart. After collecting his baskets and counting and recounting his earnings, the man finally went off.

Adrian followed him.

The old man headed down meandering avenues and moved across old bridges, but only when he entered a vacant alley did Adrian make his move. His good hand reached into the seller's basket and seized a handful of dates. The date seller looked up and blinked, as if he wasn't sure what just happened. Adrian darted away and shoved the dates into his mouth, sucking them down to the pit. *By the gods these are sweet. And that was easy. Too easy.* He wanted more. He went back for another handful. This time the old man was wary. He pulled back his basket, crooked an accusing finger, and demanded payment. Adrian tried to tell him it was all right, that he would pay him back once he found his friends, but the man was already calling for the guards. Adrian told him to stop, but the doddering old bastard wouldn't listen.

Time to go, Adrian. You need to go. Now. For some reason he didn't go. Maybe he was too weak, maybe he wanted more dates, or maybe Adrian just hated the old bastard for ignoring him earlier in the square. Whatever the case, Adrian used what little strength he had left to shove the old man against an earthen wall. He held him there, jabbing a finger into his gut and telling him it was a knife and that he'd better shut up. Well, the old man didn't shut up. He was shouting now, shouting for help like a wounded swine—no, worse, like a goddamn banshee. It was so loud that Adrian would do anything to shut him up, anything at all, but the only thing he could do was yank off his glove and grasp the man's neck with his blackened hand. He squeezed and squeezed and apologized when the man's neck and face began to smoke and crack and melt away like candlewax. Next Adrian knew he was holding the clean white bones of the date seller's cervical spine, which crumbled into dust a moment or two later.

Silence came at last . . . but it didn't keep for long.

Armor clanged as a pair of sentries approached. Adrian greeted them alone. What happened here? Who are you? The interrogation was brief. They had no victim, no witnesses, and no crime. Well, Adrian made up some bull-spit story about how he screamed because he thought he saw a monster, but that only made the sentries snicker and laugh. They called him a coward and a wretch and a few other not-so-nice names, and that was that. "It's past curfew," one sentry remarked. "Get your face out of here so I can be relieved of my duty. Some of us have to work for a living."

Adrian turned to leave, but something made him pause midway. "I'm actually looking for the Stone Laurel Inn. Can either of you kindly gentlemen tell me where to find it?"

The sentry looked him over for a good moment or two, as if surprised to hear a filthy street beggar speak so articulately. He exchanged a quick glance with his partner, then crossed his arms and answered the question.

Adrian was stunned by what he was told.

Apparently, the Stone Laurel had been foreclosed on months ago. The owners of the city's once prominent inn had since moved and reopened in the third ward of the western district. The name of this new establishment?

The Sapphire Moon, of course. Just as the strange old child had said.

Chapter Seventeen

The Sapphire Moon Inn was a large structure, over four stories high, with stout wooden pillars and gauze-shielded lanterns and a rounded common room that was alive with music and packed with patrons. Only a handful of eyes glanced Adrian's way, and every one of them was miles from sobriety. Adrian stood at the far end of the room, his eyes searching, searching, searching through the haze of smoke and the horde of bodies.

No Eldred, no Olan.

He walked up the stairs to the second story, and the third and fourth after that. He peered inside the private rooms and suites and saw nothing but drunken idiots who glared at him with drunken idiot eyes. Back down the stairs he went, back to the first floor. Adrian was exhausted now. He staggered to the nearest vacant table and sat down. His eyes absently scanned the room one last time. A squat fellow was causing a stir at a corner table. He looked like some uppity snob with his fancy brocade cap and onion-white robe trimmed in fine ermine. Who was he yelling at? Adrian squinted to get a better look. Wait a moment, is that . . .? Yes, not the snob but the man seated opposite the snob. Eldred.

The husky outlaw was sitting quietly, his hands coated in a bluish liquid. Adrian nearly smiled when he realized what was happening. *Eldred's doing what he does best, hoodwinking people—otherwise known as pyromantic examination. Only this time, he seems to have landed himself in a bit of trouble.*

The snobby man was causing such a fuss that others were beginning to take notice. Apparently, he didn't want to pay for a revelation that he deemed as utter nonsense. Adrian didn't like the way this was going. He needed to intervene. He approached the table and bowed a dramatic bow, but he was so weak that his legs wobbled and he nearly toppled over. Nevertheless, he righted himself and spoke directly to the snobby man. "Forgive my intrusion, but please don't make the mistake of denouncing this man. I've come here myself to apologize for doing just that. In fact, since denying his divine revelations, I've experienced nothing but misfortune. On the eighth day of the eighth moon, my fields were destroyed by a swarm of locusts, my workers left me, and a muntjac bit me in the rump. Now look at me, I'm starving and alone and miserable. What an arrogant fool I was for ignoring this illustrious fellow."

Eldred's frown shifted into a smile when he saw who it was, but the smile quickly faded when he saw how awful Adrian looked.

The snobby man narrowed his eyes. "But he claims I've been dishonest in my family affairs. Complete drivel."

"Is it? Think deeply," Adrian said. "No one is here to judge, my friend. You would be wise to heed his words. And also, to pay him."

The snob looked at Adrian, then back at Eldred. He seemed unsure for a moment, but in the end he handed over a string of coins. Then he left.

Eldred rose from his chair and examined Adrian from foot to crown. "By the gods, Adrian. You look terrible."

"Do I? I feel peachy."

For a moment Adrian thought the husky man was going to smack him, but he ended up throwing his arms around him in an unexpected embrace. It felt good, even though it hurt. "All right, let me go, goddamn it. You're getting your Snakelion juice all over me. Probably some grasshopper legs, too. Where's Olan?"

Eldred released him and gestured toward the smoke-infested gambling dens in the rear. "Drinking, gambling, whoring . . ."

"The usual," Adrian finished, and both men shared a laugh.

Eldred sat back down and pulled out a linen kerchief to wipe his hands. His expression turned sober. "Second dissatisfied customer in the last fortnight. I must be losing my touch. So, a muntjac bit you in the rump, eh?"

Adrian laughed. "It was all I could think of. Trust me, I know how nasty those beasts can be."

Eldred gave a soft nod. "My heart is glad to see you again, my friend. I saw that general chase you down. I thought we lost you."

"You would've, had I not given him a friendly touch." He wiggled the fingers of his gloved hand.

"You're turning out to be a pretty resilient outlaw after all. Where's the robe?"

The question stole every bit of life out of Adrian. "Gone. The robe's gone."

"Tell me what happened."

Now Eldred was the sort of man who rarely showed his emotions, a manly man, a real tough's tough. But as Adrian began to speak about Kit and his band of robbers, the anger in his eyes and the tightening of his jaw made Adrian stammer his words. He still wasn't sure which of the two brothers intimidated him more. Sure, Olan's bursts of anger were frightening enough to make you flee, but lately they've become rather commonplace and predictable. Eldred's anger, however, was controlled and calculating, an anger you knew would have serious implications. What made it more unnerving was how seldom the man showed it.

Olan emerged from the wall of smoke that separated the gambling dens. He staggered to the table, muttering to himself and rubbing his meaty fingers through his shaggy hair. It took him a moment or two before he recognized Adrian. "By the gods . . . I've seen waterlogged corpses prettier than you."

"I was robbed," Adrian said. "The robe's gone."

It seemed to take a moment or two for Olan's drunken mind to digest that. His jaw worked and clenched, and a giant fist slammed the table. Wood cracked. Voices dropped as dozens of eyes glanced their way, but no one dared say a word to the giant fellow.

Eldred spoke quietly. "Describe the knave, Adrian. I want to know everything about this robber."

Adrian did his best. Tall, thin—extremely thin. Large and ugly ears, and of course that scar on his forehead. What else? Oh, he styled himself after a fox.

"Keep going," Eldred said. "Where is he from, what is he like. Anything you can remember."

He thought for a moment. Everything Kit had told him was probably a lie, but nonetheless Adrian explained the story about his family-owned terrace and the tax collector and his father's death. Olan was so restless he began searching the room with his eyes, as if hoping to find the robber here. "He took everything from me," Adrian went on. "The robe, the Chitterer mask, my knife and all my coin. Bastard even took my boots."

"Well, we're going to get everything back. Especially the robe."

"Do you even remember it? All glittering with gems and garnets inlaid in the finest firemouth silk. Even a complete idiot would realize just how special that robe is—and Kit's no idiot. Once he learns there's a hefty reward for it, he'll be gone. He's probably gone already."

"You don't know that. Listen, I know a man here, a retired civil administrator who once served the provincial viceroy. I'll pay him as an informant, to find out everything about this robber. What do you think?"

"I think . . . I need to eat something."

"Fine. All right. We'll talk about this later. When have you last eaten?"

"I can't remember."

"What about the last time you bathed?" Olan remarked. "You stink, Deadhand. Almost as bad as when I pulled you out of the ordure pit."

"I'll get him to a bathhouse," Eldred said to his brother, "and have one of the attendants pluck the lice from his hair." He looked back at Adrian. "But first, let's get some food in you."

Adrian was served a simple meal of beancurd and wheat squares. A few weeks ago it would've been bland and boring, but today it was the most heavenly repast he'd ever eaten. Afterward, Eldred escorted him out of the inn and down a few avenues and into the public bathhouses. Once inside attendants had Adrian strip to the buff, while a petite woman with warts on her fingers used a pole to place his clothes inside a high cubbyhole. She giggled when Adrian refused to remove his glove, but he pretended not to notice. Adrian was then handed a bathing towel to wear as he waded into the large square tub of mineral-rich water. Workers also helped bathe him, using the six specific movements and techniques that were each as skillful as they were swift. Afterward they dried him, handed him his clothes, and bid him a cool farewell.

Eldred brought him back to the Sapphire Moon. Adrian staggered up two flights of uneven stairs and entered the private room. He headed right for the featherbed and collapsed on the soft coverlet. He was so tired. So goddamn tired. But all he could think about was that poor old date seller. Shame filled him. He'd broken his own precepts—he killed an innocent man. How could he have committed such a horrendous act?

The next he knew the light of dawn was flooding inside the unlatched window. Adrian's eyes squinted against the glare. Eldred was holding open the shutters, his husky frame outlined in an aura of golden light. The shaggy-haired Olan was sitting on a nearby armchair, chewing on a cruller, which was probably stale given the face he was making. He offered Adrian a hunk. Yes, it was definitely stale.

Eldred's hands were folded behind his back. "Well, I put that old administrator to work."

"And yet you sound so glum," Adrian said.

"Nothing on the description or the name Kit," he

said, still gazing out of the window. "A false moniker, just as I thought."

Adrian lay back down and closed his eyes. Eldred came over and gave his shoulder a nudge. "You've rested enough."

*T*hey spent the day combing the wards of the western district. The foul streets were filled with the same slovens and slatterns and unsavory fellows as before, but this time Adrian wasn't concerned; he had the brothers with him. The massive Olan simply lumbered forward, and men and women wisely stepped aside. He was like a hungry bear searching for its first meal after hibernation.

Adrian led them to the fountain square where he was robbed. They waited for hours beside the discolored and cracked sculptures, interrogating every miscreant that came and went. But by the end of the day they'd received nothing but scared silence and stuttering misinformation. Still, the brothers—well, mostly Eldred—refused to give up.

A fortnight passed. The late summer sun was beginning to lose its strength. Today was especially cool. Chilly, even. There were talks of freezing rain belting the northern province, but Adrian paid such rumors no mind. Only in the far, far north would one ever see snow during the eighth month. Beyond the mountains where the arctic tribesmen wandered the frozen wasteland, living off whale and walrus meat and sleeping in shelters of packed snow.

Adrian had returned to good health, but as the days continued to pass, the idea of locating the robe became no more real than the grasping of fog. Their determination was waning, their resolution dying. Eldred had little coin left, so the husky man went back to work as an examiner, while Olan found employment as a pig butcher's assistant. Adrian remained in the private room, alone and drowning in remorse.

"I killed a man," Adrian confessed to Eldred. It was late one evening, just after second watch. Moonlight peered through the crevices of the latched window. Olan was sleeping on the floor, on a cushion of sedge. His snoring sounded like the contented grunts of a wild boar.

Eldred asked for an explanation.

"An innocent man. A date seller. I *killed* him. I had to, he wouldn't shut up. I told the old bastard to shut up but he wouldn't listen."

"Why?" Eldred asked.

"I don't know, I just wanted one date. Goddamn it, I told him to shut up. Why didn't he just shut up?"

Eldred spoke quietly. "Sounds like an act of desperation."

Adrian stomped the floorboards. "He was an innocent man. I broke my own precepts. I don't deserve to live."

Eldred's thick brows pushed together. He glanced at Olan, who hadn't even woken up (though his snoring had ceased), then he turned back. "So you killed a man. Life and death is preordained. It was not your choice, but that of heaven itself. You were meant to take that man's life, just as you are meant to find that ill-bred little trickster who robbed you. Are you listening to me? Why are you looking at me like that?"

Adrian refocused his eyes. Ill-bred little trickster—those were the exact words spoken by the old child he'd met on the hill. But the name he used . . . what was it? Dravid. Could it be? The old child had already revealed the correct name of the inn . . . but no, all diviners were frauds, were they not? No man—no matter how prophetic or wise—could possibly predict something of such narrow detail. *Am I wrong? Only one way to find out . . .*

Adrian looked up. "Ask your contact to do a search on a man named Dravid."

Eldred frowned. "Who?"

"Dravid. Just do it, please. I have a hunch."

"I've already spent a lot of coin on this man's services, I don't want to pay him more based on a hunch. You have to be sure about this. Are you sure?"

Adrian wasn't sure at all, but he did his very best to appear so. "Just ask him. One more time."

Eldred sighed. "Why didn't you mention this before?"

"I didn't know until now."

Three days later Adrian returned from the privy to find the two brothers waiting in the room. The grin on Olan's face was like an overgrown pea pod. "Found the prick," he said.

"Damn you both for startling me," Adrian said. "Found who?"

"Your 'hunch,'" Eldred said. "Dravid—he's your robber. Turns out he's also the leader of the ragtag group of strong-arming scoundrels called the Snake-heads. That little sob story he shared with you? Bastard wasn't the poor little farmhand who had his land taken from him. He was the goddamn tax collector. Amassed his wealth through years of extortion and appropriation and about a thousand other vile acts."

Adrian snapped to attention. "Is he still in the city? He's probably gone. He's gone, yes?"

Eldred smiled that rare smile of his. "As a matter of fact, he's not gone. A recent illness has left him bedridden. Typhoid fever, I'm told. Can you believe it?" The smile widened just an inch. "What do you think of fate now? Are we not destined to retrieve the robe?"

Adrian gave the husky man a stern nod. "Where is the prick?"

"A cozy little manor just outside the city's inner wall."

"What a fine morsel to land in a mutt's mouth," Adrian said. "We're hitting this bastard tonight."

Chapter Eighteen

The manor stood in a concealing grove of about a hundred weeping willows. That was the good. The bad was the forty-foot double wall of rammed earth and yellow clay protecting it.

The only visible entrance was through an immense double gate, but of course it was closed and barred and utterly impregnable. Force was useless here—the only way inside was through means of deception.

The three men quickly devised a plan.

Days later, as nightfall descended like the wings of a thousand black thrushes, Adrian and Olan crept along the shadows of the outer wall, sidling toward the gate, while Eldred approached the manor in the open, lantern in one hand, sealed document in the other. He was dressed in a close-fitting garment of sable and gray, which was ornamented by a silver badge of office and matching epaulettes. Now a constable's uniform wasn't easy to find, which meant it was rather expensive—but what drained their coin pouches most was the scribe they hired to pen the false edict, as well as the sealer who imprinted it with the city's 'official' mark. It was all very detailed and sophisticated work—not to mention illegal—but Adrian knew its authenticity was vital in the success of this little ploy.

A lone figure appeared on the parapet above, asking for the visitor's identity. He sounded young, maybe twenty or so. Eldred held up the sealed document and demanded an audience with the lord of the manor. The gatekeeper studied him for a long moment, then said, "His Lordship isn't receiving guests this evening."

Eldred crossed his arms, feigning the impatience of a busy constable. "Orders from the prefect. Open the gates at once. I am not asking."

The young man kept looking around. Hesitating. Clearly he was in over his head. "Why are you alone? Seems rather odd for a constable to appear alone."

"This is a private visit arranged out of respect for your lord's illustrious status. But if you prefer I can return with fifty armed officers at my side. The choice is yours."

The gatekeeper looked utterly intimidated—but to

his credit, he didn't give in. "Leave the edict with me. I'll hand it to His Lordship. I'll dare not unroll it."

Eldred shook his head. "I am sworn by imperial law to personally deliver the edict. This is no small matter."

"Well, His Lordship is ill, so I'm unable to grant your request. Please extend my apologies to the prefect. Have a good evening." The gatekeeper lowered his head and disappeared.

Damn this stubborn bastard, Adrian mused. For a moment he thought the plan had failed, but Eldred wasn't so quick to give up. "Very well. I'll leave the edict with you. But I must place it in your hand directly. If you deny me this, then I will be forced to return with my chief officer. And I assure you, he will not be happy about having to leave the comfort of his household to ride across the city and deal with some minor affair."

The gatekeeper's head reappeared, but he remained quiet for a long moment. "The postern door is up the ramp, west of the gate. Wait there."

Eldred began walking. Adrian and Olan followed, hidden in the shadows. The big man's footfalls were surprisingly quiet, but his breathing was loud enough to make Adrian wince.

The gatekeeper's voice sounded muffled through the door. "A simple warning. I am well armed and well trained in the sixteen weapons of military warfare. Constable or not, if you play me false in any way, I will cut you down."

Eldred acknowledged the warning, and after a

long and tense moment the door creaked open just a bit. A pale and nervous hand emerged from the gloom . . . waiting . . . waiting . . .

Olan shoved the door open and burst inside.

The gatekeeper flinched and fell back and landed hard on his rump. In a flash Olan was on top of him, thrusting a knee to his chest and holding the blade of his ox cleaver a breath away from the apple of his neck. "You alone? Nod if yes."

At first Adrian thought the young man might cry out, but when his trembling lips parted, no words came out. His entire face turned grayer than a storm cloud, and his head began bobbing up and down repeatedly.

Olan's bulbous nose crinkled in disgust. "You pissed yourself, didn't you? Goddamn it, why'd you go and do that?"

Adrian stepped inside the compound and looked around. Four single-story houses were positioned in four equal quadrants whose doors faced the four cardinal directions. A large inner courtyard stood in the center of the houses, fringed by a series of wooden walkways that meandered through beautiful gardens and around tall rockeries. The generous size of the property left a bitter taste on Adrian's tongue. *How much space does a single man need?*

Eldred leaned in and glared at the young gatekeeper. "How many summers have you seen? Look at me. How many?"

The young man opened his mouth, then closed it,

then opened it once more. "N-nineteen," he said in a mousy whimper.

"Good. Nineteen. Now listen to me. You still have a lot of summers ahead of you, and I'm sure you don't want to die for the wretch you're protecting. So just be calm, be quiet, and answer a few questions. Can you do that?"

He nodded and nodded and kept nodding.

Olan was scowling. "Look at him. Shaking like a sheep after a shearing. He's of no use to us."

Eldred shook his head. "No, he's calm. He'll listen." He stared pointedly at the young man. "You'll listen, yes?"

The man's frightened eyes combed Eldred up and down. "You're not a constable, are you?"

"That's right," Eldred said. "I'm not a constable. I'm just an associate of the man who was robbed by the lord of this manor."

The young gatekeeper, for some reason, begged for forgiveness.

"Stop it," Eldred told him. "Listen closely now, I need you to answer a few questions. Can you do that?"

Nod, nod, nod.

"Good. These are simple questions. Very simple. Are you ready?"

Nod, nod, nod.

"Is there anyone else assigned to night watch duty?"

The young man's mouth opened but the words just didn't seem to come out.

"Calm yourself. Look at me. At me," Eldred said. "Good. Now once more, are you the only man on duty?"

The gatekeeper nodded about a thousand times.

"Good. Next question. Where do we find your lord?"

"The rear hall. He's ill, h-he's very ill."

"Are you sure?"

More nodding. "H-he's ill, he's very ill."

"No—I mean are you sure he's in the rear hall."

"Oh, yes, yes. He's there, he's bedridden, he's ill, he's very ill."

Olan scowled. "If he says *ill* one more time, I'm going to rip out his goddamn tongue."

Panic filled the young man's eyes. He began to gibber like a drunken fool. Olan's frustration grew, and he pressed the blade closer to the young man's neck, drawing a thin line of blood.

Eldred said, "Look at me. Look at me. Good. Last question. Is he alone?"

"W-who?"

"Your lord. Is he alone?"

"H-his headservant is there, well, his father actually. Oh, and His Lordship's being treated by a master herbalist. Wait, no, the master's gone, he left at dusk."

Adrian cut in. "I thought his father was dead."

"N-no, he's as old as death, but . . ."

Eldred stood up and crossed his arms. "That's all the questions I have. But I'm not quite finished with you, so don't get comfortable just yet. I need you to take us to your lord's hall. Once you do that, you're done. Do you understand?"

Nod, nod, nod.

"Good. Now hold out your hands. Like this. That's it." Eldred tied the gatekeeper's wrists together with a length of cord. "If you stay calm and do as we say, this big fellow here won't use his big blade to split your head like a melon. You got that? Don't try to run from us, or alert anyone in any way. Very simple, eh? Now move it."

Olan hoisted the young man to his feet. Adrian couldn't help but pity the poor bastard. He brushed the dirt off the young man's padded tunic, then motioned forward. "Go on then."

Their boots clunked across the wooden planks of the walkway. No one spoke. A narrow gate and a bronze-bound door led them into the three-bay rear house. Adrian was struck by the overwhelming smell of garlic and wild ginger and also a hint of basil, too. An old man was slumped in a chair in a small anteroom. The sudden intrusion barely roused him. He lifted his bald and mottled head, smacked his lips together, emitted a few old-man groans, and reached over to scratch his backside. His rheumy eyes eventually squinted at the young gatekeeper and the three armed and dangerous men. "My son is indisposed. What do you idiots want?"

The gatekeeper spoke quickly. "The good constable here demands an audience with His Lordship at once. He bears an official edict."

"He bears a what?"

"An edict."

"What?"

All four spoke at once. *"AN EDICT."*

"Oh." The old man motioned for it. It took a while for his feeble fingers to break the seal and unroll the document, but once done his old eyes darted back and forth across the parchment with the swiftness of a lettered scholar. After closing the scroll, he reached back with his free hand to give his behind another scratch. "Well, fine. Go on in, but I doubt he's in a pleasant mood. The man's ill, you know. Typhoid. The infection is weakening though, thanks to the herbalist's remedies. Still think the crook's over-charging us, but what do I know. You're all still here? If you idiots don't mind . . . my featherbed is beck-oning to me. I must've fallen asleep on this chair again. Damn thing plays havoc on my piles."

He rose, scratched his backside once more, and wandered off into a private room, not bothering to lower the door curtain behind him.

Adrian exchanged a curious look with the broth-ers. Then they entered the rear hall.

It was as luxurious as a palace chamber, complete with fine sandalwood couches and elegant wall tapestries and fancy openwork étagères on which stood an assortment of objects—mostly onyx stat-uettes of foxes and she-foxes and other vulpine crea-tures. The bed was curtained in gossamer silk, highly detailed and tasseled and probably as expensive as those owned by the highest ministers of the noble court. Behind the curtain a silhouetted figure sat up and pulled down the coverlets. "Father?" It was a man's voice, weak but irritated.

Adrian yanked the curtain so hard he tore the fringes. A familiar face stared at him—it was Kit or Dravid or whatever the hell his name was. The man looked terribly gaunt and terribly exhausted, and while his face was as pale as pigeon poop, his giant ears were pinker than a piglet's rump. Lower, a spattering of tiny red dots covered the bare skin of his torso, which was visible between the folds of his unfastened robe.

Adrian leaned forward. "You know who I am?"

Dravid gave him a hard look, but otherwise remained silent.

Smash. Olan's cleaver split a dressing case that was sitting on a nightstand beside the bed. Dravid quailed as wood splintered and look mirrors broke and brushes and flacons clattered to the floorboards. Adrian spoke louder. "Do you know who I am?"

"Yes."

"And do you remember robbing me?"

"I do."

"I want it back. All of it."

The robber gestured across the room with his eyes. "Through the alcove . . . beside the writing desk."

Adrian went and found a large brassbound chest and dragged it back into the hall. The catch was rusty and the splitting spring padlock—cast in bronze and shaped like a fox's tail—wouldn't budge. "Locked."

Olan walked over and smashed it open with the butt of his weapon. "Unlocked."

Adrian knelt down and riffled through the container, pulling out an assortment of clothing and weapons and smaller coffers that contained coin and jewelry and other stolen items. He found his belongings wrapped in a sheet of sackcloth. Everything was there: his traveling cloak, belt, boots, knife, Chitterer mask—and of course, the haversack. Adrian untied the leather thongs. Inside, the glittering garment was neatly folded and untouched. *By the gods . . . he never opened it. He didn't even know what he had.*

Dravid spoke while Adrian was fastening his cloak. "You're a resourceful fellow, I must admit. How did you find me?"

"You're not the only fox in this city."

That made Dravid laugh. "Damn your lambent wit."

"It looks like your father is back from the dead. You must know a talented necromancer."

He gave a shrug like a child caught eating a honey cake. "Well, the man is a prick, I wasn't lying about that. He may be a doddering old fool now, but in his younger years he was a savage. He beat his brother to death with a cauldron. Bastard used to beat me, too. What a cruel and miserable wretch, don't you agree?"

"Sounds like another sob story," Adrian said.

"Yes, well, it is what it is. Does the big guy have to be so rough?"

Adrian turned. Olan was ransacking the place, flipping couches and tables and tearing open cushions and searching through everything from cupboards to trunks and various strongboxes. So far he hadn't found much—a few pouches of coin, a handful of trinkets, a small figurine of a dancing girl that he seemed to like.

Adrian looked back at Dravid. He didn't like the unruffled attitude the man was giving off. In fact, it downright angered him. "You *deceived* me," Adrian said. "You took everything I had and left me to starve. I had to do terrible things to survive because of you." The anger rose like bile in Adrian's throat. "You should be thrown in a hole and left to die." A sudden smirk lifted his lips. "A foxhole, how fitting."

Dravid smiled and looked at Eldred. "Does his wit ever run dry?"

"No," Eldred replied. "But your sarcasm bores me."

Dravid frowned at that. When next he spoke, his tone had become grave. "You three are the only criminals here. To rob a prominent man in his very own home . . . you will all face a rather agonizing death. Try to run and I will hunt you down like the dogs you are. Even you, big man."

A shadow passed over the robber's face. It was Olan rising to his full height, his meaty hand wrapped around that terrible ox cleaver.

"Don't do it," Adrian told him.

The big man squeezed the handle so hard his knuckles turned white. "There's no innocence in this man, Deadhand. We're not breaking your precious precepts."

"Precepts?" Dravid asked curiously.

"I said *no*."

"Only a fool would allow this miscreant to draw breath," the shaggy man argued. "He has to die."

All Adrian kept thinking about was the old date seller. He couldn't explain it, but a part of him thought that letting this vile man go would somehow cleanse his soul of that old date seller's death. It made no sense—well, it made a little sense, in his mind at least. "I don't care," Adrian told him. "Don't do it. Come on. We're leaving."

Olan scowled and cursed and stomped an angry foot, but thankfully Eldred was there to pacify the big man. It didn't take him long to persuade his brother to let the wretched robber live. Soon the three men were exiting the rear house and hurrying out of the manor. It wasn't until they were out of the grove of willows that their pace slowed to a walk. Adrian used his good hand to squeeze the haversack to his breast. They'd done it. Their prize was back, their focus renewed, their partnership restored. The feeling was hard to describe—a wellspring of pure jubilation that coursed through Adrian's body and sent his heart soaring like a caged songbird set free.

Maybe Eldred was right about all that fate talk. Or maybe it was something else. Something a bit more . . . supernatural.

Adrian turned to Eldred. "I'm ready to tell you how I knew the scoundrel's true name."

Chapter Nineteen

"For the last goddamn time, Adrian, there are no true men of divinations. You know that better than anyone."

Adrian only gave a half-turn to regard the trailing Eldred. "It's just beyond this ridge. Come on."

The husky outlaw cursed as his foot became caught in a tangle of undergrowth. "A gifted diviner living as a recluse in the hills," he growled, reaching down to pull himself free. "Sounds like a load of moonshine. No, worse, like a trite and unoriginal work of poetry."

Adrian shook his head and continued on. They'd already ascended hill after hill and were now moving through the stands of blue-black junipers. Shouldn't the cottage be just over this crest? Maybe they'd strayed too far east. All of these hills looked the same, goddamn it.

"I'm dead tired, Deadhand." It was Olan, calling from somewhere behind them.

Eldred placed a hand on Adrian's shoulder. "This so-called diviner of yours simply made shrewd predictions based on careful deductions and insider knowledge. It's a skill, I told you that. He played you false. Why can't you see that?"

Adrian halted. There it was, the small cottage of knotted gray wood nestled against a stand of wild plum thicket. No one was around. Eldred began to speak but Adrian shushed him. "Do you hear that?"

"No," he said, though he was breathing rather heavily.

Adrian listened closer. It was a rhythmic sound, the unmistakable *chop-chop-chop* of a woodcutter at work. The three men followed it to a tranquil copse where a diminutive figure stood before a stout hardwood, hatchet in hand. It was him—the little fellow who'd made those astounding predictions. He was dressed in undyed trousers and a tattered straw hat, but his upper body was bare and his boyish chest glistened without a speck of adult muscle. He took a long, curious look at the visitors.

Adrian bowed his head. "I wish to talk, my friend."

The old child rested the hatchet against a nearby stump. Every movement he made was nimble and childlike—picking up a gourd-bottle from the ground, removing the clay stopper, leaning his head back to take a swig, swallowing, lowering his head, stoppering the bottle, placing it back on the ground. "I see you brought friends this time," he said. "I must admit, you look different from the man who came scrambling up the hill, eyes wide and hands shaking as if a bugbear was after you."

"And you look different from the little monkey who stole my mask."

The old child lifted his hat to thumb the sweat from his brow, then he grabbed an old tunic hanging from a branch and put it on. "Is that why you came back, to insult me?"

"No, I didn't mean that, but—"

"To hell with the little brat," Olan growled. "We're wasting our time here."

Eldred agreed. "This is your man of divinations? He's not even a man. Is he?"

Adrian didn't answer that because he wasn't sure himself. Yes, the little fellow had the body of a boy, but his face looked as old as he remembered. Older even, since the radiant light of the midday sun illuminated the deeper wrinkles that went unseen in their previous encounter. "I came back to thank you," Adrian told him. "For telling me the name of the inn, and also the name of the man who robbed me. How do you know such things?"

"I don't. My associate does. You see, the world speaks to my associate every day, and every day my associate listens. He is what a devout Argalist would call a Seven Times Awakened Soul. Free from all limitations and full of sublime wisdom. It's not something one can acquire through esoteric study. No, my associate holds the answers to imponderable questions of infinity and eternity, of life and death and of course the Great Rivers of Transmigration."

"He sounds like a man of great talent. May I meet your associate?"

The old child shook his head. "He's not receiving guests today. I'm afraid he's been rather busy this year. Ever since he met a wealthy landowner who was concerned about what little rain the season had brought. As they say, no rain, no grain. Well, my associate told him not to fret. The days of drought would end on the evening of the first quarter moon, and the earth would provide a bountiful harvest. Of course that's exactly what happened, but ever since that day, crowds of needful men and women have sought out his wisdom at all hours of the day. You see, my associate is a true altruist and egalitarian, one who helps others without ever asking for anything in return."

"Sounds like nonsense," Eldred said. "It is not difficult to predict a good harvest. I've been observing the swallows flying in and out of the open window of your cottage. They are nesting in the rafters there, yes? I'm sure you know that the size, shape, and arrangement of a swallows' nest is quite indicative of the warmth of the coming autumn—which tells you whether it will be a good harvest or not. Now if that's what you mean by listening to the world, then by all accounts, your associate is correct. But spare the supernatural drivel. It's all a sham."

The old child blinked at Eldred. "My associate's prognostications are beyond the realm of guesswork."

"But not beyond simple deductions and probability. Or better yet, you and your so-called associate are in league with that bastard robber."

The old child frowned.

Adrian gave Eldred a stern look, then he asked the old child for forgiveness. "I didn't come here to quarrel. I certainly didn't come here to make accusations. I only wish to speak with your associate. When can I meet him?"

"I don't know. Is this about your hand? Please, show it to me."

Adrian flinched at that.

That made the old child smile. "Oh, don't fret, I am quite familiar with your case. My associate has taken a keen interest in you. You can say our meeting is providential. Now go on, show it to me."

For some reason Adrian did. He gingerly pulled off the glove, revealing the burned and blackened hand beneath. The old child studied it for a time, his eyes combing the disfigurement not squeamishly but with cold precision, like a veteran physician tending the wounded after a grueling battle. "The eschar . . . it's deeply rooted into the flesh, but yes, this is something my associate can relinquish. But I must note this is no ordinary condition, and as such, it will require an extraordinary treatment."

"That is good news," Adrian said. "What sort of treatment?"

His voice softened to a murmur. "Oh, it's actually just a little thing . . . a tiny little polypore is all."

"A polypore . . ." Eldred said. "You mean like a mushroom?"

"Yes, a red cloud mushroom."

The husky outlaw's brows came together. "Does it have another name?"

"Oh, it has many. Phoenix tail, scarlet saddle, heart of the woods. It's a relative of the bracket conks and sulfur shelves found in the north, though it's much rarer, and far more potent. In fact, its potency goes beyond—"

"Phoenix tail," Eldred interrupted, as though speaking his thoughts aloud. "I've heard the name. In the annals of the second era of rule, a phoenix tail mushroom was presented to the young emperor after fearing a coup from his own ministry. From what I recall an assassin crept into his private bath to slit the emperor's throat, but the blade shattered against his bare skin like warm glass." The husky man didn't try to hide the expression of cynicism he wore. "A mushroom of immortality—is this a jest?"

"Not immortality," the old child corrected. "The gift of true immortality does not exist, and yet for centuries the most powerful men have scoured the ends of the realm in search of it. But the silver lakes said to wash away the years only brought on an insidious poison, and the white blossoms meant to enliven the heart only made it weaker. No, immortality can never be attained because heavenly law states that all life that begins must end. That said, the red cloud mushroom is a supermundane antioxidant and supernatural preventative. He who holds possession of it is rendered impervious to the constraints of pain, illness, and death. But there is a notation next to death, as in death by all unnatural occurrences. Do you understand?"

"Yes, I do," Eldred said. "But this is stupid, and you are mad."

The old child didn't bristle at the insult. "Your one-gloved friend asked for help. I am simply answering his query."

Adrian spoke. "All right, I'll play along. What exactly does this mushroom look like and where can I find it?"

"The red cloud is a hard and corky fungus that resembles a nimbus with a bright red varnish. It lacks gills but releases its spores through the white tubes underneath the cap. Its ancient binominal name, *Vethel Anor*, translates as 'devil's food,' because the mushroom is quite toxic if outright consumed. In fact, even a complete steam distillation of the mycelium will still cause various ailments including blurred vision, mydriasis, hallucinations, dry mouth, nystagmus, and neuralgia. No, the red cloud mushroom works only if used like a talisman. Very simple. But I must note, the mushroom alone will not heal your condition. Only my associate can do that."

"Fine. And its location?"

"I'm afraid it's found only on a single log of

undying deadwood that stands on the summit of a remote mountain peak. Even then, it requires centuries before the fruiting bodies are mature enough to retain the properties of invulnerability. In the last century alone there has only been one to blossom with such supernatural properties, but that was over five years ago now, and it has since been harvested. Now that is good news, my friends, since you don't have to risk the perilous journey to fetch the mushroom yourself. But there is one issue: my associate doesn't know who this harvester is, although there are rumors of a—"

"Wait a moment," Eldred cut in. "Let me understand this better. Your associate somehow knew the name of the inn my friend was looking for, as well as the identity of the man who robbed him . . . but he cannot clearly identify the fellow who harvested such a precious and magical fungus?" He turned to Adrian. "Do you still believe this isn't a scam?"

Adrian didn't know how to reply to that, so he remained quiet.

"Listen carefully," the old child said. "A being of clairvoyance can only see what he focuses on seeing. He cannot recall past or present events. Only the greatest of deities are gifted with omniscience. That said, we do know that it wasn't some bumbling neophyte. Arcane knowledge does not come cheaply, and I say that because the harvesting procedure is quite complicated. Not just any fool can approach the mushroom and scrape it off the log. No, the mushroom must be approached between the vernal and autumnal equinoxes, specifically when the tubes of the underbelly are dilated and the fruiting body is glossed over in a pale pink. After receiving a series of whispers in a specific order using a precise inflection, the mushroom will take on a faint phosphorous glow, which means it's ripe for removal. Now, as I was saying, rumors tell of a wealthy misanthrope who was assaulted on a mountain road and suffered a tragic plunge off a high cliff. Well, it would've been tragic, but miraculously the man wasn't injured at all. No broken bones, no fractures, nothing. He simply got up and walked off. Now, we believe this fellow is your harvester. But I must warn you, some say this man is more than just a man. Some say he is a demon made flesh."

Adrian looked down and sighed. This was all becoming too much. He simply came here for a simple solution to his condition, not to go on a hunt for some stupid demon who surely wasn't a demon, for the odd chance of recovering some stupid fungus that surely didn't do anything special. "Well, I thank you for your information. I don't think we really have time to search for magic mushroom thieves. We have other obligations."

"You know, the alleged harvester makes his home in a cave just outside the southern city of Swallowtail. Isn't that where you're headed, Swallowtail, yes?"

Adrian tried his best to remain expressionless, however surprised he must've appeared. "It is," he said at last. *How the hell did he know that?* His eyes dropped to the ground. "Even if we agree to this, we have no idea how to find this man. And if he's wealthy he must be powerful, and so he must have powerful friends. There are but three of us."

The old child's face brightened at that. "I assure you I won't cause any trouble. I'm a diffident fellow by nature . . . just don't mistake my timidity for a lack of shrewdness."

"Wait, you're coming with us?"

The old child nodded. "For a modest surcharge to cover my traveling expenses. Like I said, my associate has taken a keen interest in you, my friend. Flattering I know, but don't let it go to your head. Remember, he is a true altruist."

Eldred crossed his thick arms. "How stupid do you think we are? You're using us because you want that mushroom for yourself. Either that or there is no mushroom, and you simply want to run off with our coin."

The old child's wrinkled face, for the first time, tightened with agitation. "I care nothing for you or your possessions, but my associate I dearly love, and it is my associate's wish to help your friend find relief from his condition."

"We don't have time for this nonsense," Olan growled.

The old child nodded as if expecting to hear that. "The alleged harvester's cave is located near a rather luxurious brothel. It is said some of the most beautiful women in the realm can be found there."

Olan's eyes widened. "Well, I suppose we have a *little* time . . ."

"Wonderful," the old child said. "So, we are in agreement then."

There was a brief moment of silence. "I don't even know your name," Adrian said.

"Temil. Some call me Timid Tem, others call me by my milk name, Little Dawn, but that might be a bit cutesy for the likes of you three hardened men. Anything else?"

"Yes, I have a question," Olan said. "What's wrong with you, are you a boy or what? I thought you were, but you don't talk like any boy I know, nor have I ever seen one with a face so old. So, which is it?"

The little fellow tilted his head back to consider Olan's words. "I don't know why I am the way I am. Perhaps I'm the punishment of some past sin. But enough about that." He looked Olan up and down. "What about you? Why the hell are you so big? You look like one of those wild trolls of the deep forests who like to snack on lost children."

Olan stared at him for a long moment, then his thick lips spread into a smile. "I think I like this one."

Adrian did, too. He liked him even though he didn't trust him. Was he just a skillful liar and master manipulator? Maybe. Of course Eldred seemed to think so. Still, the opportunity to find relief from Adrian's condition was too tempting to ignore. To end his hideous disfigurement and that cruel pain, to stop the recurring nightmares of fire and death and that damn three-legged dog, to free his mind from sadness and worry and fatigue and lack of focus . . . yes, it was a chance worth taking. Besides, the trip to the cave would be just a minor detour—it probably wouldn't really put them off too much. And with Olan and Eldred by his side, Adrian wasn't concerned about what sort of 'demon' might be waiting for him. They'd simply purchase this mushroom from the man, and that would be the end of it. What harm could come of it?

Fine. Done. Now Adrian could focus his mind on matters of a much greater importance.

And what matters were those? Well, the answer was threefold. One, arrive safely to the city of Swallowtail; two, sell the imperial robe to the southern privateer with the crooked eye and horseshoe mustache who answered to the name of Broden; and three, bask in a life of wealth and privilege for the rest of his glorious days.

Chapter Twenty

he farther south they traveled, the more the hindwings of summer fought against the season's change. It was like a drunken tavern-goer who simply refused to leave . . . but in the end, as with all things, nothing could stop the passing of time.

The air was chilly today, borne from a wind that screamed down the eastern highlands and plastered Adrian's trousers to his legs. All around him stands of powerful broadleaves began to disrobe, sending variegated shades of copper and gold and red spiraling to the ground. The nearby pond rippled like a scorned lover whenever a fallen leaf touched her otherwise tranquil surface.

Adrian no longer feared the sound of passing riders. They were too deep in the south now—certainly far beyond Lord Haroden's grasp. The military garrisons and outposts they saw now all displayed the embroidered standards and olive green banners of the southern warlord. Samos the Stormbringer ruled the lower provinces with his skilled generals and fierce naval armada, though he himself was nothing more than a power-hungry fool with an unsubstantiated claim to the throne. Supposedly, he was the late emperor's distant nephew.

Adrian didn't care about that, nor did he care about the civil strife that currently plagued the realm. And yet, every wine shop and roadside inn they visited was packed with unsophisticated fellows who blathered on about issues they had no business blathering on about. Adrian did his best to remain invisible, but it was a near-impossible task when accompanied by a giant bearded fellow who took pleasure in raising a row and drinking teams of men under the table.

Still, to his credit, Olan promised to behave—and he did. In turn, the people of the south proved to be rather accommodating, even if most kept a wary eye on the giant man. As far as the tiny fellow at his side, only children seemed to show any interest. When they looked at Temil's wrinkled face their eyes lit up and their mouths twisted into expressions of confusion and wonder and sometimes terror. One little girl actually broke into tears when the old child cracked a smile at her.

"Children always notice me," Temil remarked later. "The older folk, not so much. But children . . . their eyes are still fresh, their minds still open to the wonders of the world."

Temil was generally a squirrel around strangers, but in private he had a tendency to be talkative and digressive and longwinded. Sometimes he said or did things that made Adrian question his level of maturity; other times he expanded on a comprehensive treatise of the astral divisions, which left Adrian in awe of his rhetoric. He was certainly an odd sort—one part shy and courteous rustic, another part bold and pompous scholar. Adrian concluded that Temil was just a strange little man who spent most of his life buried in books. *Well, he is a recluse. Isn't this how a recluse is supposed to act?*

Olan didn't seem to mind the old child's company, but Eldred never warmed to his presence. Adrian remained somewhere in between—he still found Temil rather likeable, but there was also an odd, discomforting aspect to his personality. Being around him was like being around someone who knew too much about you. You never wanted to displease or rile him, for fear that he might reveal all the nasty little secrets in your life.

Another week of uneventful travel passed like a flicker of candlelight. Swallowtail was no more than a fortnight away now. Everything Adrian and Niall had arranged months ago would soon come to fruition. Sure, the journey across the realm didn't happen exactly as planned, but all that mattered was getting there, and Adrian was about to do just that. Every step he took now was filled with a renewed sense of determination. Nothing could stop him from marching inside Swallowtail's gates and selling the robe to the southern privateer with the crooked eye and horseshoe mustache who answered to the name of Broden. By the gods . . . Adrian could almost taste the riches on his tongue.

Then, Olan vanished.

It happened during the second night of their stay at a seedy little hostelry in a seedy little hamlet called Three Tarns. Adrian awoke at cockcrow and noticed Olan's featherbed hadn't been touched. He didn't think much of it then, since the big man had a habit of spending his nights either soused and chasing women or soused and gambling with men or soused and doing whatever the hell he did. The giant man would eventually turn up, no doubt with some grand story to tell.

But the day came and went and Olan's featherbed remained vacant.

Eldred looked into the matter with the proprietor. The proprietor directed him to the game master of the gambling dens. The game master was an unlikable man, small and balding and seemingly not too happy about either. "Of course I remember him," he said, picking at his lower lip with a dirt-encrusted fingernail. "The drunken oaf who tossed all his coins and lost every bet. Instead of handing over his purse, he threw his fists at me and chased the collector into the river."

Eldred moved closer. He wasn't a giant man, but he still towered over the game master. "Watch your tongue. That drunken oaf is my brother."

The game master's eyes widened, but when a pair of tall bruisers under his employ took a few steps closer, his fear melted into a look of disdain. *I'll do whatever I damn well please*, his eyes seemed to say.

"Forgive my friend," Adrian said. "He is distraught. Please, go on."

The game master hesitated, as if unsure how to handle Adrian's politeness. "Yes, well, there was a lot of drinking and a lot of chatting, and what else do drunken men chat about besides women, eh? Well, your big friend wanted to know about the courtesans of the Bluebell brothel. So, we told him and he left."

"Wait a moment, what exactly did you tell him?" Temil asked. He was standing behind Eldred, so small that Adrian had forgotten about him. And yet, for all his four-foot stature, he seemed to cut a rather intimidating figure right now.

The game master's eyes narrowed. "We told him what we know about the place."

"And that is?"

"That it's a secret pleasure house employed by some of the most beautiful women in the realm. The five infamous singsong girls of Moonflower, the twelve mistresses of the southern ministry, the harem of golden concubines once bedded by the late emperor himself. All are trained in the nine levels of pleasure, and a few are said to know two or three more. Is that enough for you?"

"Yes, but that was nearly a year ago. Did you tell him what the brothel has since become? Did you happen to mention the Night of the Red Death?"

"What is the Night of the Red Death?" Eldred demanded.

Temil's eyes remained focused on the game master. "The night a fire-spitting hellbeast swooped down from the sky and burned the brothel to the ground. Did you forget to mention that macabre little detail?"

"I don't know anything about that," the game master said.

"Of course you don't. And of course you don't know that the master of this hellbeast is a demon, and this demon now uses the enslaved courtesans as sirens to lure travelers into a nearby cave, only to rob them to the bone and feed them to his beast." He shrugged. "Now, if you had told our friend all of that, do you think he still would've gone there alone?"

The game master's scowl meant that he wasn't used to having his integrity questioned. "Like I said, I don't know anything about that. None of us do. We are honest folk, hardworking and simple by nature. Are we done? I'm a busy man."

No one spoke until the three men returned to the privacy of their rented room.

Eldred immediately lashed out on the old child. "You little bastard, why the hell didn't you tell us about all that?"

"I did, I said the man is rumored to be a demon made flesh."

"Yes, but you didn't mention his little fire-spitting pet, or that the goddamn brothel was burned to the ground."

Temil opened his mouth to reply, but the husky man spoke over him. "Those bastards may have sent my brother to that cave, but it was you who planted the idea that there was a brothel full of beautiful women to begin with. You withheld the truth. Why? Why, goddamn it."

"I didn't want to frighten you," Temil said at last. "If I had told you the truth would you have agreed to go? Besides, it's all rumors and speculation. We don't know if the alleged harvester of the red cloud is actually a demon."

Eldred looked ready to throttle the old child, but thankfully he didn't. Instead the husky man clenched his fists and paced the room for a while, angry and restless and beyond frustrated. Then an idea must've come to him, because he dropped to his knees and began rummaging through his rucksack. Adrian had never seen him like this, and only now did he begin to understand just how deep his brotherly devotion ran. It was unlike anything Adrian had ever witnessed before—and it made him feel rather empty for never having that kind of bond with his own kin. Still, to see such a normally stoic and emotionless man become so unhinged . . . well, it certainly was a bit unnerving. You could almost feel Eldred's thoughts racing in a thousand different directions.

But were they rational thoughts? Olan was an absolute powerhouse, a giant slab of impenetrable stone. How many men would it take to overwhelm him? And his captors weren't even men! And there certainly wasn't any demon, not to mention a giant fire-spitting hellbeast. No, this was no different from the Chitterers. *Men in masks, nothing more, just as these sirens are lawless women and nothing more.* Adrian wasn't worried—in fact he was rather annoyed by it all. How could that giant lecher go off on his own when they were so close to the end?

Adrian turned to Eldred. "Listen, I don't know what to believe. But there's one thing I am sure of. That bald prick of a game master must be fattening his purse by sending unsuspecting travelers to that brothel."

Eldred wasn't listening. After handing the old child a mortar and pestle, he dove back into his rucksack and began searching through the various pouches and pockets. "Tell me what you need," he said. "Milfoil, wormwood, tortoiseshell, nightshade, anise, bloodroot—tell me what you need. You have to find my brother. *Please*."

Temil refused. "Only my associate has such an ability, I told you this."

Of course that didn't sit well with Eldred. "Stop lying, you little runt. I need your goddamn help. If anything should happen to my brother . . ."

Temil didn't seem to be the least bit intimidated, but not for any showing of courage. In fact, the expression on his face was rather curious. It resembled either the confidence of an all-powerful being who couldn't be harmed by mere mortals, or the incomprehension of a halfwit who didn't know he was being threatened. "I told you, I can't do it," he replied.

They stared at each another for a long moment, but in the end Eldred shook his head and sighed. "I can't lose him. I can't lose that big bastard."

The old child spoke softly. "Listen, my friend, your brother may yet be alive—in fact, I'd wager that he is. But if you want to save him then we need to go to this cave at once. You have coin, yes? Use it to hire some swords. We'll save your brother and retrieve the mushroom in one heroic assault."

Adrian placed his good hand on Eldred's shoulder. "We'll get him back." He had no idea why he said that, but it seemed the right thing to say. "I promise you, we'll get him back."

Chapter Twenty-One

Traveling without Olan was odd and unfamiliar. There was a certain comfort in the man's giant stature—a comfort in knowing that Olan could overpower any fool who dared threaten the group. He was a great fearless bear of a man, and Adrian and his companions were that much smaller now that he was missing.

They had no shortage of coin, but every sellsword they'd approached wanted nothing to do with the demon of the cave. Not even the most desperate or vainglorious of men, no matter how drunk or reckless they appeared to be. Adrian couldn't make much sense of that. These were grown men, many ex-military and all with significant skills in swordsmanship. How could these fireside tales of demons and sirens and ferocious hellbeasts infect them with such fear?

Eldred stopped to unfold the block-print map purchased from a gruff cartographer who demanded a high price while being immune to haggling. The map had taken them south by southeast for the better part of an hour now, and the going was relatively tame, aside from Temil's frequent chattering about everything and anything. Still, the little man quieted the moment they approached a mass of stones reaching skyward like the teeth of some giant carnivore. Eldred paused to check the map. "This path will take us into the heart of the Saberfang Forest. Once there we head east until we hit the springs. Just north of that is the brothel."

The late-afternoon sun bathed the land and made the stony peaks glimmer like magical scepters. It was a rather breathtaking sight—like Adrian's first view of the northern alpenglow—and yet he said not a word about it, not even when Eldred halted for a drink and was splendidly silhouetted against the rosy light. The three men simply continued on, maneuvering around jagged stones and climbing over slabs of mossy rock, again and again until at last they were greeted by the sound of a babbling spring.

It was as if the light of dawn had melted into the earth only to bubble up as a liquid. A shimmering blend of soft pink and bright white and gentle aquamarine, the waters evoked a scene of bucolic tranquility one wouldn't expect to find in this otherwise bleak area. *A truly beautiful place*, he mused. *But also a fine place for an ambush.* Still, there was no time to ruminate. Just beyond the spring the path brought them to a small clearing where the lonely remains of an old fire-gutted building sat. The Bluebell brothel may have been glorious in its day, but now it was nothing more than a heap of blackened and broken wood, half buried and overrun by fungus and fireweed.

The three men immediately split up. They toiled like laborers before an overseer, searching the crannies of the surrounding rock faces, cutting through creepers and vines and carpets of kudzu, peering through openings in the jutting walls of stone. They searched and searched but there was nothing to be found. No cavern, no sirens, no demon, no hellbeast, and of course, no Olan.

At twilight the three men reconvened by the springs, sitting motionless on lichened stones as nightfall descended like a heavy mantle upon their shoulders. Eldred was staring down at the map, while Temil was absently pulling at willow catkins and humming a tune like a bored child.

Adrian didn't notice her at first. A lone woman quietly approaching the water. She wore an undyed silk blouse, sleeveless and short—but it wasn't her attire that drew Adrian's eye. It was her skin. Smooth and shiny and remarkably pale—it was as if she'd been painted with a brush that was dipped in the clouds. In contrast was her hair, which shone as black as polished iron. She was certainly a pretty thing, but not the supreme vision of pulchritude that was supposed to make a man like Adrian run amok with desire. No, in fact, he'd known far comelier women. *Lady Amelia for one. Beautiful Lady Amelia and her bright eyes and perfectly curled hair. Yes, I'm such a spoony idiot.*

The woman knelt to fill a bronze ewer cast as a flower. She was no more than twenty spans away, and yet she took no notice of her onlookers. The three men began skulking through the outer brush of the spring, edging closer. They made it about halfway when someone's boot scraped a stone and alerted the woman. She stared briefly in their general direction, then went back to filling her ewer. "You don't have to hide." Her voice was as soothing as a summer breeze.

"Shouldn't she be afraid of us," Eldred whispered.

"I don't know. Of you, maybe," Adrian said.

Eldred emerged from the brush and cleared his throat. "My brother came this way. A big fellow, angry and hairy and all stages of drunk. Your people took him. I want him back."

She looked up at him with gentle eyes. "If he's half as manly as you I certainly would've remembered him. I'd be glad to—"

Eldred's cudgel shot forward, halting mere inches from her face. The woman recoiled, knocking the ewer into the spring.

"I know who you are, and I know what you do to people," Eldred said. "I *want* him back."

For a moment she looked longingly at the sunken ewer, as if intending to retrieve it, but when Eldred motioned her to rise, she decided to let it go. She was taller than Adrian had first thought, her legs long and shapely and paler than two carvings of kiln-fired porcelain. She also seemed more indignant than afraid, but Eldred was too impatient to care. He demanded to know where the entrance to the cavern was, and she replied by gesturing to the stone formations behind her, the ones they'd already combed through a dozen times. Eldred nudged her forward, and she began moving in defiant steps.

Adrian leaned close to his outlaw companion. "This reeks of a ruse. Are we this stupid?"

The husky man shrugged. "I think we are."

The entrance to the cave was a narrow cleft footed by ferns and balsams and strange plants bearing only a single leaf. Inside, the musty passageway was narrow and uneven and the walls were curtained with flowstones and clustered with feathery crystals. Floor cressets cast tiny flames that sputtered for breath in the thinning air. Above, long-legged spiders scurried in and out of the shadows, while bats occasionally squeaked from the darkness of the high alcoves. Adrian spotted a centipede as long and thick as his arm, and his first thought was to remove his glove and incinerate the nasty thing.

She led them down a dozen different passageways, which meandered in a dozen different directions. Deeper and deeper into the cave they went, deeper and deeper until Adrian was no longer sure which direction they'd come from, or how exactly to get out. Just as he began to panic, the passageway opened into a massive chamber. Twisted and towering rock formations rose like gold-gray icicles, casting shadows over nooks and grottos and forming overhead accretions that looked like grotesquely melted candles. It was strangely quiet, the only noticeable sounds being the rhythm of Adrian's own breathing and the constant dripping of stalactites.

Two main sections divided the chamber. The closest was bare and empty save where the cavern floor was overlaid with thick wooden planks that were covered with mats and rushes. The second section was farther back, and that area was furnished in the most luxurious of comforts. Silk-curtained beds, upholstered chairs, five panel screens, elegant wall rugs, expertly carved cherrywood couches—only the very best that coin could buy.

As striking as the furnishings were, Adrian's eyes were drawn to the score of beautiful women who lounged freely around them. They stared at the guests as if they'd never welcomed a visitor before. No one had a weapon—well, none that Adrian could see—and yet, he couldn't ignore the cold hand of fear that pinched the back of his throat. He didn't like this. The darkness was too thick, allowing too many crannies and pockets and cavities to hide an ambusher. At any moment that fire-spitting hellbeast could leap out of the shadows and Adrian wouldn't have a moment to react.

Eldred, however, seemed to ignore all sense of danger. He pushed his captive inside, one hand clutching a fistful of her hair, the other pressing his weapon to her back. He shouted for his brother, a thunderous roar that was ingested by the cavern and fired back in a series of sonorous echoes that went on and on until at last the chamber decided to return to quiet.

No reply.

Where the hell are you, Olan?

A figure stumbled out from behind a wall of sinter columns. He was a dumpy fellow, probably only a head taller than Temil, which was still quite short. One plump hand held a twisted goosefoot cane while the other struggled to fasten the clasp of his red robe. His skin was also red—not ruddy but a deep crimson hue that was as unnatural as it was disconcerting. Still, he didn't look like any sort of demon, although he did possess a strange, vacant stare that examined the three intruders with mild contempt, the way a warden might look at a lifer.

"Her name is White Rain," the dumpy man said. "Pretty, isn't she? One of my favorites, you know. Why don't you let her go, I won't harm you."

"The big fellow with the shaggy hair," Eldred said with a scowl. "I know he's here."

"We can have a discussion about that if you like. Just let the lady go. She's my wife, you see. Well, these women are all my wives, but the point is, she's not yours."

"Bring out the big fellow and we'll talk."

The dumpy man gave a sigh. "Why don't you come closer, sit with me. Your companions, too. Is the little one your son? We have noisemakers and pinwheels to play with, and for us there's plenty of wine, clear or cloudy, whichever pleases your palate."

He turned and motioned to one of his wives, who immediately went off.

Eldred gave a yank of White Rain's hair. "My brother first."

The dumpy man lowered his head and clasped his hands together. "Please, don't hurt her."

Eldred snorted at that, but Adrian was more curious by the man's reaction. "I must say, you're the most pathetic demon I've ever met. Surely the smallest, too."

The dumpy man's vacant stare fell on Adrian. "A demon? Is that what you think of me? You shouldn't listen to rumormongers."

Adrian looked around the chamber. "Well, I'm a bit torn, in truth. For one, you do have that fabulously demonic skin tone, but you also look a bit too tubby to be a demon. Now that doesn't mean I think you're an upstanding man . . . you do live in a cave, after all. But I don't see this infamous fire-breathing hellbeast of yours, so I don't know what to believe."

The dumpy man seemed amused. "It's difficult, you know, having so many beautiful wives. Lesser men tend to covet what I possess. And who could fault them? Still, in these uncertain times, rumors have their place. I need to protect myself from all the marauders and thieves and scoundrels of the realm." He really was a roly-poly little thing; there was nothing intimidating or fearsome about him. *Are we making a mistake?* How could this defenseless meatball and his dainty wives subdue a giant warrior like Olan? It didn't seem possible. Well, not unless they drugged his wine or something. Yes, that would've been easy to do.

Eldred's face began to twitch, not unlike how Olan's did whenever he was itching for a fight. "You're a liar. You're a fat little varlet who's brainwashed a harem of hapless whores. I want my brother back. You lured him to this filthy hole and you took him from me." With White Rain still in his control, he approached the demon. Adrian and Temil followed, their boots tapping hollowly across the floorboards. Adrian didn't like this at all. "Wait."

"Why, Adrian. Don't tell me you think there's honesty in this bastard, too?"

"Of course not," Adrian said, and it was the truth. He didn't believe this little demon's words . . . no, not after everything he'd been through. The deceitful abbot, the masked Chitterers, the crooked viceroy, the thief who befriended and robbed him— need he say more? Point was, Adrian may not have been a cold-blooded outlaw, but he certainly wasn't some naïve adventurer either.

"Then what is it?" Eldred asked. "And don't talk about your goddamn precepts, because I will gut this prick and every last one of his whores in order to find my brother. I hope you'd do the same."

"Of course I would, it's not that. This . . . doesn't feel right. Something's wrong here."

"What's wrong is this bastard has my—"

White Rain tore free of his grip and bolted. Eldred stood there blinking, his extended hand still clutching the empty space where her hair used to be.

For a second he seemed poised to give chase, but the woman was too fast. She ran to the safety of the dumpy man, who took her in his arms, caressed her pretty face, and gently placed her behind him. Turning back, he stood straight and tall—well, as tall as the little fellow could stand. A strange mirthful smile touched his face, like an aging man given a secret elixir to restore his youth. "I don't recall meeting this brother of yours, but if I had then he's already dead, just as you three will soon be." He butted the tip of his cane on the cavern floor and shouted some sort of command. Then, still smiling, he said, "The fragrance of your burning flesh will serve as my evening incense, and the sound of your dying screams will serenade me as I bed my many wives."

Something groaned beneath Adrian's feet. It was an immense sound, like the gearwork and chain drives of a thousand-part mechanism suddenly jolting to life. The ground began to tremble, then judder, then *whine*. Adrian looked down. *The floor . . . is it opening? It can't be.* But it was. Wood groaned and splintered and clumps of rushes scattered and dust sputtered into Adrian's face. He pawed blindly at his eyes while struggling to stay balanced, and next he knew he was sliding down the inward opening slabs. *Don't fall, don't fall, grab something!* He wedged his good hand between two floorboards and dangled over the pit like a rat caught in a loop snare.

Someone was calling his name. It was Eldred—or maybe it was Temil. Both were clinging to the wooden planks and hanging over the pit as Adrian was. The dumpy man sauntered over to Temil without a trace of urgency. His goosefoot cane came up, then down, smashing the old child's hands and dropping him into the darkness.

Next he sauntered over to Eldred. The cane came up, then down, smashing Eldred's hands and dropping him into the darkness.

He approached Adrian last. The cane came up—

"*WAIT!*" Adrian shouted.

The cane froze.

Adrian cocked his head to meet the man's eye. "How do you get it so red? Your skin, it's really quite spectacular. Is it a bloodroot extract? No, it can't be. What is it?"

The man's eyes narrowed for a long moment. Then, slowly, he smiled a wicked little smile. "Madder," he said.

The cane came down, *crack*, smashing Adrian's hands and forcing him to release his grip. With a painful cry, he plunged into the open arms of darkness.

Chapter Twenty-Two

It wasn't so much a fall as it was a slide down a rocky chute, and by the time Adrian tumbled and rolled and jerked to a halt, the floorboards above had already groaned to a close. He found himself in a dank and lightless area that reeked of spoiled meat and old gristle and other nauseating things. When he rose his head bumped a jutting shelf of rock, which caused an avalanche of bones. Human bones. Skull pieces, femurs, shoulder blades, rib cages . . . all clattering to the ground, causing Adrian to leap back and bash his heel against the wall. *Damn this place —where the hell am I anyway?*

It was a small circular cell, maybe seven or eight paces across. The rough-hewn walls were shored up with wooden braces and beams, but it wasn't an entirely enclosed space—no, Adrian could feel a gentle waft of cool air tickling his face.

"A simple system of ropes and capstans," a voice was saying. It was Temil. "That's all that's needed to make the floor open and close like a trapdoor."

"So the bastard baited us after all," Eldred said. The husky man grunted as he rose to his feet. "Adrian, you all right?"

"I think so. Smells awful down here. Worse than that goddamn ordure pit." He rubbed his head to dull the pain, then rose and combed the walls with his good hand. He was surprised to find a rectangular opening, about eye level and just wide enough for a slender man to fit through. *Now why would something like this be here?* A passageway lay beyond, though the darkness made it difficult to see where it led. "Hey, there's a way out over—"

A growl rose from somewhere down the passageway, a powerful, inhuman sound, like the collective snarl of a hundred rabid wolves. Adrian spoke in a deadpan tone. "What the hell was that."

"The hellbeast," Temil whispered, in a voice choked by fear.

The floor began to tremble. The walls, too. Something large was obviously approaching, and yet the movement wasn't the rhythmic stomping of powerful legs, but more of a grating sound, like something dragging itself across stone. Whatever it was, it frightened the hell out of Adrian. "Sounds like the beast is eager to say hello," he said.

Temil looked horrified. "How can you jest at the hour of our death?"

"It's what he does," Eldred said. "His way of coping with situations of peril."

The advance of the creature was like a battalion's charge: slow, loud, and utterly inexorable. Twenty feet away now. Fifteen. *There's no way it's a fire-spitting hell-beast*, Adrian thought. *No goddamn way.* But those awful sounds were making his mind run over with terrible images, and the louder they grew the harder it was to picture anything except a bloodthirsty monster of inordinately large size. Ten feet away now. Nine. Temil wrapped his arms over his face and scrunched his body like a pill bug. Adrian's legs were quivering like congee. The creature was just outside the cell. There was nowhere to hide.

The grating came to a sudden halt. Everything became still. Everything became silent. In the sludge-thick darkness Adrian saw a faint outline of what could only be an enormous beast of some kind . . . and then, it sparked.

It was so bright Adrian shielded his eyes and recoiled as though someone lit a man-sized matchstick in his face. Through blurred vision he saw a sphere of fire pulsing inside the giant open maw of a giant black creature. The spreading light revealed a truly horrifying thing: six glowing eyes, a lupine muzzle, four deadly horns, and a hulking, segmented body covered in imbricated scales.

Fear chilled Adrian to the bone, but for some stupid reason, he didn't back down. No, he unslung his haversack and removed his glove and handed them both to Eldred. "Stay behind me," he said, before turning back to face the beast. His thoughts screamed at him. *What are you doing? What the hell is wrong with you!?* But he ignored all that and raised his blackened hand like a protective buckler, and then . . .

Fire burst from the creature's mouth.

Adrian saw it in slow motion, his mind detailing every bit of that rushing stream of flame. Pain drilled into him, waves so terrible he thought his skin would burst. *It hurts, it hurts, please make it stop, please.* But it didn't stop . . . and it wouldn't. Not until Adrian's skin melted from his bones and his eyes oozed from his sockets and his heart spilled from his chest and every living tissue in his body became a charred and blistering lump of—

Something gurgled. An abrupt sound, like water down a plughole. The gurgling ended with a final slurp, and with that, the pain was gone.

Adrian opened his eyes. Tiny tendrils of smoke rose from the fingertips of his upraised blackened hand, but there was no fire and no heat. His chest, his legs, his good arm—everything remained intact, save the minor singeing of his clothes. *It worked. It worked, goddamn it.* Adrian turned. His two companions were staring at him through the darkness. "Your hand . . . what the heck just happened?" Temil asked.

Adrian didn't reply; he tried to, but his throat was dry as dust.

Eldred hawked and spat and cracked a smile. His lips were black. "Our friend here has just absorbed that goddamn flame." He seemed pleased to see the old child so mystified. "I know, such a blatant display of the supernatural arts offends me, too."

Temil didn't respond to that. He continued to stare at Adrian with childlike wonder. Adrian swallowed and cleared his throat and swallowed again, repeating the process until the moisture returned. "All right, well . . . I was wrong. Apparently there *is* a fire-spitting hellbeast."

The three men turned their eyes back toward the hole. The smoke was beginning to dissipate, but all you could see of the creature was a hulking silhouette. It made no motion at all, not until the grating sound returned, only this time it swiftly faded as the beast retreated back down the passage.

Eldred moved frantically around the chamber. Bones rattled and earth shifted from his rough hands. Adrian thought he was looking for another way out, but when asked the husky man said he was searching for his brother's remains.

"But how will you recognize him?" Temil asked. "It's all bones. Piles of charred bones."

"I'd know my brother by the sight of his big stupid bones." Eldred's tone may have been rough, but there was no hiding the grief in his heart.

Adrian wanted to help, but he found himself drawn to that rectangular opening. He hoisted himself up, pushed himself through, and landed on the rammed earth of the dark passageway.

"Where are you going?" Eldred called.

"To kill this goddamn beast."

"You'll be chomped into mincemeat."

"I appreciate your faith in me."

He moved through the short passage and approached the shadowy outline of the creature. It seemed not to notice him; its great lupine head remained lowered and its six eyes were all closed. Still, a single incautious step would no doubt awaken the beast's wrath, and the last thing Adrian wanted was to find out was if he could absorb a second blast of fire —and this time at a much closer range. Still, if he could just get near enough to touch the beast . . . *That's it, a little more, you're almost there . . . that's it. Now grab it.*

His blackened hand seized a scaled foreleg. The damn thing was harder than any limb he'd ever touched before. Worse, nothing happened. His hand went higher, but all he found were more scales. He grazed the creature's head and muzzle, but then a gust of hot air puffed from its mouth and Adrian spun and ran.

He moved as swiftly as the dark and uneven passage allowed him, and all the while he couldn't stop imagining the creature's six eyes opening and its hot breath drawing in air to blast him with another torrent of flame. But when he squeezed back into the cell and regained his breath, he saw the beast hadn't moved. Eldred and Temil both stared expectantly at him.

"Well, I touched it. It didn't die." Adrian wasn't sure if he was scared or simply winded, but he couldn't stop his legs from shaking.

Eldred snorted. "The hell you mean it didn't die? You sure you touched it?"

"Yes. I don't know. It was covered in scales . . . I don't know."

A sudden noise startled them, but it wasn't from the hellbeast. No, it was an eruption of cheers from the chamber above. *They're celebrating*, Adrian realized. Music filled the air, muffled yet melodious fiddles and panpipes accented softly by chimes and bells. Voices sang in harmony, lilting and feminine voices. The vibrations of the cell meant there was dancing, too. Adrian was transfixed by the sounds; it was like listening to the joyous welcoming parade at the annual spring festival.

The three men neither moved nor spoke for quite some time. They just listened. It wasn't until three or four songs later that Temil began humming along. Eldred glared at him, but the old child deflected his eyes with an innocent shrug. "Ghost of the Raven Lord. It's a unique choral progression taught to the freshmen of the Second Star Academy. What? It's a captivating tune."

For some reason, Adrian laughed. A small laugh that turned into a great whooping guffaw, and before long Temil was laughing, too. Eldred didn't join in. He simply stood there, arms at his sides, deep-set eyes staring at the two men as if they'd gone balmy. Adrian didn't care; he laughed and laughed and he didn't even know *why* he was laughing. But slowly the laughter unraveled a deep-seated anger, and as that anger reared, Adrian pounded his fist on the wall and exclaimed, *"WE'RE STILL ALIVE DOWN HERE, GODDAMN IT."*

The music died, slowly, in parts. First the pipes and fiddles trailed off, then the bells and chimes ceased their ringing and tinkling. The singers stopped singing, the dancers stopped dancing. Soon all that remained was a silence that was more uncomfortable than before. Adrian spoke in a murmur. "Probably shouldn't have done that."

The growling returned from the passage, an angry, urgent growling, joined by that familiar grating of movement. Swiftly the beast advanced, its six maniacal eyes glowing like will-o'-wisps of moonlit blood. Adrian didn't think; he simply threw himself into the opening, squeezed inside the passageway, and ran toward the hellbeast. But it was dark and he couldn't see, and when he tripped over a wooden beam he stumbled headlong to the ground. Looking up, he saw the hellbeast bearing down on him. *Idiot! You're doomed.* But no, the creature ignored him. Not one of its six eyes even glanced his way; they all had that same lifeless forward stare. *What's going on here?*

The growling was dreadfully loud now, but strangely enough, it wasn't coming from the creature's mouth. Adrian could hear other noises, too. Subtle noises. Mechanical sounds, the clunking of a piston bellows and the gurgling of a liquid pumping through a tube. When the beast's mouth opened it was with a hinged metallic groan. The spark ignited. Adrian shoved his blackened hand over it and closed his eyes. The insides of his eyelids flashed brighter and redder and redder and brighter, and then . . . *WHOOSH*. Flames backfired into the creature's throat. *BOOM*. Adrian's world spun and screamed and crackled. Next he knew he was curled on the ground and covered in a blanket of soot and ash, while cracked wood and mechanical parts and broken scales rained down like a shower of brickbats around him.

When it was over, Adrian sat up. He checked to see if his ears were bleeding. They weren't. Through the hissing he could hear Eldred calling his name. He went to reply but his attention was drawn to a figure sprawled out behind the wreckage. It was the dumpy man. When he saw Adrian he gasped and rose and limped off in a hurry. Adrian gave chase. Despite his awful aches and poor balance, he was gaining ground on the man. *I'm coming for you, little bastard.* Closer, closer, he reached out with his good hand—but then the ground shuddered and knocked Adrian off his feet. The dumpy man glanced behind him. It was just a brief glance, but the moment he turned back around a broken beam swung from the ceiling and smacked him in the mouth. The impact lifted him off his feet and the momentum drove him forward a good two or three yards before he hit the earth like a sack of discarded meat.

The dumpy man didn't move after that, but when

Adrian came closer, he saw that his legs were twitching. For a moment Adrian wanted to help him, but he decided against it when the wooden wall braces snapped and jagged chunks of solid rock began crashing down around him.

The passageway was collapsing.

Eldred appeared out of nowhere. Temil stood behind him like a frightened hare. Adrian tried to speak but the rumbling was too loud. Eldred pointed at something in the distance and they ran. Boots thudded soundlessly across the earth. Clouds of dust choked Adrian's lungs and stung his eyes. *Faster, FASTER, goddamn it.* But his legs wouldn't go any faster —in fact they were ready to fold. No, he ignored the pain. He had to. He pushed on and on until a tiny sliver of distant light widened into an open cleft of rock, and without hesitation Adrian flung himself through.

He was out.

The cavern was behind him now. He was outside and he was running free . . . but just as the moonlight poured down around him and the crisp autumn breeze filled his lungs, the ground gave way and now Adrian was sliding down the scree of a roaring mountain.

His heart pushed up his throat. Rocks the size of a man's head zigzagged past him, some bouncing perilously close. He blinked once and was no longer sliding but plunging feet-first into a raging river of whitecaps. *CRASH.* The world became wet and muffled and dark. Adrian flapped his arms and struggled to break the surface, and once he did he struggled even more just to keep his head above it. *Help me! Eldred, Temil, where the hell are you!*

The water was so cold it could freeze a man in minutes. But the powerful current wouldn't let him escape. Instead it jolted and jostled and carried him like a criminal tethered to a horse. Adrian never felt more helpless in his life. All he could do was extend his good hand and hope to grab onto something, anything, and finally, after slicing his palm and smashing his fingers on projecting rocks, he managed to tangle himself in the twisted branches of an uprooted willow that had fallen into the river. He coughed and belched and spat mouthfuls of freezing water, and when he finally lifted his head, he spotted Temil on the shore.

The little man was frantically attacking the bent bough of a sapling. *What the hell is he doing?* Adrian wondered. *I don't need that.* After about a thousand stomps the limb finally snapped, and Temil carried it toward Adrian, all while shouting and pointing and pointing and shouting.

What the hell? I don't understand. Behind me?

Adrian turned. Eldred was floundering about in the river like an overturned turtle, arms flailing and head bobbing as fistfuls of white water spurted into his mouth. *Damn it, I can't get to him. He's going to drown.* Temil crawled across the fallen snag and passed Adrian the sapling limb, and together the two men guided it like an oar into the river. Six or seven attempts before Eldred managed to get a firm hold on it, and despite the current fighting like a devil to pry his grasp, Adrian's persistence eventually won, and Eldred was pulled to safety.

The three men crawled out of the river and collapsed onto the muddy banks.

Chapter Twenty-Three

When Eldred nudged him awake it was still dark, and in the predawn chill the three companions made their way back to the cavern.

Adrian's head was still fuzzy and his ears still hissed like a midsummer downpour. Worse were the aches . . . his arms, his legs, hell, every goddamn joint and muscle in his body hurt. Still, these were minor complaints. For one he was fortunate to be alive; and two, he was even more fortunate to still have possession of the imperial robe. Eldred was to thank for the second point. When they'd pulled the husky man out of the river, the haversack was fastened to his belt in a tight overhand knot. He even had Adrian's glove, too.

Temil wasn't convinced that the dumpy demon-man was dead, and even though Adrian did his best to explain otherwise, the old child said he needed to see for himself. Now finding the brothel wasn't difficult at all since Eldred still had the map, but locating the entrance to the cavern was another matter. They'd already lost half the daylight and accomplished little more than searching the same stretch of stony pillars at least a dozen times. Adrian was tired. He could only carry on for so long. "No more," he said. "We have to go back."

But Temil was a stubborn little fellow who refused to give up. And when Adrian defied him by resting his weary body against a nearby slab of stone, the old child frowned and whined and looked ready to raise a quarrel. But Adrian didn't care. "We're exhausted, we're hungry, and we're—" he stopped. Something in the rubble caught his eye. He craned his head to get a better look. Then he smiled. "By the gods, look where we're standing." No more than five spans away were the half-buried ferns and balsams that footed the cavern entrance.

They cleared the debris and made their way inside. Temil led them through the maze of dark and twisted paths, and only after a lot of effort and a little luck did they finally reach the main chamber. It was in ruins. The explosion of the fire machine had ruptured the cavern walls and destroyed the lavish furniture and toppled the limestone pillars and sinter columns. Cressets lay extinguished beneath the debris, but the cavern wasn't entirely dark—no, light was trickling in through the cracked fissures in the ceiling, just enough to allow visibility of the wreckage.

The three men were careful to avoid the multitude of obstacles. The center area was especially treacherous, as the floorboards were broken in such a way that gaping rifts and jagged planks of wood all threatened to twist an ankle or slash an incautious foot. But steadily they moved, and steadily they made their way across, until eventually they halted before a heap of rubble that was piled conspicuously against a far wall.

"I know he's in there," Temil said.

Adrian wasn't so sure, but he offered to help clear the blockade all the same.

It took nearly an hour to dislodge a substantial number of loose stones and remove the cracked timber. Thankfully, no one was injured—well, nothing more than a few scratches and bruises, but Adrian had plenty of those already. He crawled through the opening and dropped down to join Temil and Eldred in what appeared to be a secret chamber. A small figure lay wrapped in a silk shroud on the ground. Eldred motioned for Adrian's knife, then he bent down to cut the fabric open. He sighed. "It's him."

Temil dropped down for a closer look. "So he didn't have the red cloud after all."

"Why is that?"

"Well, if he did, he wouldn't be dead right now."

Adrian spoke after a long moment. "So that's it then."

Eldred shook his head. "Where are his wives?"

Temil's tiny eyes drifted up.

Adrian hadn't noticed them earlier, but there they were, about three-dozen women dangling above his head, noosed in thick hempen rope that stretched and empurpled their necks. It was a grim sight, an awful sight . . . like a group of condemned witches hanging from a gallows tree. Adrian couldn't help but pity these women. He pitied them even though he knew they were conniving she-devils who stole the life of a dear friend. But right now, in death, they looked so frail and helpless and pitiable . . . were they truly the monsters everyone said they were? Maybe, maybe not. Still, it was sad to know that these poor women had hanged themselves around their husband in a final act of devotion. Or maybe it was done out of sorrow or desperation, who could say.

The three companions salvaged a few bushels of grain before heading back to Three Tarns. It was a quiet and uneventful trip, the air thick with sorrow and regret. When they returned to the hostelry, Eldred wanted to go to the dens and bash the game master's skull, but Adrian talked him out of it and ushered him into their private room. A storm passed that night. Howling winds and roaring thunder and rain that pounded against the upper roof tiles like an unrelenting swarm of locusts.

At cockcrow Eldred entreated the village elder to organize a funeral for his brother. It was a modest ceremony filled with heartfelt threnodies and genuflections and clouds of incense. There was a coffin, but of course it was empty, and as the funeral cortege halted before the gravesite, the director offered a brief prayer for Olan's swift and safe passage through the Great Rivers of Transmigration. The ceremony came to a close as Eldred knelt with a flagon of wine to offer the final libation. Adrian watched the purplish-red liquid sink into the earth, and next he knew the surrounding monks were intoning a farewell chant while the pall-bearers lowered the casket into the ground.

Eldred spent the remainder of the evening alone. By the next morning, the husky man no longer seemed angry or combative or hungry for vengeance. Had he somehow found some semblance of solace in all of this? Well, Adrian did not. Since the day of Olan's disappearance, Adrian had refused to accept the truth. He'd ignored it, denied it, never truly acknowledged it. But now, after participating in the funeral rites and committing the seven showings of reverence and respect, he realized he'd been lying to himself. Olan was gone. *He's gone . . . he's truly gone.* The ache in Adrian's chest was like the strike of an arbalest's missile. He couldn't think of completing the journey to Swallowtail without the big man. No, it wouldn't be the same. Not at all.

Was he to blame for Olan's death? No, he wasn't, and yet it took all of Adrian's strength to convince himself of that. *The brothers knew the risks . . . they damn well knew it was a dangerous journey.* Still, he couldn't help but think that Olan's death was wrong. That it shouldn't have happened. That it wasn't meant to happen. By the gods Olan wasn't a bad man. A drunken lout, sure, but he was a drunken lout with a decent heart.

The following day was cold and rainy and the three men spent it in their private room. They were low on coin, overdue on payment, and quickly losing favor with the proprietor. When Adrian addressed the issue, Eldred just stared out of the unlatched window, his deep-set eyes fastened on the drenched country-side. What could Adrian do? Eldred obviously needed time to grieve. Problem was, there was no time. Adrian wanted to make that clear, but he couldn't find the courage, so they sat, as they usually did, in silence.

It was sometime later when the wooden door burst open. At first Adrian thought it was the propri-etor and his bruisers coming to collect, but no—it was a huge, shaggy-haired, and rather bedraggled man who entered the room.

Olan.

The big fellow ignored the wide-eyed stares as he lumbered by and flopped face down on the feath-erbed. The wooden frame groaned in protest, and globs of mud from his boots splashed onto the floor.

Eldred rose slowly, like a statue cast to life. His mouth fell open. "Brother? You . . . you're alive?"

Olan's reply was both loud and unexpected. He broke wind.

Chapter Twenty-Four

"It was late," Olan explained. "I didn't want to disturb any of you. I just wanted to see the women for myself."

The shaggy-haired man was sitting on the edge of the bed, his oversized feet planted firmly on the floor. The corners of his bulbous nose were encrusted with grime, his tunic and trousers were spattered in mud, and truth be told, he smelled worse than an over-worked draft horse on a hot summer day.

"Olan, tell me what happened," Eldred insisted for what seemed like the hundredth time.

"I told you, I don't remember much. The old winegrower said I must've slipped and hit my head."

"What old winegrower?"

"I don't know, some old bumpkin. He took me to his home and fed me stale bean curd. He did have quite an assortment of wines and ales and toddies, mixtures made from rice and grapes and sorghum and rare millets grown as far as Mistlake Point. He had some dead seagull wine, too . . . you know, the kind drunk by the northern arctic folks. But I must say that stuff tasted nastier than—"

"Olan," Eldred snapped.

"What? I stayed there for a while, and then I left. That's it. Oh, I gave the winegrower's brother a good drubbing. He deserved it . . . bastard was a real sawed-off prick." His massive body leaned to this side as he broke wind once more.

"So, you never even made it to the brothel?"

A glob of mud fell from Olan's beard when he shook his head.

Adrian looked down. A flurry of emotions ran through him, but he couldn't focus long enough to sort through them. There was a lot of joy but there was also a lot of confusion and apprehension. Yes, Olan was alive and well, but what did that mean for the dumpy man and his harem? Perhaps they weren't such a vile lot after all. Adrian gritted his teeth. *What have we done?* He exchanged a long look of concern with Eldred.

"Don't, Adrian," the husky man said. "You know they were scoundrels, all of them. They lured inno-cent people to that cave and incinerated them with that goddamn fire machine."

"We don't know that," Adrian said. "We've no proof of that."

"Do you not remember the giant trapdoor we fell into? Or the piles of charred bones?"

"He said it was for protection. Maybe he was telling the truth."

"Seems a rather cruel and excessive form of protection," Temil put in quietly.

For once Eldred agreed with the old child. "It was a fate well deserved."

"Maybe, but we're not the ones to decide that," Adrian snapped.

"Well, it was decided," Eldred countered.

"Yes, I suppose it was."

Olan interrupted. "What the hell are you two going on about?"

"Never mind," both men said at once.

Eldred's expression softened when next he spoke. "Brother, my heart is glad to see you alive and well. I'd offer you to a hot bath and a warm bowl of wine, but we're rather low on coin, so a wash basin and day-old rice gruel will have to do." He turned back to Adrian. "Tomorrow at dawn we leave this wretched place. Swallowtail is the end."

When Adrian agreed, Eldred's deep-set eyes settled on Temil. "What about this one?"

"What about him?"

"We've done what he's asked of us, so this must be the end for him as well."

"No," Temil exclaimed. "We haven't found the red cloud yet."

Eldred frowned. "We haven't found the red cloud because there is no red cloud. It's a stupid legend that faded into a stupid myth, and only a fool or a madman would believe it. So stop playing us false, I know just what sort of person you are."

"And just what sort is that?"

"A two-face. A sham. You appear timid yet in spirit you are bold. You speak as a gifted scholar yet shuffle around like an immature rustic. Clearly you know well the laws of the esoteric and the exoteric, so why spend all your time playing the fool?"

"I never studied as a scholar, never took the official examination, never claimed to be a lettered individual, but just because I am small and strange doesn't mean I lack the critical thinking required to decipher the sacred Argalist Scriptures of the World of Life and Unlife."

"I don't care. The only reason you are alive right now is because you saved my life at the river. It was your deceit that nearly caused my brother's death. You lied about the brothel, you withheld the truth about the hellbeast, and you're lying about your associate. What more needs to be said?"

"I'm *not* lying. You know what, never mind. How could I explain myself to a man who has such little belief in anything beyond his own earthbound senses?"

"I believe in what I see, what I hear, what I can touch. I believe in the five senses."

"Why just five? What about equilibrioception or thermoception or nociception?"

"I don't know what you're talking about."

"I'm talking about the sense of balance, of relative warmth or cold, and of pain. There are more than that, you know. There are many, in fact. What about the sense of hunger? Or pressure? What about the sense of when to urinate and defec—?"

"That's *enough*," Eldred growled.

Temil looked down. "My point is there is so much more out there than what you might believe."

"Well, I believe in Adrian's hand. I saw him use it to absorb a stream of fire that would've reduced us all to ashes. You saw it, too, did you not?"

"I did. And I am aware of his condition. That is why I am here, that is why my associate entreated me to help." His old yet childlike eyes drifted to Adrian. "It can be done, I assure you."

Adrian looked down at his gloved hand. He didn't speak for a while. "I don't know," he said at last. "Holding on to false wishes makes a man weak, and a weak man is susceptible to guile. I don't want to be weak. I think it's time for me to accept this curse or gift or whatever the hell it is."

"These are not false wishes," Temil said. He seemed distracted by something for a long moment. "Listen, your friend is right. I haven't been entirely truthful with you. Healing your condition is not so simple as acquiring the red cloud. Are you familiar with the Five Faces of the Ever-changing and Everlasting Cycle? Fire, metal, wood, earth, and water. Life and land cannot be ordained or sustained without these agents."

"It's from the ancient Argalist law," Eldred cut in. "The Five Faces form the conceptual order in which all things are balanced, everything from the smallest droplet of rain to the grandest of cosmic phenomena. It is the very basis of geomancy, music, biology and biota, medicine, military strategy, and countless academic fields. The Five Faces work in a state of constant flux with one another . . . wood feeds fire, fire creates earth, and so on. What does that have to do with Adrian's condition?"

Temil nodded at the informed reply. "I see you know the horns of history well. But let me share something that you may not know. There are things in this world that can disrupt the balance. An overacting or dominant cycle can restrain, weaken, or destroy another cycle. Now this disruption occurs only by the actions of a forced agent, which is generally at the hands of earth's most destructive force: mankind. I know how foolish and impractical this sounds, but an unexpected and unintended shift in the cycle can leave a sort of residue in the realm of life and unlife, and this residue travels like an air-borne pathogen into a receiver's spirit through insufflation. Now according to my associate, this is the cause of Adrian's condition."

"So, this 'disruption' is just an elaborate way of calling it a curse," Adrian said. "And forgive me for such a tedious follow-up question, but are there others? Please, don't tell me that I'm special. Even *I'm* not foolish enough to believe that."

"It has nothing to do with being special, as it's

neither a curse nor a gift. In the ancient texts your condition is known as *Sa'vareth*—one who is touched by the Insulting Fire. Everything you suffer from, not just the disfigurement but the nerve pains and inner disharmony . . . it is all directly related to this residual energy from when you endured a great disruption of fire. That last part, was I correct to assume that?"

Adrian's nod was slow and sincere.

"Now, in order for you to become a receiver of this condition, two primary requirements of the overacting cycle must have been met: one, in this great disruption, you were victimized by an act that was both premeditated and deliberate; and two, in this great disruption, you suffered an irreparable loss of a loved one. So, to answer your question, yes, there are other receivers. They are found in every overacting cycle caused by a great disruption, be it fire, water, wood, whichever. I know it is difficult to understand."

"Adrian . . ." Eldred cut in, exasperated.

Adrian raised his good hand to stifle Eldred, then to the old child he said, "Difficult to understand? No. Difficult to believe? Yes. But please, don't let my skepticism hinder you. You have my attention, so go on, tell me how someone can mend this so-called disruption."

Temil took a moment to brush down his cowlick, but the tuft of hair refused to obey. "Well, in order to do that, I must touch upon another matter. I'm sure you are all aware that when a man dies his soul ascends to the Great Rivers of Transmigration, but did you know that each of the three celestial rivers has its own name?"

Eldred spoke. "I don't recall the ancient Argalist texts giving specific names to the Great Rivers."

"Modern versions omit the names for the sake of brevity, but the ancient tomes do list them. The first of the heavenly rivers is the External, the river of moonlight, where the newly departed souls begin their journey. The second of the heavenly rivers is the Supernal, the river of starlight, where the souls are judged by the Five Deathkings of All That Becomes. The third of the heavenly rivers is the Eternal, the river of stardust, where the soul is transposed from everlasting life into another earthly body, to be reawakened as new.

"Now the receivers are invariably tied to those who died in the great disruption. You see, these disruptions are so powerful they prevent the spirits of the deceased from fully transforming into celestial matter, which means they cannot fully pass beyond the External River. Instead they become stranded in a sort of purgatorial threshold between mortality and spiritual liberation, and this celestial disharmony is the direct connection to a receiver's condition. There is an exemplary tale in the annals that predate the first era of rule, but the tome is back at my cottage so I'll have to spare you the longwinded narrative."

"I think I get the gist," Adrian said. "To mend my condition the stranded spirits must be freed, but to free the stranded spirits the overacting cycle must be restored."

"Exactly."

"Great. That sounds easy enough," he quipped. "And I'm assuming the red cloud mushroom has something to do with all this, yes?"

Temil nodded. "To the east is the Mantis Vale. Inside this vale the receiver must pass his disrupted energy into the Tree of Transposition. Doing this will summon the White Whirlwind, which will take him to the External River. Now it is the red cloud that allows the receiver to endure the fury of the whirlwind. Do you understand? I also wanted to note that one *can* survive without the red cloud, but I won't lie, it is unlikely. Still, since the red cloud itself is normally found at such a remote location, it's almost as difficult to acquire it as it is to survive the White Whirlwind without it. But since the red cloud had already been harvested, I was hoping to acquire it without much difficulty. Unfortunately, I was wrong. Once the receiver ascends the whirlwind and touches upon the Eternal, he or she must confront the guardian, the Shepherdess of the Stars, and only after dispersing the darkness and opening the sky will the cycle be rebalanced and the spirits freed. Now I know this is a lot of information, and I know I've withheld these complicated truths from you, but I hope you can at least understand why."

No one spoke for a long moment. Adrian was simply staring at the old child, a long and thoughtful stare—but then, without warning, he laughed. An unintentionally scornful laugh, brimming with doubt and derision. "You and your associate are crazier than I imagined."

"My associate speaks the truth."

"No, he doesn't, and I'll tell you why. I'm not this receiver or whatever it is that you think I am. I say this for two reasons. One, this great disruption was actually just a terrible accident, not some premeditated and deliberate act. Two, I saw a lot of people burn that day, but I didn't love any of them. Hell, I didn't even *know* any of them. So, you are either misinformed or misguided or you are simply playing me false. Given our history together, I'm inclined to believe the latter."

"Perhaps it is you who is misinformed. There are no accidents or errors in the Great Path of the Sacred Argali."

"I've heard that quotation before," Adrian said. "Unfortunately, the venerable abbot who had spoken it turned out to be a deceitful wretch just like everyone else we've encountered on our journey. But I made a grave mistake in believing that holy man, and I'll be a goddamn fool before I make that same mistake again. I'm sure you can understand that, yes?"

Temil's nod was slow. "I do, but—"

"Then you must also understand why we must part ways. Look, I'm done hunting false demons and I'm done chasing mushrooms and I'm tired of all your mystical bull-spit. Swallowtail is within reach and I'll not let you alter my course now. I'm going to be very wealthy soon, and as a wealthy man I'm going to live the rest of my days with the world in the palm of my hand. It may be just a single palm, but I assure you I will come to terms with that. Besides, Eldred was right. You deceived us. How can I possibly trust you again?"

Temil looked like a berated child ready to burst into tears. For a moment Adrian regretted his words, but the moment passed and the old child seemed to gather his resolve. "A shame our partnership didn't have a more meaningful end," he said. "If you decide to abandon the pursuit of wealth and instead embrace a much greater truth, you know where to find me."

"Thank you, but I won't." Adrian offered a rather stern nod of farewell, but inside he was aching with indecision. He didn't wish to part ways with Temil in this manner. Somewhere along the journey, this mysterious old child had become somewhat of a friend to him. Adrian wanted to tell him that, but the right words just wouldn't come, so he said nothing at all.

Temil bowed his head, took a step back, and looked at no one in particular. "I thank you, all of you, for satisfying a meager hermit's wanderlust. I am eternally grateful for the opportunity to share the path of such experienced and resourceful men. It was an often joyous, sometimes harrowing, but always exciting adventure, and I'll not soon forget it."

Olan went over and gave the old child a hearty squeeze, a rather comical sight given the difference in size. Eldred, however, offered little more than a cursory nod. Temil looked one last time at Adrian—

and then at his gloved hand. His mouth opened as if he were going to speak, but whatever it was, he never said it, and in the end he simply turned and headed for the door.

And just like that, Temil was gone.

Chapter Twenty-Five

They exited the hostelry at daybreak. The sky was gray and overcast and the earth was swollen and muddy from the recent rains, but the company of three men slogged through it with silent determination. They ate when they were hungry and drank when they were thirsty, and many a night was spent in the debt of generous villagers who offered them a bed of straw beneath a roof of thatched sea grass. After another long week on the Centipede Road, the soggy ground plunged into dense floodplains and crescent-shaped bayous that were permanently cut off from the surrounding waterways. Thick vegetation curtained these sluggish holes, which were dotted by meandering cypress and wild pecan whose boughs were strangled by twisting vines. Experience kept them wary of the occasional threats. Crocodiles lurking beneath the cover of pondweed. Water moccasins gliding across the surface. Prehistoric turtles with jaws so powerful they could snap a man's toes clean off. Still, it was nothing a little caution and common sense couldn't overcome.

Once out of the marshlands the group moved briskly along the rocky coastline of the Sawtooth Sea. Thick tumbling dunes rose in the distance like golden mountains, hump after hump of storm-swept sand that carved out a plethora of lagoons and cays and finger-like sandbars. Beach grasses and wild holly were found along the protruding headlands, casting shadows over tiny crab holes that appeared like pock-marks on pale skin. An occasional oak was spotted, but it was always stripped bare and covered in tangles of brown moss and sculpted by years of salt spray.

The longer they traveled the busier the seacoast became, and the past few days the sheer number of vessels crowding the water was awe-inspiring. Swal-lowtail was the heart of southern seaborne trade, so Adrian had expected this, but even still, it was a rather magnificent view. Near the shores were an array of small coastal flatboats and single-oared fishing skiffs, while farther out in the heavy swell were cargo-carrying barges and three or four-masted merchant ships that ranged from large to enormous. Cutters darted in and out of the white lace of wave trails, swift boats used for couriering information in a timely manner.

A city rose in the distance, appearing as if out of nowhere. It wasn't a large metropolis surrounded by imposing stone walls, but a cluster of short salt-stripped buildings huddled on a cape that stretched to the storm-tossed sea. There was a wall, but it was disjointed and red and made of river rock and sandstone, and the buildings it protected showed only a grungy hint of the piquant blue color they once proudly displayed.

Was this the great Swallowtail? It had to be. It was.

They entered through a sturdy land gate that was positioned to the west of a sturdy river gate. All Adrian could focus on was the giant behemoths of wood and rigging and sailcloth on the wharves, along with the hundreds of workers who scurried around them like mice. By the gods there were so many ships —in fact, there wasn't a single empty berth in sight. Inside the city, Adrian immediately noticed the cleanliness of the streets. These weren't the broken down ghettos of Beetleburr but high functioning wards filled with prosperous businesses and well-to-do citizens. Horse-drawn carriages and loaded ox carts moved along the rutted avenues, which were still wide enough for travelers and sightseers to amble unimpeded. Adrian, for the first time, found himself in a foreign city and yet he didn't feel the need to clutch his haversack to his breast.

And the people! Adrian saw men and women and

children of all sizes and shapes and skin tones, but it was the oddness of their attire that kept his eye drawn. Women strolled the avenues in flared skirts and silken shawls while men hastened by in loose-fitting tabards and patchwork capes. Aristocrats wearing frock coats barked from inside beribboned palanquins while wealthy graybeards moseyed along the streets in fluffy hats and oversized pantaloons. And where the fabrics of Beetleburr and even Scarlet Sun were drab and gray, Swallowtail's colors were quite the opposite. Yellows so bright they seemed to be dyed with something more than dandelion. Purples so bold they were rumored to be extracted from a rare and expensive mollusk, and reds so warm they could put a sunset to shame.

But this was only a taste of the true exoticism that lay in the heart of the city: the bazaars.

There was nothing Adrian could think of that wasn't for sale here. Rare bristle-skinned fruits from far-reaching tropical jungles, strange sweetmeats and candy-coated insect delicacies of insular origin, shark-skin boxes and deer-tail fly whisks and fancy gewgaws from the remotest parts of the realm. You could buy a gold-threaded dress of the highest quality silk, calfskin boots the color of the sky, or a leopard-skin hat expertly edged in the finest gold brocade. There was such a vast assortment of unusual wares that Adrian had trouble focusing his attention on just one thing.

But then he found that one thing. A sculpture of a winged wolf meticulously carved from grayish-green bowenite—though it was being sold falsely as northern jade. Still, the craftsmanship was impeccable, even down to the tiny nicks that gave the appearance of craquelure. It was so inspiring that all Adrian wanted to do was sit down at his workshop and get out his tools and start carving, but then he looked at his gloved hand and remembered that he wasn't an artisan any longer. What a shame.

It mattered not, since he wasn't here to gape at all the wonderful baubles or fill his belly with foreign fare. He was here only to find the southern privateer with the crooked eye and horseshoe mustache who answered to the name of Broden. And after selling the precious imperial robe to this man . . . well, we all knew the rest.

They entered the nearest inn and rented a room with the little coin they had left. After washing themselves and sharing an overpriced meal of vermicelli stew, the three men spent two or three hours in the dimly lit common area. It was odd not having Temil around; Adrian truly didn't realize how accustomed to the little fellow he'd grown. Sure, Temil was often immature and sometimes overly talkative, but he was a kind soul, and one of the few who could make Adrian laugh.

"You shouldn't have been so cruel to him," Adrian remarked to Eldred. "Temil could've let us drown in the river, you know. He revealed his true heart to us that day."

Eldred gulped his drink before answering. "Yes, but that doesn't mean he can be trusted. I may not be as gifted as his associate, but I know when a man is lying to me. All men, no matter their size or perceived age, are inherently selfish. It's in our nature. You know this, Adrian. You made the right choice. You would've ended up disappointed."

"Maybe," Adrian said, staring down at his wine.

"Don't fret about it," Olan said. "Once we find this privateer of yours, we'll all be as happy as turtles in an ale keg."

The shaggy man was right, and Adrian told him that.

"What if your contact proves unreliable?" Eldred asked.

Adrian shook his head. "I've known Niall my whole life. He's not a man to abandon his word. Trust me, we've planned this out for nearly a year. The southern privateer with the crooked eye and horse-shoe mustache will be waiting at the bazaars. We'll find him."

"Good, then we drink," Eldred said. "To a most fortuitous end to a most fortuitous journey. We've made it at last. We've made it to Swallowtail."

Gourd-cups were raised, and wine was drunk in hearty measures.

Chapter Twenty-Six

A week later, on an especially brisk autumn morning at the bazaar, Adrian spotted two men standing before a vendor's stall of pickled shrimp and honeyed crabs. One fellow in particular had an off-center gaze and the thickest U-shaped mustache Adrian had ever seen.

Adrian jogged Eldred's arm and gestured.

"Looks like our man," Eldred said, nodding.

"What's the name again," Olan asked. "Brody or something?"

"Broden." Adrian repeated the word to himself. "I think." *The southern privateer with the crooked eye and horse-shoe mustache who answers to the name of Broden—wait, was that correct? The southern man with the crooked eye and horseshoe mustache who answers to the name of Brody.* Now Adrian wasn't sure. It had been a long damn time since leaving Scarlet Sun, and well, Adrian's mind wasn't as sharp as it used to be.

Still, it mattered not. They had found their man.

"There's two of them," Adrian said.

"So?"

"Niall said our man would be alone."

The three companions moved closer. The man with the misaligned gaze and horseshoe mustache wasn't an imposing fellow, but he did look rather fit and rather confident. When he turned to regard Adrian, his salt-encrusted cloak crackled in protest. "I don't know you, friend," he muttered, sucking the meat from a hairy crab leg. The briny smell of the sea was all over him.

"I'm looking for a fellow stationed here in Swallowtail, a privateer who commands the wooden bones of a lady called *Morning Shadow*. Known as Broden."

The man's good eye narrowed just a touch. "My given name is Broden. My mates call me Salt Spider." He leaned back and looked Adrian up and down, then turned and counted his coins before paying the vendor. That done, he and his taller muscle-bound companion moved across the busy roads, away from the buzz of the bazaar and into the private seating of a wine shop's seaside pavilion. Adrian and the two brothers joined him there.

Adrian said, "I was told you'd be alone."

Broden licked his chapped lips and gestured to a

serving boy for wine. "I was told the same." The man's no-nonsense attitude went well with his no-nonsense mustache, and those misaligned yet thoughtful eyes made you wonder what he'd seen in his day. His partner, however, was much less of a mystery. The brawny fellow had a mercenary's look: big, stoop-shouldered, square-jawed, scarred, ugly. Broden called him Catfish, and he certainly had the face of one.

The wine came but Adrian didn't drink. Neither did Eldred. Olan's refusal seemed to be much more difficult to handle. Adrian shot him his typical *it-might-be-drugged* look, which made the big man grit his teeth and ultimately refrain from his vice.

Broden was eyeing Adrian so intently that the entire pavilion could've been under attack and he probably wouldn't have noticed. "Been waiting a long time for you."

"It was a long journey." Adrian opened the haversack and drew out the imperial robe—just enough for Broden to catch a glimpse of the shimmering firemouth silk and the sequined rows of garnets stitched along the sleeve. The privateer's eyes lit up—until the haversack closed. "The coin, do you have it?"

Broden snickered. "What's the point of a lucrative business deal if it's not celebrated with a measure or two of wine?"

"I'm not here to chat," Adrian said. "Do you have the coin or not?"

Broden glanced at Catfish for a moment, then

nodded. "Ten thousand ounces of gold, a king's ransom."

Adrian nodded. "Good. Take us to it so we can complete this little transaction."

Broden gestured once more to the wine. "I will. But first . . . I'm a simple man who likes to indulge in simple pleasures. Grant me this small request. It's not too much to ask."

Adrian stared at the rim of the goblet but made no move to pick it up. This Broden fellow was polite enough, but his constant urgings to share wine were beginning to look suspicious. And Adrian wasn't a goddamn fool. "We're in a hurry."

Broden drank and exhaled. "Niall was right. You are a stubborn young man. Always running, running, running. Sit. Relax. Take a breath and enjoy the day, I promise you the southern sun will be kind to your heart."

"I've seen enough of the southern sun," Adrian said. "Olan, don't."

The big man had the goblet in his hand, and this time he wasn't so easily dissuaded. "You think everything's drugged," he said. "I'm tired of it." He took a huge gulp and followed it with a huge belch. "Good wine makes good blood, so why let it go to waste?"

Broden smiled and drank and gestured in return. "Smart fellow, this one."

The wine wasn't drugged, and in the end it did its job and softened the mood. Still, while the others drifted into idle chat, Adrian didn't feel comfortable enough to speak freely, so instead he leaned back and let his eyes wander across the lovely seaside esplanade. The clouds were plump and white, the breeze was fresh and invigorating, and the waters were undulating gently beneath the pearly sun. Gulls squawked and swooped overhead, while minstrels serenaded a crowd of spectators from an open-air theater. Closer, a trio of raucous sailors ogled and whistled at coquettish wenches, while a pair of bald bruisers chatted amiably with regular folk. It was nothing less than a storybook scene of seaside tranquility.

"Of course there were unexpected storms," Olan was saying. "Highwaymen, swindlers, forest monsters, cave demons—you name it, we put it down. No goddamn greengrocers in this group." He placed an oversized arm on Adrian's shoulder. "Not to boast, but our little friend here wouldn't have made it without me or my good brother."

Broden leaned back and nodded in fascination. "I assume that warrants a share of the coin?"

Olan didn't seem sure if he should answer that, but in the end, he nodded. "An agreement was made. Though I should receive twice as much just for Beetleburr. Lovely goddamn Beetleburr." He snorted in disgust. "Place is a goddamn hole. And Deadhand left me alone with crusty old Murden so he could go play with a bunch of masked fools."

Broden smiled and savored another long drink. "Yes, the bitter provincial viceroy of the north. I wouldn't be so hard on him, my friend. It's not simply the vicissitudes of life that weigh him down, but the stress of his daughter's upcoming marriage. I wouldn't want to give my daughter's hand to the Rhinoceros Lord either."

The men laughed—all except Adrian. He looked pointedly at the Salt Spider. "How do you know that?"

The directness of the question gave Broden pause. "Oh, I've heard things here and there, you know, rumors and criers and pillow talk with a whore or two."

"No, you couldn't have," Adrian said. "That little tidbit wasn't yet made public."

The pavilion grew quiet. Tense.

"Easy, Adrian," Eldred said softly. "It's probably not true anyway."

"It *is* true," Adrian said. "Lady Amelia's union with Lord Haroden is planned for the evening of the Midwinter Festival. But the announcement hasn't been made, so as of now such information is privy to very few." He looked squarely at Broden. "So how does a southern privateer know about it? And don't tell me about some bogus expedition to the north, Niall told me you'd be stationed in Swallowtail until the spring thaw."

The man gave a shrug. "Niall said that? He must've made a mistake, you know how he is."

He's lying to me. Adrian knew it because he knew exactly how Niall was. A fastidious little steward, sure, but he was also a detail-oriented man who would never impart false or unverified information. Something about this whole thing began to stink, and Adrian suddenly feared for his safety. He rose and swallowed what felt like a giant pebble in his throat. "Forgive me, but I think it's time for us to leave."

Broden told Adrian to sit back down. "Too soon. We haven't finished yet."

"Yes, we have." Adrian stared at the man. The man stared back. No one moved. The silence dragged on for a moment, a long moment, so long that every living person seemed to fade away, a strangely surreal feeling, as if a great black cloak drifted down to cover the entire esplanade . . .

Something flashed in Catfish's hand. A dagger. He lunged for Adrian's throat.

Adrian winced. Something warm splashed his face. He thought it was his own blood, but when he looked up he saw the man's dagger had never reached its mark. No, Olan's ox cleaver had sliced its way through Catfish's head, opening it up like an overripe honeydew.

Everything happened so fast. Broden scrambled from his seat and bolted, but Eldred was there to tackle him to the ground. "Brother, *brother*," Eldred called, over and over and over, but the big man wasn't listening. He couldn't get his cleaver free—not until he threw the bloody corpse to the floor and used a booted foot for leverage. At last the blade slid out, and with it came an arc of blood that spurted into Olan's face. He pawed at his eyes and stumbled around like a clumsy fool, but a goddamn terrifying one at that.

On the esplanade, panic spread like wildfire. The minstrels' music ceased and the party of sailors gasped and shouted for the sentries. A throng of bodies soon crowded the white stone walkways, men and women screaming and weeping and pushing and falling as they fled the gruesome scene. Wine ewers and flagons crashed to the ground with shattering clangs.

"Time to go," Adrian said.

Eldred pointed at Broden. "Take him with us."

Olan dragged the Salt Spider along the waterfront's outer boardwalk. Wooden planks thudded beneath their heavy tread, and once far enough away they leaped off and crouched behind a tall stand of reeds no more than a yard or two away from the low tide's clawing fingers. Eldred grabbed the Salt Spider by his salt-encrusted cloak. "You have three breaths before this big fellow here opens your throat. Talk."

The man cursed under his breath. "I had no choice. Lord Haroden knew . . . rumormongers said he spoke to the sky and learned the truth of your escape. I had to serve his will. I had to. He *knew* everything."

"Lord Haroden knows about Niall?" Adrian asked.

The man nodded. "Did you not hear me? He knows *everything* . . . Niall, me, even that bawd who gave you the horse."

"Jessamine?" Adrian felt a pang of ache in his chest. *Oh no . . . I didn't mean to include you in this, Jessa.*

Broden began mumbling to himself. "Forgive me, Niall . . . forgive me, old friend."

Olan looked ready to throttle him. "A bit late for remorse, you traitorous dog."

Adrian raised the man's head by the ends of his mustache and locked eyes with him. His privateer's skullcap had fallen off somewhere on the boardwalk, and what little hair he had was waving in the autumn breeze. "Keep talking," Adrian said.

"We were supposed to lure you to the wine shop and hand you over to Lord Haroden's hired swords. That's it. There wasn't supposed to be any bloodshed."

"Well, there was." Adrian swatted at a dragonfly that zipped past his ear. "And I didn't see any hired swords."

"That's because the lazy bastards drank themselves blotto again last night and overslept."

"So that's why you were playing the good host. You were stalling us."

"Someone's coming," Eldred hissed.

Sentries hustled down the boardwalk, their heavy boots hammering against the planks. Broden gave a look as though he were going to shout, but one glance at Olan's gore-painted cleaver made him decide otherwise. When the sentries were gone the subdued man went back to murmuring a stream of apologies to Niall.

Olan looked disgusted. "What are we going to do with this prick?"

Eldred spoke. "Best to end this, Adrian."

"No, we've ended too many lives already." Adrian looked down and sighed. "It's over. Lord Haroden's won."

"What the hell are you saying?" Eldred said.

"I'm saying it's over. I was a fool to think I could get away with this. Poor Jessamine, I didn't intend to put her in any trouble. I have no choice but to turn myself in. Lord Haroden is nothing if not an honorable man. He will grant me an honorable punishment."

Broden laughed at him. "Honorable? You think Niall and that whore received honorable punishments?"

"What are you saying? He *executed* them?"

"Lord Haroden didn't just execute them, he paraded them into his private hall, stripped them to the buff, beat them, flayed them, plucked out their eyes, sewed their mouths shut, and cooked them in a vat of boiling oil."

"Horse-spit. Utter *horse-spit.*"

"No, and that's nothing compared to what he has planned for you, my friend."

Adrian didn't believe him. "You're lying. Everyone knows the Rhinoceros Lord is a man of steadfast honor and righteous—"

"Are you dense? Lord Haroden is a *monster*. No sin is too vile for that man. He tortures his loyal subjects at the slightest displeasure, abuses their wives and sisters, and eliminates all traces of evidence by murdering entire bloodlines."

"Stop it. Stop talking—"

"I'm sure you are familiar with the Black Gorge Barbarians, yes? Who can forget the famed story of Lord Haroden riding into battle and single-handedly unhorsing the cruel barbarian leader after forty grueling clashes of combat. Well, truth is, he eliminated the barbarian threat by *paying them off*. But wait, that's not even the despicable part. After the barbarians left, Haroden hired mercenaries to ride into his own villages and decapitate all the male farmers of a specific age and size. Haroden then returned to the capital with the severed heads claiming they belonged to the barbarian leaders. He's a monster, I tell you. A monster who masquerades as a saint. By the gods, he burned people *alive*. Worthy ministers and loyal men —even children."

"What are you talking about—burned who alive?"

"You're from Scarlet Sun, surely the Conflagration of the Twilight Hall holds some meaning to you."

The words hit Adrian like a bolt in the chest. He stammered before answering. "The fire was an accident, a spark from an untended cauldron that leaped onto a mat of sedge."

The man looked at him as though he were no smarter than a very stupid dog. "Was that the official story? How droll. The truth is far different, I'm afraid. You see, paranoid Lord Haroden suspected that a handful of his ministers were conspiring against him, so he invited them and their clans to the Twilight Hall and burned the entire building to the ground. I know most northern folk are deluded, but goddamn it, just how blind are you?"

Olan thwacked the man's jaw with the handle of his cleaver to shut him up. But it was too late; the damage was already done. Adrian dropped to his knees. His eyes caught the reflection of his gloved hand in the gentle wavelets, and the terrible memory of that terrible day came rushing back at him. The black smoke . . . the sweltering heat . . . the acrid stench of burning flesh . . . the men and women and children running and screaming and dying. Adrian tried to help, by the gods he tried . . . but the fire was too powerful and the bodies kept dropping like sacks of pitch all around him. In the end, he could do nothing but watch in horror . . .

The old child was right. It wasn't an accident. It was Lord Haroden all along.

Chapter Twenty-Seven

"Y ou can't just leave," Olan argued. "The robe's not sold. Payment not received."

Adrian handed him the haversack. "Take it, sell it yourself. Should fetch a fair price from one of the many silk-stocking aristocrats in this city."

"That wasn't the arrangement," Olan growled. "You promised us a fortune, enough coin to buy fifty households, one hundred plots of land, two hundred—"

"I know what I promised. Look, the plan failed, Niall is dead, and the southern man with the crooked eye and horseshoe mustache is a traitor."

"So? You can't just give up."

"It's over, Olan. Done. Let the Salt Spider go."

Olan hesitated, his white-knuckled hands still gripping the haft of his ox cleaver.

"Let him go," Adrian said. "The wretch is too racked with guilt to give us any trouble."

Olan hemmed and hawed and grumbled a few curses under his breath, but in the end he kicked the Salt Spider in the rump and told him to be gone. The man dashed off down the coastline. Adrian began walking the opposite way.

Eldred caught up to him. "What's the matter with you, Adrian? You can't just leave like this."

"I'm going back to Beetleburr."

"What the hell for?"

When no answer came, Eldred seized Adrian's arm to halt him. The outlaw's deep-set eyes searched his companion, as if desperate to make sense of all this. "After all we've been through . . . after the crooked abbot and the Chitterers and the fire machine and all the hours we spent in the wilds . . ." His head shook disappointedly. "You're a good man, Adrian, but don't pretend to be driven by something more than material gain. Now tell me, why Beetleburr?"

Adrian hesitated. He watched as Olan came lumbering over, wiping the blood from his face with a dingy kerchief. The big man took his place next to his brother. Clearly, Adrian wasn't getting out of this without offering some kind of explanation. "There are many eyes about," Adrian told them. "Come, we'll talk in private."

The sentries in the bazaar were on high alert, but the avenues were so crowded that the three companions moved unnoticed—well, once Olan bent his knees and slumped his shoulders. Adrian ruminated on how to explain his Beetleburr decision, and in his mind he'd organized the best words in their best order, but by the time he returned to their private room he'd forgotten nearly everything. And after spending far too much time washing his face and changing into a fresh tunic, he could sense the brothers were thin on patience. Finally, Adrian sat down on an armchair and gave a defeated sigh.

"I was there, the day of the conflagration," he began. "A score of us, master carvers and craftsmen and artisans, a veritable who's who of talent all attending an imperial auction in the outer courtyard of the Twilight Hall. I remember watching Lord Haroden exit through the palatial gates in a silk-curtained carriage . . . outriders moving ahead, guardsmen flanking the sides, the powerful High Commander Krall Vyren riding postilion. Word of the fire came shortly after. The artisans thought it was a jest. I did too. But then I heard the shouts, faint at first, but louder and more urgent by the minute. And then the smoke . . . thick tendrils of smoke, like shadowy fingers reaching to the heavens. Guardsmen went running past, shouting to open a path for the teams of carriers. But the gigantic water vats were strangely empty, and the great double doors of the hall just wouldn't open."

Adrian paused to swallow. "I remember the

screams the most . . . the ministers and courtiers and women and children . . . they were all trapped inside. All burning alive." He fought back a sudden surge of emotion. "A handful of us . . . we used a bloodstone pedestal to ram open a small postern door. I crawled inside but the smoke stung my eyes and the pressure crushed my lungs. I couldn't help them; I tried but I couldn't even stand. All I could do was cough and wheeze and watch as the flames devoured them until they were nothing more than charred husks of dead flesh. When I made it back out I saw my arm had been scorched nearly to the bone. I remember . . . I remember thinking it was a mistake. That it wasn't *my* arm. Just a hideous, unrecognizable thing, a red-black lump of undercooked meat. Funny thing was, I didn't feel any pain. I don't even know how it happened."

The room was left in silence, but it was a brief silence, since Olan grunted and jabbed a finger at Adrian. "So Lord Haroden killed some innocents and now you want to set yourself to revenge." His cavernous eyes pierced Adrian like two burning coals. "Have you gone raving mad or what?"

"The bastard murdered without compunction," Adrian shot back, though his tone immediately softened. "But it's not just that. The fire . . . it destroyed my life. Everything I've ever worked for was taken from me that day. The old child was right about one thing: the Conflagration of the Twilight Hall was an evil act borne out of premeditation. I know that now. I know that and I . . . I need to get back what that bastard took from me."

Eldred spoke calmly. "Do you truly believe regicide is the best way to do that?"

The notion sounded absurd, sure, but for some reason, Adrian couldn't tell him no.

"Recompense, Deadhand," Olan said. "You stole the bastard's coveted imperial robe. Is that not enough?"

"No, it's not."

Olan stroked his shaggy beard. "How do we even know that goddamn Salt Spider was telling the truth? Gods know a frightened man will say anything to save his neck."

Adrian shook his head. "It's the truth. And Broden's right, I *was* blind. By the gods I should've seen it sooner. When Lord Murden groused about Haroden's negligence, I thought him bitter. When Lady Amelia spoke of his cruel temper, I didn't believe her. Even Temil, the day he left, I told him the fire was an accident. I was sure of it." He shook his head angrily. "By the gods it was all there . . . all but spelled out for me. The prime minister of Scarlet Sun is a cruel and murderous despot. But I didn't listen. Why didn't I listen?"

"Old bones," Eldred said. "The past is nothing but old bones and dark tentacles. Don't let yourself go there."

"I can't let this go," Adrian said. "I just can't." He raised his gloved hand and tried to make a fist but his nerve-damaged fingers barely moved. Pain flared up in his hand but he grimaced it away. "Not until I kill the bastard. I can do it. I can kill him."

Olan scowled and snorted and spat. "Listen to me, you can't just show up and touch the bastard's hand and be done with it."

"He's right," Eldred added. "The Rhinoceros Lord has over twenty decoy rooms in his palace alone to deter assassins. Not only that, he's under constant supervision by the most experienced sentries of the empire, and he's personally guarded day and night by a picked team of bodyguards. Even if you somehow make it to his private bedchamber, your throat will be slit the second you enter."

"True, but there's another way. The marriage ceremony is said to take place in Beetleburr . . . Lord Haroden will be vulnerable then. But I won't be hasty or reckless about this. In fact, I intend to return to Temil's cottage first. Since this mysterious associate of his was right about Lord Haroden, perhaps he can offer me further insight."

Eldred frowned. He obviously didn't like this at all, but after a long moment of deliberation, he seemed to understand there was no changing Adrian's mind. He turned and took the haversack from his brother's hands and tossed it back to Adrian. "How do you plan to make it back to Beetleburr?" he asked. "You have nothing, no coin, no food, not even the proper winter clothing, and winter is less than a lunar month away. Best to wait until the spring thaw."

"I can't wait. I told you, the ceremony takes place on the evening of the Midwinter Festival."

"You'll never make it alone."

"So be it then."

Eldred's eyes narrowed in frustration. "You *are* damn stubborn, aren't you?" He exchanged a quick glance with his brother. "Fine. We're going with you."

"I didn't ask for your company."

"I don't care. Look, we've traveled together for months. I've seen you in the wilds, Adrian, wolfing down poisonous berries and lapping up contaminated water. You're a bit of a fool to think you can make it all the way back to Beetleburr alone. If I let you go, I might as well be killing you myself."

Adrian's expression softened. It was true, there was no way he was making it to Beetleburr without the brothers' help. Still, why would Eldred, after enduring such a long and futile journey to Swallow-tail, choose to risk his life once again for no gain? It made no sense. Actually, it made a great deal of sense, but Adrian wasn't prepared to accept the truth. He'd always been on his own, from the latchkey child who lacked a mother's compassionate touch, to the cold professional who spent his days alone in his workshop. Aside from his late wife, no one had ever showed him such an outright display of devotion. Adrian didn't know how to respond.

Thankfully, Eldred didn't wait for one. "We won't get far without the proper supplies. How much will this fancy little robe sell for?"

Adrian had to think about it. To an uninformed buyer its worth was but a fraction of its true value— but that was still quite a lot. "For a gem-studded robe of rare firemouth silk . . . an estimation of six to seven hundred ounces of gold seems reasonable," Adrian told him. "And that's if we sell it to an uncommonly affluent collector. Preferably a transient one. We must be careful, wealthy men tend to have sharp eyes, and the last thing we need is for someone to grow suspicious of the robe's true origin."

"Seven hundred ounces of gold will get us to Beetleburr and back on the swiftest palominos," Eldred said. "And no less than thirty times over."

Adrian nodded. A brief silence followed. Strangely enough, Adrian found it difficult to meet Eldred's eyes. "Thank you, my friends. I couldn't do this without you."

"We know," Eldred said.

*T*hey spent the next eight or nine days at the bazaar, surrounded by vendors and browsers and buyers whose long days consisted of dickering and gossiping and arguing and more dickering. It was such a vast melting pot of disparate cultures that Adrian could probably spend a year here and still meet someone from a new and distant kingdom. He learned quickly that it took a certain level of finesse and experience to hawk your wares here, as many merchants were polyglots, or at the very least had interpreters under their employ to assist in matters. Adrian had no help. Worse, he had to avoid interacting with anyone who looked overly sophisticated or spoke too eloquently or just had a general swagger about him or herself. One little slip and the three companions might end up in shackles.

An hour before dusk they were approached by a dark-skinned fellow who introduced himself as a foreign dignitary who'd just arrived in the city days ago. He looked like a walking cloud with his puffy white outer robe and puffy white pantaloons and rounded silk shoes that had heels like a woman's heels, but what truly gave away the extent of his wealth was the puppyish yes-men who followed him around with embroidered satchels and fancy coin boxes and floral-patterned parasols.

Now in order to successfully hobnob with the wealthy and self-important types, one needed a certain degree of charm and etiquette. And since Adrian had the most refined tongue of the three—despite Eldred's dissent—he elected himself as the resident snoot. "You got to play the constable," Adrian reminded him. "It's only fair."

Inside a high-end and low-lit infusion house was where Adrian and the potential buyer talked business. Here, the prices for herbal tonics and extracts were downright insulting, but Adrian put on his most obliging face whenever the dark-skinned fellow called for another offering. Adrian hated the man, not because of his fancy cloud clothes or his fancy accent, but simply for the way he prattled on about his own wealth—as if his money were his secret key to a gateway of eternal happiness. Hell, maybe Adrian was just envious.

In the end, the drinking and the dining and all of Adrian's stupid cajoling paid off. The man just had to add this fine gem-studded robe of rare firemouth silk to his already exquisite collection. But for all his immeasurable wealth, the bastard turned out to be quite the haggler. It took hours before a price was agreed upon, and when Adrian finally left the establishment and rejoined the brothers outside, the hour was already growing late. "It's done. Told him it was a rare artifact from the private burial cache of the northern capital's late Imperial Steward."

"How much?" Olan questioned at once.

"Eight hundred ounces—"

"Eight hundred," the big man cut in with a smile, "that's more than your estimation."

"—of silver."

"*SILVER?!* Are you mad? No, that goddamn robe is worth a hundred times that."

Adrian shrugged. "It was the best offer we've had all week. Look, only a fool would spend a fortune on an alleged imperial garment with no proof of authentication."

"I don't care. It's not enough."

"Well, it's done. And it's more than enough to get us to Beetleburr."

Olan lowered his head and began grumbling to himself. Was the shaggy-haired man having doubts about all this? It certainly appeared that way—and they were heavy doubts that threatened to sap Adrian's own resolve. *Did I make the right decision?* Adrian wasn't so sure any longer. A part of him said yes, but another side—perhaps the flawed side—regretted parting with a possession worthy enough to purchase fifty households, one hundred plots of land, two hundred servants, and the best guard dogs around. But Adrian couldn't go back now. The transaction had been completed; the robe was gone. The luxurious imperial garment . . . the key to all the riches a man could ever desire . . . gone, gone, gone.

Olan's nostrils twitched. "Deadhand, you sure you don't want me to rob the prick? I have experience in that sort of thing, you know. Just something to consider."

Adrian gave a soft chuckle. Sad thing was, he did consider it.

Chapter Twenty-Eight

*P*arting with the robe turned out to be an unexpectedly liberating relief . . . one that the old and selfish Adrian would've never thought possible. And yet, it was hard to pinpoint why he felt this way. Not only had Adrian abandoned his only opportunity to attain great wealth, he also had committed himself to a task that was as dangerous as it was absurd. Burning touch or not, what sort of a clodhopping fool attempts to assassinate the Supreme Lord of Scarlet Sun?

Maybe Adrian was a fool. Or maybe he was just determined. For the first time in his life he was inspirited by a sense of purpose . . . a *true* purpose. A purpose that was greater than all his shallow wants and narrow-minded ideals. It was like all his life he'd been pushing and fighting and struggling against the current . . . but now, he was moving with it, flowing in harmony with the natural cycle of things. Water nourishes wood, wood feeds fire, that sort of thing. Yes, it sounded idiotic and senseless, and yes, the skeptic in him flinched at such thoughts, but he couldn't deny the clarity of his path, or the sudden and unflinching desire to end one of the great evils in the realm.

The silver ingot they'd received was melted down and exchanged for strings of copper coin, and the coin was used to purchase winter clothing and supplies and provisions. A semi-retired stable owner sold them three riding horses—certainly not palominos, but the roan, buckskin, and blue dun were all compact and strong-legged crossbreeds of the northern steppe horses. At the outfitter's shop the beasts were equipped with the proper tack and their saddlebags were stuffed with dried fruit and smoked meat and griddled wheat cakes. While this was being done the owner rambled on about the northern barbarian clans and how they would put raw steaks between their saddles and ride for miles and miles until the steaks became tender and edible. "A fascinating tale," Adrian commented, "but we're not going to do that."

They set out early, when the sun was still dormant and the air was quiet and cold, and by eventide the group found shelter in one of the many roadside inns nestled along the Centipede Road. After stabling the horses and sharing a meal of cold bean jelly, the three travelers retired to a drafty room where they wrapped themselves in moth-infested blankets. Disgusting, sure, but it was far better than roughing it in the wild.

The days moved quickly. The endless *clop clop-clop* of their horses' hooves removed the need for talk. The farther north they traveled the colder it became, and after another week or so they encountered the first touches of hoarfrost. Two days later, snow. Fat white flakes that drifted to the ground or gathered on the boughs of the surrounding broadleaves. The sky was a gray sheet that stole the warmth of daylight, and as the winds grew fiercer and more urgent, the once abundant wildlife simply vanished. Well, not entirely. A snow leopard prowled along the high ridges, emitting a string of mournful roars that sent the three men working the reins to soothe their frightened horses.

But the company stayed close and pushed on, even as the cold worsened. Rime glistened off tree trunks and icicles hung from branches like pale fingers. The ground beneath their horses' hooves was a rutted morass of black slush, yet they never saw a single porter or traveler. Well, not until a lone fellow appeared on an intersecting path of a gentle hill.

The stocky man was struggling with a shoulder pole from which hung two covered buckets. His feet slogged through the snowdrift, taking slow and difficult steps as he descended the hill. He stopped just as he touched the outer edge of the Centipede Road, then set down the pole, exhaled a frosty breath, and began brushing the snow from his fur-trimmed waistcoat.

Olan thrust a sausage-like finger at him. "What have you got there?"

The man flinched in surprise before looking up. He had a round and gentle face, fat antelope eyes, and plump cheeks that looked rosier than a pair of summer poppies. "A smoky brew of dark blackberry and currant with a warm oak spice," he said. "A wine made to melt away the sorrows of winter."

"How much for a full bucket?"

"Olan . . ." Adrian warned.

Olan raised a hand to stifle Adrian. "How much?"

"Three strings of coin and not a copper less."

"I'll give you two," Olan said.

"I don't bargain, my large friend," the wine seller replied. "Three strings or nothing."

Adrian pulled Olan aside. "Don't, we don't know who this man is. The wine could be—"

Olan cut him off. "I know. You say it every time. *Drugged.* Listen, Deadhand, we've been on the road for weeks and all we've had was rice wine so flat and tasteless even a steer would refuse it. Why should we let this fine winter brew go to waste? We have the coin, and more important, we have the ladle." He dismounted from his roan, tethered it to the nearest tree, and began searching through the saddlebags.

Adrian turned to Eldred. "I don't like this."

Eldred folded his arms across his chest. His eyes spent a long moment examining the hilly path the wine seller descended from. "Adrian might be right on this one, Brother."

"I don't care," Olan said. "Why don't I care? Because I'm cold and tired and thirsty and the aroma of that goddamn wine is making me—ah, here it is." Ladle in hand, he walked over to the merchant. "Pour me a taste, so I can decide if the price is worth the flavor."

"Sorry," the wine seller said. "Three strings for the bucket or nothing at all."

For a second Olan looked ready to whack the wine seller with his ladle, but in the end he simply tightened his jaw, grumbled something to himself, and opened his coin pouch. "Here's your damn coin. Now give me the bucket."

The exchange was made and the wine merchant thanked him while stepping aside to count the coins in the strings.

Olan sat down at the foot of the hill and ladled out a bowlful. Adrian and Eldred dismounted and joined him there. Adrian refused a taste, but his resolve weakened whenever his companions downed another measure. Olan was even passing his compliments to the wine seller, who nodded mechanically, as if he'd heard those words a hundred times a day.

Maybe Olan was right. Why should they let such a fine brew go to waste? Despite all his suspicions and concerns and trepidations, not once had their wine actually been drugged. And why would a random traveling merchant making a routine hike to some insignificant hostelry want to drug them? No, those were foolish and paranoid thoughts, and Adrian was tired of them. "Well, are you going to give me a taste or not," he said.

Olan scratched his belly with the tip of the ladle. "I knew you'd come around, Deadhand."

"Just give it to me." Adrian snatched the ladle and fetched himself a measure. The liquid warmed his throat as it went down—smoky and rich and full-bodied, yet balanced by moderate tannins. Delicious. Adrian handed the ladle back to Olan, who smiled approvingly. Just then, Eldred spoke. "Who are they?"

Adrian looked up. Figures . . . at least twelve, standing on the slope of the hill, half hidden behind a stand of white-robed pines. Adrian turned back to the wine seller. "Are those—"

The merchant was gone.

Adrian smacked the ladle out of Olan's hand.

The shaggy man scowled at him, but when Adrian pointed out the strangers, Olan rose to his feet. Well—he meant to rise, but what he actually did was wobble and teeter and stumble about. Adrian was about to scold him for his antics, but a moment later the big man fell forward and hit the ground with an awful *thump*. He lay there, unmoving. *No, no, no, no, no!* Adrian spun. Eldred collapsed a few yards away. *Thump.*

Son of a mother-raping fool. Adrian wanted to laugh, but the strength in his body was already fading, and his legs were like two pillars of curd melting under the sun. The figures in the distance were coming closer. He could hear them now . . . the sounds of men talking and laughing. "Down, down, down they go," one called. He kept repeating those words, while the others laughed like children entertained by a nursery rhyme. "Down, down, down they go."

Fight it, Adrian . . . you only drank a little. He tried and tried but his body was barely a usable thing. *You only drank a little, you weak-willed wretch. You only drank a little . . .*

He was on his knees now, though he didn't remember how that happened. The figures were so close Adrian could see their grungy gray wools and ragged trousers and the red neckerchiefs tied around their necks. Wait a moment. *Red neckerchiefs? Oh no.* It was that gang . . . the goddamn—what was the name again? Snake something . . . yes, Snakeheads. He tried to cuss the bastards out, but at that exact moment his body decided to fail him, and down, down, down he went, down until the ground smacked his face and force-fed him a mouthful of black slush. The world flickered and flashed, and his mind teetered on a hazy threshold of darkness . . . but Adrian never went out.

No, he was still awake when the Snakeheads dragged him and his unconscious companions into the forest. There were only eight or nine of them now, as three had galloped off with their horses. Adrian's vision was a foggy blur, but his hearing seemed more acute than ever. Not to say that was a good thing, since every grunt and snort of snot and hack of phlegm was loud enough to make him wince, and every crunch of booted feet across the snowpack was like the scraping of teeth across slate. When at last the scraping stopped Adrian was thrown to the snow and trussed up like a swine. The brothers received the same treatment, with extra attention paid to Olan's bonds, as expected.

Adrian lifted his head and blinked away the snow in his eyes. His vision was clearing. A fence of coppiced timber stood around them like a crude palisade. Crows cawed from the limbs of a nearby deadwood, which clashed eerily with the ebullient song of a winter wren. *You're alone, Adrian. Your friends are all drugged. Do something. Your bonds, can you loosen them?* Adrian tried but there were hands on him now. Calloused hands . . . one pair removing his warm wool coat, another lifting the heavy tunic over his head. A third pair yanked off his boots. There was a lot of scuffling, and soon voices rose and arguments broke out, but Adrian didn't listen; he was too busy wriggling his wrist to loosen his bonds. But he only had one good hand, and the cord was too goddamn thick.

A familiar voice rang out to end the arguments. Adrian looked up at the speaker. The man's tall frame was hidden beneath the heavy folds of his fur-trimmed cloak, but there was no mistaking those big stupid ears and that scarred forehead. It was Dravid.

"Still awake," he said in his posh accent. "Good. You didn't think I'd let you go so easily, did you?"

Adrian unclenched his jaw. "Actually for a while there I thought you just might."

"I see you still have that same witty tongue," Dravid remarked. "You know someday that wit of yours is going to cost you." He stood up straight and smiled at his cohorts. "And it just so happens that day is today."

The gang members snickered at that, but Adrian wasn't so easily amused. "You know, I never did apologize for barging into your manor. But what can I say? It was just too easy. That little bantling you keep as a sentry . . . I'd wager that a blind and toothless hound is worth more. And your old man? Hell, I could've been a branded criminal carrying a bloody halberd and he would've let me pass."

Dravid chuckled at that, but you could tell the jabs wounded him. "Yes, well, I've been known to occasionally succumb to nepotism, even if that lessens the quality of my personal protection. I also admit I can be a bit arrogant, and I certainly underestimated your cunning. But impersonating a civil officer and ransacking a respected man's private household? Those are the actions of the lowest mongrels of society." He pointed at Olan. "That big oaf smashed my dressing case and shattered my precious collectibles. Some of those took years to acquire."

Adrian had given up trying to loosen his bonds, but now he was trying to pull off his glove. It wasn't working. "Took years to steal, you mean."

Dravid didn't like that. "Yes, well, they were *mine*, however acquired. Most things owned by a powerful man are stolen in some way, are they not?"

Adrian feigned a look of awe. "Such profoundly philosophical words, my friend. But wait, before I begin to unravel the many layers of genius behind them, I would like to backtrack a bit. You spoke of my actions being low, yet you and your toughs robbed me on the street in the middle of the day. What do you call that?"

He exchanged a sly look with his gang members. "A profession."

"Interesting. I was thinking it was more the actions of the lowest mongrels of society."

Dravid bristled at that. He called out a one-syllable name, and a huge and tattooed fellow came shambling over. In his hand was a five-pointed mace, a weapon large and heavy enough to crush a few bones without difficulty. Adrian's heart thumped in his chest. Only now did he realize just how brutal his death would be.

Dravid stepped back and gave a bored frown, as if he were about to watch a toad hop across a patch of moss. "Make sure you do it right," he ordered. "I don't want his goddamn brains spurting all over the place like that fat fellow the last time."

The tattooed man's voice was like a slab of granite dragged across gravel. "Let it go already, will you?" His calloused hand absently pushed Adrian's head into a better position. "I showed you the goddamn angle of the blood spatter." He widened his stance to line up the blow of his mace evenly with Adrian's skull. "And then I told you to move. You didn't move." He was so calm, so casual—it was as if he were preparing to do a routine action, like a butcher at his block.

"I *did* move, but I'm not going to grouse about it,"

Dravid replied. "Now hurry up. It's cold and I'm dog-tired."

Adrian wanted to spit to show that he wasn't afraid, but his mouth was dry as desert salt. Hell, he *was* afraid. But not of death . . . no, death no longer moved him as it once did, not after all he'd been through in the last months of his thirty-four years. It was more the fear of failing—both himself and his companions. Eldred and Olan had blindly put their faith in him, and now they would die for it. But it was more than that, it was the realization that Adrian would die while Lord Haroden would live . . . and worse, the bastard would go on to marry a beautiful woman whom he didn't deserve. How was that fair at all? It wasn't. But life was often cruel. Adrian knew it all too well. He finally found a purpose beyond his own selfish desires, and now he was to die before achieving any sort of redemption. A senseless death, truly. But when is death not senseless?

No, it can't end like this. I have to do something. Think, you idiot, think. He glanced up at Dravid. "Wait. I need you to remove it for me. Please."

Dravid's scar tightened when his small eyes squinted at Adrian. "Remove what."

"At the tavern, you said I shouldn't hide my scar. You said it only strengthens the very thing you wish to forget. Well, you were right. I don't want to die as cowardly as I lived. Remove my glove. I want to be free of my earthly fetters when I ascend to the Great Rivers of Transmigration."

"We'll remove it after you're dead," Dravid said, and the gang members laughed.

Adrian spoke quickly. "Listen, I know there was some truth to that bull-spit story you spun. You meant what you said because you lived through it. I understand that now. So please remove it. I've been a worthy little quarry, haven't I? Grant me this final request."

Dravid examined him with those tiny eyes. A slender finger reached up to touch the pink wormy scar on his balding pate, and then the big-eared robber gave a nod. "No one can tell me that I lack honor, my dear dead friend. Here, you and you. Hold him." Two gang members clamped down on Adrian's shoulders. Dravid went around to cut his bonds. When the cordage fell away, Dravid yanked Adrian's hand in front of him, gave a single scrutinizing look, and pulled off the doeskin glove.

It was over quickly.

Chapter Twenty-Nine

$\mathcal{A}$drian was weary and footsore as he climbed the bleak and snow-flecked pathways. He'd already ascended hill after hill and was now moving through the stands of frost-laden junipers. He was sure the cottage was just over the next crest—but it wasn't. Maybe they'd strayed too far east? All of these hills looked the same, goddamn it.

"I'm dead tired, Deadhand," Olan groaned from somewhere behind them.

"Almost there," Adrian said, and thankfully he was right. When the three men crested the next hill they were greeted by a familiar cottage of knotted gray wood. The familiar *chop-chop-chop* was absent from the nearby grove, which was odd considering how surprisingly warm it was today (even at these alpine heights). Still, the pale golden rays of the midday sun weren't strong enough to persuade Adrian to shade his eyes, and the wintry landscape was rather devoid of wildlife, save a covey of white-tailed ptarmigan that wandered the mountain meadows in search of vegetation.

When the three men approached the cottage, the cedar door creaked opened and a child-sized figure stepped out. "You came back," Temil said, brushing down his cowlick. "Without the red cloud."

Adrian nodded. "I want to speak to your associate. Is he inside?"

Temil lowered his eyes. "He's still not receiving guests."

Olan's breathing was loud and labored. "This is . . . stupid. Are we . . . still going to pretend . . . this associate of his exists?"

"He's right, Adrian," Eldred chimed in. "What are we doing here?"

Adrian answered that while staring at Temil. "I suppose there is no associate."

"Only one way to be sure," Olan said, making a rush for the door.

Adrian dashed in front of him. For a moment he feared the big man would bowl him over, but thankfully Olan came to a halt. "Damn it, Deadhand. Why are you always spoiling the fun?"

Before Adrian could respond, Eldred approached

the old child with his arms folded across his chest. "You're alone here, I know you are."

Please don't do this, Eldred, Adrian thought.

Temil stammered. "N-no, I'm not, but I told you, my associate is not receiving guests."

"I don't believe you," Eldred said.

"Eldred," Adrian warned. "That's enough." He looked at the old child. "Back at the village, all that talk about cycles and disruptions and receivers . . . well, your associate wasn't entirely wrong. The Conflagration of the Twilight Hall—it wasn't an accident. It was a deliberate and premeditated act, and Lord Haroden was behind it. But that doesn't mean I'm ready to believe I'm some kind of receiver or whatnot. No, I just . . . I want to speak to your associate. I have some questions that I hope he can answer."

Temil looked at him with strangely pitiable eyes. "I'm sorry, Adrian."

Adrian's jaw tightened. "And I'm sorry to have come back." He spun, motioned to the brothers, and began walking off. He could hear their heavy tread behind him—or at least he did for a good moment or two, until someone stopped and muttered, "Ah, the hell with it."

Adrian turned. "Olan, don't. *STOP!*"

Too late. The shaggy man pushed past the old child and kicked open the door. Adrian called out his name, but the big man was already inside, with Temil clinging to his hip like a creeper on a trellis. Eldred looked at Adrian, shrugged, and casually went after his brother. For a long moment Adrian remained outside, until at last his curiosity got the better of him.

Inside the cottage was dim and damp; the earthen floor was strewn with cookware and crockery and straw baskets and stands of cobwebbed bookshelves that were laden with tomes and piles of scrolls. There was so much clutter Adrian almost didn't see the ragged curtain that separated what appeared to be an adjoining room. A moment later Olan came lumbering out of it, his big bearded head shaking in disappointment. "No one in there either. Unless your associate happens to be that crippled old mutt."

Temil emerged behind him, his face redder than a rhubarb stalk. He ordered Olan to leave, but when he saw the other two intruders standing in the main room, the old child stopped and sighed and slumped his shoulders.

"What crippled old mutt?" Adrian asked.

Olan gestured behind him. "It's just sitting there. It didn't even bark at me. Damn thing only has three legs."

"Three legs? Olan, did you say three legs?"

"Look for yourself," Olan said, but Adrian had already crossed the space and yanked aside the ragged door curtain. The small and musty room was bare of furnishings save an old openwork chair and a single rattan bed. The dog was huddled in the corner, resting on a cushion of sedge. Adrian's heart reached up his throat. *Could it be?* Black fur, brown hocks and brisket, a flat muzzle, one chewed ear, and one missing rear leg—yes, without a doubt this was the same dog that plagued Adrian's dreams.

"I didn't think . . ." Adrian murmured. "I didn't think you were real."

The dog didn't look up at him, didn't even move its head. Adrian felt like a fool for speaking to it, but he couldn't help himself. "So, here we are. You're sitting there and I'm standing before you." He went closer; the dog's ears perked up a bit, but its head remained lowered. "The words you said to me, all those nights, I need to know what they mean. Please, you have to tell me." When no response came Adrian recited them: " 'Save us, save us, save us the innocent from agony. The gods know we've suffered enough. Only the rivers can carry us home.' " He moved a step closer. "You have to tell me."

Silence for a while, then at last the dog twitched its ears and slowly raised its head. Two glossy black eyes settled on Adrian . . . mindful eyes, intelligent eyes. The animal's hindquarters moved. Yes, it was attempting to stand, perhaps to formally present itself like a master orator at a lecture. Adrian held his breath. His hand was trembling. *How long have I waited for this moment? At last I've found you, and at last I'm ready to learn the meaning of your cryptic message, and perhaps to comprehend some profound truth about my condition. Yes, I'm waiting . . . I'm waiting and willing and entirely ready . . .*

The dog shifted its weight, raised a single rear leg, and proceeded to lick itself.

Adrian sighed. *How lovely.*

Lick, lick, lick, lick, lick, lick, lick. Over and over

again, until Adrian's patience thinned and his frustration overbore him. "I know you can talk. You've done it before, many times, goddamn it. Do you not recognize me? I know you can—"

"Deadhand?"

Adrian spun. Olan was leaning against the doorframe, one bushy eyebrow raised. "Are you talking to a dog?"

Adrian's cheeks warmed with embarrassment. He opened his mouth to reply, but the sounds of arguing from the main room nabbed his attention. The two men headed back to find Eldred squaring off against the meek little Temil. "You were right, Brother," Eldred said. "That mutt *is* his goddamn associate. Do you believe it?"

Olan coughed. "What?"

Temil tried to defend himself but Eldred cut him off. "Stop talking rot. Never before has your madness been so plainly revealed."

"Oh yes, I'm such a madman. Don't forget that I'm also a trickster and a fraud. Tell me again, I have cheated you out of what, time? A paltry sum of coin? I told you I have no interest in such superficial matters."

"I don't believe you or your sanctimonious bullspit. Fetching that stupid mushroom was nothing more than a smoke screen. You wanted that pudgy little troglodyte dead. I don't know why, but you did."

"And why would I want that?"

"I don't know, perhaps you're just a perverse little

creature. It was terribly convenient that the mushroom was never found, wouldn't you agree?"

"I didn't lie about that."

"Just like you didn't lie about your associate?"

"I didn't lie about that either."

"It's a goddamn *DOG*."

"It's not just a—"

"ENOUGH," Adrian shouted. *"PLEASE.* No more. I've had enough."

Surprisingly, they all listened. Unsurprisingly, the truce lasted only a moment or two.

"I know why you despise me so," Temil said to Eldred. "You are intimidated by my associate's gifts. Intimidated because you're the only deceiver here . . . a man who makes his living handing out false examinations to desperate souls." His sudden burst of childlike laughter caused the three-legged dog to raise its ears. "Look at yourself. You are so terribly untalented and mediocre that over the years you convinced yourself that everyone else is untalented and mediocre as well."

Olan cut in. "Watch it, little one. My brother stands among the most gifted of pyromantic examiners in this realm. Don't you dare insult him."

"Forgive me," Temil said with overblown sincerity, "but maybe you should ask him for the truth of his profession, my big friend."

Eldred unhooked the cudgel from a loop in his belt.

Adrian stepped between them. "Eldred, put it away, what the hell's wrong with you?"

The husky man wasn't listening; he was gnashing his teeth and squeezing the handle of his weapon. Fortunately, Olan was able to calm him enough to take a few steps back.

Adrian spoke. "Listen, the next person who opens his mouth gets a touch of my blackened hand. I mean it. I'm tired of all this . . . tired of the arguing and resentment and distrust between you two." He turned to Temil. "I need the truth. The dog . . . is it your associate or not?"

Temil didn't answer. He was focused on Eldred's brandished weapon and aggressive stance.

"Temil. *Temil.*" Adrian repeated his name until eventually the old child gave a slow nod.

"Not in a direct way, not as one would think. But—"

"Your associate communicates with you, yes?"

Temil's beady eyes squinted at that, as if unsure how to answer. At last he said, "I know how it will sound, but—"

"Just answer the question."

Temil winced. "Not in the way that you and I communicate. My associate speaks to me when he wills, not when I wish him to, and only in an Argalist's meditation mudra, a complete stillness and detachment achieved by ascetic discipline. Only then am I able to comprehend what—"

"Oh by the devil's hairy red sack," Eldred cut in.

Adrian scolded the husky man. Then he told Temil to continue, but the old child no longer seemed willing. "Why? So you all can mock me, scorn me, think me dancing mad?"

"No," Adrian said, and it was with such firmness that no one argued the point. After a long pause, Adrian looked down and said, "I've seen that dog before."

"What?" Olan asked.

"When?" Eldred asked.

Adrian waited a moment before replying. "It started right after the Conflagration of the Twilight Hall. The three-legged dog . . . it came to me in my dreams and in my nightmares, and sometimes I even glimpsed it while awake. It frightened me at first. I won't lie, I thought it was a grim portent of my own death. In my dreams I ran from it, every night, until eventually my fears dwindled and dwindled and turned into an odd sort of curiosity. It was obvious the dog was trying to tell me something. Eventually I forced my subconscious mind to stop running, and when I finally gathered the courage to approach the dog, its mouth opened and a ghostly voice came forth. Never the same speaker, but always the same words. 'Save us, save us, save us the innocent from agony. The gods know we've suffered enough. Only the rivers can carry us home.' " Adrian looked down. "I never told anyone about it. How could I? I would've been reviled, scorned, branded as a lunatic. But I'm not a lunatic . . ." He turned to Temil. "Because now I see the same dog in your cottage. What the hell is going on?"

Temil scurried over to the wooden shelves and

began searching through the tomes. "I know I have it. I just recently perused it. Ah, all these damn cobwebs. This it? Yes, the Compendium of Primordial Attachments and Immortal Familiars, volume two, as compiled by the Argalist monks of Blue Bee Mountain." He glanced up. "You know some of these texts are nearly as old as the oracle bones used by the record keepers of the very first era of rule." He blew the dust off the cover and opened the tome, his beady eyes darting across the foxed pages until he found the one he wanted. "Here it is. *Immortal Ones, Neverdeads, Plane Gazers, Otherlings . . . these are among the many appellations given to a distinct class of spiritual psychopomp entities that are borne from the radiance of the sun's chromosphere and the void of the moon's black ocean. When the star of the heavens is called to descend upon the heart of the earth, the celestial matter is granted form and shape and the'*—wait, this isn't important, let's skip all this." His finger jumped farther down. "Ah, here it is." He held the open tome closer to Adrian before reading on. " '*The immortal psychopomps traverse the plane of the living with the sole purpose of guiding the receiving Sa'vareth toward the World of Unlife, in order to restore the*—' "

"Wait a moment, psycho-what?"

"Psychopomps. Guides who can pass between the Worlds of Life and Unlife."

Adrian shook his head. "I don't understand. Are you saying the dog is one of these beings? If you knew about all this, why did you try to hide it from me?"

"Because I didn't know," Temil replied, and he sounded terribly disappointed. "I didn't know you've connected with my associate, in dreams or however it was done. How could I possibly know that? In truth, I thought I'd been appointed as some sort of heavenly liaison, specifically tasked with fulfilling a grand and heavenly request. I was sure the matter of my success would resonate with the celestial deities and result in some divine reward . . . perhaps the deification of my own flesh and blood, or the uncovering of a vast and long-forgotten mystery of mankind, or even a personal revelation concerning my own meager existence." His old face dipped into a frown.

"So you do have a motive, as far-fetched as it sounds," Adrian told him.

"Yes of course, I am no different from any of you. But now I find out that my associate has been reaching out to you all along. I don't know what to think about that."

"I don't know either. So what does all this have to do with all that tripe you spouted before? The Five Faces and overacting cycles and all that."

"Yes, well, as I was explaining earlier, when a cycle is broken, the guardian of the Great Rivers, the Shepherdess of the Stars, will seek to reunite it. Now the deity herself cannot pass unto the realm of the living, so she uses the corporeal essence of the spirits that are stranded in purgatorial shadow. Now I've a question for you. Do you remember seeing my associate during the Conflagration?'"

"The dog? Yes, I remember . . . the poor thing died of smoke inhalation. But it wasn't missing a leg.

If this is the same dog, why doesn't it have four legs? And why doesn't it recognize me?"

"Many scholars theorize that the materialization of a stranded spirit is a clumsy, imperfect affair, and this often results in a physical flaw or defect in the psychopomp's outward appearance. A dog with three legs, a bird without wings, a rat with two tails, these sorts of beings have all been recorded in varying degrees over time. My associate also doesn't recognize you because psychopomps are simply conduits of the Shepherdess of the Stars. Mortal shells that have limited recollection of their own lives." The old child looked away then. He was quiet for so long that Adrian wondered if he was ever going to speak again. "The different voices you heard were obviously those of the stranded spirits," he said at last. "They are pleading for salvation, so they can continue their journey through the Great Rivers of Transmigration. I hope this proves that you are a receiver, Adrian. If you do what must be done you *will* heal your condition."

"Sure, all I have to do is travel to a remote vale, touch a magical tree, fly up a magical whirlwind, and stand upon a river in the sky," Adrian remarked. "But without the red cloud I'll not likely live through it, isn't that what you said?"

Temil gave a reluctant nod. "A receiver without the red cloud has very little chance of surviving the White Whirlwind. But it can be done. In fact, I have the written account of the first such feat here some-where . . ." Temil began searching through his shelves, opening more tomes and flipping through more pages. "Yes, yes, this must be it. No, maybe this one. Darn it." His movements were so frantic that Adrian's head began to ache.

"Temil, stop it. Please. Just stop."

The old child froze. Slowly, he withdrew his hands from the bookshelf.

Adrian didn't speak for a time. When he went over and opened the only pair of shutters, a gust of wind rushed inside, blowing about some scrolls that were strewn upon the desk. Adrian moved to pick them up. When he was done he looked down at his gloved hand and said, "The dreams . . . the three-legged dog . . . it's all too tightly interwoven to be a coincidence. I realize this now, Temil . . . but it may be too late. I have something I need to do first. Something in Beetleburr. Something that *I* believe will relieve all the disharmony in my heart, without any of your whirlwinds and mushrooms and disrupted cycles."

"Don't do it," Temil said at once. "Don't go after the Rhinoceros Lord."

Adrian was about to ask him how he knew such a thing, but he decided to save his breath. "I don't care what you or your three-legged associate says, I have to listen to my own heart."

"Adrian, consider your hand, your supernatural ability. Clearly you've been touched by the Insulting Fire. You are a receiver of the *Sa'vareth*. How can you blatantly ignore the truth?"

"Because of the second requirement," Adrian said

at length. "You said one becomes a receiver only when two requirements are met. Your associate may have been correct about the first requirement, but what about the second? It states that the victim of the disruption must endure a terrible loss of a loved one. But I never endured such a loss. So how is it possible for me to be this receiver?"

"Adrian, there are no accidents or errors in the Great Path of the Sacred Argali."

"You can say that until we all sprout wings, but it doesn't change the fact that I *did not* lose a loved one during the Conflagration of the Twilight Hall."

Temil looked down. For once he was without reply.

"I will consider your words," Adrian said, "but right now, my heart is set on revenge."

Temil's childlike head shook softly. "Please reconsider. If you think taking Lord Haroden's life will ease the disharmony in your heart . . . well, I'm sorry to tell you it won't. Revenge is glorious for the ego—but meaningless to the spirit."

"I'll take my chances with that," Adrian told him.

Chapter Thirty

𝒯he city of Beetleburr was as run-down and miserable as Adrian remembered—worse even, since winter's icy jaws had clamped down on it. The avenues were rutted pits of gray slush, the buildings all shoved together and weighed down by heavy white mantles. The people looked no better. Filthy, ragged, hungry people, plodding along like herds of diseased antelope. Even the foul odors that lingered in the streets weren't completely abolished by the cold— and damn, it was *cold*.

The company headed to the Sapphire Moon and managed to rent the same private room as before. Third floor, left, third door. It took them days to settle in, warm their bones, fill their bellies, and rekindle their focus. Now Adrian had expected to encounter a snag or two when arranging this private audience with Lady Amelia, but he never imagined the gate sentries being impervious to persuasion, immune to deception, and unaffected by bribery. Apparently, Viceroy Murden, for all his shortcomings, kept security tighter than a crab's bunghole. Adrian even turned to memorizing schedules and waiting until shifts changed, but every sentry he approached—the youngest and most inexperienced included—was equally dismissive, and no less kind. "Why would a common street slug have any business with the daughter of the virtuous Lord Murden?" a stout sentry barked. "No documentation, no entry. Got it? Good. Now get out of my sight before I give you a good drubbing."

And that was that. Adrian wasn't there under any official business, and since he was too hesitant to reveal his true name, he ended up being treated as another worthless cur in a city of worthless curs.

Days passed. Bleak and frigid days that drained his confidence and sapped his motivation. A midday snowfall turned into an evening of freezing rain, and as Adrian sat in his room listening to the endless clinking of the tiled roof, his mind ran through every possible avenue of how he might get Lady Amelia's attention. All were dead-ends. What could he do? Short of just loitering near the tall palatial walls in hopes that she might somehow spot him, Adrian had nothing.

So naturally he had grown idle, stagnant, and next

he knew he was waist deep in a morass of doubt and self-pity. *What the hell am I doing here? Did I really think I could do this? How could a meager fool like myself think to accomplish something so grand?* Yes, it was *those* sorts of doubts. You know, the debilitating ones.

Now Adrian wasn't a man who waved the white without a fight, but the ache of his failed ambitions quickly became as harsh as this goddamn winter. It was so painful to see the plans that had begun so boldly in Swallowtail dwindle down to the delusions of a small-minded clod. Without the lady's help, Adrian had no chance of attending the wedding cere-mony, which meant he had no chance of ever getting close to Lord Haroden, which meant he had no chance of ending the reign of a great tyrant, which meant he was stuck in this miserable city with limited coin, which meant his whole journey had been in vain, which meant he was a stupid, cursed, worthless goddamn—

Tap, tap, tap.

Adrian looked up. *What the hell was that?* It wasn't the howling wind or the hammering rain . . . no, the sound he heard came from the opposite end of the room. From the door. *Tap, tap, tap.* Adrian rose to his feet, threw a heavy wool robe over his bedclothes, and moved across the room. He waited . . . listening, listening, then his good hand reached up, and the door opened with a creak.

Half hidden in the dim light was a petite figure cloaked in a heap of wet rags. A hand reached up, and the figure's hood came down . . .

Lady Amelia.

Her face was as pale and flawless as Adrian remembered, her features as dainty and cheerful and her hair as dark and curly. Those high cheekbones, those full lips . . . he must've been staring at her for a little too long, because the lady motioned inside and said, "May I?"

Adrian bowed his head and stepped out of the way. She entered the room in small, soft steps, like a lotus petal drifting across a pond, and when Adrian gestured to the wooden couch, she decided instead on a dark corner where the moonlight couldn't touch her. "I planned on carrying an alms bowl, but I thought that too much," she remarked.

Her smile made Adrian smile, even though he didn't wish to smile. Still, he couldn't help it; he was like a nervous boy around a schoolyard crush.

"Before you speak, I need to say something," she told him. "What happened at the fortress garrison . . . I wanted no part in my father's scheming. He forced it on me. But our time together, it was meaningful. You know that, yes? It was meaningful."

"I know. How did you find me?"

Her eyes squinted just a touch, as if she were unsure of the question. "It was your friend, the little one. My courtiers and I were enjoying our daily walk through the gardens. A group of children ran past, heading to the academy for the day's lessons. The little one must've been hidden among them, because he came to me in my private lakeside pavilion shortly after. I thought he was a child . . . but his face . . . it wasn't a child's face. Anyway, he told me a friend is waiting at the Sapphire Moon. 'Third floor, left, third door,' he said. 'The brave one with the single glove.' " She brushed aside a lock of wet hair and smiled. "You sent him, didn't you?"

Adrian paused before nodding. *Damn it, Temil. You're making it difficult for me to believe I made the right decision in not trusting you.*

"Well, I'm here," she said. "You wanted to talk, so talk."

Adrian stumbled over his words before getting the right ones out. "The wedding . . . your promise to Lord Haroden. I intend to stop it."

"It's too late, Adrian. The betrothal gifts have been exchanged, the seven etiquettes completed, the dowry sent, and the contracts signed. Lord Haroden's courtiers are already preparing the imperial procession. There is talk of economic rebirth in Beetleburr, but to me it reeks of empty promises."

"No, you don't understand. By stopping it, I mean to take his life."

She stared at him for a long moment, her normally cheerful features slowly fading into an expression of sorrow. "Why are you telling me this? Do you know how deeply the idea of hope punishes me?" She made a disappointed click of her tongue. "I assure you there is no reaching that man. Lord Haroden's veteran guardsmen cling to him at all hours of the day. Even a hundred men at your side wouldn't be enough to lift my doubts."

"I don't have a hundred men. I don't need a

hundred men. It's just me, and I plan to strike during the wedding ceremony, when the tyrant is most vulnerable."

"Strike . . . with what? Every man or woman who enters the imperial hall will be subject to a thorough search. Nothing will get inside that Lord Haroden doesn't want there."

Adrian gave a small but sly smile. "I won't be carrying a weapon."

Her eyes flickered, and a bewildered yet hopeful expression lifted her face. "Listen, you know I admire your courage, Adrian. I do. But you have to under-stand, I—"

"This isn't about us, my lady."

"Then why are you doing this?"

"Because the Rhinoceros Lord is a tyrant and a murderer and he must be stopped."

"How noble. But don't insult me. What is the real reason?"

Adrian looked away. "The Conflagration of the Twilight Hall . . . the day that bastard Haroden burned all those innocent people alive. I was there and I almost died with them. But that's not all; the fire ruined me, robbed me of everything good I've ever had in my life." He paused to collect his emotions and swallow the lump in his throat. "I need you to tell me about the performances. The entire schedule of events, in order, from beginning to end."

Her face tensed when a gust of wind rattled the shutters. "The entertainment begins in the outer courtyards at high sun. Poetry is first; the academy is presenting the four themes of scientific nature recited by the newest graduates. Next is the display of callig- raphy and landscape painting, to be presented on handscrolls and lacquerware and folding screens. The afternoon banquet is served after that. Then the acro- bats and funambulists and other daredevilry, followed by the jugglers and jesters and pratfall artists. At nightfall the spectators fill the theater hall for the betrothal banquet. After that the sconces are extin- guished for the most spectacular act of the day: the fire masters."

"The fire masters," Adrian repeated. "Can you get me on stage with them?"

She looked at him as if he'd just told her he could fly. "You want to perform as a fire master?" She almost laughed. "Do you have any idea of the requirements? A lifetime of physical and mental training along with an uncanny ability to endure the pain of blisters on your tongue and lips and throat. Hell, even if you were prepared in those aspects, you still won't have time to learn the complexities of the utilizers and transfers and extinguishers." Her hands moved as she announced formally the various maneuvers: the Nine Dances of the Sun, the Six Tongue Transport, the Candlelight Bringer, the Ghost in the Mist, the Five Retentions of the Flame." When she stopped, she gave Adrian a slightly patronizing look, as if he were a naive little child.

Adrian didn't blink. "Obviously I won't take part in the main performance. I'll close the show, performing my own special act . . . though I'll need their help, of course."

She frowned at the idea. "Is your mind completely frazzled? Lord Haroden will see your lack of skill as an affront, and he'll have your head for it. I thought you knew the difference between bravery and foolishness?"

Adrian rose. He used the light of a candle to ignite a torch, and when the flames flashed to life and hungrily licked the air, Adrian removed his glove and placed his blackened hand over it. Instead of burning his hand, the fire was drawn into it, disappearing like water down a tube, leaving nothing more than a trail of smoke that rose from his fingertips. "My lady, my question stands, can you get me on stage with the other fire masters?"

Her eyes were huge. "H-how did you just——"

Adrian put the glove back on, clenching his teeth to ward off the pain in his blackened fingers. "Can you get me on stage with the other fire masters or not."

Her eyes were still locked on his hand. "I-I don't . . ." She blinked. "There's a certain protocol, Adrian. Very strict. The waiting list is long, years long, and every aspiring fire master must pass a series of rigorous auditions. It is unheard of for someone to just leap ahead."

"My lady, you are the daughter of an illustrious provincial viceroy. If something can be done, you're the one to do it."

She thought for a while longer. "One of our lead

performers is fighting a bout of fire lung, it's a rather insidious condition caused by the prolonged aspiration of ethanol. The physicians generally treat this with herbs that widen the bronchi, but if treatment were to be obstructed or delayed . . . well, the lead will be forced to retire from the performance." She turned and began pacing, her heeled shoes streaking across the floor. "I'd have to hire criers and scribes to pass the word of a new fire master. It shouldn't be an issue. People love mysterious strangers, so a mysterious stranger is what I will give them." She thought for a moment longer. "You'll be the Wanderer of Ash and Smoke, a mysterious vagabond from the north. A recent poem immortalized the Wanderer as an other-worldly being whose lungs cannot be poisoned by smoke and whose body cannot be burned by fire."

"What about Lord Haroden, will he be accepting of this?"

Lady Amelia nodded. "Of course. A revealing dress and a dash of confidence can go a long way with that brute." Her hands moved to straighten the folds of her attire, but she stopped and shrugged when she realized how tattered and filthy it was. "The other fire masters won't be happy about this alteration, however, so don't expect a warm welcome."

"Understood."

"I suppose you'll need the proper raiment, and a mask. If something should go wrong—"

"I have a mask. Don't worry, my lady, Lord Haroden doesn't even know my face. His high commander Krall Vyren did, but Krall is dead."

Lady Amelia nodded, but she remained thoughtful for a moment. "Still, if somehow the truth of your identity is revealed to Lord Haroden . . . well, let's just say that my death will be a slow and torturous event, as gruesome as the most heinous traitors of the realm."

The image made Adrian frown. "I won't let that happen."

She gave a nod. "You have my faith, Adrian. Do this for me, and you'll also have my heart."

Chapter Thirty-One

*A*drian stood in awe of the imperial procession.

It was a massive train . . . a remarkably organized sequence of vehicles and footmen and heavy draught animals that roared across the countryside and left the very earth to tremble beneath its might.

Outriders moved at the head. Powerful men in polished steel plates and spiked halfhelms with feathered headplumes that matched the barding of their caparisoned horses. Behind them were the columns of ministerial carriages, each a marvel of gilded framework and studded wheels and dark damask curtains, and each drawn by a team of horses beribboned in lace and bedecked in flowing silks. Next marched a regiment of pike-wielding infantrymen, along with a host of standard bearers who waved three different sets of colors: the earthy taupe of the northern empire, the bold red of Scarlet Sun, and the pale blue that signified Lord Haroden's personal sigil. After that was a second regiment of infantrymen, followed by the teams of drummers. Next were the carts whose loads of cookware and miscellaneous trinkets clinked and clattered like the bells and chimes of an orchestra. Next and last of all was another host of mounted soldiers—the rear guard.

Adrian observed it all from an overlook on the nearby hills. A knot of disgust twisted in his gut when he saw the rows of civilians all lining up to pay their respects to the imperial procession. *If only these people knew just how much of a monster Lord Haroden truly is,* Adrian thought. The knot grew tighter when the gates of Beetleburr groaned open and a small honor guard of mounted men emerged to escort the prime minister into the city. This was all done amid a grand display of music and fanfare.

Shortly after, Lord Haroden delivered a welcome speech from the private balcony of the provincial viceroy's imperial tower. The charismatic ruler waggled his magnetic tongue and crowds of men and women kowtowed with tears streaming from their eyes. Adrian stood among them with a clenched jaw and balled fist. Were all men so easily deceived? No, surely one person in the audience had the shrewdness to see through all the false promises of the tyrant.

Maybe there was more than one, maybe there were quite a few, but fear kept them smiling and bowing along with the rest of the sheep. Yes, that was more likely—and more believable. Adrian needed that comfort; he didn't want to feel alone in all this.

The prime minister soon retired to his luxurious guest accommodations, and the city eventually returned to its usual doldrums. Adrian himself had become busy with his upcoming performance with the fire masters, and since he had so little time to prepare, the days of course passed quickly, one after another, until the morning of the wedding ceremony was suddenly thrust upon him.

He was standing backstage in his private dressing area, concealed behind a screen but not isolated from the commotion of his fellow performers and their busybody assistants. Eldred and Olan were with him; the big man was chuckling at Adrian's garb—and with good reason. Adrian had attempted to modify his robe and trousers to match the Wanderer of Ash and Smoke's famous fuliginous attire, but the end result was a mess of torn and oversized rags that looked no better than the threadbare tatters of a street beggar.

"You look like a fool, Deadhand," Olan said.

Even Eldred couldn't resist a jab. "I don't recall the fireside tales ever describing the great Wanderer of Ash and Smoke as an indigent fellow."

Olan tapped the mask that was strapped on Adrian's face. "Is that the Chitterer mask? It looks even more hideous."

He was right. Adrian had altered the mask using

strips of leather that were taken from the scrap piles of a puppet workshop. The strips were strung together and dyed black using iris root and oak gulls, but the dyeing process was rushed and the color ended up looking more like a sun-faded gray than black. Still, its primary purpose was to conceal Adrian's identity, and for that it served well enough. "I'm glad that both of you find this so amusing," Adrian remarked. "But be warned, if I make a mistake tonight and end up facing the axeman, I'm taking both of you down as co-conspirators."

Olan guffawed at that. "I tried to talk you out of this madness. Tell me, Deadhand, are you stupidly brave or just stupid?"

Eldred was the one to answer that. "He's a bit of both."

Adrian nodded. It was probably the kindest compliment he'd get from the husky outlaw, so he took it with good grace. His hand reached up to adjust the fit of his mask, then came back down to retrieve a small look mirror. The face that appeared in the reflective glass was ragdoll hideous, but it was also an emotionless and expressionless and inhumanly confident face—even though the man behind the mask was anything but confident. In truth, Adrian was scared. He was scared and he wanted to leave this place. Every moment of every hour of every day —it was all he thought about. *Get the hell out of this wretched city and never look back. Get the hell out of this wretched city and never look back.* But he didn't get the hell out . . . he didn't because he knew he wouldn't be able to live with himself. Well, maybe he could. No, probably not.

Eldred remained with Adrian in the dressing area, but Olan wasn't so patient. The big man wandered off to observe the daytime art exhibitions in the outer courtyard, only to return several times to grouse about the sappy poetry and uninspired landscape paintings. But when the afternoon's physical entertainment commenced, Olan didn't reappear until the sky began to glow with the oyster pink light of dusk. "By the gods, what a spectacular show," he said breathlessly, his deep-set eyes glowing with wonder. "Blindfolded acrobats juggling double-edged knives while balancing on giant wheels, and gymnasts dressed in bright gold leotards forming human pyramids that looked like stacks of bullion. There were tightrope walkers, lion dancers, trapeze artists . . . let me think . . . yes, contortionists, hair hangers, tumblers, sword masters . . ."

Adrian stopped listening. Instead he focused on a growing din coming from the main hall of the imperial theater. He exited the dressing area, walked the length of the narrow wing, and peered out from behind the backstage curtain. Spectators were taking their seats along the rows of wooden benches. A haze had already begun to blanket the area, but it wasn't thick enough to obscure the sight of Lord Haroden, who emerged from a door at the far end of the hall.

The overweight prime minister sat down on a cushioned seat with a high openwork back and carved ivory armrests. His company of personal guardsmen fanned out protectively around him, strapping men strapped in polished steel breastplates and faulds and pauldrons and greaves. They were cold-faced and hard-eyed and intimidating men, the kind you didn't want to tangle with.

Viceroy Marius Murden stood on the dais and announced the schedule of evening events with all the pomp and charisma of a trained master of ceremonies. When he was done he turned to the Rhinoceros Lord and bowed his head in an obsequious manner that Adrian never imagined him doing. "Your Supreme Lordship," the viceroy declared. "I assure you the evening's banquet and performance will surpass the banality of the day's entertainment."

Olan leaned in to whisper to his brother. "What does 'banality' mean?"

"Boring, unoriginal."

Olan frowned. "I thought the entertainment was good."

Lord Murden bowed once more and headed to his seat, but a thought must've come to him because he turned back to the audience and said, "I have one final announcement, and it is an unexpected treat for all of us. Closing tonight's performance is a stranger known throughout the six provinces as the Wanderer of Ash and Smoke." He stopped as the crowd cheered, waiting patiently for the opportunity to continue. "I see many of you are familiar with his name already. That is good, I don't need to waste your time with explanations then, do I? Now this man has come to us from far beyond the Caddis Mountains, where the land is dead and the sun never touches the sky. This will be something to see, don't you think?"

The ovation was so loud it gave Adrian a start. *Get the hell out of this wretched city and never look back*, he told himself. *Get the hell out of this wretched city and never look back.*

The banquet commenced shortly after, and it was the typical lavish affair filled with luxurious dishes and opulent drinking vessels. Servers came and went with pearl-enchased salvers and gold leaf tureens, delivering course after course of piping hot fare that was as extravagant as it was rare. The smells made Adrian's stomach rumble, even though his nerves had long quashed any semblance of an appetite. To relieve his tension he did a lot of pacing, back and forth, back and forth, and every few minutes or so he'd go to the far window to observe the sky. Nightfall was swiftly devouring the purplish twilight, which meant the performance of the fire masters was soon to begin. Adrian paced back and forth a hundred more times, maybe a thousand, his heart constantly battling the waves of panic and nausea.

A hand touched his shoulder to stop him; it was Eldred.

"I could sure use one of your nerve-calming tonics right now," Adrian said. "Hell, you can even throw in some Snakelion blood or a few grasshopper legs if you'd like."

Eldred smiled at that. "The show's about to start."

Drums breathed to life, a faint but steady rhythm that quieted the audience and drew all eyes to the stage. The soft cadence soon perked up in tempo, as female performers in scanty gowns of red silk emerged onto the stage, waving and twirling two or three-armed batons of flickering flame. When the tips of the batons ventured in and out of their mouths, the crowd gave a fierce applause. It was a perfectly choreographed display, and one that was further enhanced by the coordinating melodies of panpipes and strings and woodwinds.

From his position backstage Adrian watched the performance rather absently, his mind roaming, roaming, roaming the realms of uncertainty. *What if my hand doesn't do what it's supposed to do? What if I fail to impress the crowd? What if my mask slips off and someone recognizes me? What if Lord Haroden decides to get up mid performance and leave?* So many ways this plan could go wrong. Adrian was pacing again. Eldred tried to stop him, but this time he had no luck.

WHOOOOSH.

A great flash drew Adrian's eyes back to the stage. Male performers dressed in loincloth skirts were breathing gouts of flame into the air, illuminating different sections of the audience. They moved rhythmically, never once out of step, in and out of the wisps of smoke that streaked across the stage. The smell of alcohol was all but dripping in the air.

The tempo pulsed faster now, faster and faster as the flames began to flicker and dance with increased aggression. To the left, to the right, performers breathed like angry dragons. Faster and faster they went—never once out of step, never once a miscalculated or wasted breath. And just as the drums were pounding their hardest, just as the strings were singing their loudest, the music rose to a final crescendo, and the performers blew a unified cloud of flame that lit up the entire theater hall.

Then, darkness.

The eruption of cheers was so loud and so sudden that Adrian moved back a step. He steadied his nerves, looked down through the eye slits of his mask, and stared at his blackened hand. *This is it, Adrian.* He drew in a deep breath and exhaled, then stepped out onto the stage.

A circle of flame rose around him: six fire batons held by six fire breathers. The sudden blaze of light left Adrian's vision impaired and spotted—but he didn't quail. No, for some reason he remained calm. His mind was clear. He knew what he had to do.

WHOOSH.

A stream of flame rushed at Adrian. He raised his blackened hand and drew it in like wreckage in a maelstrom. A second flame, this time from the opposite direction; Adrian spun and his hand absorbed that stream as well. A third flame and a fourth. A fifth and then one more. Smoke curled from the fingertips of Adrian's blackened hand. The heat had singed the cuffs of his gray robe and left the inside of his mask reeking of burnt hair, but he was otherwise unscathed. *It worked. By the gods, it worked.* His once frightened heart was now engorged with confidence, and that confidence flowed through him like a river in full spate.

The six fire breathers repeated their oral assault, breathing stream after stream of fire just as they'd been instructed to do. Each and every stream was absorbed by Adrian's hand, resulting in the same diffusion of light and the same spreading of smoke into the air. After a third round of this, the crowd was on its feet and chanting the Wanderer's name. Another round, another six breaths absorbed. The cheering grew louder, louder, louder. Another round. Another, and at last, after one final assault, the fire batons dimmed and dimmed and the hall fell into a hazy darkness, leaving the crowd cheering and chanting like drunken zealots.

Adrian sneaked out of the circle, hopped off the stage, and skulked along the western wall, beneath the tiger pen shell sconces. He was quite close to the outer row of spectators, but they were all too busy cheering to notice. It was also hard to see—especially with this damn mask—so Adrian advanced slowly and with caution, and before long he was ascending the dais and sidling past the outer ring of Lord Haroden's guardsmen. Now most of these men were rather large, but one bodyguard in particular was truly a colossus, appearing every bit as tall and even wider than Olan, although most of that bulk was probably armor. Still, Adrian shrank away and almost fled at the site of him and his ugly face, but when he noticed that the bodyguard's attention was distracted by all the clamor, Adrian held his breath and sneaked past.

He found Lord Haroden slumped in his throne-like chair, elbow perched on an armrest, plump hand lazily holding up his round head. He wasn't paying attention. Was he even awake? It didn't matter. Adrian's blackened hand spidered up the base of the chair and rose over the armrest, reaching, reaching, reaching . . .

Got you, bastard. Adrian squeezed the tyrant's arm.

It was too dark to see, but Adrian didn't need to see. He could *feel* the prime minister's flesh bubbling, peeling, melting away . . . could feel his bones disintegrating into ash. In his heart he felt every nuanced bit of the tyrant's gruesome end, but one thing that struck him as odd was how quiet the prime minister was. The bastard didn't make a sound, nor did he make a move—not even to flinch or pull his arm away. *You vile wretch, are you dying in your sleep?* Adrian wondered.

It was then the prime minister spoke.

They were calm and confident words. Words that lacked any trace of pain or suffering. Lord Haroden simply called for light. A moment later the tiger pen shell wall sconces flashed to life, one after another, *whoosh-whoosh-whoosh*, in rapid succession like the hanging lanterns of a midsummer festival. The last pair of sconces illuminated the tyrant himself, and no, he wasn't a bubbling, peeling, melting mess of flesh. In fact, he was unscathed and unruffled and—by the way his big bull eyes glared murderously at Adrian—rather unhappy.

I don't understand, Adrian thought. *I'm touching you.*

I'm touching your skin. He blinked and blinked and refocused his eyes. Yes, his blackened fingers were clearly wrapped around the tyrant's plump forearm—he could *feel* the man's cold and clammy flesh. And yet, nothing was happening. *Why not? Why not, why not, why not, why not?* Adrian didn't have time to consider an answer. The prime minister wrenched free his arm and squealed with bloodcurdling rage: *"HOW DARE THIS IMPERTINENT DOG ACCOST THE IMPERIAL HAND?!"*

Adrian staggered back. Guardsmen swarmed from every direction.

Chapter Thirty-Two

*H*ands seized him, armored hands, spiked and articulated and hard as steel. One moment Adrian was thrown facedown to the cold tiled floor, the next he was back on his feet and staring up at a handful of imposing guardsmen. The Rhinoceros Lord was behind them, poised at the edge of his seat and yelling out all the ways he wanted the offender to die. Words like bludgeon, flay, and boil were being tossed around, along with other, more gruesome methods that caused the officials to gasp in abject horror.

The guards dragged Adrian through dark corridors and down spiral stairways, passing landing after landing and doorway after doorway until he found himself in the dank lower dungeons. The air was heavy with the smell of must, as most underground chambers were, but there was an underlying foulness to that smell, as if it were continuously tainted with the reek of unwashed bodies. Three scrawny jailers were sitting at a table and engaged in a heated gambling game. They glanced up at the disturbance, but remained silent as the guardsmen dumped Adrian in a rear holding cell, stripped him of his mask and robe, bound him in leg irons, and barred the iron grate door.

Adrian's eyes wandered down to the black and withered fingers of his black and withered hand. *I touched him. I felt his flesh. The bastard should've burned and died, the same way Dravid and that Chitterer and Krall Vyren and that old date seller had all burned and died.* But no, Lord Haroden hadn't burned—in fact he hadn't shown even the slightest hint of discomfort. *What the hell went wrong?*

He replayed the events in his mind. The prime minister was slumped in his seat, elbow perched on an armrest, head cupped in an open palm. The sleeves of his loose-fitting pachyderm robe were hiked down to his elbow, and his pale pink flesh was exposed. Adrian used his blackened hand to reach up and seize the tyrant's forearm. Yes, that was exactly how it happened . . . and yet, nothing happened.

What the hell went wrong?

Maybe it was a prosthetic limb. Sure, in these modern times arms and legs were carved and crafted with marvelous detail, and the flexibility of the joints provided by bronze catches and hinges made it quite easy to mistake the artificial for the actual. Certainly Lord Haroden, in his ever-reaching influence and immeasurable wealth, could've had such a realistic arm constructed for him. Couldn't he have?

No, you idiot. Wood is not soft and metal is not sweaty. You touched his flesh.

Adrian gave a long, despondent sigh. *So what the hell went wrong?*

He couldn't decide on an answer, so he decided that an answer no longer mattered. What did matter was that he had failed, and now only death remained for him—and what an agonizing death it would be. But the pain, like all things, would eventually end, and with that his soul would journey through the Great Rivers of Transmigration, to be judged by the Five Deathkings of All That Becomes.

How would he fare under this mysterious judgment? Adrian wasn't sure. Of course in his life he'd committed his share of sinful acts . . . but what man hasn't? He knew that his heart was pure. Surely the Five Deathkings in their all-knowing wisdom would see that. Or maybe they wouldn't. Hell, maybe all this talk of journeys and rivers and immortal beings was nothing more than bunkum and balderdash, and the dead and gone were simply dead and gone. Adrian didn't want to believe that; he wanted to believe the Argalist Path of renewal and rebirth, but he couldn't stop those pesky what-ifs from gnawing at his heart. *What if the rivers are nothing more than manmade comforts for dying men? What if death is no more real than the darkness before birth? What if you are forever eradicated from all worlds, spheres, realms, and planes of existence?* Goddamn it, Adrian was standing on the precipice of death and he still couldn't muster the slightest touch of faith. One thing was certain, however; afterlife or not, he would finally be free of this cursed hand.

The main door opened and a jolly-eyed and jelly-bellied fellow entered the room. He chatted briefly with the jailers, then turned and approached the cell. He was bald as a bunion on top but had thick red hairs at his temples that reached outward like fiery branches. He also had the thickest monobrow Adrian had ever seen. It was like a giant black caterpillar slunk across his head. "I'm Barik," he said in a strangely pleasant tone.

"Bark. Like the dog?" Adrian asked.

"No, like the tree. I'll be escorting you to the other side."

"You make it sound like we're taking a midsummer stroll."

The man lifted his monobrow and laughed a single, short laugh. "Twenty-seven years ago I received my grand master's certification in the advanced methodologies of torture and execution, so you can be assured that I know what I'm doing. Now I understand His Supreme Lordship wants the worst for you, and yet that bastard refuses to give our viceroy the funds to pay what a man of my caliber and experience deserves to be paid, so I'm inclined not to give a rat's puckered bunghole about what he wants. Tell you what, work with me I'll give you a nice dose of Paradise Tea to dull your mind and ease your pain."

"How do I work with you?"

"Don't talk, don't squirm, and don't fight back. Basically don't do anything that disrupts my concentration or pisses me off. Oblige my request and your death will go as smoothly as possible. Got it? Good. Now—questions. Make it quick. I have things to do."

Adrian was quiet for a moment. "By what method am I to die?"

The jelly-bellied executioner spoke with no more compassion than an elderly master ordering around a servant. "The Longest Death."

"That doesn't sound good, Bark. What exactly is it?"

Barik gave a sigh, not out of compassion, but as if he had better things to do than explain his methods to the very man he was going to execute. "You'll be taken to the Hall of Winter Tranquility and tied up before the Supreme Lord himself. I'll be using a series of precise instruments on select organs and orifices. Nothing lethal at first. No, the Longest Death is done in a very slow and lingering manner, so that you will remain alive for as long as Lord Haroden wants you alive. I'll start off lightly, probably yank out a tooth or two, then bludgeon your face a bit, maybe break an orbital plate. Things pick up after that. I'll cut out your tongue and fasten a mask over your mouth, then

I'll pluck out an eye and chop off a few toes and slice off an ear. After that I'll move lower, carefully shaving off the excess flesh on your pectorals and biceps and upper thighs. At this point the pain becomes unbearable, and clemency usually dictates a final stab and twist to the heart, but Lord Haroden wants no mercy for you. I have to exact every drop of agony from your body before death takes you." He gave another sigh, and not because he was a man who didn't like torturing other men, but because he did it for too little pay. "Of course my duties don't end there. Your remains must be dismembered and boiled, and your bones must be triturated. We have a high quality pressure pulverizer for the latter . . . though I'm not sure if the goddamn thing is functional right now. Well, it needs to be, because there's no way I'm going back to that oversized mortar. Last time it took me three days to grind down a damn femur. No, I'm not doing that again. I don't care what Haroden says, he can go suck a loach."

Adrian gave a sympathetic nod, as if he were commiserating with an old chum. "The whole process sounds very efficient, but there is one flaw in your methodology. I don't see the point in covering my mouth with a mask. A man can't scream without a tongue."

"Not true. A man can most certainly scream without a tongue, but that is not why it is removed. Do you know nothing of the teachings of the Sacred Argali? Covering the mouth prevents a man's spirit from exiting his body upon death. You'll not be able to ascend to the Great Rivers of Transmigration. It is a punishment that lasts an eternity, hence the Longest Death."

Adrian swallowed a lump of cold dread. "Well, I was hoping to return as a squirrel or chipmunk, you know, to live meekly and harvest the seeds of future life."

"Sorry, friend. It's eternal damnation for you."

"Great, looking forward to it. When will this little jaunt of ours begin?"

"Tomorrow morning. Anything else?"

"No, that's all, thank you. Wait. Yes, one more thing. Any chance you could just let me out of this place? I promise I won't tell anyone."

Barik the executioner rubbed his shiny pate before laughing a single guffaw. "I should, just to piss that fat bastard off." With that he turned and toddled off.

*A*drian spent the evening wrapped in the same recurring dream. He was standing outside the same imperial hall and staring at the same rising tide of dark smoke. From inside the double doors of the hall, he could hear the same men and women and children screaming and burning and dying. The same three-legged dog appeared to stare at Adrian with the same black-pooled eyes, and when its mouth fell open, a ghostly, disembodied voice poured out: "Save us, save us, save us the innocent from agony. The gods know we've suffered enough. Only the rivers can carry us home."

Adrian opened his eyes and sat up. Normally, he'd just shrug off the dream and continue on with his day, but he was in a cell waiting to die, so a deep and desperate anger gnawed and gnawed at him until it erupted like a white-hot geyser. Adrian slammed a heel into the latticework bars, again and again and again. Dust stung his eyes, but he didn't care. He grabbed the latrine bucket and clumps of straw and threw them and anything else he could find in this mother-raping cell. He yelled and yelled and yelled some more, and eventually he grew hoarse and tired, so he dropped to his rump and began to moan and whimper. "What do you *want* from me? I can't help you. Can't you see I'm going to die? Just go away and *LET ME DIE*, goddamn it."

A gruff voice responded from across the room. "Tomorrow you die, tonight you have a visitor."

Adrian squinted at the approaching light. A jailer was holding up an oil lamp; behind the scrawny man was a familiar young woman. "My lady . . ." Adrian said. "Forgive me, I . . ."

Lady Amelia was wearing an emerald-green gown that matched her studded green shoes and complemented the flecks of green in her eyes. Her dark locks of coiffured hair dangled loosely in the front while a portion of it was gathered in a twist at the back where a pin kept it in place. She looked as comely as ever— and yet, there was a touch of exhaustion in her eyes, maybe even illness.

The lady thanked the jailer before sending him away. She approached the cage and knelt before the latticework bars, reaching in and taking Adrian's good hand in hers. Her touch was so warm, so comforting —for a moment Adrian forgot about everything else in the world and thought only of her. But when her hand drew back from his, it felt like thorns jabbing at his heart.

"Does Lord Haroden know?" Adrian asked. "Does he know who I am?"

She said no. "My father has sworn to keep your identity a secret, but only for the sake of my safety. Not that it matters, the 'Wanderer of Ash and Smoke' will still receive the most heinous of executions. What you did was considered an egregious offense. Adrian, what went wrong?"

"Would that I knew."

She looked at him as if expecting a better answer. "Well, I pleaded with my husband, remonstrated with his ministers, exhausted every avenue of dilatory tactics with my advisors," she said. "I can't stop this, Adrian."

He wasn't sure which bothered him more—the thought of his impending execution or her mentioning of Lord Haroden as her husband. "It matters not. I've failed you, my lady, I've failed you after everything you've done for me. Arranging the fire masters, rousing the public's interest, working all the little details to get me on that stage. You put your faith in me . . . and I failed to fulfill that faith. It saddens me to know that you've become the tyrant's wife."

She glanced behind her to make sure the jailer

was gone. "Me as well. Not only is he a foul-tempered and violent man, he's also quite repulsive. He sweats a lot, snores a lot, eats like a hog, and, oh, he *smells*."

Adrian, despite the overwhelming despair in his heart, managed a soft chuckle. "I thought regular bathing was a standard luxury of the high nobility."

"It is, but that's not why he smells. It's this little locket he keeps tied around his neck. He never takes it off. Ever. He says it enhances his vitality and virility and other such nonsense." She gave another quick glance behind her. "The smell isn't noticeable when he's adorned in his silks, but when he undresses and climbs into bed with me . . . well, it's awful. Don't look so surprised, he's been performing his conjugal duties since the day he arrived. I know it's not an acceptable custom, but who's going to tell that to the Supreme Lord of Scarlet Sun? Certainly not my father, or any of his cowardly advisors. Anyway, it's like sharing the coverlet with a swine that was dunked in a vat of sulfur. The smell gives me headaches. Terrible headaches." Her eyes wandered to the floor, an uncharacteristically bashful action. "Forgive me. Here you are awaiting a terrible fate, and I'm blathering on about my insignificant troubles."

Adrian gave her a sympathetic look. "Talk to him about the headaches. Maybe he'll take it off for you, or simply stop wearing it altogether."

Lady Amelia sighed at that. She looked at him in a way that she never had before. It was as if her fiery little spirit had run out of fuel, and all that remained was the shell of a desperate woman. "Three nights ago Lord

Haroden drank himself blotto and had his way with me. When he was done he fell asleep, and that's when I removed the locket and put it in a keepsake box. Well, the next morning he awoke in a panic. When I retrieved it and began explaining about the headaches, he snatched the locket from my hands and gave me this." She brushed the hair back from her face to reveal a small purple welt on her left cheek. "It didn't hurt much, not really, but what he said afterwards scared me to the bone. He told me if I ever take his locket again, he would cut off my legs and leave me in a field for the wild dogs to pick at."

"What a bastard," Adrian said. "Let me see. Turn your head."

She did. "I don't know what's so special about the stupid thing anyway. I opened the locket. It's just a red mushroom."

Adrian was still examining her face. "I can't believe he struck—wait a moment. Did you say red mushroom?"

She gave a nod. "Yes, a red mushroom. It's not like any mushroom I've seen though. It has no stalk, and the shape is rather strange. It looks a bit like . . ."

"Like a cloud?"

"Yes. It looks like a red cloud. How did you know that?"

Adrian's eyes dropped to the ground. He couldn't believe it. *No, no, by the gods, no.* He shook his head, as if to somehow deny the truth of why Lord Haroden didn't burn to ashes upon Adrian's touch. He recalled Temil's words: *The red cloud mushroom is a supermundane antioxidant and supernatural preventative. He who holds posses-sion of it is rendered impervious to the constraints of pain, illness, and death.*

Lady Amelia snapped her fingers in his face. "What's wrong? Adrian."

He looked up at her, a movement so sudden that she nearly gave a start. "I need you to do something for me. The mushroom, can you steal it from him?"

"Please, Adrian. Don't concern yourself with me, they are just headaches . . ."

"It's not that, my lady. There may still be a way to stop the tyrant, but I need that mushroom."

"Adrian, you are sentenced to die tomorrow morning."

"I know. That's why I need it. You have to believe me."

Her face formed a scowl—a pretty scowl, but a scowl nonetheless. "I've had enough of your false promises. You're worse than Lord Haroden. I've accepted my fate, you need to accept yours."

"No, you don't understand, I—"

The jailer cleared his throat from the neighboring room. "It's time, my lady," he called.

"I have to go," she said, rising to her feet.

"The mushroom," Adrian whispered.

She paused, hesitating.

He wanted to tell her why he needed the red cloud—he wanted to tell her exactly what it did and exactly how it could help him, but he didn't have enough time. Why was there never enough time? "I know how this sounds, but you have to do this," he told her. "Please, you *have* to do this."

She seemed to deeply consider his words, but in the end, she simply said, "I've already risked my neck for you. I can't risk it again." With that, she turned and left the room.

Chapter Thirty-Three

They came for him the following day.

A pair of soldiers pulled Adrian from his cell, removed his leg irons, hoisted him to his feet, and led him up stairway after stairway until they were out of the dark of the underground and into the sunshine of an open footpath.

It was a serene and balmy morning—certainly not the kind of morning you'd expect to be your last. Plump white clouds drifted dreamily across a robin eggshell sky, and the stout cherry trees that lined the walkways shimmered and sang with blossom and birdsong. The rebirth and renewal of the coming spring seemed to flourish everywhere—well, everywhere except in Adrian's heart. Sadly, he had reached the inevitable nadir of his adventures.

The soldiers escorted Adrian across two court-yards, three orchards, and four stone bridges before stopping at the studded double doors of the provincial viceroy's inner palace. The doors groaned open, revealing a spacious hall with four rows of finger-like pillars and a bas-relief ceiling depicting a wonderfully detailed scene of a frozen moonlit lake. Adrian's bare feet pattered softly across the tiled floor, while the booted heels of the soldiers at his sides clicked and clacked with vigor and purpose. They halted in the center of the room, stripped Adrian down to his ragged undershorts, and tied together his ankles and wrists, careful not to touch his blackened hand. This was done not out of respect for Adrian's supernatural ability, but because the soldiers feared catching an infectious disease. *They think me a plague-ridden rat,* Adrian mused. *Perhaps that's just what I am.*

Lord Haroden was seated on the center dais, on a throne-like chair wide enough for two average-sized men—or one grossly overweight prime minister. He was clad in his typical horned headdress and thick pachyderm robes, and surrounded by his typical host of soldiers and bodyguards and civil and military offi-cials. The tyrant's big bull eyes were focused on a salver of persimmon slices, which were being fed to him by the loving fingers of his newly wedded wife, Lady Amelia.

Adrian admired her low-cut gown and cloud-coiffed hair and powdered face, but he was sickened by the way she clung affectionately to the tyrant's side. She was like a child cuddling an oversized doll. Had she been playing him false all this time? *Goddamn it, you are no different than your father, aren't you?* Adrian wanted to lash out at her, to condemn her and to call her a deceiving whore, but he decided not to waste his breath. *It matters not what she does. I'll soon be free of my earthly torments.*

The stillness in the hall was disquieting. Obviously this wasn't a public square, and obviously Adrian's execution would not be a loud, riotous affair filled with throngs of hostile spectators who hurled imprecations as well as old fruit rinds at him. Would Adrian have preferred that? He wasn't sure. He would've wanted the citizens of this city to witness publicly the punishments enacted by Lord Haroden. Perhaps then they'd see just what sort of ice-blooded monster he was. Still, it was a foolish thought, since the prime minister was a bit too clever to let that happen.

A small man with a long beard rose from his seat and introduced himself as the Chief Officer of Punishments and Executions. He offered a few trite words, then broke the seal of a scroll and read aloud the official sentencing. "This nameless accused, the man known only as the Wanderer of Ash and Smoke, has offended against heaven's principles by laying his shriveled and diseased fingers upon the sublime skin of the Supreme Lord of Scarlet Sun. And so this man must . . ."

Adrian stopped listening. His focus shifted to the jelly-bellied executioner, Barik, and his tabletop assortment of ghastly torture instruments. There were so many different shapes and sizes and alloys and tempers on display—everything from lung piercers to orifice stretchers to spine twisters and thumb screwers —and all were designed for a single, specific purpose: to inflict as much pain as possible. Adrian didn't know which instrument frightened him most, so he decided that all were pretty goddamn frightening in their own special way.

After the convictions were presented, fabric rustled and chair legs scraped the floor but the hall was otherwise silent. Well, except for the sudden sound of Lord Haroden's tittering. Adrian looked up. Lady Amelia was wrapped around her husband's overweight frame, her tiny fingers caressing him playfully beneath his robes. Adrian ground his teeth and tensed his arms as if he intended to break his binds. Barik took notice and issued a quiet warning. "Remember what I said yesterday, about working with me and all that."

"To hell with you," Adrian shot back in a contemptuous whisper.

"Fine, but I offered to make things easier."

"Yeah, you're a real model of rectitude. Just get started already, will you? I'm ready to die."

Barik gave a sigh. "Of course you are. Death is easy. It's the part before it that's hard."

There was a sharp metallic *clink* as Barik grabbed a rusty pair of pincers from the table. "We're starting off slowly, remember? Open your mouth. Good, that's it." He leaned in so close Adrian could smell the sour wine on his breath. The pincers whined as they clamped down on a tooth—and then somebody screamed.

It came from a cleaner, a young man with the thankless job of gathering Adrian's bloody bits as they fell to the floor. Well, this fellow was now the one lying on the floor, and he was shrieking and thrashing about as if tormented by some unseen sorcery.

Officials rose from their seats, pointing and gasping. A handful of soldiers unsheathed their curved swords and cautiously advanced. Others began a hasty search of the area, confused and wary of an ambush. Barik was cursing and ordering the cleaner to be still, but the young fellow wasn't listening; he was too busy convulsing.

What is going on? Just then Adrian felt something brush against his arm. He turned and saw Lady Amelia kneeling beside him. She had placed something in his good hand. It was the mushroom. He couldn't see it but he knew from the shape and the hard texture and of course that sulfurous smell. "It's yours," she whispered, "though it may be too late to do any good." She disappeared a moment later, slipping back through the crowd toward her husband.

The young cleaner's convulsions eventually lessened to an irregular twitch, and it was then a handful of soldiers carried him off. It was all very quick and efficient, and within a few minutes the hall had returned to its usual state of order. But no, not entirely—there were whispers now, whispers of ill omens passing around the room. Lord Haroden rose from his chair slowly, like a great rhinoceros rising from a waterhole. "Any man who contaminates my hall with foul portents will pay with his life. Do you hear me? I don't want to hear a single whisper. Not one." He didn't settle back down until he seemed sure his point was understood. "Executioner, get on with it. Forgo the formalities and begin the real torture already. Take the ears first."

Barik bowed his head. A white-robed assistant offered him a long-handled knife with a deeply curved edge. Barik took the blade, examined it, and gave a nod of approval. The assistant held down the flap of Adrian's ear, while Barik positioned the blade. He gave a single grunt, and flicked the knife down to slice off Adrian's ear.

But the blade didn't slice off Adrian's ear—in fact it didn't cut him at all.

For a moment Barik looked terribly bewildered, as his giant monobrow kept wriggling like a hungry silkworm. When he decided it was a simple miscalculation, he shrugged and flicked the knife down once more. But this time he slipped, and worse, the blade fell out of his hand and struck the floor with a loud *clang*. The civil and military officials began murmuring to one another.

Barik bent down to retrieve the blade. He kept his back to the small crowd, probably because his face was redder than a very red apple. His eyes turned on his assistant. "The hell is this? I told you to sharpen them *all*."

The assistant was a snub-nosed fellow with a bad

attitude. "I did, I worked that damn grindstone to hell. Here, give it to me." He placed the knife against a swatch of linen pulled from his belt. The fabric tore like a reed. "Look at that. Told you, it's damn sharp."

The executioner glared at him. "Are you saying that my skill with this blade is in some way lacking or rudimentary?"

The assistant snorted. He certainly wasn't without a spine. "I didn't say that."

"Well, if you're not saying that, then this man's ear should be lying on the floor like a fresh cutlet, yes? Give me another. Steel edged and chromium plated. And make sure it's sharp this time. Do it."

The assistant went back to the table and began searching. The executioner was left rubbing his balding pate and apologizing to the officers.

"So much for thirty years of torture experience," Adrian said archly.

A handful of soldiers within earshot grinned at the remark, but Barik only glared at Adrian. The assistant returned and handed him a large knife with a cleaver-like blade. The jelly-bellied man examined the weapon with expert caution, then he smiled and said, "Let's see how witty you are after this." He lined up the blade to strike. Adrian shut his eyes and squeezed the mushroom in his hand . . .

CLANG. The blade snapped from the hilt and crashed to the floor.

"That tickled," Adrian said. The soldiers burst out laughing. Barik threw the broken weapon to the ground and demanded another. The assistant placed it into his hand and the scene repeated itself, over and over, with each failed attempt resulting in a clever gibe from Adrian.

CLANG. "Are you truly an executioner, or are you a court jester?"

CLANG. "Maybe your assistant is more qualified to do this."

CLANG. "Who knew a master executioner would have the clumsiest hands in the realm?"

Barik began to panic. He had accidentally sliced open his own thumb, and now his assistant was using a swatch of silk to staunch the bleeding. The poor executioner's hands were shaking, and his eyes were darting back and forth in disbelief. At some point he began to ramble to himself. Adrian had to lean forward to hear him over the uproar of the civil and military officials. "How . . . how could it be possible? I once used that knife to remove the ears of ten different men, all in row. That's twenty ears. How could it just break?" Barik went quiet then, his eyes lowering to the ground like a sad puppy.

Adrian smiled. He smiled not at Barik's shame— though that wasn't unpleasant to witness—but because Temil was once again correct. Not only did the red cloud mushroom exist, but it had done exactly what the old child said it would. Adrian's smile widened when he realized that today wasn't his day to die. No, today was just another warm and cheerful day, a day of rebirth and renewal and all those wonderfully corny things that came with the warm spring—

"BE SILENNNNTTTT!!!!!"

Lord Haroden sat clenching the armrests of his seat, his shoulders trembling, his big bull eyes wide and livid. The reddish yellow juice of a persimmon dripped down his chin, but he didn't seem to notice or care. He rose from the throne and waddled over to the edge of the dais. The hall was so silent that even a scampering mouse wouldn't go unheard. The prime minister made a quick motion, and soldiers seized Barik.

The jelly-bellied man didn't resist. His face went white. It was as if someone sucked all the color out of it. "Your Supreme Lordship . . . I don't understand . . ." He kept glancing at his assistant, as if this was all just a clever gag, and he was simply waiting for the truth to relieve him of his shame.

Lord Haroden ordered them executed. Barik, the assistant—hell, even the metalsmith who initially forged the instruments, wherever he might be. No one was laughing now.

Advisors pleaded with the prime minister, but Lord Haroden threatened their lives as well. When Lady Amelia whispered something into his ear, Haroden pushed her away and shouted, "I don't care about that. No one makes a mockery of my private affairs." He turned to his soldiers and ordered the condemned to be taken to the dungeons. When a pair of guardsmen went over to Adrian, Lord Haroden stopped them. "Not him. I'm not done with him yet." He turned to Viceroy Murden and demanded the services of his most skilled axeman.

Bo-boom Boom, Bo-boom Boom. A giant man with a giant axe came stomping across the tiled floor, which all but vibrated beneath Adrian's bare feet. A ragged hood covered his face from the nose up, revealing little more than crooked yellow teeth and a jaw crisscrossed with scars. He shoved Adrian over a chopping block and brushed aside his hair to expose the neck. His buckskin boots were black and stained with what could only be splotches of old gore from former victims. *How the hell will I survive this?* Adrian wondered.

The man's legs spread apart and the shadow of his giant axe rose. A moment later the blade came screaming down—only to smash into the tiled floor beside Adrian's head. The axeman lurched forward, grunting and cursing and pawing at the dust and debris in his face. He tried again, and failed again, and already Haroden had seen enough. He sentenced the axeman and his entire bloodline to death. After that he called for a master hangman.

It was high sun by the time the workhands set up the frame and crossbeam and accurately measured the length of the drop. After that the hangman made Adrian stand on a square block and put his head in the noose. Death seemed all but certain now. Adrian's body would drop but the running knot would tighten and break his neck. *How the hell will I survive this?*

The hangman removed the block, and Adrian dropped.

The lower platform rushed up to meet him, but

just as the noose grew taut there was a *snap*, and Adrian dropped harmlessly to the floor.

The hangman swallowed hard and lowered his head, afraid to meet Haroden's murderous stare. When he finally did, the prime minister spoke to him through clenched teeth. *"Do it again."*

The hangman retrieved the heaviest rope in his arsenal. Arm-thick hempen braids that looked strong enough to suspend an ox. Adrian was hoisted up once more.

The hangman removed the block, and Adrian dropped.

The floor rose up, but this time the running knot tightened and Adrian's body gave a sudden jerk. He dangled in the air, his legs frantically kicking out, his windpipe being crushed by the weight of his own body. But just as quickly as the panic began, the rope snapped, and Adrian fell. But when he landed this time, the mushroom popped out of his hand and went skittering across the floor.

Lord Haroden's eyes widened. A plump hand went to his chest, pulling out the necklace from beneath his pachyderm robe. He opened the locket. Empty. Thunder filled his eyes. *"THIEFFF!!!"* he shrieked, charging headlong at Adrian like an elephant in musth. Soldiers and ministers and attendants all leaped aside, and those who didn't were either knocked out of the way or thrown to the ground. He was a juggernaut, an out-of-control chariot, his mouth open wide, his jowls bouncing with every powerful step. *Boom, boom, boom, boom.* He wasn't stopping—he couldn't stop. Adrian didn't want him to stop. *Come on, you bastard. COME ON.*

Adrian raised his blackened hand—but the tyrant plowed into him, lifting Adrian off his feet and sending his world spinning. Next he knew he was lying on his back and gasping for air beneath Lord Haroden's smothering frame. Giant fists poured down—three, four, five blows before Adrian heard his nose break and his lungs wheeze. He swallowed clumps of blood that made him nauseous, yet somehow he continued to fight back. But Haroden was too goddamn big and too goddamn strong, and eventually his giant fists pounded so hard that Adrian's body stopped responding and his world began to fade like a dying candle, flashing from light to dark, light to dark.

In this stuttering, half-closed view, Adrian saw Haroden reaching for the mushroom. Reaching . . . reaching . . . his crazed mouth hanging open, his tongue lolling out between silvery teeth. He had it. No, he didn't. Just as he was about to seize it, just as his fingertips were about to close around his prize . . . Adrian's blackened fingers grabbed the prime minister's chubby cheek, yanking him back.

Lord Haroden's great body turned. His eyes fell upon Adrian with that murderous stare, but it was too late. Why? Because his flesh had already begun doing exactly what it was supposed to do.

It began to burn.

Chapter Thirty-Four

It took an eternity or two before the Rhinoceros Lord's ample flesh and ox-thick bones disintegrated into ash.

But when it was done, when all that was left was a smoking pile of pachyderm robes and a horned head-dress, panic seized the hall. Ministers wept and covered their eyes in horror while military officers screamed curses and jabbed fingers at Adrian. When someone called for the murderer's head, guardsmen charged from all directions, but Adrian raised his blackened hand and sent them skidding to a halt.

They began to circle around him now, like hungry wolves with hackles raised.

I won't die like this, Adrian thought. *Not now, not after all I've done.* But the guards were growing bolder and moving closer, and the red cloud was lying out of reach near Haroden's smoking robes. *No, I won't die like this. Goddamn it, somebody help me, please!*

It was then Lady Amelia shouted a command, and moments later the tall double doors burst open and a host of soldiers with pink-streaked capes stormed inside. Leading them was none other than General Layne Rey himself. *The Pink Pangolin! Thank all the goddamn gods in the goddamn sky.*

General Layne's men crossed the room swiftly and methodically, and before Lord Haroden's guardsmen could regroup they were outnumbered and surrounded. Weapons fell to the ground with deaf-ening clangs. Hands were raised in surrender. It was over. At last.

Lady Amelia ran to Adrian. He embraced her with his good hand; he couldn't say how long it lasted, but only that it eventually had to end. When she pulled away, she looked at him the way she might look at a pitiful child, and only then did Adrian recall the battering he took from Haroden. "I must look like a rotten gourd," he admitted.

She ran her hand through his filthy hair and smiled that spirit-lifting smile of hers. "You look like a hero."

"It was you, my lady. You're the hero this time."

Her smile widened. "It was me, wasn't it?"

A small side door opened and Viceroy Marius Murden entered in a fit of coughing. Amelia went off to reunite with her father. Adrian bent down to retrieve the red cloud. He held it in the closed palm of his good hand, then turned to greet a familiar pair of outlaw brothers. Olan threw his huge bear arms around Adrian in a warm embrace, while Eldred stood back to offer a respectful bow his head. "You look terrible," Olan said, "worse than the last time you looked terrible."

"Well, I could've used your help a little sooner, you know, when my face was getting pounded into mush. But I must say, I'm glad to see you again. Both of you."

"So are we, Deadhand," Olan said. His giant hand came up and mussed Adrian's hair.

General Layne came over and greeted the three companions with an overdramatic bow. When Adrian thanked him for his assistance, the general smiled that sly smile of his and said, "As I've said before, pink has the uncanny ability to neutralize disorder and calm hostility, in any situation, in any heart."

Adrian smiled. "I'll never doubt you again, General."

"Glad to hear it. Listen, it's best if you leave this hall at once. Lord Murden has a bit of mollifying to do. I'll have a physician tend to you at once."

"Can we share a measure of wine first?" Olan asked.

Adrian chuckled. "Yes, I think I can manage that. Eldred, what do you say?"

The husky outlaw didn't answer. His deep-set eyes were fixated on the dais, where Viceroy Murden was addressing Lord Haroden's civil and military officials. There were a lot of frowns, a lot of crossed arms, and a lot of disgruntled voices. "That man murdered the Supreme Lord of Scarlet Sun," a high minister argued. "No crime is more wicked than that of regicide."

"Don't be as blind as the populace," Lord Murden told him. "All of you. You all know what sort of man Lord Haroden was. His cruelty knew no bounds, his transgressions towered to the heavens and beyond." He coughed a few times, then extended a hand to indicate the area around him. "Just look at my hall. Look at all the pain and suffering he has brought upon us."

It was true. The Hall of Winter Tranquility looked like something out of a night terror. The lacquered tables were covered in torture instruments, the elegant platforms were ruined by an executioner's block and makeshift gallows, and the tiled floor was littered with broken blades and frayed coils of rope. Not to mention the puke and piss from the terrified men Lord Haroden had ordered executed. It looked like someone had spilled stale rice wine and old pottage all over the place.

"Looks better this way," Olan said, examining Adrian's nose. His left eye closed for a more precise look, and then his bearded face split into a grin. "You know, I always thought it was too straight." He slapped Adrian's cheek playfully. "Now you look like an outlaw."

Chapter Thirty-Five

*N*ews of Lord Haroden's death left a fissure in the heart of Beetleburr . . . a deep, cavernous fissure that refused to mend even after the Hall of Winter Tranquility was refurnished and redecorated and scrubbed spotlessly clean.

Weeks later, when Viceroy Murden ascended the terraced tower to placate the populace, rioters erupted in the streets, torching buildings and spilling blood. The fierce groundswell of opposition left the viceroy and his city officials disheartened and in despair. It wasn't the violence but the underlying statement that was so troubling: the people were afraid. Lord

Haroden had been their protector and their savior—with his death, reprisal from the southern warlord and his menacing armada loomed higher than ever before.

But as the days came and the nights went, the shock of Lord Haroden's death began to wither and fade. Adrian spent his time with Lady Amelia, either in the elegant pavilions of the imperial gardens, or in the quiet comfort of her private chamber. He found a peacefulness with her that he'd desired for so long, and yet it wasn't enough to shake the restlessness from his heart. He wanted to leave, yet he wanted to stay. The constant contradiction of emotions left him drained and beaten, even weeks after his physical aches and bruises had all but healed.

Not to say Lady Amelia wasn't an exceptional woman—she certainly was, but was there more beyond her highborn status and comely face and incredible confidence? Adrian was no longer sure. For all of Lady Amelia's admirable qualities, she was also a cunning and calculating woman who would always place her own ambitions over the needs of others. And so, for all their joyous evenings and intimate moments together, Adrian knew—just as before—that it wouldn't last. And this time, strangely enough, he didn't want it to last.

It was a particularly blissful evening; the cloudless sky stretched into an endless midnight sea, and the stars twinkled like tiny white beacons. Lady Amelia leaned in close while they sat together on a knoll beside a white-latticed bower of the imperial garden. "Adrian, you will always have my heart," she said, "but you can never have my hand."

Adrian didn't reply to that. In fact, he was quiet for so long that she had to ask if he'd heard her. When he told her yes, she said, "It's not my decision. You know that." She raised a hand to caress his cheek. Her head tilted slightly and her warm green eyes sparkled like peridots in the moonlight. "My father plans to extend my hand to Lord Haroden's eldest son."

"Eldest? The boy's no more than sixteen," Adrian said.

"Fifteen, and I'm not pleased about it either, but he's a kind and gentle boy, and uniting our houses may be the only chance at reconciliation. My father . . . he's always been an ambitious man, even now in his advanced age. He plans to take the cord and seal of the prime minister and use his rank to regulate the northern provinces."

"While keeping the boy in the shadows, yes?" Adrian didn't wait for an answer. "There are a number of ministers in Scarlet Sun hungry for that same position. Does he think it will be so easy?"

"Of course not, that's why he's leading the imperial procession back to the capital. He intends to personally offer my hand to the young successor, and later deliver his inaugural address to the people."

"Your father may be shrewd, but how brazen is he to think he can win over the capital? The people of Scarlet Sun *loved* Haroden."

"Yes, but Haroden's dead, the realm is split, and fear of a southern assault runs ever rampant. My father's not looking for love. The people . . . once their grief has passed, they'll be searching for a new face of leadership. You see, deep down, people want to be controlled. It gives them comfort. Farmers and merchants and moneylenders—they desire nothing more than a simple life under the protection of an evenhanded lord. Do you think they will bow their heads and offer their undying loyalty to a callow young brat, or some old armchair minister who's never held a weapon in his life? No, they want a man with experience in all aspects of civil and military office. My father is that man."

Adrian turned his head and studied the stars for a while. A streak of silvery light caught his eye, but it was gone in an instant. For some reason it made him sad. "And so we stand on the precipice of a new age. And you, Lady Amelia Murden, you will rise ever higher, leaving me buried deeper in the dregs of your past."

"Don't be so melodramatic," she said with a chuckle. "I don't want to leave. But my father, I can't turn him down for something so petty as love."

The words should've pierced him like a bolt in the heart, but they didn't. In fact, Adrian was expecting them. "So, that's it then," he told her, in a voice that wasn't nearly as compassionate as he'd intended.

A long moment passed before she spoke again. "There is a poem about a famous highborn woman who fell in love with a handsome but lowly servant. The problem was the woman was already married to a powerful lord. Still, passion won over restraint, and she secretly gave herself to the lowborn man. But after months of affection and intimacy, her conscience forced her to reject her lover and send him away. Do you know what happened to this man?"

"I believe I'm about to find out."

"He went on to win the heart of another high-born woman, and this woman gave him three strong sons and two comely daughters, and when he died he was aged and at peace and surrounded by his loving family."

"An end longed by every man," Adrian remarked. "What of the lady?"

"She died fifteen years earlier, murdered by her husband after the truth of her affair surfaced. They say her husband had her beaten and publicly humili-ated, then he locked her in a tiny storeroom and denied her even the smallest morsel of food. Every night, a private banquet was presented in the small hall right next to her room, so he could listen to her pitiful wails while he dined."

Adrian didn't know how to react to that. At length he said, "Why are you telling me this?"

"Because it was none other than the lowborn servant himself who informed the husband of the affair. Unrequited love is cruel, Adrian."

He squeezed her hand. "If you think I would ever do something so vile . . ."

"I don't," she said. "Not any longer. In fact, I don't think you'll be heartsick at all. Am I wrong?"

Adrian didn't look at her, nor did he answer right away. "No," he said at length, and the two remained there for a time, quietly observing the stars.

*A*fter exiting the palace grounds, Adrian wandered the streets for a time, listening to his booted footfalls on the flagstones and observing his shadow loom and twist beneath the waxing moon. The buildings around him rose like drawn and lonely faces, and many of these faces were burned and bashed and gutted from the recent riots. Farther down the avenues, however, the wine shops and inns and taverns all looked livelier than ever—even those in the western district. Adrian entered the Sapphire Moon through the newly constructed door, a thick carving of rounded ash that was lacquered in a soft eggshell white.

Inside the common room, the stained and ramshackle tables had been replaced with spherical and crescent designs that complemented the nightscape tapestries and starry wall sconces. Every face here seemed full of smiles. Adrian still hadn't gotten used to seeing this place so full of spirit, but after Dravid's death the Snakeheads crumbled and disbanded, which meant their hold on all the local establishments had finally lifted, the Sapphire Moon included.

Adrian joined Eldred and Olan in their usual section. The three men shared a few measures of crisp hawthorn wine, and as the hours passed the conversation deepened into the recounting of past events, both pleasant and unpleasant. Adrian didn't speak much, nor did he pay much attention. It wasn't the wine, and it wasn't because of Lady Amelia. No, he was truthful when he said he wasn't heartsick about their parting. Nor would he miss the privileged life of an aristocrat. Viceroy Marius Murden had bestowed on him more than enough coin to get by, along with an official exoneration of all crimes and offenses. Such generosity was only accepted when the same offer was extended to Eldred and Olan.

"Did someone spit in your wine, Deadhand?" Olan's sonorous voice cut through the common room's low murmur of conversation.

Adrian looked up. "No, of course not, why the hell would you ask that?"

"Because that sour mug on your face is dampening my spirit." He belched, then leaned close. "Coin, freedom, laundered clothes, warm fare—we have it all, Deadhand. All those nights out in the wild, eating snails and grubs and sow thistle and acorns . . . this is what we talked about, all of this, and now, finally, we have it. Why sit around and sulk?"

Adrian sighed. "I'm not ungrateful."

"That's not the answer I'm looking for."

When Adrian hesitated, Temil's words back at the cottage suddenly popped into his head. *If you think taking Haroden's life would ease the disharmony in your heart .*

. . well, I'm sorry to tell you it won't. Revenge is glorious for the ego—but meaningless to the spirit.'

Temil was right. Of course he was. Adrian was still the same broken man with the same strange condition. He looked down. From the corner of his eye he thought he glimpsed the three-legged dog sitting on its haunches near the entrance, staring pointedly with those black-pooled eyes. Adrian didn't acknowledge it. Instead his good hand wandered to the pouch on his belt, where he kept the red cloud. When he spoke his voice was no louder than a whisper. "It was no accident how I survived that day." He brought the mushroom out, gently and cautiously, like a child holding a flower for the first time. "Forgive me for sounding so trite and melodramatic, but if there is even the slightest chance of truth in everything Temil has told me . . . well, I have to try. I know how it sounds, trust me, I do."

Eldred unfolded an arm and motioned for the mushroom. The husky man examined it for quite some time, while Olan looked on and occasionally scratched his beard. When Eldred was done he exchanged a knowing look with his brother, but Adrian couldn't interpret it. Finally, Eldred said, "When do we leave?"

Adrian was stunned. For the first time in his life, he couldn't think of a clever response. "You don't have to do this," he murmured at length. "You two have done so much for me already. Why would you do this?"

The husky man furrowed his brow, as if the question were too preposterous to answer. After a long moment, however, his mouth widened into one of those rare smiles. "Because we are brothers, you clod."

Olan reached across the table and placed a huge hand on Adrian's shoulder. "From this day forward. This is our oath of brotherhood."

Chapter Thirty-Six

"I'm dead tired, Deadhand," Olan called from behind. "How much farther is it again?"

Adrian replied without turning. "We're almost there."

The three men had already ascended hill after hill and were now passing through the stands of blue-black junipers. They stayed close to the eastern paths (even though all these hills looked the same) and when they crested the next rise, they spotted the familiar cottage of knotted gray wood. The familiar *chop-chop-chop* of a woodcutter's axe rang in the air, a comforting sound, and when Adrian and his companions entered the nearby grove, the old child stopped his laboring, put down the hatchet, wiped his brow with a small kerchief, and smiled at his guests.

Adrian didn't speak; he didn't even reach into his pouch and retrieve the red cloud. Neither were necessary. He knew the old child was expecting him.

"So here we are, four mismatched travelers together once again," Temil said. "But wait, this journey will consist of one more. Stay a moment while I inform my associate."

The old child went skipping off in a carefree manner, and when he returned the three-legged dog was gamboling at his side—well, if gamboling looked anything like a marionette being dragged across the ground. Olan smiled at what he saw while Eldred rolled his eyes and grunted, and with that, the five companions were off to the Mantis Vale.

*I*t was a rather uneventful and slow-going journey, since their guide was a three-legged dog that moved as quickly as a three-legged dog could move. But Adrian couldn't complain; the weather was warm and welcome and the scenery was among the most pristine he'd ever encountered. Tall-grass prairies with humus-rich soil, crackling forests filled with rich conifers and maples and beeches, warm sphagnum bogs ringed in stately larches, and steep watersheds with rocky mountain slopes and multi-leveled waterfalls. The gorges they crossed were gorgeous, the ravines they skirted were ravishing, and the valleys they traversed were marvelously carpeted with radiant wildflowers—as if arranged by a master artist's patient hand.

Occasionally they found shelter at a roadside inn, but those were becoming rare, so their evenings of late were spent beneath the stars. Temil had so much to impart during these quiet respites, about how Adrian must approach and interact with the Shepherdess of the Stars. Every movement and gesture had to be so precise and so timely and so this and so that . . . it all seemed so stupid. Worst of all, the old child's relentless onslaught of questions made Adrian feel like a pupil cramming for an official exam. Still, Adrian listened to them all, even though a part of him refused to believe what he heard.

"Are you even listening?" Temil demanded.

Adrian shifted his gaze from the night sky to Temil's disappointed expression. Behind him, the brothers were resting before the smoldering firepit. Olan's boar-like snoring fit well with the usual orchestra of nocturnal denizens.

"You didn't answer me."

"I'm tired, can we continue this tomorrow?"

Temil gave a heavy sigh, like a frustrated schoolmaster whose lectures went unheard. "If you're not going to take this seriously, we may as well turn back now. You need to understand, there is a certain protocol that must be followed when a receiver presents himself to the Shepherdess of the Stars. This isn't child's play."

It was the third or fourth admonition Adrian had

received in the last fortnight, and for the third or fourth time he apologized like an indolent servant. What else could he do? Of course Temil didn't seem convinced of his sincerity, but the little fellow continued on nonetheless. "What will you do once you touch upon the External River?"

"I will approach the Shepherdess of the Stars."

"And then?"

Adrian had to think about the answer, even though Temil had spent the last week or so drilling it into his mind. "I will greet her using the sacred Argalist gesture of reverence and respect," he said at last. "Arms crossed, palms flat against the chest, right shoulder slightly lowered, head tilted down and directed to the left. My movements will be graceful and smooth, but not overly confident as to appear arrogant or vainglorious. I will also not exude awe or diffidence, as that may be seen as an affront."

"Good. And just who is this deity?"

"The Shepherdess of the Stars oversees the Great Rivers of Transmigration, commands the processes and materializations of the World of Life and Unlife, and knows the sacred truths of all the heavenly realms and beyond."

"And what exactly will this deity do for you?"

"The Shepherdess of the Stars will allow a receiver to attain the state of enlightenment needed to open the sky and free the stranded spirits of the over-acting cycle."

"And how does a receiver reach such a state?"

"By offering statements—not questions—to this

deity, and formulating his conclusions based on the deity's response or lack of response."

"Yes, and why must you offer such statements?"

"Because the Shepherdess of the Stars doesn't have the verbal ability to answer mortal questions. The deity will only offer a single gesture."

"And what gesture is that?"

Adrian crossed his arms and repeated the Argalist gesture of reverence and respect.

"Good, and what is the literal translation of this gesture?"

"There are no accidents or errors in the Great Path of the Sacred Argali."

"Correct. And what exactly does this gesture mean as a response?"

"It means the statement offered by the receiver is false, and as such, it will not bring the receiver closer to enlightenment."

"What sort of response will bring a receiver closer to enlightenment?"

"Only a statement met without response will bring a receiver closer to enlightenment."

"Excellent," Temil said. "You may be a bit lazy, my friend, but you're certainly a swift learner. Perhaps I can make a scholar out of you yet."

"Wonderful," Adrian quipped. "Third watch is over. I'm going to sleep."

*A*fter another uneventful week of travel they descended upon the Mantis Vale. The once lush and colorful landscape swiftly faded into drab ridges and lifeless plateaus. Adrian should've been joyful, since these sights meant they were getting closer to their destination. But he wasn't joyful. Truth was, over the past month the four travelers and their canine companion had become quite close. Hell, even Eldred and Temil had spent many a night sharing wine and chatting like old chums. How could that not put a smile on Adrian's face? On nights like these he didn't care if they ever reached this so-called Tree of Transposition. No, simply reveling in the brotherhood and comradery of these fellows was enough. It was a shame that all this had to eventually end, for better or worse.

Huge rocky slabs of granite narrowed their path and ushered them into a perfectly flat plane of a dried-up lake. The area was dim and desolate and foggy—an arid dust pocket dotted with black rocks that had been pushed around by the wind, leaving what looked like the trails of desultory snails. There was so little life here . . . so little of anything. How could a tree of such magnificence tolerate these conditions? Truth was, it probably couldn't.

And yet the three-legged dog hobbled along without care or concern, and Temil followed closely behind with an eager expression on his old face. Once they crossed the arid dust pocket, the company spent the next hour or so weaving around boulders and crags in the winding path. They climbed two or three rises and dropped down four or five outcrops, and occasionally Adrian's ears popped and often his eyes stung from the dirt and dust. Finally, at the bottom of the last drop, their journey appeared to have come to an end, and oh . . . what a disappointing end it was.

There was a tree, a single tree, but it certainly wasn't what one would expect when envisioning the great Tree of Transposition. No, it wasn't a massive broadleaved thing with lush foliage and a canopy that rose into the clouds, but a leafless and withered and weeping old beech. Was Temil lying again? It certainly seemed like it. Adrian snapped a glare at the little man. "Don't tell me this is it. Don't tell me this is the Tree of Transposition."

Temil nodded, although he seemed a bit unsure himself. "This is it."

Adrian scoffed—he didn't mean to, but it just came out. No matter, the old child didn't acknowledge it. The little fellow's eyes were focused on something on the bole of the tree. A tiny white lesion, easily unnoticed unless you knew what to look for. "There's a canker here," he explained. "It's killing the wood beneath the bark. See it? Here, look here. The bark is sloughing off and the spore mats are being exposed." The little man sounded strangely upbeat. He raised a little hand to brush down his cowlick, then he stepped back to examine the withered tree as a whole. "Don't you see? The wound is indicative of the disruption in the over-acting cycle."

Eldred grumbled something unintelligible under his breath.

Adrian shared the husky man's sentiments. He was angry; he felt cheated. This tree was just a regular old tree, undernourished and frail like everything else in this barren hole.

"Go on, Adrian," Temil urged.

Adrian didn't remember taking the mushroom out of the pouch, but it was sitting flat in the palm of his good hand, all red and rough to the touch. He moved close enough to the tree to study the details of the tiny white lesion. When he was done he turned back for a final glance at his companions. Eldred and Olan looked bored and tired, while Temil's old face was bright with expectancy. The three-legged dog sat with its single rear leg raised in the air; it was licking itself.

Adrian turned back. He removed his glove. All the horrors of his black and withered hand stared back at him. He placed his palm against the wounded tree, right where Temil told him to place it. Of course, nothing happened.

Adrian readjusted his position, this time covering the entire lesion with his palm. Again, nothing happened. "Am I doing something wrong?"

"Try it again," Temil said.

Adrian did. He angled his palm so it fit snugly against the grooves of the surrounding bark, but still nothing happened. Stubbornly he held it there, waiting and waiting and waiting, and still . . . nothing.

Eldred folded his thick arms across his chest. "Are we done with all this nonsense now?"

Temil's old face reddened. "It's not nonsense——"

"We've traveled for over a *MONTH*," Eldred roared back. "Only to stand before a stunted tree that looks no different from every other stunted tree we passed. Yeah, I'd say it's quite a bit of nonsense."

Adrian withdrew his blackened hand and sighed. *There goes the comradery.* Still, it was hard to argue with Eldred's assessment, even though it was harder to believe that all this wasn't for nothing. "I don't understand . . . the red cloud, the three-legged dog . . . is it all just a meaningless coincidence?"

"It's not," Temil said, although he sounded as though he were trying to convince himself. "That wouldn't make sense." He sat down before the three-legged dog, closing his eyes and crossing his arms in a meditative posture.

"What the hell are you doing?" Adrian asked.

"Quiet. I'm attempting to connect with my associate."

The dog didn't seem very receptive. It sat there with a vacant look on its face, then turned to bite at something on its haunch. Fleas, probably.

"The afternoon sun is weakening," Eldred pointed out. "If we leave now we might be able to get out of this hellish place by nightfall. Adrian, are you coming?"

Adrian told him yes, but his eyes were still on Temil. The old child had given up on trying to contact his associate, and now he was left staring at the tree and babbling to himself. "I don't understand . . . I don't understand it."

"Adrian," Eldred called, already moving off. "Time to go."

Adrian was about to follow but then something tapped the top of his head. Rain. Tiny droplets of rain, soft and sparse at first, but growing more intense by the moment. Looking up, he saw a wave of angry gray clouds devouring the sky from the north. The wind began to howl. Lightning flashed; thunder boomed. The rain was sheeting down now, soaking Adrian to the bone. He didn't care. He didn't care because when he turned he saw the tree was bending and creaking and crackling, and somehow, the tiny white lesion was *glowing*, a faint but phosphorescent glow, like the reflection of starlight in water.

The old child was capering about in the rain, shouting, his little boots sloshing through the mud like a necromancer summoning the dead from their graves. "The White Whirlwind! The White Whirlwind!" he kept shouting, over and over again.

A flash of lightning blinded Adrian, disoriented him, and a sharp crack of thunder knocked him off his feet. Next he knew he was lying on the wet earth with mud dripping from his hair into his face. He tried to wipe it off but his good hand was also muddy so it only made things worse. The cold winds of the norther screamed at him like a great aerial beast. He covered his eyes, but when he looked back he saw that Eldred and Olan were somewhere below him, both men bracing themselves against the gale. Were they shrinking? No, Adrian was rising into the air, higher and higher into a terrible, spinning vortex of cyclonic winds. He squeezed the red cloud but the storm was too strong; it pried the mushroom from his fingers and stole it away.

Oh shit.

Waves of pain wracked his body, a suffocating pain, unlike anything he'd ever felt before. Higher and higher he went, higher and higher as his throat tightened and tightened and his lungs shrieked and begged and pleaded for air. But the air never came, and suddenly the clouds became so thick that Adrian couldn't see, and the wind roared so loud he thought his eardrums would burst, and then, just as the pain grew to an unbearable climax . . . the rain ceased, the wind died, and the world fell silent.

Chapter Thirty-Seven

*C*ough, cough, cough.

  It took some time for Adrian to realize that the coughing he heard was in fact his own. It took a bit more time for him to actually *stop* coughing, but eventually he did, and only then did he notice that the terrible storm had been replaced with a sulky silence. Adrian lifted himself onto his hands and knees, heaved out a few more coughs for good measure, and rose.

  He was no longer in the vale but on the summit of a mountain—or at least he thought he was, although he felt neither the wind nor the pressure of altitude. The vast maw of the night sky yawned down on him, and it was a deep and lonely and terribly oppressive yawn. In the dark distance he could see flecks of starlight, hundreds and thousands of them, but all were shimmering mutely, like the faintest flickers of candlelight observed through a window of over-stretched horn.

As expected his companions were nowhere to be found, but that didn't mean Adrian was alone. No, farther along the path walked a solitary figure, a woman, leaning on a crook and slightly hunched as one of great age would appear. *Must be the good shep-herdess,* Adrian thought. *Well, I'd better get this over with.* He began to approach, but then he stopped and recalled Temil's lessons. *Arms crossed, palms flat against my chest, left shoulder slightly lowered, head tilted down and directed to the right. Yes, that's it. Or wait, was it right shoulder slightly lowered and head directed to the left?* Indecision gave way to anxiety, and anxiety jumbled his thoughts even more. *Calm down, Adrian. Calm down and clear your mind.*

When that didn't work frustration took over, and before long he ditched all the fancy protocol and simply strode forward. His approach was rather strange, even dreamlike, and for a long while the female figure seemed to never get any closer. But suddenly she *was* closer. Very much closer. Such a strange thing to experience . . . it was a terrible slow-ness that was also quite sudden, like the onset of old age to a perpetually busy farmer. Adrian was now standing before the figure and the figure was now standing before him—and by the gods she was the most frightening old woman Adrian had ever seen.

For one she was bone thin and extremely tall, a good head taller than Adrian despite the obvious hunch. Her hair was long and steely and her body was covered in rags that looked as old as anything could ever look old, but what was most off-putting was the woman's face—she didn't have one. Just the tiniest indents of where the eyes and nose and mouth and ears should've been, and that was all.

Adrian didn't know whether to flee or piss himself, and if he had a bit less control over his faculties he would've done both. But then he remembered the Chitterers and their masks, and somehow he found the strength to stand firm. *But what the hell do I say to an all-knowing deity?* Adrian thought about that until the most sensible greeting and introduction came to mind, but when he opened his mouth he'd forgotten it all and only a single, stupid word was left on his lips. "Hi."

The shepherdess didn't respond.

Idiot! Don't exude awe or diffidence. Adrian did his best to stand tall and look the deity in the eye—well, to look where the eyes *should've* been. "I know you're not one for idle chat, so I plan to make this quick." His voice sounded strangely deadened, as though speaking from behind a thick curtain. "I've come seeking the summit of enlightenment so the Five Faces of the Ever-changing and Everlasting Cycle may be repaired and the stranded spirits of the Conflagration of the Twilight Hall may continue their journey through the Great Rivers of Transmigration." *Damn, that was a mouthful.* "But wait, before we get started . . . I wanted to share one small criticism. Obviously I'm not an expert on the celestial material-izations of immortal psychopomps, but surely there is a more efficient way to reach out to a receiver? You know, a rather direct and concise explanation would save a lot of time and trouble. But again, I'm not an all-knowing deity, I don't command the processes and materializations of the World of Life and Unlife, and I don't know the sacred truths of all the heavenly realms and beyond. You do of course, and yet you don't speak. I find that rather amusing, don't you?"

Adrian didn't know what the hell he just said, or why he didn't stop himself from saying it. His nerves were on edge so his mouth was saying stupid things. Of course the shepherdess didn't respond to any of it. The old woman's head remained lowered, long tresses of silvery hair concealing most of her faceless face.

"I also have an admission," Adrian went on without thinking. "I don't believe I'm the receiver you're looking for. Perhaps I'm just a partial receiver. Is that possible? Forgive me, I know you don't answer questions. It's better to be a listener anyway. I should listen to others more. You know, you wouldn't be so mysterious if you could talk. You'd probably just criti-cize my earlier comment and pontificate about the limitations of celestial materialization. Or maybe you'd say something trite and insulting, yes, you seem like a cantankerous old lady, judging by your expres-sion. Forgive me, that was a jest."

The shepherdess didn't respond.

"I feel like this is a one-sided conversation, so I'll

speak plainly. I want to heal my condition. My burned hand. I'll do whatever is required of me. Can you help? Sorry, that was another question. I'm supposed to speak in statements. So let me start with this. I'm not the receiver you seek but you will heal my hand all the same."

The old woman remained motionless for a moment, then she crossed her skinny arms over her chest, leaned her left shoulder back, and inclined her head to the right. Then the arms uncrossed and the woman became still once more.

"I know what that gesture means. Temil told me. It means there are no accidents or errors in the Great Path of the Sacred Argali. Is that correct? Yes, I know it is. So, my statement is false. Are you saying I *am* a receiver? Wait, let me redo that. I *am* a receiver."

The shepherdess didn't respond.

"No gesture—that means my statement is true," Adrian said. "But that's where we have a problem. You see, I was told there are two requirements needed to become a receiver—and well, the second require-ment was never met. Like I said to Temil, I saw a lot of people die the day of the Conflagration, but I didn't love or even know any of them."

The old woman's hands came up, crossed over her chest, and went back down. *There are no accidents or errors in the Great Path of the Sacred Argali.*

"But I'm telling you the truth. I didn't know any of those people."

The hands came up, crossed over her chest, and

went back down. *There are no accidents or errors in the Great Path of the Sacred Argali.*

Adrian took a step back. He paused for a long moment before speaking. "Fine, let's try this. I lost someone I loved that day."

No response.

"How is that possible? I'm telling you, I've never lost someone I loved. Well, no, that's not true. I was married once. My wife died during childbirth. But that was ten years ago—it has nothing to do with the Conflagration of the Twilight Hall."

The hands came up. *There are no accidents or errors in the Great Path of the Sacred Argali.*

"How is that false?" Adrian almost laughed at the ridiculousness of this conversation. "My wife and son both died because of complications during childbirth."

There are no accidents or errors in the Great Path of the Sacred Argali.

Adrian grunted. "Do I have to oversimplify every goddamn statement? Fine. My wife died during childbirth."

No response.

"Good, I'm glad we both agree on that. Now, the second part, our son was stillborn."

There are no accidents or errors in the Great Path of the Sacred Argali.

"No, no, that *is* true. It's true because I remember every detail of that awful night. I remember rushing into the rear hall and finding my wife covered in blood. I remember how tired she looked, I remembered every droplet of sweat on her face, every strand of hair that lay out of place. I remember the way the midwife wept when she explained that my son was . . ." He paused. "If the babe wasn't stillborn . . . what happened to him?" Another pause. "My son was stolen."

No response.

"It was the midwife, wasn't it?" Adrian growled. "Wait, damn it, Adrian, speak in statements." He cleared his throat. "The midwife stole the babe."

No response.

"I should've known. That jealous hag couldn't have a child of her own, so she stole mine." Adrian stepped back. "So that means my son is still alive."

There are no accidents or errors in the Great Path of the Sacred Argali.

"Oh, so my son is dead."

No response.

"Why even bother with this then?" He shook his head. *My son wasn't stillborn, he died sometime later. That's so sad.* Adrian's thoughts meandered for a while. It was hard to believe there was a time in which he actually had a son in this world. *I wonder how many summers he'd seen? Well, let's find out.* "My son saw more than six summers."

No response.

"My son saw more than nine summers."

No response.

"My son saw more than eleven summers."

There are no accidents or errors in the Great Path of the Sacred Argali.

"So, ten summers it is. Such a brief glimpse of life." Adrian was quiet once more. Such news should've made him heartsore, but in all honesty, Adrian wasn't sure how to react. Yes, his son didn't die at birth, but he was dead now and Adrian never knew him. What did it matter? And what did it have to do with the Conflagration? Was there somehow a connection? "Please tell me I'm wrong about this," he said. "My son died at the Conflagration of the Twilight Hall."

No response.

"That's it then. The second requirement, the loss of love. It was my son. The son I dearly loved but never knew. I suppose Temil was right . . . I am a receiver after all." Adrian gave a shrug. "So, are we finished? Have I reached the enlightened state needed to mend the overactive cycle and free the spirits?" Adrian looked around. The darkness was still thick and oppressive, and the distant lights were as dull and dreary as ever. Adrian turned back to the old woman. "Let me try a statement." He cleared his throat with a pronounced cough. "With these truths I've at last reached the enlightened state needed to open the sky and mend the Five Faces of the Ever-changing and Everlasting Cycle, which in turn will allow the stranded spirits of the Conflagration of the Twilight Hall to journey through the Great Rivers of Transmigration."

There are no accidents or errors in the Great Path of the Sacred Argali.

"Goddamn it," Adrian growled. "What am I missing? What else must I know in order to fix this goddamn cycle?" When the old woman didn't respond Adrian gritted his teeth. "Fine. Let me rephrase that, because I know you like statements so much. How about this? Our whole meeting is a sham, our conversation is bull-spit, and you're just a stupid old crone in a stupid mask."

There are no accidents or errors in the Great Path of the Sacred Argali.

"Oh, the hell with you," Adrian groaned. "I don't know what you want me to say. I give up. Damn it, I wish Temil were here."

There are no accidents or errors in the Great Path of the Sacred Argali.

"Now what? I said I wish Temil were here. Nothing false about that. Clearly he's not here."

There are no accidents or errors in the Great Path of the Sacred Argali.

Adrian's head tilted back. "Is this some sort of jest?" He looked this way and that, as if expecting his companions to emerge from the darkness and laugh at him. But no one appeared, and suddenly Adrian never felt more alone in his life. At length he muttered, "Temil *is* here."

No response.

"No. He can't be here. I don't see him. Look, I was told only a receiver can call upon the White Whirlwind and rise into the empyrean. Well, no, the three-legged dog can do the same, but that's because the dog is one of your little psychopomp-familiar things." Adrian ruminated on that for a moment. "If

Temil is in fact here, then that means he must also be a . . ." He swallowed. *The dog with three legs, the bird with a broken wing, the rat with two tails.* How did he not realize this sooner? He looked back at the shepherdess's faceless face. "Temil is also a psychopomp sent to guide the receiver."

No response.

"But if that's true . . . then that means Temil is a stranded spirit, which means Temil died at the Conflagration of the Twilight Hall, which means Temil was a boy of no more than ten, which means Temil is my . . ." Adrian faltered. "He's my son."

The old shepherdess didn't respond to that—but something else did. The darkness—it began to crack and crinkle and curl, revealing a hidden glow of something that seemed to have been yearning for years for release. When it finally got its way, a blaze of milky light whooshed from the sky and ripped the darkness apart like old fabric, and suddenly the ground at Adrian's feet became a swollen cloud, and the mists of this cloud unveiled a great river of moonlight, and this river was more beautiful than anything Adrian had ever seen in his life, more beautiful than birth or life or love itself. And this river wound its way into the radiant sky, a divine channel banked by divine clouds as it climbed higher and higher and farther and farther until distance no longer seemed a thing worth measuring, as time itself had no meaning or purpose or truth.

The Shepherdess of Stars flung out her arms, and Adrian saw not an old woman but a beautiful one, and with pale and beautiful arms she directed the stars like sheep in a celestial fold, culling them in a massive gathering of constellation and comet and cosmic stardust. And in this gathering, every living organism on every known planet extended their most sacred and intimate of treasures—the light of creation. Every living man, woman, animal, and plant—from the tiniest aphid to the largest leviathan—all surrendered themselves without prejudice and without selfishness and without hesitation. Adrian knew this because his soul gave its own light, and in doing so he became privy to the divine and universal celebration of life and all of its ephemeral necessity and eternal glory.

Shapes began to materialize in the light. Shapes of men and women and children and birds and rodents and cats and insects and even a dog with four legs. Dozens of spirits, at least three score or more, were suddenly drifting across the river of moonlight, never quite touching the surface but floating across it like seedlings carried by a gentle breeze. It was all so breathtaking, so absolutely mesmerizing—but then, one particular spirit caught Adrian's eye. The spirit of a young boy.

Temil.

Adrian dashed along the outer banks, his feet moving across clouds that refused to let him fall. When he came upon his friend he saw that the old child was no longer old. He was just a child now, a young boy with a young boy's face, which matched well with his dark mop of brown hair and stubborn cowlick. By the gods, even now, at no more than ten years, he looked so much like his father.

"Who are you?" the boy asked.

Adrian fell to his knees. His good hand reached out to his son, but all it touched was a cold shroud. "You don't remember? No, of course you don't. Temil told me—" He paused as his heart shot up his throat. "I didn't know. How could I have known?" His voice was quavering. "Had I the slightest notion of who you were, I never would've doubted you, never would've sent you away. No, all these months, we could've been together. If only I wasn't such a stupid, stubborn, skeptical fool."

The boy looked at him with that same tight-lipped expression his late wife used to give him. Adrian smiled at the semblance, but inside he wanted to weep. He tried to speak but couldn't, and soon the boy was glancing back at the other spirits, eager to depart. That made Adrian even sadder. He didn't want Temil to go. Not now, not after discovering the truth.

"I don't know you," the boy said at length. "I'm only ten. I have to go now. Journey and judgment are waiting. I'm scared, even though I shouldn't be. Is it wrong to be scared?"

"Of course not, but you shouldn't fear the journey through the Great Rivers of Transmigration, for I know how you will be judged by the Five Deathkings of All That Becomes."

The boy beamed hopefully at that. "Perhaps I

may return with the soul of a master artist, or a master dancer, or maybe I'll return as a tiger!"

With that, the boy turned and joined the other victims of the Conflagration of the Twilight Hall, and together, guided by the Shepherdess of the Stars, the spirits drifted down the External river, farther and farther until they were no more than a speck of light that twinkled like a distant star.

Adrian's gaze dropped to the ground. He began to weep. He wept and wept as grief ripped apart his insides and squeezed his heart like a vise. The fist of his good hand slammed into a ground made of clouds, again and again despite the soft and unsatis-fying impact. He continued to weep, so inured inside a deep well of his own sorrow that he didn't notice the changes around him until it was too late.

The world had grown cold and dark and distant, and suddenly Adrian knew no more.

Chapter Thirty-Eight

"*D*eadhand. Hey. Wake up." The voice was gruff and deep and familiar.

Adrian opened his eyes. The world was a blur. He rubbed away the warm tears and then frowned as the familiar gray vale unfolded around him. The hour was late; the sky was dull and overcast.

"What a hellish goddamn cloudburst," Olan muttered. "No warning at all."

Adrian coughed up a few mouthfuls of phlegm, then looked up at Olan's upside down face. It made him laugh.

"Am I that ugly, Deadhand?"

"No," he replied at length, "but from this angle you look a bit like an angry troll."

The shaggy-haired man helped Adrian to his feet. "You should've seen yourself a few moments ago. Whimpering like a yearling and flopping about like a fish out of water." He raised his arms and fluttered in a way that a man his size should never do. "Must've been some dream."

"No dream," Adrian said. "No, it certainly wasn't a dream." He reached down into his belt pouch. Sure enough, the red cloud was gone.

"Temil's missing," Eldred remarked with downcast eyes. "No tracks, no trace. The dog too. Maybe the storm took them, or maybe they fled. Can't blame the little fellow . . . not after wasting our time the way he did. But I know you wouldn't want to leave without him, Adrian, so we'll break here tonight and search again in the morning."

"No need," Adrian said. "We won't find him."

*T*he three men traveled for a week before they spotted their first roadside inn. The common room was crowded but comfortable, and the proprietor was actually a proprietress who entertained her patrons with her sultry charm and skillful playing of a cucurbit flute. After a brief supper Adrian left the company of his fellow brothers for the solitude of the outdoors. He ended up chatting with a pair of grooms by the stable yard, but the conversation was brief and regrettably dull, as

Adrian could focus on little except Temil. Sadly, the memory of that night had already begun to slip away . . . swiftly, like how a dream fades from one's grasp. But it wasn't a dream. Was it? As the days came and went Adrian had become less and less sure. Of course that was the skeptic in him . . . the old skeptic's mindset that gnawed and gnawed until Adrian began to doubt things that he shouldn't doubt. But he didn't fret over it. The truth was here, waiting to be unveiled. All Adrian needed was the courage to do it.

He kept walking. Whatever the outcome, not even the skeptic in him could ignore the changes in his heart. Truth was, since that night in the vale, a warmth had begun to blossom inside Adrian, an unexplainable warmth that lifted all the shallowness that once weighed him down. Coin, societal status, fancy trinkets . . . all of that meant nothing to him now. Wealth was nothing more than a fleeting and superficial thing to be coveted by the grasping and small-minded. Yes, deep down, Adrian finally understood a simple truth that had eluded him all his life: One must never mistake the changeable for the eternal.

The footpaths narrowed as Adrian continued walking, and as nightfall descended, shafts of moonlight peered down through the shadows of the overhanging trees. A wood owl hooted from somewhere and nocturnal birds chittered from somewhere else, but it was the high-pitched call of peepers that led Adrian to a gentle pond. He sat down on a slab of mossy shale. The peepers went silent. Adrian waited a while longer to make sure he was alone. He was.

It's time, he told himself. *Time to reveal the truth of the river, the shepherdess, the disrupted cycle, and all of the stranded spirits. But most of all, it's time to see if little Temil was, once more, telling the truth.*

Adrian pulled off his glove.

HE END

About the Author

M.A. Liguori is the author of *Virtue and Vengeance: Empire of Cinders* and *Rivers of the Sky: An Epic Fantasy Misadventure*. He was raised in New York and currently lives in North Carolina with his longtime partner and three playfully defiant cats. He spends a good portion of each day exploring faraway lands with incredibly epic battles and remarkably grand quests, and then he rises to slog through the waking world.